BETWEEN
COMMITMENT
AND
BETRAYAL

BETWEEN
COMMITMENT
AND
BETRAYAL

USA TODAY BESTSELLING AUTHOR
SHAIN ROSE

PAGE
&
VINE

Page & Vine
An Imprint of Meredith Wild LLC

Paperback ISBN: 979-8-9877583-2-8

Note on Content Warnings

As a reader who loves surprises, I enjoy going in blind with each book. Yet, I also want to give my readers the opportunity to know what sensitive content may be in my books. You will find the list of them here: www.shainrose.com/content-warnings

For every woman who can take all that is thrown at them in the world and still come out on top...way to take it like the good girls you are.

CHAPTER 1: EVERLY

"She won't be coming over," I heard from the doorway of the yoga studio room. The smile on my face dropped off like a ton of bricks.

It'd been only two months of me living in sunny Florida with my estranged father, but it felt like two lifetimes. I met his blue-eyed gaze with my own. The color of them was about the only thing my father had handed down to me. "Carl, seriously?" I whispered.

"Mr. Milton, don't you think your daughter can make the decision herself?" Wes Bauer rolled up his yoga mat and stood up near me.

"I *can* make that decision myself," I pointed out, combing a hand through the waves of my hair that had succumbed to the rigorous workout.

My father scoffed, his face turned beet red. "I agreed to you working here at the fitness center for us to build a relationship, Evie. This isn't the way to do it."

I sighed. "Can we talk about this later, Carl?"

"We'll talk now." He shook his finger at me.

This was why I hadn't seen him in eighteen years. Carl Milton was truly a baby, an only child who had inherited a fortune from grandparents I had never met. He'd gone on to live a life where no one defied him, leaving my mom and me when I was just six years old because we weren't "good listeners."

He'd actually only agreed to have me come work for his

fitness center after my mother guilted him into it. She'd said I needed to escape my hometown and start a new life away from the graduate school I'd dropped out of.

She was right, of course. I knew that. I was drowning under a deep sea of pain that I couldn't swim above. I'd planned to leave and start anew somewhere else, but I'd never wanted it to be here.

Yet, Carl had insisted. Said he was going into heart failure, that he should be getting to know his only biological daughter.

I'd given in to the naive hope of the little girl still wanting her father's love and relocated halfway across the country to Florida two months ago.

Like an idiot.

"If you go, I'll call Declan." Carl announced, and Wes groaned as he tightened the dark man bun on his head.

"Call me for what?" Declan Hardy's voice was always strong. Deep. Authoritative enough that it commanded all the attention in the room, even as all six foot three of him leaned casually against the doorframe. With chiseled muscle and a famous, beautiful face, the retired NFL star had not a care in the world—even though he'd intruded on someone's private conversation.

My seething father huffed as he walked over to his business partner. "Evie thinks she's going to a party at this asshat's house again. Please, for my sake and our business, take care of it."

With that, he walked out, leaving me with that word *again* bouncing around in my head.

Again. That was the real problem. This wasn't the first time my father had intervened in my dating life. He'd called Declan a month ago and had him fly in to retrieve me from Wes's house.

Fly. Like in an airplane. And Declan had just gone along

with it, knocked on Wes's door, and demanded I leave. That was the world I was living in. To them, I was Carl's precious daughter, breaking a cardinal rule.

Wes chuckled and winked at me before he said, "I'll swing by and pick you up at the end of your shift, Evie." He stalked out of the studio, holding Declan's gaze as he murmured back to me, "Maybe you can stay the night."

My father's business partner flicked his vivid green eyes to me with that comment, capturing my stare and holding it hostage like he owned it. I saw the spark of anger, the question, and the entitlement.

"Everly," he ground out, his voice rumbling so deep in his throat before it emerged that I shivered.

Tension ricocheted off the windows and the mirrors as I stood nonresponsive, the silence engulfing us. I let the quiet stretch on and on, unwilling to give him an iota of the information that I knew he must want. He didn't deserve it nor was he entitled to it. Yet, even still, my whole body practically shook with the need to submit to him, to give up control to him.

Did he have this effect on everyone? So dominating and attractive that he could bend most people to his will? He thought he could just silently lean against a doorframe and make a person answer a question he hadn't even asked yet.

His jaw ticked up and down, up and down before he dropped the question so casually, I wasn't sure I'd heard him right. "How many times have you slept with him?"

I blinked once. Twice. Three times before the words registered. Anger, hot as molten rock, flowed through my blood as my mouth dropped open at his audacity. "Are you serious?" I breathed out, twisting the towel I held in my hands. Then I wiped it over my face, trying my best not to freak out. With a wet sports bra that had the HEAT logo on it, my curls frizzed out, and only twenty minutes until my next one-on-one training session, I shouldn't have even been entertaining the ridiculous conversation.

And yet, it was technically with my boss.

"Yes, Everly." He pushed off the doorframe and stepped toward me. Hissing my full name like no one else would was another show of him trying to grate on my nerves. I just knew it. And on top of that, he came close to tower over me like he could intimidate me. "How many times did you sleep with that fucker?"

I stood toe-to-toe with him, meeting his gaze right back even if he was a whole head and a half taller than me. My body never reacted in fear the way it should have with him. It got stupid butterflies in my gut instead. I figured everyone got those, though.

Declan Hardy was a global sensation for a reason. It wasn't just that he was an investor in my father's hospitality and fitness empire either. That face, his thick dark hair, those piercing green eyes that stared into my soul every time he glanced my way. "That *fucker*?" I emphasized his language and lifted an eyebrow as I glared at him.

He shook his head like he wanted to chastise me and waited for me to explain. Yet, I'd learned long ago not to indulge in idle conversation around my personal life.

He breathed out when he realized I intended to stay quiet. "You're Carl's *daughter*, Everly." He said it like I should know better.

I shoved the plush towel into my duffel while grumbling, "I can't believe he tattled to his partner about where I'm going again."

Declan pointed at a sleek gold bin. "There are clean towels in the locker room. You can dispose of that one there."

The luxury this man was accustomed to made me wrinkle my nose. "I'm fine reusing."

He wiped a hand over his face. "You're going to make us all go insane."

"Seriously?" I scoffed. "You barely see me."

"And yet every time I do, you're ruffling feathers," he pointed out.

I tried not to raise my voice as I hiked my duffel bag up onto my shoulder. "If you're talking about the meeting you couldn't attend last week, I'd simply requested an empty yoga studio for the Sunville kids in this town to utilize for children's yoga."

"I—" He narrowed his eyes. "Your father didn't say it was for kids."

Could I roll my eyes at this point, or would that have been too disrespectful? Sunville Elementary was an underserved school that was in desperate need of more after-school activities. It was a way for the HEAT Empire to give back to the community. A win-win really. Yet, my father had immediately shut down the idea.

"Had you not skipped the meeting, you would know that, *Mr. Hardy*."

"Declan," he corrected, his eyes flashing with irritation. "I'm busy. I train athletes, have shareholder meetings, and—"

"Yes, a skydiving appointment seems like it should take precedence."

That chiseled jaw ticked fast. Maybe he thought because I was quiet that I would back down, that I would roll over since he was a major shareholder of this elite fitness and hospitality brand. HEAT stood for Hardy Elite All-Access Team and supposedly spanned the nation with resorts, fitness centers, restaurants, and more.

My backbone wasn't impressed and was still very much present when it came to what I'd be doing while I was here. I intended to make an impact where I could even if I didn't plan to stay forever.

"I'm sure it wasn't skydiving."

"Fine. Racing a car." I shrugged and squeezed the bag's strap on my shoulder when he dragged his gaze up and down my body like he was measuring me up.

"I'm not going to argue with you, Everly," he said softly. Still, it somehow felt like he was grinding salt into a wound.

"It's Evie," I threw out, knowing it wouldn't matter.

"Look, have more classes for the kids. I'll never say no to that." He scratched the back of his neck, his bicep bunching and showing off a few of the tattoos he had on his upper arm beneath his white T-shirt. "I just had other meetings. If you need to discuss implementing new classes that you know your father is going to disagree with, you should probably make sure I'm available. Do you check the schedule?"

Could I smack the condescension out of his tone or would I lose my job for that? "I'll make sure to double-check it next time."

"See that you do. And let's not get your father's heart worked up. Wes is probably twice your age. You can't be seen with that asshole." He said it offhandedly, like he could slide one extra request in.

I combed a hand through my waves. "Twice my age? Get real, Mr. Hardy," I sneered his last name since he couldn't be bothered to listen to my request either. "I'm twenty-four. And just because I'm his daughter doesn't mean I'm not going to date people I'm interested in."

He tilted his head, like he needed to study me all of a sudden. Like he was realizing I was more than ten years old. His gaze dragged over me, licking up every curve of my body, and then he shut his eyes tight as if seeing what appealed to another man was painful. It infuriated me that my body even responded to his perusal. "He's not just a guy, Everly. He's an asshole. Being seen with him is bad for press. You're a part of HEAT now."

"Really?" I cocked a hip and lifted an eyebrow, ready for this to be over. "So, there are rules already regarding who I date because of a headline? You're going to continue to come to his house and drag me out because you're nervous it might tarnish a brand name? Do you hear how ridiculous that sounds?"

"We barely accepted him into HEAT based on his reputation and how he's played in the NFL. He plays a dirty game and his fuckboy reputation—"

"I don't watch football and can make my own judgments on a person. I don't need the press telling me who to date." I cut him off, furious that my father's business partner thought I'd let the media's story on a person sway me.

I wouldn't let journalists or the internet paint someone's story like they had mine once before. In my hometown, I wasn't trusted, wasn't looked at as a person, wasn't given the benefit of the doubt.

"You don't watch football but you know how to rehab an athlete?" He really hated that I was working in his gym with no credentials when it seemed all his other employees were overqualified.

"I provide stretching techniques, not full rehab." As he

knew. I'd gained client after client for the unique way I handled each of them and there'd not been one complaint since I started. "And I'm going to be late for a one-on-one. So, if we're done here..."

I brushed past him, but before I could walk away, his voice rolled over me cold enough to freeze me mid-step. "You didn't answer my question."

I turned to look at him. In the middle of this yoga studio, he was a beautiful sight among the mirrors reflecting around him with the backdrop of floor-to-ceiling windows that overlooked the Atlantic. "What was it?"

"How many times have you fucked him?"

My whole body tightened at how he phrased it this time. My stomach, my throat, my nipples, my sex squeezed and ached in hate but also something more. The visceral reaction I had to this man was dangerous, tempting, and completely wrong.

"That's absolutely none of your business." The answer was zero and would probably remain that way. We'd casually gone on a few dates that led to nothing because Wes didn't cause a reaction in me at all.

"So, you haven't. That answer changes, Everly, and I'm coming for him." Declan's voice was low in warning, like I shouldn't question him, and I felt the vibration of it shoot through my body, giving me goose bumps everywhere.

I considered giving him the finger as I left him in the studio by himself. But he was my boss.

My off-limits boss I hated and wanted all at the same time.

CHAPTER 2: EVERLY

A hot shower after my shift didn't help to scald away any of my frustration. Nor did brushing through the tangles of my hair harder than intended.

Putting on my tennis skirt and a coat of lip gloss and mascara before I texted Wes I was on my way over, though, had me feeling much better.

Po and Noah saw me exit the revolving door of the fitness center as they sat on the fountain's edge in the circular drive. "Evie, you coming to Vibe Club with us later?" Po asked.

I pointed toward a small path that led down to HEAT Health and Fitness that was sitting atop an ocean cliff, providing beautiful views and connecting to their Oceanside Resort. "I'm walking over to Wes's actually."

"See, bro. Everyone's going to Wes's. Let's just go." Noah shoved his friend.

"Goddamn," Po grumbled, combing his big hand through his wavy mess of hair. It looked styled, but I knew for a fact neither of them cared a bit how they looked. Instead, they both lifted most of the day at the fitness center, ran, took yoga classes, and then they trained on-ice a few times a week. Their lives, even in the off-season, revolved mostly around hockey.

Noah cajoled, "You know puck bunnies are going to Wes's. Let's just go. Plus, Evie will be there."

Po reached for my duffel, then hiked it up onto his shoulder. "Fuck it. We'll walk with you."

I chuckled as we stepped onto the sand and started our trek along the water, waves lapping softly along the way. "Are you both going just to hook up with women?"

"If I say yes, will you think less of me?" Po asked.

Sighing, I stopped to pick up a white shell and grabbed at the pocket of my duffel bag to slide it in. "No, because I already think pretty low of you and your hookup habits."

Po glanced at me collecting the shell. "You realize there're better ones up at the tourist shop than that?"

I shrugged. People stepped all over the shells like they weren't beautiful pieces to be reused, and what was the use of buying them when I could have the experience of finding one myself?

A seagull hopped close but jumped back as we stepped toward it. So, I waved at the guys to stop walking and tried to give him and his flock a wide berth. I made sure to do it every day when jogging to work so as not to scare them off.

"Evie," Po deadpanned, mirth in his dark eyes. "Just go through the gulls. They'll fly away and come right back."

I sighed and fell into step with them again. "They're different from the blue birds and cardinals back home in Wisconsin. You scare them and they're gone to another feeder for a whole season."

"Florida's filled with seagulls that'll never leave. You'll get used to it soon enough," Noah said as he nudged me on the way up to Wes's oceanfront property.

Getting used to hanging out with people who owned homes five times the size of my apartment, like Wes's, wasn't going to come easy.

Getting used to everything at HEAT Health and Fitness was near impossible. My mother and I had owned a run-down yoga studio that we charged a five-dollar fee to attend. Here, members paid hundreds of thousands in dues each year. They got access to private clubs, spas, hotels, and red carpet events like they were celebrities.

When I walked into Wes's house, I saw that many of them were in fact celebrities. Athletes. Moguls. Millionaires, all of them. The kind of people who dressed in their best just to hang out with friends.

Wes met us right away and introduced me to some of his team. Po and Noah draped their arms around women immediately, which would have been impressive if it hadn't been so gross. Yet, when Wes wandered off once or twice, Noah appeared near me right as I started to wring my hands. "Got you, Evie. Want to go sit by the pool?"

In that first hour, Noah and Po demonstrated their acceptance of me not simply as a yoga instructor but as a friend. They stayed close while Wes was off hosting, and they didn't let me out of their sight.

Women and men walked around in bikinis and swim trunks but somehow still managed to look like they belonged.

"I probably should have gone home and changed," I mentioned to Wes when he came back over, but he shook his head.

"Oh." He dragged his gaze over me before he hummed, then smirked to himself. "People always want to dress up for shit like this. No worries. One sec. I'll get you something."

Po rolled his eyes at Noah. "Bet he brings one of his fucking jerseys."

They both laughed seconds later when Wes came bounding down his sleek floating stairs carrying a small Cobras jersey and a beer. He held it out to me as Noah teased him. "How many of those you got upstairs? You have every size?"

"Fuck off," Wes chuckled. "We get a few boxes for fans, dumbass."

Po grumbled, "More like you bought a few boxes."

I didn't want to be rude, so I slid on the fabric and smiled. "Thanks." But I shook my head at the beer. "I'll just have water."

He nodded and skirted around the island's white marble counter to grab a glass with ice and water. From there, it was like I had a golden ticket. Women tried to engage in conversation with me, men offered me drinks and places to sit, always trying to be accommodating. The jersey seemed to hold a lot of status.

"Evie?" I winced when I heard the high-pitched voice behind me. I actively had been avoiding that voice since the first time I'd been introduced to my stepsister Anastasia. Her blonde hair swung as she walked over from the backyard pool area in her pastel-pink dress that hung loosely enough to show her bikini underneath, and then she hooked her arm into my other stepsister's arm.

Clara and Anastasia were two years apart in age, and they couldn't be more different. Clara wore bright florals and had a permanent smile on her face as she called out a soft, "Hi, Evie," before her sister elbowed her.

Noah glanced between us and must have seen my discomfort because he draped an arm around my shoulder and said, "Happy I get to hang with you Milton ladies tonight."

He probably thought he was defusing tension, but Anastasia practically stomped her pink high heel. "She's not a Milton, Noah."

"My mother changed our last name back to her maiden name when my parents divorced," I explained since Noah looked a bit confused. Clara's face turned pink, but I wouldn't feel ashamed for someone else's rude behavior. I stood tall and sipped a bit of the water before continuing. "Anyway, Carl was gracious enough to let me come stay in the guesthouse for a week, but our families really haven't mixed since he left when I was six and you both were...?"

"I was ten and Clara was eight when Carl came into our lives," Anastasia announced like everyone needed to know. "He's been a great stepfather."

I nodded and chewed my lip, trying not to feel any sense of disappointment. Anastasia had made it very clear we'd never be sisters. Nor did she care to get to know me.

Noah, being the laid-back guy he was, squeezed my shoulder and lifted his drink. "Well, to Carl bringing us all together then."

Anastasia eyed us both up, though, and wrinkled her nose when she saw my attire. "Where did you get that?"

"Wes let me borrow it." I shrugged because it didn't mean anything to me honestly.

"Make sure you give it back before you leave. We don't wear Cobra gear," she ground out before pushing past me. I wasn't sure if she was actually mad about what I was wearing or the fact that I was being accepted into her circle in the slightest.

I glanced at Clara whose green eyes rolled before she murmured, "I'm sorry about her. She's in a mood."

The freckles across her nose had started to peek out from under makeup as she wrinkled it, looking at her sister like she was disgusted with her behavior.

I waved it off. "It's fine. I came straight from work and was underdressed."

She blinked twice, her fake eyelashes noticeable but still doing a great job of framing her eyes beautifully. She'd inherited her mother's high cheekbones and tall frame, and I could see how she was appealing to the masses even if she didn't see it herself. "Not underdressed when you're in the quarterback's jersey. Are you two a thing?"

"Not really. Just seeing where things go, but he knows it's casual." I played with some of the string bracelets on my wrist, but she hummed like she disagreed.

"Carl will get over it if you are. He always huffs and puffs first, then deflates after a bit. Anyway, I'm still sorry about Anastasia. She just hasn't gotten to know you." She pointed to a plush couch where we could sit and waved Noah off.

"Why should you be sorry?" I shrugged and swirled the ice in the glass while I glanced around for Wes. He was taking a shot with his friends, and a girl was leaning on his arm. It was another indicator that this was casual flirting between us and nothing more.

She sighed. "Because she's rude, and she's my sister. So, I should probably teach her some manners."

"She's old enough to know." I pushed the waves out of my face and smiled. "I learned manners like that the first time I listened to *Bambi*."

"Listened?" Clara tilted her head and her dark red curls fell from her shoulder.

I couldn't help but smile at the fact that Clara was attempting to talk with me even knowing her sister wouldn't like it. "My mom was weird about TV and movies. So, I listened on headphones to them."

She gave me a once-over. "That makes a lot sense."

I waited for her to elaborate.

"You do this"—she motioned in front of me—"a lot." Again, I waited. "You don't fold in a moment of awkward silence, like you have a much more controlled attention span than we do."

I laughed at the assessment. "I'm just waiting for you to finish."

"No, no. It's really true."

I glanced at a woman laughing near the pool, reluctant to get in. "I was homeschooled for a long time and not around other people much. Makes me a bit awkward, I guess." I wasn't ashamed of that anymore. "I had my mom and a few friends who came to her small yoga studio, but that's about it."

"Were you lonely?" Clara whispered, like she shouldn't be asking.

"Sure. I wanted..." I sighed. Carl used to send cards of him with his new wife and the children she'd had with her first husband. I'd have those childhood dreams of Christmases together, that I would have sisters, that my mother and their mom would become friends. Yet, I'd overheard my mother asking, heard her agree with my father that maybe it wasn't such a good idea. I saw Anastasia glance over at us and roll her eyes. "An only child gets lonely sometimes, but I also learned a person can keep themselves company probably better than anyone else can."

"Clara, get over here!" Anastasia yelled, waving her manicured hand in the air for Clara.

"I see." Clara leaned in and whispered, "Well, sometimes having Anastasia as a sister can get lonely too." Before I could pick apart what she'd said, she nudged my shoulder. "Oh, don't start reading into it, Evie. We'll talk later. Come to the bakery sometime next week."

I couldn't help but smile at the idea until she stood up and gasped. I followed her line of sight. "What?"

"Probably won't talk later since he's coming this way."

I heard whispers, felt the air in the room shift and, like a parting sea, saw how the crowd moved for him.

He towered over most everyone as he paced through the room, straight up to me without looking away. Anastasia murmured something to him, but his laser focus couldn't be deterred.

"Everly." Declan breathed my name out sternly as he came toe-to-toe with my running shoes.

Why hadn't I changed again? Sitting there in my workout gear with one of Wes's jerseys draped over me now felt a bit ridiculous as he glared down at me. "Yes?"

"Get up. I'm taking you home."

Commands from a man that didn't have any authority over me. Couldn't he see that people were listening, were watching, that he had no claim on me whatsoever?

He'd done this once before, come to Wes's and told me to leave. It'd been with far fewer people to witness it though. This was beyond disrespectful. I'd made that clear to him. So crystal clear it was freaking transparent. He might have been business partners with my father, but he wasn't my dad. We weren't even friends. We were barely even colleagues.

"Hardy, man, you come to have a good time with the wrong team?" Wes called out from behind the counter. He'd had enough to drink that it seemed he was willing to put all rivalries aside.

"No. I came to take Everly home," he growled.

An hour. I'd been gone from the gym for an hour. That meant he'd found out and come straight here. No hesitation, no thought of the repercussions. Not one ounce of consideration for how embarrassing this might be for me.

I stood up and Declan gave me a once-over, his eyes

widening before he pinched the bridge of his nose through a grimace. I saw how his cheeks blew out, too, like he needed a couple deep breaths. "His jersey, Everly? Jesus fucking Christ."

"Mr. Hardy," I ground out his name. "Thanks for stopping by, but I'll take an Uber home *if* I leave. But you being here is completely unnecessary," I whispered angrily, trying to reason with him without everyone hearing.

"You being here when your father forbade it is even more unnecessary." He folded his arms over his chest.

I grabbed his big elbow and led him to a corner of the house, caring too much that eyes were on us. Then I squared up to him. "Forbade his estranged daughter from going to a house with a guy she's been seeing? Do you even hear yourself? I'm here just like Clara and Anastasia." I poked his shoulder, because at this point, everyone was watching us anyway.

"Clara and Anastasia know better than to date Wes." His eyes flashed. "Why can't you just listen?"

"Listen to you like everyone else does?" I threw out my hands. "What? Because you own HEAT?"

A few people gasped, and Anastasia chose that exact moment to walk up to Declan and wrap her arm in his, her pink saccharine smile condescending as she pointedly said to me, "I know you haven't lived here long, Evie, but Declan does a lot for all of us."

"Not me," Wes chuckled, his drink sloshing in his hand. "Declan, chill. I can get you a glass of whiskey if you're—"

"I'm not staying." He stared at me, a fire of determination in his eyes. "We're leaving."

"And if I don't?"

"Oh, I'll carry you, Drop. Try me." With a warning tone, he used the nickname he'd come up with the first time he'd met me. I tried my best not to roll my eyes. He knew I hated nicknames other than Evie, and that one associated me with being as small as a raindrop.

All of it was too juvenile, too over-the-top to argue about.

"Wes, can you walk me out?"

"Really?" Wes suddenly sobered like he couldn't believe I'd leave his party. "I mean, sure. Sure. Let's go."

I looped my arm in his and brushed past Declan. Weaving through the people still watching the confrontation was bad enough but walking outside to hear Declan say, "You can give him his jersey back," was nearly my breaking point.

Still, I gripped the sides of it. Causing more of a scene wasn't worth it. None of this was. Yet, Wes smiled big like he wanted to piss Declan off and announced, "Keep it, Evie. I've got more." Then, he pulled me close and kissed me in front of Declan. It was our first. We'd been strictly friendly before that moment.

His lips tasted of bitter beer and were all wrong. It was like we were playing a game, and Wes simply wanted to win the prize. I stepped back and let him know I'd call him, even though I considered not.

Declan opened the door of a black SUV idling in the driveway.

I gave myself one pass with my anger when I stepped into it and grabbed the door from him, slamming it hard behind me.

He rounded the hood of the car and slid in next to me while announcing to his driver, "Peter, Everly lives at Carl's."

"I don't," I corrected. "I moved."

"Moved?" he questioned but quickly waved it off. "Tell Peter your address so we can get you home." I turned my gaze on him, waiting for him to at least apologize. He waited too, like he was studying me as I was studying him. "You're pushing the wrong boundaries, Everly."

"There shouldn't be boundaries outside of work with my boss," I pointed out.

"You were at work when you decided to come to this fucker's house," he ground out, his jaw working up and down.

He was angry? *Great*, I thought. *Me too.* "Are you going to apologize?"

"For what?" His nostrils flared as he breathed out.

"For the scene you caused," I almost screeched, my composure slipping a little as I pointed toward Wes's house. "For embarrassing me *again*."

"I don't really give a fuck what scene I cause. And if that's embarrassing, don't go to a dumbass's house and expect I'm not going to come for you. I'll come every fucking time, Drop." He clenched his fists like he was holding on to his fury just as I was.

I almost told him to stop calling me that, but we were barreling toward an explosion if one of us didn't do the mature thing. I ignored his comment and told the driver where he could find my apartment.

His eyes bulged. "But you've been jogging to work."

"Yes." I shrugged and played with the edge of the jersey.

"That's a four-mile run and some of the side streets aren't great neighborhoods. What are you thinking?"

"Excuse me for enjoying the morning and evening breeze."

"The damn breeze..." he grumbled. "When I have you work overtime—"

"I'm capable of taking an Uber. I'm smart about running, not that I should have to be. Female runners are notoriously blamed for others' behavior. Studies show sixty percent of us have been harassed on runs, yet we're told to know when to run, to run in groups, to—" I paused, realizing I was rambling and then waved myself off. "It really isn't that big of a deal."

"Jesus, is nothing a big deal to you?"

"As opposed to you acting like everything is a big deal and storming into a party to demand I leave?" I pulled my hair back, combing it up to put into a bun, but when I grabbed at my wrist for a hair band, I growled, realizing I'd forgotten to add one to my wrist.

"You shouldn't have been at Wes's party."

"Oh, Jesus. Not this again." I sighed, so tired of him and my father. "I'm trying to see if we're compatible."

"You're not. He's not your type," Declan concluded for me.

"That's not your call." I blinked slowly and tried to calm my frustration. "I'm being reasonable, Mr. Hardy."

I heard him breathe out like a frustrated bull. "Well, it's tiring being reasonable," he shot back.

How did he get by acting out like this? "Is it really that hard to do?"

"Fuck yes," he bellowed. And then he shut his eyes for a moment. "Your father cares about you, and I care about—" I waited. If he wanted to admit more, I'd let him. "Our brand. About your father's wishes. He's done a lot for me. So he expects when you're working in the gym I manage that you'll be taken care of."

My heart sort of crumbled hearing his justification, though I didn't know why. Declan and I were colleagues, nothing more. "You're getting heated for no reason. We're in this situation because you're an absolute hothead with no one to rein you in."

"What's that supposed to mean?"

"Tonight's a perfect example. You have no hold on me and shouldn't get to dictate where I go, yet no one questioned your antics at Wes's party. You're the king of this elite empire you've built." I motioned out at the city lights passing us by.

"Right." He nodded. "So you should be listening to me."

"Oh, Mr. Hardy. I'm not part of your empire. I'm a short-term transplant just passing through. I intend to be out of your hair in no time." That was the plan at least.

He narrowed his eyes as the SUV came to a stop in front of my apartment building. "Everly, do me a favor. While you're in my empire, please don't wear that fucking jersey and stop going to his place."

I sighed. "You should learn to not let things bother you so much."

He leaned in. "What's bothersome to you? Because I'd really like you to feel exactly how you make me feel."

CHAPTER 3: DECLAN

"And how is it that I make you feel?" she whispered.

Everly Belafonte. My business partner's *only* biological daughter. Although they were estranged, he looked at her like she was a treasure, something so precious that he even thought he could taint her in some way. He'd told me the first time I'd met her that he'd stayed away from her and her mother after he'd realized he could do them no good.

It was a twisted way to parent, yet I couldn't disagree with him.

Everly was pure and unmarred by the world in a way I couldn't really articulate. She had waves of curls that framed her face with a braid or two mixed in with the brown and black and blonde that flowed all around in ringlets so wild you wanted to tame them. Then you caught her gaze and saw how calm and focused it was. Sapphire blue and piercing against her tan skin while completely steady, like she couldn't be knocked down no matter how anyone would try. And then she spoke, and the rasp in her voice soothed even though her words grated on my every nerve because they made total sense.

She held my gaze now with a mix of determination and what I think mirrored my lust. I was hooked. Trapped. Captured by the way she bit her bottom lip waiting for my answer.

"How do you make me feel?" I repeated her question back to her, trying to get ahold of myself, but I knew the fight was futile. I'd danced around her for two damn months and still couldn't avoid wanting her to myself. "It feels like I have my business partner's daughter sitting in front of me, riling me up, driving me near madness, and still my adrenaline is pumping, my cock is rock solid, and I'm scrambling to find any reason I shouldn't be tasting those lips. Why I shouldn't demand that you come sit on my lap for a minute."

Her reaction to my words was instant. She looked at my cock and then licked her lips. "Demand? You forget that I'm one person you don't control, Mr. Hardy."

I leaned in a fraction more, so my mouth was at her ear, and murmured, "I'm starting to think you'd like me taking control, Everly. There's a reason I'm the boss, right? A reason you got in the car willingly?"

She wiggled in her seat as we stared at each other like she was considering it, like she needed a release as bad as I did. "And that's the reason why this can't happen." She pointed between us. "Boss and employee. Partner's daughter. Lavish lifestyle... and mine not so much."

"You underestimate how easy it is for me to plow through obstacles." I leaned close to her neck now, mesmerized at the thought of what her skin would feel like against my lips as I gripped her bare thigh. Smooth, soft, and willing as she spread her legs for me to massage farther and farther up. "I think we could both enjoy me controlling you for a night."

She whimpered but rolled her hips when my hand cupped her pussy. She pulled my head closer to her neck and moaned out, "This is wrong, Declan."

"Not Mr. Hardy anymore? She finally says my name... But the question is whether you're using it to get me to stop or keep going."

Her hands found their way into my hair, like she needed

to hold me close as I grazed kisses over her collarbone. "I don't even like you," she breathed.

I chuckled. "Oh, but your pussy loves me." She gasped at my words, but I kept going. "It's begging for me, babe. And you don't really know me. I could make you like me."

She scoffed at my confidence like I was ridiculous, but when my thumb brushed over her clit, she clawed at my shoulders. "You're a hothead when I'm not at all like that. I think you enjoy a game and an adrenaline rush, Mr. Hardy. I don't enjoy either of those things."

I sat back to watch her as I did it again and threaded my other hand through her hair, yanking it so I could tilt her face to be lit perfectly under the city lights. They shone through the window, illuminating the change of her expression as I worked her up toward an orgasm that would unravel the composure she always asserted around me. "I could make you enjoy the game and an adrenaline rush too, Everly." I didn't prepare her for my mouth, descending without further warning.

I wanted to catalog how her body responded. How she met me taking what I wanted without apology with her own vigor. How she hung on to my shirt like she relished the moment as much as I did and wasn't worried about the repercussions for once.

I wanted her lost in what I was doing to her and only stopped long enough to grab her hips and move her onto my lap. With her back against my chest, I wrapped my arm around her waist and went back to working her pussy at the perfect angle. I thrust my cock up, not being able to control feeling her ass against it, and she moaned in pleasure like the outline of it would be enough for her.

Her hips rolled as she grabbed the front seat, but then she

immediately froze, and I saw her staring up front. She'd been too lost in what we were doing to remember Peter.

He was on the phone, completely ignoring us. It was his job to do so, but it was a goddamn wake-up call.

This was a woman I didn't want to fuck and duck nor would it be a good business decision. My mind swirled with the consequences. I needed to make it right. I barked out for Peter to take a walk. He immediately left, but she glanced back at me, her ass shifting on my dick enough that I had to mash my teeth together.

"The moment's ruined," she pointed out, pushing her hair to the side, and I caught a whiff of the sweet coconut shampoo she must have used. Her ass wiggled again as she bit her bottom lip and my dick wasn't giving up after that.

My hard length rubbed right where I wanted it to as I shifted and desire flared in her eyes. "So, let's make a new moment, Everly. Let the last one go. Let me help." My hand was still cupping her, but I took that second to slide my fingers under her skirt and panties.

"I don't let things go," she breathed out as my fingers explored how wet she was.

"You should, babe," I hummed close to her ear. "Why worry about a past you can't change? Just listen to me instead, huh?"

I was asking her to hand over control. Asking for permission before I took.

She hesitated, mulled it over, took her time, all while rolling those hips into my hand before acquiescing. "I'm listening this one time, and if someone sees—"

I didn't even wait for her to finish. My finger dipped into her fast, and she gasped. "Let me worry about that. You just focus on this." I rubbed my thumb over her clit hard, creating a friction she couldn't ignore. "That's what's important now."

The fear of being seen wasn't going to guide her orgasm. I was going to make sure of that. I wanted her every worry to be chased away by me this time. She was too composed all the goddamn time, too fucking perfect and pure, and she needed an outlet.

I was the best fucking one.

Not a party.

Not Wes.

Me.

"I want that damn jersey off you now. It shouldn't ever be his name on your back," I growled in her ear. "Take. It. Off."

I indulged her wet pussy so good that she didn't even hesitate. She whipped it over her head and threw it on the ground while I took in the zip-up tank she'd worn from work underneath.

"I'm doing this one time." She said it like we needed a damn reminder. "Take over, Declan. And don't make me regret it."

"She commands before she hands over control." I nipped at her sensitive skin near her collarbone, and a smile spread across my face before I said, "I think I'm going to have a hard time only wanting you this once, Everly."

I grabbed a fistful of her hair then, making her arch against my chest as I devoured her neck and worked her pussy at the same pace my tongue slid against her skin. "Unzip your shirt."

Her damn HEAT sports bras and tanks always zipped in front, driving me fucking insane.

She hesitated.

"Listen, Everly," I ground out, "or I'll make you work a lot harder for this orgasm you want so badly."

SHAIN ROSE

She whimpered as I circled her clit much more slowly this time, bucked into my hand like she couldn't wait, and then did as she was told.

"That's it. Such a good girl already. Look at those pretty tits." I stared over her shoulder at them as the one hand I'd had on her hip slid up to work her nipples, pinching and rubbing them back and forth, back and forth just like I did her pussy. Her own hands went into her hair as she arched while I picked up the pace. Then I sucked on her neck while thrusting my fingers to her G-spot over and over, faster and faster until she screamed my name.

Loud, uninhibited, and out of control.

She crumbled back into my chest, her sex spasming again and again around my fingers.

Her losing control for me the way I'd been fantasizing about since the first time I met her had me murmuring my next command. "Come back to my place."

Her thighs clenched closed on my hand as she whipped around, her eyes still cloudy blue from her first orgasm with me. "There's no way."

"Why?" I knew why even as she scooted off me and rearranged her clothing.

"Because this is it." She waved between us and then reached for my waistband, but I grabbed her wrist.

"We're not just doing this," I said. "I'm not fucking you in the back of an SUV, Everly."

"You got me off back here. What's the difference?" Her eyes widened and her voice raised one octave. Wrenching her wrist from my grip, she zipped her top back up hurriedly and reached for the jersey on the floor.

"Yeah, foreplay." I decided this wasn't going to be the end

for us. I needed more of her. "Before you come home with me."

She chuckled, slipping the jersey I hated back over her head, and then sobered when she realized I was actually serious. "I can't... We can't do that."

"Why the fuck not?"

"Because I'm me. You're you. You're a freaking celebrity. I don't want anything to do with you outside of this car."

But she'd just had my hand so far up her pussy, she'd screamed my name?

She laughed at what must have been my look of confusion. "Mr. Hardy, not all of us want to be in the spotlight. Not all of us are turned on by the fact that you own this weird HEAT community and are plastered on the front of every magazine in town."

"And yet, here I am with the arousal of your pussy still on my fingertips, babe."

"Jesus. I can't with you." She pulled the handle on the door. "I don't like the press, Declan. And I hate being seen as less of a human than someone else. I had that in my last relationship—"

I cut her off because that was never going to be her and me. "You dwelling on someone before me?"

She glanced away as a gust of wind whipped by, hiding what she wanted to but not before I saw it, the ghost of a past still haunting her.

"Now I see pain in your eyes and that hesitation. You're pushing me away because you're stuck in a past."

"You have no idea." She shook her hair back over her shoulders, like she could use it as a shield to hide from me.

"I don't dwell, Drop, and I'm going to make sure you don't one day either."

"Stop calling me that." She slid out of the car and shut the door on what she didn't want to be.

Yet, I rolled down her window. "Get rid of that fucking jersey, Everly."

"Let's not get carried away. It's a jersey."

"I had to stare at his name on your back right before you ground your ass against my cock and moaned my name. I won't let that happen again."

"Oh, well, it won't be happening again. So, that solves that," she said over her shoulder, and I had half a mind to get out of the car and follow her to her apartment. "Good night, Mr. Hardy."

"Everly," I yelled after her but she didn't turn around. "Don't jog to work. I'm sending a car for you on Monday."

"Please don't. I'll just ignore it." She waved it away like she was waving us away too.

I swore ten times before I yelled at Peter to get back into the vehicle.

She was already inside by the time I finished cursing out our whole situation. We shouldn't have indulged. I was quick to temper, and it looked like Everly maintained her composure even after I'd unraveled her.

Still, I was already figuring out a way I could do it again come the very next day.

CHAPTER 4: DECLAN

Me: It's been two weeks of you ignoring the car I'm sending for you.

Everly: How did you get this number?

Me: You're my employee. I have all your numbers.

Everly: That's not what the employee directory is for.

Me: I can use it how I see fit. Take the ride home from work today.

Everly: I don't need a car when I like to jog. I appreciate the thought though.

She appreciated the thought? I'd appreciate bending her over my knee and spanking her ass for defying me every chance she got. Could I send her that?

The bouncing dots showing she was typing something stopped and started a few times at the bottom of my screen before I got another text.

> Everly: I appreciate the extra time in the studio with the kids too. It was nice of you to open self-defense on Tuesdays and yoga on Wednesdays.

She shouldn't have to thank me for that. I wanted HEAT to do more with the community, and Carl knew that. He'd mumbled that he didn't know whether Everly was ready when I brought it up to him the day after Everly confronted me about it.

When I told him she was, he'd smiled big and said, "Okay! I'm glad. See? This is going to work out fine."

Yeah, except I couldn't figure out how to stop thinking about how my dick would feel inside her every chance I got. This "working out fine" was a long shot with bad aim in the middle of the night.

I glanced up as the elevator doors opened and saw her smiling at a kid at the front desk where she was setting her water bottle down. Wearing a zip-up bra.

It was a damn problem that I couldn't look away.

"You did great today, Grayson." She high-fived him, and he spun in a circle with his mom standing there before his eyes lit up as he saw me.

"Declan Hardy! No way!" He ran toward me, his chestnut hair flopping fast, and then stuttered to a stop. "Mom! Do we have a football?"

She smiled bright before digging in her bag and whipping out a marker and pigskin like she walked around ready to run into retired NFL players.

"You have fun at class?" I asked, and he nodded vigorously as I signed the ball. "I did the best downward dog ever. And

35

Ms. Everly says if I breathe properly, my emotions won't get all squiggly sometimes."

When I finished signing, he gave me a hug and his mother thanked me before they walked out as Piper walked in. I didn't have a chance to turn around to talk with Everly about taking care of the kids, about how she was making a difference by teaching them how to handle emotions with exercise, how utterly brilliant it was.

I had no chance because my PR exec was a viper of a woman who didn't care that I wanted to deal with Everly in the least. "You ready to talk?" Piper flipped her bone-straight raven hair and kept walking without scanning in her watch to check in as she walked by the front desk.

Everly ducked her head immediately to look at the tablet instead of us. She really did hate the spotlight and attention of any sort. I sighed because I didn't catch the blue of her eyes or even a small smile from her that I would have liked to see after two weeks of us playing professional.

Piper droned on as she followed me to one of our all-gender locker rooms. My brother had implemented privacy throughout with expansive stalls and private showers so all genders could utilize the shared space. As we weaved past the sauna and into my office, I wondered if Everly would text me again.

Could I text her and thank her for being good to the kids? Could I tell her I appreciated her?

"Are you even listening to me?" Piper stopped and crossed her arms over her blouse as I loosened my tie. This was where I normally changed, but when I saw her eyes dip before a small smile played on her face, I halted.

Fuck.

Piper and I were over. I'd made it pretty clear to her once

or twice. Or maybe three times. We'd been on and off for years, but only one girl consumed my mind these days and it wasn't Piper. This girl had waves cascading down her small back, fire in her blue eyes, and a composure I was sure no one could crack, but I damn well wanted to try.

Even so, Piper stepped up with her expert hands and undid my tie before she started unbuttoning my shirt. "I see now why you're not listening."

"No." I grabbed her hands and stopped her. "I've got a lot on my mind, Piper."

"Okay," she whispered. "Let me clear it for a bit then."

She'd get on her knees in a second, I knew that. But my dick didn't even twitch at the thought. "Piper, I said last time was the last time. I meant it."

She rolled her eyes and scoffed. "Fine. I'm confirming the sponsorship with the shoe company." Back to business because the woman was better at her job than most, I'd give her that. "HEAT Resorts needs to push the Pacific Coast hotel soon too. You need to talk with your brother about it." She glanced at her watch. "I'm late for a meeting, but if we're not dating, you need to consider Anastasia because my bestie will be good for press."

She left me more irritated than I'd been before, so I changed into gym shorts and a T-shirt. Then my irritation turned to pure rage when I saw Everly across my damn gym, bending over to adjust the height of the punching bag.

For Wes.

"Everly." I tried to keep my voice calm, but I had just arranged schedules so she'd be up front permanently, aside from the children's classes. She was great at greeting guests, and that way guys wouldn't be staring at her ass all the damn time like he was at that very second.

It was wrong, but I wasn't above that shit. I saw the way every guy in my gym looked at her. She was in shape, had curves for days, and those fucking deep-blue eyes. So deep, they looked like sapphire sirens that mesmerized you before she pulled you in and devoured your soul.

Plus, she was my partner's daughter. I was looking out for her. That's what I'd keep telling myself. And what I told my brother Dom when he asked me what I was doing when he saw me switching the schedule the other day as we went over shareholder business.

No one needed to know about the night in the back of that SUV. Even though I couldn't forget about it. I'd held her composure, her control, her damn undoing in my hands. She'd given it to me. And ever since, I wasn't sure I could keep control of myself. I'd made her leave another man's house. And she wasn't even mine. Yet.

I could blame Carl for it. He'd called and practically designated me to be her guard dog, but she'd stirred something different in me the moment I'd met her. The girl was beautiful, nice, quiet, and had a take-no-shit attitude. Most of the men at my gym thought she was a catch. I heard the damn whispers.

But I couldn't figure out if she was fucking with everyone's minds or just mine. I was convinced that even if she was younger than me and half the guys in the gym, she was smarter than all of us combined.

"What do you need, Mr. Hardy?" She held a hand up to stop Wes from continuing to pummel the bag she was holding, and then she wiped the sweat from her forehead, her breath coming fast.

My eyes flicked over her, lingering on the fact that she couldn't for the life of her wear a T-shirt or a tank top to the gym. Instead, she was in tight yoga leggings and bright-red sports bra, her curves on display so perfectly that I couldn't look away. At this point, I was considering a new employee dress policy expressly so others wouldn't stare at her like I was.

Her dark wavy hair was up in a pony, ensuring everyone could admire the slope of her neck too. And I knew her hair was long, could imagine how it fell down her back or that it would have covered the way her chest rose and fell if it cascaded over and in front of her shoulders.

I hated that she did these classes at my gym for our business, showing these guys flexibility and strength when those fuckers weren't even there for that. Noah didn't need a damn yoga class for balance in the NHL. He only wanted to stare at her ass.

Much like I did.

Fuck.

And if I wasn't daydreaming about grabbing her hair or her ass, I imagined running my hands over her bare stomach...the one that currently glistened under the gym's lighting, showing off her muscle tone, the small curve of her waist, and how her ass swelled perfectly from it.

"I thought I told you to assist at the front desk."

"Right. I didn't have a chance to tell you when you walked away with Piper." Her cheeks were flushed, and she chewed her lip in an effort to not give anything else away. But I heard the dip in her voice when she mentioned our names, felt the tension like she might be jealous. She pointed to my front desk where I saw one of my seasoned employees. "Juna took over because Wes needed help sparring so..." She shrugged and smiled at Wes.

Big man that he was, he stepped in to defend her. "I just needed a little extra motivation today." He winked at me like I would understand.

Oh, I understood his dumb ass all right. "Motivation?" I chuckled and rubbed my jaw, trying my best to temper my response. To see reason. To act composed like she did all the time.

Everly was an employee. She was my partner's daughter. She should have been completely off-limits and not at all mine.

Yet, my dick responded every time she was in the room. My mind had started to scream that no one could look at her but me. And my body obviously didn't react to anyone else at this point. It'd been two weeks since our time in the SUV, and I'd jacked off to her countless times since.

"Declan," she whispered like she knew something in me was brewing. When her hand grazed my bicep gently, she probably figured it would calm me.

Her touch instead ignited the flames of jealousy that licked through my veins and made me spew the bullshit I said next. "How about I motivate you to get the hell out of my gym before I beat your ass for flirting with my partner's daughter?"

One of our security guards who meandered around incognito stepped forward. In the NFL and in the empire I'd built, I reigned supreme. No one wanted to come into HEAT Health and Fitness and upset one of the owners. Everyone, even Wes, knew that.

I wouldn't apologize for it. He should have known his place.

"Bro, you know you're a legend to me. I still think you could take another Super Bowl if you decide to come back in a year or two." That fucker knew I was retired and that he was part of the reason for it. "This can't be that big of an issue that you, me, and Carl can't look past—"

"It is." I cut him off. Wes was a snake. Everyone in the NFL knew it. His ass should have been happy he was a HEAT member at all. He knew it too, because he was already backing away, grumbling to Everly that he'd call her later. He didn't want me sharing his reputation with her, didn't want me tarnishing what he thought they had.

What he didn't realize was they were about to have nothing at all.

"Are you a complete imbecile?" Everly ground out, her small hands fisting at her sides as Wes practically ran to the locker room. "We're seeing each other. You can't just come over and scare him off."

"Your dad wants me to." I shrugged. Damn, her eyes turned a vivid crystal blue when she got mad. "I told you the other night, and I'll tell you again, he's not your type."

"I don't care what Carl wants," she spat. "You and my dad aren't my keepers."

"Wes is an asshole," I found myself saying, although I didn't have to defend my actions to her. Carl Milton had made it clear that Everly was not allowed to date any guy from Wes's team.

He and I were partners. The man had lived and breathed by my team. When I'd mentioned that I was thinking about retiring to the press, he'd hunted me down to invest in his hotel and gym empire. That was five years ago and I hadn't retired then. I'd played four more years while we'd built up the gym and hospitality brand together. In that time, he'd been smart enough to plaster my name on everything.

Hardy Elite All-Access Team. Hardy Hotel. Hardy this, Hardy that. My face everywhere and America went wild.

Carl was a mentor and a friend, and I was going to make

sure his daughter wasn't dating someone he didn't want her to. At least, that was the reason I was going with for now.

"How would you even know? You never talk to him here," she pointed out.

"Exactly. Because he plays a dirty game of football, and he's cheated on every single woman he's ever been in a relationship with. He's not your type." I turned and started to walk back to the front desk, but she grabbed my arm and yanked me to turn and continue the conversation.

"Totally my type," she threw back, her poise suddenly slipping.

I leaned in close. "Was he your type when your pussy got wet for me? When you screamed my name, not *his*, after leaving his house the other night?"

Her eyes widened at my question and then narrowed like she was ready to go to war. "Great. So, you're assuming I want a serious relationship? That I'm concerned he cheated on someone before me?" She leaned in and whispered, "Maybe I just want to fuck someone in the locker room once or twice like you and Piper have."

Her sapphire eyes blazed a blue fire now, her jealousy burning to the surface with mine. Two storms brewing to make a damn hurricane. She wanted to goad me; I saw it in how she squared up to me, but she must have realized her mistake. I felt my heart pounding, my body reacting to her, my anger mingling with the desire to be the one to take her back to the locker room and do exactly what she wanted.

She took a step back as I took one forward, and then she spun on a heel, navigating her way to the locker room as she undid that long hair and let it cascade down her back before the doors swung shut behind her.

I swear she was taunting me to come back there, playing a fucking game with my dick that I couldn't win. Everly was the mastermind, and I was the dumb man being led by lust rather than reason.

But I followed her into that locker room, rounding the corner fast, ensuring no one saw me, before I grabbed her by the elbow and shoved her into the first private shower stall I could without saying a damn word.

"What the hell, Declan?" She turned and faced me, tilting her head up to stare at me as I stepped close to her. We'd been pushing each other for too long now. I wanted to taste her, smell her, feel every part of her. I took my time nestling into her neck, and she gasped but angled her head, giving me access to her neck.

She may have wanted to fuck someone else.

She may have been ten years younger than me.

And she may have been my partner's daughter.

But Everly was going to be only *mine* right then and there.

"If you intend to fuck someone in my gym, babe, you can bet your ass it's going to be me."

She shook her head and stammered out, "I wasn't talking about doing *anything with you* in here."

"If you're talking about fucking someone, it better only be me, Drop." I took my time dragging my lips across her neck as I moved my knee between her legs. She immediately whimpered in response to the pressure of my thigh against her pussy, even with the fabric between us.

"We're at work." She stared up at me, and I saw lust in her eyes, saw how she licked her lips. "And contrary to what I said out there, I don't fuck at work like some—"

"Piper does my PR. She was giving me an update. Not—"

"It doesn't matter." She looked away and one of her hands went to her neck full of necklaces to play with them. She dragged her teeth over her bottom lip and it glistened enough that I had to lower my head to taste it. To taste her.

I took her lips in my mouth, and she opened them immediately, ravaging me like I did her, taking what she wanted from my kiss like she needed it as much as I did.

When my hand brushed over her breast, though, and I felt that nipple pebble, she pushed me back, breathing fast. "We're at work. My father's gym. Your gym. I'm barely a part of this community. I don't want to make waves by sleeping with the king of it. Especially when the king is friends with my father."

With that, she pushed past me.

I called after her but she didn't listen.

And she didn't listen to my text from earlier about taking a car home either.

I didn't text her about it. I couldn't. Instead, I tried to let her go, because I knew everything Everly had said was right.

It was just a matter of time before I figured out if we could ignore the pull of being wrong.

CHAPTER 5: EVERLY

"Carl, I'd rather not talk about it right now," I blurted out and then patted his shoulder so he could calm down. I'd found it helped him in a weird way, like he was an overzealous puppy that needed a pat on the head every now and then.

"Well, you can't date him."

"That's not really up to you," I repeated in a matter-of-fact tone, trying not to cause a scene. "You can't meddle in everything."

He scoffed as if he was affronted, but we both knew how he was. "So sue me for caring! I held my tongue when you went for coffee and on a few dates, but this is another month in, Evie. He's not a good man."

That was a lie. He hadn't held his tongue at all.

Juna walked by, pulling her arm across her chest in a stretch when she decided to stop and listen. She couldn't steer away from the gossip magazines, and we were turning into a live one for her viewing pleasure. "How you doing, Mr. Milton?" she asked, knowing full well he was irritated since his cheeks were bright red.

He immediately looked to her for help. "Tell Everly how bad Wes is."

Juna smiled wide, her purple pixie cut swinging back and forth as she opted to give him hell instead. "Mr. Milton, Wes is sort of hot." The girl was a breath of fresh air in the stuffy gym. She had a foul mouth and loved to play devil's advocate, but that's not what Carl wanted. "I mean, I know he pulled that move last year on Dec—"

"We're not talking about that. We don't talk about that at HEAT." Carl cut her off and then groaned. He waved her off, and she fluttered her fingers before skipping away. Carl turned back to me. "The media has painted the right picture of Wes, and I'm not having you associated with that."

Media. That word. The press and publicity that came with working at HEAT made me cringe. I repressed a small shudder and went through the tablet's schedule to make sure all our tasks were in order for the day.

"What did Wes do that could be so bad?" I didn't really believe Wes was it for me, but it was my intention to get out there, to start dating again, to embrace love instead of bitterness.

And to forget about Declan. Mostly that, even though my body couldn't seem to do so.

"He plays for the other team! That's all you need to know." Carl threw up his hands like this was the end all be all.

"The team doesn't define him," I pointed out. We were at the front desk bickering, and I knew a client would walk in any second. "We've talked about this. Just calm down, okay? We can discuss it more later when we aren't at work."

"You know I'm your father, right?" His gray eyebrows furrowed together above his glasses. He never trimmed them, but somehow, they suited his boisterous attitude.

"Of course." I nodded, suddenly uncomfortable.

I'd moved out of his guesthouse as fast as I could and hadn't accepted any help financially to get what he felt was a nice apartment. I didn't want to owe Carl any more than I already did.

"I wasn't always there, but I'm still your dad, Evie, and I

have a lot of experience behind me." His voice sounded pained.

How could I tell him that he'd gained all that experience without me though? That my childhood had been filled with nights spent hoping I'd get one phone call that wasn't on the holiday. What I would have given for one visit from him for no reason other than he wanted to see me.

I scanned my watch into the system so I could get to the employee login quickly, trying not to dwell. "I know you do, even with Melinda by your side."

He sighed and laughed a little. The man loved acting like his wife was a bit of a burden, and I knew it would ease some of the tension between us. "You're good, Everly. Such a good kid. I only want what's best for you. You understand? And I'm telling you, even if it's the last thing I'll ever do, I'm going to make sure a Cobra isn't in your life. Have you thought about those Hardy brothers? Because—"

"No." I cut him off. He was not going to meddle that hard.

Thankfully, the revolving glass door began to move and an older woman waltzed in, immediately smiling at my father. I dropped my hand from my hip and tried to shake off his words.

I patted his shoulder one last time and whispered it would all be okay. Carl needed reassurance more than I needed a father now. I'd lived long enough without one to know that I'd survive. Unfortunately, Carl had probably been reassured his whole life. My father came from old money, knew he'd be provided whatever he wanted for the rest of his life.

As the woman spoke to me across the front desk, my father murmured he was going to the sauna. I waved him away and continued to check-in Mrs. Johnson, a nice woman who frequented the gym daily with a vigor I could only hope to possess at her age.

"I'm so thankful to be a part of this gym, Everly." She winked her extra-long black eyelashes at me. "Your dad is doing so well by all of us."

I didn't know about that. I'd been there for three months, working at the most luxurious, beautiful gym on the planet. It had also been the most ludicrous three months too. The technology, the swag, the events they came up with to justify the membership price tag were insane. It was like the adult version of Disney.

"I see you don't have your watch with you today." I held out the fingerprint scanner and she offered her print as if it was normal. "Would you like another HEAT watch for tracking today?"

Her answer should have been "No, I don't need a freaking heart monitor that's the equivalent of a smart watch but engraved with HEAT on it like I was suddenly somebody worthy."

Yet, people truly believed it was a status symbol. They all wanted to be a part of HEAT. She nodded vigorously and then scanned the kiosk next to our marble counter. "Give me a pin, too, would you, dear?"

She grabbed for the gold-and-sapphire emblem with *HEAT* molded there and pinned it to her white collar immediately with a smile on her face. "Now, don't sell Lucy one when she comes in. I want to have more HEAT gear than her today." She chuckled at her own joke. "I'll be at the tennis courts if you want to tell Carl to stop by and say hi. I need to give him a bit of hell again for having me on a wait list for two years even after Declan took over before he accepted me."

There it was. The underlying truth of why everyone wanted to be a part of HEAT Health and Fitness. They thought Declan might grace them with his presence, like he was a god here amongst mere men.

The sad part of it all was I was starting to want his presence around too.

He hadn't lingered by the front desk, hadn't texted me, hadn't really looked my way since our locker room encounter. He'd stopped by a self-defense class for the kids and even lingered to throw a few balls with them. Yet, he'd only nodded at me like I was any other employee.

Which I was. Which was what I wanted to be. It was for the best.

"Give him all the hell you want, Mrs. Johnson." I smiled at her.

She chuckled. "Oh, you know I never would. Carl and that guy, Declan, have done so much for all of us. You know Declan had every opportunity right out of college, right?"

I nodded. I was well aware of his story, considering my father would drone on and on about how America loved Declan, about how he played both defense and offense in college, how he was first-round draft pick his senior year, how he played for a total of twelve years and could have kept playing.

"Declan made a name for himself, and then, well, you know your father wasn't doing too hot with everything. I'm his lawyer, you know?" She preened at mentioning that. "I always tell Carl that stamping Declan's face and last name on everything when he let Declan invest in the business years ago was the smartest move he made, even if he had to dole out some of the shares to Declan's brothers. Those Hardy brothers are a dream."

She sighed and I ground my teeth together, trying not to think about the man who'd kissed me senseless in the locker room and then had avoided me ever since. He'd been at the gym since seven this morning and had greeted everyone with a hello except me. The only remnant of him in my life now seemed to be that a car still idled in front of my apartment daily and followed me to work, although I tried not to pay any attention.

"You'd know better than me, Mrs. Johnson," I said because the woman had known my dad for years.

"Oh, right. Right." She patted my hand with a smile on her face. "But you're all getting along fine, it seems? I know your father loves you so much, and Declan's wonderful with everyone, right?"

The woman was as nosy as she was gossipy, so I stayed quiet.

"Well, even if you've only come to live here just recently, you'll be one of us in no time. Which reminds me, can you go grab him, actually? I need to tell him all the changes he made last week are worked out."

"Okay." I tried not to sigh as I waved Juna over so that I could go bring my father back out to the front desk, but just as I was rounding the corner, an alarm on my HEAT watch went off.

I took off at a sprint toward the sauna.

CHAPTER 6: EVERLY

Even in the hot sauna, his body was cold. Lifeless.

Dead.

Carl was dead.

The alarm from a HEAT watch must have alerted the medical staff because people streamed in but nothing registered.

I know I rattled off instructions as I stood there while people moved around me like a swarm of angry bees, furiously trying to protect their queen. In this case, their queen was my dad.

Carl Milton.

Deceased in the sauna.

Someone said it had to be a heart attack. I said someone should administer CPR, pointed at coworkers, gave directions.

None of it mattered. The buzzing and the talking and the screaming of employees all seemed to fade away to silence.

They laid him down to do chest compressions, but he didn't gasp for air. His body remained lifeless in his HEAT shorts and sweat-soaked T-shirt.

I fell to my knees and whispered to wake up. This time I called him Dad. This time tears fell for my father, praying he'd come back. I crumbled as my breath came faster and faster, but no oxygen filled my lungs. It was brutal, ugly, and pathetic the way I wanted it to not be real. We weren't close, but he was family. He'd been my saving grace when my world fell apart months ago.

"What the hell is going on?" The growl from behind me was full of authority, like he owned the place and we were all inconveniencing him. I turned my tear-stained face toward him and found myself face-to-face with Declan. "Everly?" he whispered in confusion.

I saw when he realized. I saw it in the way his face paled as he looked over my shoulder, how his cheeks hollowed. He let out a breath and then barked orders. "Resuscitate him."

"Sir, he's gone. It looks like a heart attack. We've been trying—"

"Try again," Declan cut him off.

There wasn't the pain in his eyes that I felt yet. That would wallop him in another minute. Death knocked like a demon ready to breathe fear, outrage, and shock into our souls first. Then, it stabbed us with that torturous grief.

I sobbed quietly like a wretched child, inconsolable at the loss.

"Get her out of here," Declan commanded. "She shouldn't see this. Call his family. He's going to need their support—and our support—when he wakes up."

"He's not waking up." I shook my head, trying my best to keep my voice steady as I whispered, "Don't you see he's not waking up?"

His greenish eyes searched mine as I stared up at him on my knees. His voice cracked as he said, "We have to try."

And try he did. Over and over again. I watched as the despair took over his face, like he couldn't handle this. Because death can't be handled.

He stood stock-still as the medical staff pronounced my father's death. Yet, his jaw worked, his hands fisted. I saw him trying to bundle up his emotions while he told everyone to get out.

When you were a part of HEAT, you were family, part of the team. It was in the pamphlet they gave everyone when they joined. Declan believed it here with my father. He and my dad were father and son in every way that counted, and he'd lost him.

I'd cry, I'd mourn the loss of what could have been with my father, but Declan's grief would be catastrophic. Even if he didn't want to admit it.

As I walked out of the sauna to allow for the medical staff to do their job, I knew my life was about to change. The only tie I had to this place was my father. And now he was gone.

I'd be gone soon too.

Or so I thought.

CHAPTER 7: DECLAN

Carl Milton passed at 8:01 p.m.

Authorities were directed to call his wife.

By about 8:02 p.m., his wife, Melinda, called to ask who was taking over his shares of the company.

I would give the press about ten more minutes until they called with questions. Vultures. Every single one of them. They swooped in on a wounded animal, ready for their feeding frenzy immediately. I may have been wounded, but I wasn't dead, and I would protect our legacy—Carl was my family for all intents and purposes—at all costs. Even if it meant going up against his wife, the press, and the whole damn empire we'd built together.

Carl had given me a place to call home during my years in the NFL. He'd made me believe in myself more than anyone ever had. He'd accepted my father and mother not just as working-class Greek immigrants, but as equals—treated them the way they always should have been. He gave us all purpose and trusted us with his business.

He was family.

And we didn't scavenge on family even when they passed.

I knew I had to call my brothers, figure out the staff, the press release—I had to do a million things.

All the things Carl was good at. He'd been the charmer, the type who could soothe the press, handle the administrative work, and focus on the business when I didn't want to. I played ball, I worked out, I posed for a shot with my Super Bowl ring and smiled at people who got in my face. I didn't organize things. I didn't want to.

Yet now I'd have to.

I'd need to be the man to make everything work, even if I couldn't incite my staff to resuscitate the person we needed most. I couldn't get a heartbeat. I couldn't bring him back.

I prompted them to try more times than I could count before the doctor called it. Then, I snapped at my staff to get out. I heard an announcement not long after that the gym was closed until further notice, that everyone needed to evacuate the premises immediately.

I stood in that hot sauna as they loaded his large body onto the stretcher. As they carted him away, my life changed before me.

It might have been seconds or minutes or hours when I heard her voice so soft behind me. "You're going to overheat, Declan."

The name she never spoke left her lips out of compassion, trying to pull me back from the darkness that was enveloping me.

When I turned, I saw how she bit her lip as she looked at me. Then, as she stepped up and wiped at my cheeks, I saw the tears there. Yet, I felt cold, numb, in shock. I blurted out, "Did you close the gym?"

She nodded. "I thought it best given the circumstances."

Something ugly brewed up inside me. Cold and vicious and hardened from losing the man who'd given most everything to me. "He wouldn't have wanted us to close down the gym. Not even for a minute."

"Oh. Well..." She pulled her hand away and fisted it. "We have to mourn him, and we have to take the right steps. We can't just drive forward."

"We've always driven forward. It's Carl's way, Everly." It sounded callous coming from my mouth. Yet, the woman hadn't been here. She hadn't seen how hard we'd worked for this, how much we put in to get here. "We open first thing tomorrow. It'll be an all-hands-on-deck situation to deal with his passing. So, make sure to look your best. The press is going to have a field day with this one."

Her jaw dropped as I started to walk past her. "You can't be... Are you even going to take a moment and stop to consider that my *father* has died?"

I dragged a hand over my face and took a deep breath. Carl Milton would have wanted us to play ball. Always. The man was all about the legend and empire. "No, because my business partner wouldn't have wanted me to."

"You knew him much better than I did, Declan." She took a breath, and it quivered like she knew what it might be like for me to grieve him. "You can't bury the pain and loss deep inside like it hasn't happened. You have to feel the past and—"

"You know that from experience, Everly?" Something shuttered behind her eyes, and she shut down the emotion, closed me off to it like she had the night in the SUV.

When she glanced back at me though, her blue eyes burned with a new fire. She glared at me when I brushed past to close down the sauna. The medical staff was now talking with the police, and we had to deal with press, call lawyers, figure out next steps. We didn't have time for mourning.

Everly was on my heels. "What are we going to say to everyone who loved him? 'Mr. Hardy doesn't care. It's still time to work'?"

"Everyone employed here will understand. Most of us have

been on this team for years, and just because you came in a few months ago—"

"What? I don't know or care enough? Is that what you were about to say?" She crossed her arms over her chest. "You know what, Mr. Hardy? Fuck you."

"Good. You're finally getting it. Feel the anger rather than the sadness and hang on to that pride you have. When the press gets ahold of the news, you're going to need it."

She was too pure for this world, too foreign to understand that an empire like this one would crumble and rip you apart if you weren't careful.

"Everly!" I heard Wes's voice before I saw him. It grated every nerve. "Jesus, I came as soon as I heard."

I glanced at my watch. Two hours. Her father had died, and it took her "casual" hookup two whole hours to get here when I know he doesn't work a nine-to-five.

"You shouldn't be in our gym right now. It's closed," I pointed out.

"Come on, man," he grumbled as he tucked her in under his arm.

At the same time, she mumbled, "Oh my God."

Still, she curled into him like he might be able to comfort her. Like his arms would be enough. "I'm sorry to hear about—"

"You both can go." I turned away from them as Melinda, Anastasia, and Clara arrived.

"What happened? Who was on the medical staff tonight?" Melinda buzzed in. Her coiffed blonde hair perched and wrapped perfectly in a bun told me she'd gotten ready for the press. Her pantsuit was black, like she knew she had to mourn, and Anastasia and Clara were dressed the same.

Anastasia—hair as blonde as her mother's, the perfect face

of makeup, and the woman I'd always entertained because she was related to Carl—gripped my arm with tears running down her face. Suddenly, her touch made my skin crawl, like she was poison ivy that I needed to get away from. "I'm going to miss him. I can't even understand how this happened."

I couldn't help but look over my shoulder to see if Everly was still there, if she was going to console her family.

She chewed her cheek with her plump lips pursed before she sighed and pulled Wes with her. She cleared her throat, and instantly Melinda's and Anastasia's eyes flew like daggers to her.

"I'm so sorry for your loss. We did everything we could but he..." Everly's voice shook as she bravely held Melinda's eye contact and wrung her hands in front of her bare stomach since she was still in her damn workout clothes.

"Why are you even here?" Melinda spit out the question like an accusation.

"I... What? I work here."

"So? You think that affords you the right to be here?" She smoothed one manicured hand over the strands of her bun. "Get employees off the premises, Declan. This is a private family matter now. We need to make sure we handle this correctly with the press for our company."

"Melinda—" I started.

"Look outside, Declan." She pointed, and when I did, the swarm in front of the windows around the ambulance and police cars was intense. Photos were being taken, flashes going off I hadn't previously noticed.

Shock of losing a man as close to you as your father doesn't hit in the first few minutes. Or maybe it does and that's what keeps you from crumbling.

None of this was good for Everly. She wasn't used to it. "Go home, Everly. I'll make sure we contact you about Carl's funeral arrangements."

"If you're invited," Melinda added.

Everly's face paled and then reddened.

"Melinda." My voice snapped out like a whip getting them in order just as Clara grumbled that Carl was her dad too and not to be so cold while Anastasia elbowed her. "I'm going to say it once so we're clear. Carl made it known to me the day I met Everly. She's a part of the HEAT empire. She's a part of the family. Our family. You treat her that way or you answer to me. You understand?"

Melinda raised her chin and pursed her lips. "We'll see about that."

"Mom!" Clara screeched at her mother's boldness, and they all started bickering, but I was only focused on Everly. She had backed away, shaking her head at me. She held in the tears, refusing to let them fall, refusing to give us an inch of her emotion. The way she didn't engage, the way she still stood tall, and the way she glanced at me and mouthed "Goodbye" made me want to grab her hand and pull her back to stay.

Carl would have been proud of her.

And I was certifiably in awe with her after that moment. She was strong in a way I didn't see from other women around here. It made something deep in my gut burn as she walked away with Wes's hand on the small of her back.

I took a breath and tried to organize the list of things I had to do. The next few days would be brutal.

* * *

I did it all. I called our PR company, brought in my assistant, called my brothers, and worked closely with Melinda and her daughters to organize the funeral.

We all lost sleep, mourned his loss, but carried on. I saw her blue eyes at the funeral where she didn't look bothered at all again. She didn't stand next to her stepfamily, but instead sat in the pews of the church with everyone else.

A woman with long dark braids who had the same exact bone structure as Everly sat beside her rubbing her arms as the pastor gave his sermon. Then, they both approached the receiving line at the wake, told the family—and me—they were sorry for our loss, as if they hadn't lost anyone. As if they were strong enough to give sympathy even when they deserved it too.

Everly Belafonte couldn't be bothered with what should have been, it seemed. I knew she should have been afforded a moment at that funeral to break down. She didn't. She should have been afforded a damn moment to commemorate her father, but Melinda took on the whole eulogy with her daughters. Everly didn't bat an eye even.

I wanted to shake her, tell her she deserved it all, that Carl would have wanted her to have something.

But I couldn't. I had to be the king of this empire now.

Two days after the funeral, my brothers and I all got the call. "There's a will reading for Mr. Carl Milton. It's rather unique in that he wanted you and your brothers to attend with Everly first. You will each be read the conditions of the will one by one. I know it's unorthodox, but we'd like you to come in—"

"Just give me the time and the place. I'll be there if that's what Carl wanted."

I'd do anything that old man wanted now that he was gone, I thought.

Well, I thought so at least until I heard what he asked me

to do in that damn will.

CHAPTER 8: EVERLY

"Marry him? I'm not marrying him." My voice shot out but still shook as I said it. I glanced around at all of them. Mrs. Johnson sat there with a HEAT pin on the lapel of her white jacket with shoulder pads while Declan and I, along with his three brothers sat around the table too.

All four of those Hardy brothers wore black suits and black ties. Tailored perfection, they were a picture with their dark hair, each of them quiet but with varying expressions on their faces.

Dex handled the brand's security, and he smirked like this was a joke. Dom had sparred with me a few times in the gym, knew me better than the other brothers, and glanced over at me with concern. Dimitri studied Declan, awaiting his response.

I did too. Declan and I had distanced ourselves since the night of Carl's death, though he had stood up for me with Melinda by saying I was a part of the family.

I wasn't.

I didn't belong, and I didn't know if I even wanted to. I survived the press at the funeral only because my mother and I beelined it out of there as fast as possible. We'd been subjected to scrutiny before and we didn't want it again.

Yet here I was, being forced into it.

Mrs. Johnson had read the instructions after summoning us all to a large conference room within her legal firm. She'd announced that Declan and I, along with his brothers, were to be read the first stipulations of the will privately. Then everyone else, one by one, would be read theirs. Melinda, Anastasia, Clara, and my mother.

Since Mom had already flown back home after the funeral, she called to tell me she'd just video chat in. "It all seems so formal," she'd said, pushing her beaded braids away from her face. "You know how I hate all that."

I assured her it would all be fine. I figured we'd be given nothing. We hadn't been given anything in the past.

That was before Mrs. Johnson dropped the bomb that exploded in my stomach. I gripped the wooden desk in an effort to stay upright, to endure the shock of it, to breathe through it.

"That is completely your choice, Ms. ..." She hesitated, probably realizing I didn't go by my father's last name. "Ms. Belafonte." She straightened her glasses, then she sighed and her manicured fingers pulled them off her face to allow them to hang from the beaded string around her neck. "Everly, forgive me if I'm overstepping, but you know I'm a part of the HEAT organization, and I do so appreciate all the service you've given me throughout the last few months. To turn down this opportunity—"

"Mrs. Johnson, this isn't an opportunity. This is a forced marriage. This is blackmail." I felt my voice rising, so I took a breath, trying to remain calm.

"Your father wanted what was best for his family and his legacy. A marriage for one year isn't the end of the world."

"Can you please read the last paragraph to me one more time?"

"Sure." She cleared her throat. "Everly and Declan must marry if they would like the shares of my company that give them majority voting rights over the HEAT brand. If they do not, these shares will be donated to StoneArm Real Estate along with voting rights. And, I promise, I know best. I'm not having my daughter end up with a Cobra. Not when my empire is on the line. And not when her name needs to be cleared."

"He just didn't want me marrying a Cobra!" I screeched, ignoring the fact that he was trying to clear my name too. I couldn't even attempt to focus on that.

"Well, that, and you've got a bad name, it seems." Declan narrowed his eyes at me, and my heart beat fast at what I might have to tell him, at what they all might find out.

"Sure it's no worse than yours," Dom spoke up through a chuckle.

"Don't fuck with me right now," Declan threw back at him.

"I've got no name in this town, let's be honest," I ground out. "And I don't want one." The pencil I was holding snapped in half. There went keeping my composure. I'd tried. I really had. No one could agree to this though. I cleared my throat. "I won't do it."

Dom nodded like he agreed with me. "You don't have to do it, Evie."

Yet, I saw how Dimitri and Dex glanced at each other. Their careers—their brand—was on the line. This wasn't a rash decision I should make on my own anymore.

"I think you need to understand all the stipulations," Mrs. Johnson tried.

I hated to feel like I didn't care about them, like I was throwing these men to the wolves. Yet, even if I ended up homeless and without a penny of his to my name, I wanted nothing to do with this. "I don't want anything. I'm sorry, but you can all figure it out without me. I don't need his money or—"

"He owns your mother's yoga studio and home. Those will go to Melinda and Anastasia Milton if you don't agree to the marriage."

"Shit," Dex grumbled, and Dom swore too.

"What?" I whispered out. I felt my heart, the way it pounded and then dropped like a hole to hell had opened up and it was falling right down into it. The blood ceased to pump through my veins, my brain stopped working, and my life screeched to a halt. "No. Not her studio. He wouldn't."

"Oh, Everly," Mrs. Johnson tsked, then patted my hand. "He was always a bit too good at business, and he had a knack for meddling as well. But he loved you. He'll also be compensating you. He set aside a good amount of money for you once this year is through."

She pointed at an amount on a sheet of paper, and the zeros on it were dizzying.

I glanced over at Declan, ready to lay the blame on anyone. His posture was rigid, hands fisted on his thighs, jaw hard as stone. He didn't look at me, not even when there was a long stretch of silence that would have given him the opportunity to. He nodded slow, like he was deciding his own fate, and then that strong jaw worked up and down. Up and down. "I'll have the majority of shares, Mrs. Johnson?"

His words were cold, calculating, and cruel. The man everyone thought was a charmer was actually just as ruthless as my father. He wanted the business, the money, the legacy. He didn't care that it would ruin me for a year. Didn't care that I didn't agree.

I'd grown up in that house, in that studio. It was all my mother had. And although I'd moved away from it all, it was the only safe place I had at the end of my time here, the place my mother and I worked so hard for.

"Well, Declan, you'll get majority shares of the gym. Voting rights for the brand, including the hotels, the restaurants, golf courses, everything. I can give you the list, but you and your brothers will be set to make the calls you want for the HEAT empire for life. If not, you will forfeit Mr. Milton's shares to StoneArm Real Estate."

"I haven't heard of them," he said, waiting for more information.

Dimitri spoke up finally. "We don't care about any of that shit. If you don't want this, we can rebuild."

"I care, dumbass. We built this brand with Carl for years. I'm not just giving it away."

Dex chuckled like it was all ridiculous. "So what? You can do it again. You're a damn male Kardashian."

Dom loosened up and laughed at that along with Dex.

"Fuck you guys," Declan sighed as he pinched the bridge of his nose.

"What? You mad because you piss on something and it turns to gold?" Dex elbowed Dom. "Remember that one commercial he did for the spa, and we thought that shit was going nowhere because he was such a bad actor. Instead, we opened up six more spas attached to resorts that year because of advanced bookings."

"So damn dumb," Dimitri said. He was usually the brother who seemed most concerned about Declan, but he busted out laughing too. "All because you caught a few good balls."

"It wasn't only a few good balls." Declan mashed his teeth together. Then he took a deep breath, like he knew they were trying to rile him. "This isn't a joke, guys."

"We know." Dom sobered. "But it is if we want it to be

because you don't have to do shit if you don't want it."

The brothers all nodded, banded together in support of the one who needed it most in the moment.

"I'm not giving this brand away to a random-ass company." He met my gaze suddenly, his eyes blazing green with resolve. "Not if I can help it."

Mrs. Johnson cleared her throat. "StoneArm Real Estate is privately owned and very random. Not much information there. We could dig, but I'm guessing their evading skills will match our researching ones."

"One year?" Declan restated.

Dex smirked at his brother. "You'll be off getting your picture taken half the time anyway. So, not even 365 days. Don't be a whiny bitch about it."

Dimitri elbowed him. "They've got to get fucking married, bro."

"So?" Dex shrugged. "Declan acts like this gym is his baby, and he's got hundreds more across the nation. He believes these resorts and restaurants and all our golf courses and casinos are part of the team. He's going to give that up for one measly year?"

They all glanced at one another. His siblings having an unspoken conversation. About me. About my life. About a whole year of me being attached to their brother.

Then Declan finally spoke up. "Does my whole legal team agree this is the best scenario?"

"Yes." Mrs. Johnson nodded. She glossed over the details and gave us the big-picture information. I didn't need the details. I just needed air, needed time to digest, needed a damn drink of alcohol. "There are a few other insignificant details that I can have the legal team look over for you."

She shuffled the papers around, and Declan glared at her.

"That just doesn't sound at all legal."

"You'd be surprised what a trust and will can help you get away with, honestly."

Carl. He had always found a way. It's what I'd seen in the few months I'd spent with him.

She smiled softly like she was a fairy godmother, ready to help both of us. "I promise we will get through this together, okay? You two get married and try it out. Arranged marriages were the norm less than a hundred years ago and still are in some cultures. It's for the best."

"Send the papers to my legal team then," he growled. I got the sense he was perturbed but willing.

"Mr. Hardy!" I finally couldn't take it anymore, his name leaving my lips fast and loud, full of accusation.

"Yes, Ms. Belafonte?" The way he sneered my name reminded me why this would never work.

"You can't be serious?" I breathed out.

"Why wouldn't I be? This is my company. I'm not handing it over because I need to change my marital status for 365 days."

"I... I don't belong here," I whispered out the words. The walls seemed to shift inward, the air stale with entitlement, the ground too soft for someone who'd lived a different lifestyle. Then I caught his gaze and held it. His were filled with determination, and they must have matched mine. "I do not belong here." This time I said it with a fury I knew wouldn't serve me well.

Be calm. Collected. You can't show anything else.

I growled as I pushed the emotions back down and shut my eyes for a second. They wouldn't take me seriously if I cried now, if I got mad.

"One year and you can belong wherever you want. You

need to pack your things and move. Take a few days or a week. But this year, Everly, you belong with me."

That adrenaline, that same rush I'd felt with him in the SUV, snaked through me at his words.

"Actually"—Mrs. Johnson held up the gold pen she'd been using as a pointer—"this is effective immediately."

CHAPTER 9: DECLAN

"Immediately? I can't go to his place right now." Everly tried her best to stay composed, but she was unraveling, losing whatever mask she held up to protect her from the world. "I'm not—"

"It's effective immediately." I cut her off. "We do what it says or we lose the things that matter to us. That's it. Carl knew how to handle people, Everly, and he's handling us."

I don't know why that realization had me cracking the first smile since we'd lost him. It was like he was giving a solid fuck you from the grave, proving his boisterous personality stood the test of mortality. He was still getting what he wanted, even in death.

I hated him for it. But loved him for it too.

"Everly, weren't you the one who wanted to start your management job right away?" I lifted a brow at her.

She guffawed and wiggled in her pressed black dress. Other than the funeral, I'd never seen her in a dress or professional attire. The tights and sports bras were enough to make my dick stir, but the prim and proper look shouldn't have gotten as much of a rise out of me, especially when I was missing her father. "Are you enjoying this?"

"Carl was always a stickler about certain terms and such."

"If you think I'm moving in and marrying you because my father is still having a hissy fit over me dating a rival team's player, you're mistaken."

"Why don't you let me drive you to my place where we can discuss it further?" I winked at Mrs. Johnson.

Everly rolled her lips between her teeth before she responded with a measured tone. "Don't wink at her like this is some joke. This is a year of our lives."

"What's a year if we're already working together in the same city? Or are you planning to go back to your hometown?"

There it was. The way she shut down and closed off when I mentioned something she didn't want to discuss. A whole history and a whole life she wouldn't bring up.

The first time I'd met her, she'd done the same damn thing.

"No. I'm not going back to my hometown," she ground out. "You underestimate me. You did that once before and it didn't work out well for you, or don't you remember?"

Yeah, I remembered that shit all right.

* * *

Carl's estranged daughter stood in front of me at HEAT Health and Fitness after being given a tour and meeting my brothers. Everyone had accepted her with open arms except me. She was wringing her hands because she must have realized we didn't hire just anyone at this gym. "I know this is weird. I really will get you a resume, and you can interview me if you'd like."

Chewing my cheek, I figured I'd ask her a few questions. "You've taught in a gym before?"

She nodded vigorously. "Yes, I like to teach and was taking classes in college. I—"

"Did you get a degree?" It was something all of my managers had.

"Well, no. But a bachelor's degree isn't going to make or

*break my skill set. You can get life experience as the equivalent."
She squared up with her reasoning and then narrowed her bright-blue eyes at me. "Did you get a degree in football?"*

She did know I was voted the NFL's MVP for five consecutive years at one point during my career, right? "I've been playing football since I was five years old."

"I've been doing yoga since I was three," she shot back. "Are we hiring people based on a sheet of paper that says they did four years of some schoolwork?"

"If you'd interviewed, you'd know that's not the only thing I base my hiring process on. You have experience in yoga. What else?" I countered, because now I was just fucking annoyed. She had to be ten years younger than me, and she was questioning how I hired people?

She took her time looking me up and down. "I'm great with kids' yoga too. Don't forget self-defense. I'm happy to teach that too. You're twice my size, but I could easily bring you to your knees."

"Wanna bet?" My competitive streak was problematic, I admit. "You can have the yoga instructor job. If you bring me to my knees, I'll give you the self-defense position too."

"Great." She smiled wide and it was like I was seeing her for the first time, because that smile alone was capable of bringing a man to his knees. Her eyes scrunched up, her cheekbones rounded, and a pair of dimples showed that made her cute and sexy at the same time.

Cute and lethal.

She'd wreck a heart or two with it, I was sure. Mine just wouldn't be one of them.

She spun on a running shoe heel and beelined to the door. "I already put my duffel in a locker. Saw a few things. The ring in the middle of the gym is a nice touch. Shall we go there so I can earn my place?"

"Whoa. Take it down a notch, Rocky," I chuckled out.

She turned to tilt her head at me. "Rocky?"

"You don't know Rocky?"

She scrunched her little nose.

Fuck. That solidified it. She was young. Too young. It was like a bucket of ice-cold water was thrown on my overactive dick.

"He's the legendary boxer in the movies of the same name!" I pinched the bridge of my nose. "How old are you?"

"Oh, I don't think ageism can be part of an interview." She smiled softly. "Plus, it's not an age thing. My mom and I didn't have a TV or go to the movies growing up." She shrugged like it was normal and then continued out the door.

"Didn't have a TV?" I almost tripped over myself at her admission.

"Are you giving me a tour before or after we get into the wrestling ring?"

"Before. You're going to be too tired after." Because her ass wasn't going to knock me to the ground. "Now, you won't be on this floor a lot. Except for management meetings and large clients, we barely use it. If you have a question, though, the HR department is down the hall, my office is at the end of it. Although, I'm not in there much."

I pointed to the elevators and pressed the button. Almost immediately, the doors slid open for her to walk in. "I never liked an office anyway."

"Why?"

"My father belonged in one, and my mother and I didn't." The statement wasn't one of pain or animosity. It's like Everly knew where she belonged. Most people tried to claw their way into a group that didn't want them. They tortured themselves to be a part of something they weren't, only to find they would have been happier if they'd found the right fit in the first place. I'd tried it with other sports, other positions, other careers. But Michael Jordan didn't belong in baseball; he belonged in basketball.

We waited quietly in the elevator until the doors opened. I waved her forward so we could walk the premises. A few clients stopped their lifting to walk over and introduce themselves. Everly practically preened. "I'm so excited to get started. It seems you have a wonderful clientele."

"If you say so," I grumbled as I cracked my knuckles, and we went around the other side of the gym to the wrestling ring.

When she got up to it, she dove under the rope so effortlessly, I started to consider whether or not she had some skill. "Want some protective gear?"

"For what? You going to hit me?" She feigned a pout and fluttered her lashes like she was making fun of those she'd seen use that tactic.

"I don't think I'll need to, Everly. You're as small as a raindrop." I grasped the rope so I could crouch between them and walk in.

She narrowed her eyes. "Rainwater can be dangerous. It can flood...take a life, wash away cars... It can move mountains. A raindrop is small but together, with others, they're a force."

I could tell right then, Everly was going to be a problem. "There's only one of you here in front of me today."

She let a small smile escape before she straightened and widened her stance. "Let's see what you got. Come at me."

I met her gaze, determined, focused, brilliant. It held no fear, like she knew she was capable of more than I'd come at her with.

Something stirred deep within me, something that shouldn't

have at all. I enjoyed taking a woman and making her mine, enjoyed ravaging her and controlling her when she wanted it.

I'd come at a woman in just that way before because she'd wanted it, not for her to defend herself.

So, I gave a half-ass effort as I walked toward her, reaching my hand out to grab her arm. She grasped my hand in just the right way and twisted it fast. She swung it over her head and cranked on it so hard that had I not curved my body and fallen to the ground that instant, I'd have a broken wrist. "Jesus Christ, Everly, what the fuck?" I bellowed.

I didn't mean to yell, but it didn't matter. She was beaming down at me, her pearly whites so bright against her lips that I immediately wanted to say sorry for my outburst. "Rule number one—you can't underestimate your opponent and give them the upper hand. It only takes one raindrop to bring you down it seems."

I glanced up in utter disbelief. "You... You almost broke my arm. I didn't expect you to—"

"Yes, again, underestimating probably isn't a good idea."

Shit. I knew that. I'd played sports forever and the underdog was always capable of the win, could always gain the upper hand when they were underestimated. Yet, this was different. "You're not even half my size."

"I know. It's extremely invigorating to know what the body is capable of."

I grumbled, "I guess the job is yours." I snatched my hand out of hers and got up. "When do you want to start, Raindrop?"

She wrinkled her nose. "I don't like nicknames. Everyone just calls me Evie. And today if possible. I worked back in my hometown and hate to not be working."

"Right. Can I ask why you left that hometown of yours?" I

was prying, and I knew it. Yet, I needed to know the type of person I was dealing with.

Her face fell, she shut off all emotion, and she didn't elaborate. "Sometimes, people just need a change."

I had a feeling she was about to change my life in more ways than one.

* * *

Our gazes were at war with each other, like we were both recalling the first time we'd met. "Hard to forget that, Everly. You can take care of yourself in a ring, you can take care of yourself now. Let's work through this, huh? We'll ride out the marriage, and that way the shares won't be given to an anonymous company."

"If we're doing this, I'm not living with you." She almost bared her teeth as she said it, blue eyes burning bright with hatred toward me suddenly.

"I have a guesthouse. Completely detached from my own," I informed her, straightening the suit jacket I was so sick of wearing already.

"Of course you do. Everyone here does." She shut her eyes, frustrated. "I'm not like you all, Mr. Hardy. I can't... I don't live this lifestyle like Melinda and Anastasia and—"

"Don't include me in the lineup," Dom jumped in, a small smile on his face. She glanced over at him, and I saw how her eyes softened.

"Dom, you know how ridiculous this is," Evie said to my brother. Seeing how they'd became friends, how he could calm her in this moment pissed me off. It pissed me off because it wasn't me.

"It's only a change in location and a license for a year," I reminded her, stopping her from engaging with my brother any further. This was between her and me. "Have your own life. It won't really interfere with mine." She chewed her cheek for a moment, and I knew I had her. "If you can't handle it, I can try to work with Melinda and Anastasia about your mother's yoga studio."

That had her narrowing her eyes. Everly didn't want to ask that woman for anything. I understood why too. She'd been vicious to her since the moment they'd first met. "There will be rules if we do this."

I smiled in triumph. "Of course there will be."

She stood so abruptly the chair flew out from behind her, but I caught it before it hit the ground. She took a deep breath and closed her eyes. "I need to read over the will again."

"If you agree"—Mrs. Johnson cleared her throat—"there will be further stipulations that can't be read until month three of your marriage."

"What?" we both said in unison.

"It's unconventional, but I assure you, it's nothing you can't handle and—"

"We need to see the documentation."

"Legally, I'm contracted—" She glanced at my legal team. Well, they were also Carl's legal team. "My hands are tied, Declan."

I glared at all of them. "You realize I could fire you all."

"Sure. But we're the best," one of them stated. "And you know that. These are his last wishes."

Was he tearing up? Jesus Christ.

"Fuck," I swore angrily and glanced at my brothers. "Guys?"

"Your call. Everly's call. We'll be behind you the whole

way," Dimitri said, loyal as always.

"Now or never, Declan," Mrs. Johnson pushed.

"Fine."

"Fine?" Everly screeched. "Are you insane?"

"You want the damn yoga studio or not? We can always back out at three months." She had to understand we lost everything if we didn't.

She took two deep breaths and folded those clean, unmanicured fingers together. Then she pulled at the assortment of necklaces from under the collar of her dress and held them tight. So tight I knew her nails were cutting into her skin as she mumbled, "I'm gonna regret this."

"Me too," I grumbled. I met the stares of my brothers. "Don't tell a fucking soul until I say."

"One moment, then." Mrs. Johnson got up and opened the door, and in walked a tall man with gray hair in a black suit. "Meet our ordained minister. I'll be the witness, and we'll get you two married off."

The whirlwind began.

We repeated vows. We made promises that were completely empty. We made commitments we weren't sure we could keep.

Then, the lawyers put papers in front of us. They explained our prenup would keep our finances and assets completely separate in the case of divorce. We signed. They explained the conditions of the will. We signed.

They pointed to our marriage license.

We signed on the dotted fucking lines.

CHAPTER 10: EVERLY

"Welcome home," he said, and like an ominous sign, lightning cracked in the sky and it started to rain. The clouds couldn't hold the water a second longer, just like I couldn't hold in the emotion and tension from the day.

His house was even bigger than Carl and Melinda's, albeit in the same gated community. The appeal of that had been made very clear when the security guard closed the iron gates on the paparazzi that had followed us from the will reading.

I'd never known fame that intense. Sure, I'd had cameras on me once before, but they were for a news article, not glossy magazines and paparazzi. The flashes almost swallowed me up along with the crowd in that moment.

Declan didn't exactly care about me—he'd demonstrated that more than once over the past few months—but he must have had a heart somewhere in that broad chest because his hand found the small of my back as he pulled me close and rushed me to his Bugatti Veyron.

I knew the car because I'd been so shocked at seeing it the first time. I'd seen a Lamborghini and other expensive cars, but nothing like that. It was always parked in the owner's spot, and I had a weak moment of looking one day.

Its price was astronomical yet surprised me less now that I was staring at his house.

He drove us down a winding street where I saw the brick pillars with yet another bigger, black gate that stood taller than the last one we passed. Declan pressed a button on the steering wheel and the two fences swung slowly outward as we approached.

Gray brick weaved up and then fanned out toward a massive garage of dark wooden doors and an over-the-top staircase to the entrance.

I stared at the trees rustling in the wind, so high over our heads. Those trees told me that this land had been here far longer than any of us. Yet, his home had sleek lines, straight angles, and had a clean look like his fitness center.

As the water droplets pelted the windshield, I muttered, "Looks like a modern-day castle."

He glanced over at me. "It's actually your castle now, if you want to call it that, but it's really just a house."

"Declan, just because we signed a contract for a year doesn't mean it's my house in any—"

He cut me off by shaking his head. "What's mine will be yours, Everly. You can't tiptoe around me 24-7. Carl wouldn't have wanted that, and I don't either."

Hearing his name even now when Declan and I hadn't discussed him really since that night at the sauna made the guilt bubble up. "I probably should have reached out to him more."

"You take the blame a lot for a woman who was only a child when your parents divorced."

I dragged one finger down the window, following a line of a water drop on the other side of the glass. "I remember the anger I had that my father wouldn't come home. I remember consciously making a choice in my teenage years to not visit after so many years of him not visiting a single time and forbidding me to come for the holidays. I forced an estrangement too. That's on me. I was being selfish and emotional."

He sighed. "Carl was selfish and emotional—he was the adult. You can't take full responsibility. He could have pushed, insisted like a father should have."

I nodded and, as I glanced at Declan, saw the charm everyone else did right then. He was meeting me on my level, smiling at me softly so as not to push me while in a vulnerable moment. Declan Hardy was dangerous this way, sitting in the quiet pitter-patter of the rain in his expensive sports car.

The world faded away as we sat in silence, as my eyes skirted over his lips, his vivid eyes that suddenly held some sort of emotion, and that massive frame I always knew would be so easy to curl into.

"I think it's best we don't discuss this with others." I tried to veer myself in the right direction. We would have to make up rules, and I was happy to start right then. The sooner we laid out everything, the easier it would be. People were going to want answers. Why was I staying with him? Where was I sleeping? What was in the will?

"Marriage is public record. It's going to come out. But discussing the stipulations within the trust and the will isn't necessary. If asked, we can call it what it is."

"What's that?"

Cracking his knuckles, he said, "A marriage of convenience for the sake of the HEAT empire."

"Okay. So, don't talk with the media and keep things vague if asked." I had to make it clear, though. My heart wouldn't allow for anything else. For me, this wasn't about their empire. "And, just so you know, this is for my mother's studio...where my whole past life took place." He needed to understand.

"There's also compensation involved for you, Everly—"

"I would never have done this for the money."

He searched my eyes like he wasn't sure. "So, this is for a past life?"

I cleared my throat, trying to strip away my fear of him finding out about my past and dragging it here. Florida was supposed to be my new start. I sat up straighter. "Maybe that's another rule. We have separate lives. Let's leave them that way. My past is my past. Yours is yours. What you do with the present and future, totally fine also. It's not my business unless we need to discuss it for the sake of the media."

He hummed. "You plan on discussing your Cobra with the media?"

"I..." Did he expect me to stop seeing Wes? Expect me to have an answer for everything right this second? "I'm not going to change who I'm seeing because my father was acting irrationally."

"Just your marriage status, right?" Declan said in a sort of monotone voice.

"Do you really care? People have open marriages."

"Yes, and marriages of convenience all the time too," he said so softly while staring at me with those green eyes that I wasn't sure he agreed with me at all. Normally, he'd have an outburst and not handle his emotions with this well at all. Normally, he wouldn't be able to contain the fire burning in his eyes that I saw right there. "We'll make it work. Carl wanted you taken care of. I can give him that."

I shrugged. "Or he wanted his way."

"Well, he can have his way for a year." His tone was matter-of-fact, like this was one more chore he had to complete for the day.

I nodded and tried my best to mirror his emotion. "Well, should we do a press release? We could—"

"Let's keep it quiet until someone figures it out. We can keep doing what we're doing. Seems easy enough," he said.

I wouldn't agree. There were more rules we should define, more commitments, more boundaries. "I'll be living on your property and in your space for a year. I'd venture to say that may pose some challenges," I said, pushing him a bit.

"You nervous about my house, Drop?" A small smile all of a sudden played on his face.

"No. I just don't want to be intrusive, and I want to make sure we iron everything out now."

"No rules. I'm laid-back about my space." He eyed me up and down, and butterflies erupted in my stomach, fluttering around near my ovaries in a way they shouldn't have. "And maybe I'm okay with you being in it."

Immediately, I shook my head. "No. That's... Us mixing this marriage with pleasure is a bad idea. No sex or real relationship. I don't like the spotlight and you're constantly in it. I don't— This is the opposite of the life I want."

He squinted before he admitted, "You're nothing like most of the women I've met. You know that?"

"I think most everyone around here is led by their ego. I let that go a long time ago. I simply want peace."

He nodded like he agreed. "And what do you think I'm led by?" he asked softly.

Something painful flashed in his eyes, like he had secrets too, like his heart wasn't open for the world to see in all the magazines he posed for, but it was those magazines that made me say what I did. "I don't know, Declan. I think you and my father enjoy being kings. And you're interested in being the ruler of an empire I want no part of." I shrugged, trying to ignore the pull I had to him. "So, let's just keep this marriage easy. I'll live in the guesthouse, and you'll live up there, and as long as you knock, I'm laid-back about space too."

The rain pounded harder now, in sync with the rapid thundering of my heart as I waited for him to agree, as I waited for us to start a freaking year together.

"I'll make note to have my assistant get you access to everything," he grunted out. He must have realized what I was saying was for the best. "I've already texted her to get the movers going on your apartment."

My mother had texted. She'd been read her portion of the will this afternoon once Declan and I had secured her assets. Once I traded my marital status for her life and livelihood. That's what I'd signed away my life for.

My mother, who'd probably left a voice mail checking on me, hadn't even been invited to watch her only child's nuptials. I hadn't even had time to tell her I was being married never mind ask if she could be a witness. She had no idea that I had bound my life to a man—with vows and everything.

It was only a year.

I took a deep breath, but it was small. Another small one. Too many small ones to count. I whipped open the car door in his driveway and stumbled into the rain, trying my best to breathe, but no air came.

"Jesus Christ," I gasped. I tried to scramble for control. I'd had to rein in my emotions before. I could do it again.

Then he was right in front of me as I bent over. I saw his stupid expensive leather shoes and watched how the water beaded off them like he'd had them shined before the meeting. They made the air around me come even slower, although I was trying to breathe faster.

A football player turned billionaire who was everyone's

dream but my worst nightmare. I saw his house, so gigantic it felt like it was towering over me, like it would eat me alive if I stepped foot into it.

"Everly, breathe."

I gasped. "I can't. I... I married you, and it's all wrong. I don't want this. Or you. Or your expensive shoes."

He grabbed my shoulder, pulling me up to standing again. Then, he grasped my chin and tilted my face to look up at him. "Breathe, Drop."

I shook my head because the air wasn't coming in even as I gasped for it.

"Now, suddenly, something finally bothers you?" he growled. "This is when you need to keep it together, not fall apart. Do not fall apart on me."

It was a command. Forceful. And a slight at my character, as if he knew why I tried to keep it together.

He had no idea.

I stood there as water pelted us both and glared up at him, my black dress already soaked through from the rain. "Just because I'm having a moment doesn't mean you need to target my weakness."

"That's exactly what it means. It's how this empire has operated, how I played in the NFL, and how I've structured my life thus far. Everyone targets the weak and acts swiftly." He smiled softly then. "It's how you can see whether that weakness has a backbone or not. Seems you do."

He was pointing out that I was breathing just fine now. He'd saved me from my panic but angered me at the same time. "Are you proud of targeting a weakness? Proud that it got you that nice house on a hill and an empire where everyone acts like they care when really they only want to be a part of it...for what? Prestige?"

"I'm sorry. Do you not work for that empire?" he threw back.

A part of me was ashamed to say, "I do. It's a job rather than a point of pride though. That exclusivity is—"

"It's a luxury," he finished, his hands fisting. "Obviously you know that since you're here working for that luxury too."

"Yes. Declan Hardy, billionaire CEO of the most exclusive hospitality brand in the country, providing us all a luxury we can't possibly pass up." I sneered it like a child, past the point of holding in my frustration. "And most eligible bachelor... Well, not anymore, considering we're legally bound in marriage."

He saw I was mocking him. It was a taunt like he'd taunted me. "Make sure you call that Cobra boyfriend of yours and tell him that."

It was a low blow. We both had to figure out where we'd go from here, and yet him throwing it in my face right after I'd almost hyperventilated on his pavement was infuriating.

"No need to tell him when I still intend to be with him. And with anyone else I want. I don't belong to you or Wes or anyone. I've made that perfectly clear. I'll go to any guy that I want...whether my husband likes it or not." I lifted my chin and let the cool droplets cascade down my face. I didn't even back up a step when he came forward to stand chest-to-chest with me.

"Your husband, *Mrs. Hardy*, will make you regret going to another man for anything."

"Doubtful. Just because you provide the facade of luxury, Mr. Hardy, doesn't mean you deliver it." The words were whispered.

Maybe it was the rain, the smell of earth and storm clouds

in the air, or the lightning cracking at us in the sky but I felt the pull to him.

He stared at me as the storm raged between us like he was contemplating how we could move forward, how he could make me bend to his will. Suddenly, his hand dragged up the bare skin of my arm, following the rain's trail to my shoulder and then across my collarbone to my neck. Even though the water was cold, my skin felt like it was on fire. Heat flowed through every part of me.

He pulled out the gold necklace that meant so much to me, the string necklace with pop tabs, and the threaded necklace under it, turning them over in his hand. "What do these mean to you?"

"Friendship necklace." I held up my wrist also to show him I wore string bracelets too. "They match the bracelets I make. Pop tabs I collected with my mom for—"

"For cash?" He chuckled and I snapped my gaze up to meet his in shock. "My brothers and I thought we were going to be millionaires one day when we'd collected thousands of them and turned them in."

"You did it too?"

"Sure." He shrugged. "What kid doesn't want to be a millionaire?"

One of my eyebrows lifted. "Guess you got what you wanted."

A small smile played on his lips. "You think I'm only a millionaire?"

Right then, it dawned on me that the guy had billions in his bank. "Oh my God. Cocky much?" I poked him in the shoulder and he snagged my hand in his as he laughed, like we could finally release a bit of tension.

"Just about what I should be, Drop." He didn't let my hand go and I didn't pull it away as his other fiddled with the necklaces. I felt the hunger in his eyes now, the way he licked his lips like he was going to devour me.

I saw the man who'd conquered the world and how he was ready to take what he wanted now from it.

Even with me. Fuck all the consequences because Declan didn't hesitate or wait to be told a damn thing. He didn't dwell on what might be or what might have been.

"What's with your gold owl necklace?" he asked quietly.

"They symbolize change. And growth, I guess. It meant something to me once." I bit my lip as I looked at his, how close he was now, how I could feel his breath mingling with mine. "Felt like a symbol of being saved."

"Hmm. Do you want to be saved now?"

"From what?"

He didn't give me a moment to consider more. He pushed me up against the front of the Bugatti and devoured my mouth. I tasted his hate for all we were going through, his anger, his intrigue. I met it with mine. Bite for bite. Touch for touch. My hands were in his hair—pulling, clawing, consuming.

His fingers dug into my thighs as he lifted me onto the hood of his car and lapped at my neck as he shoved himself between my legs. I wrapped them around him immediately, my body latching on like a starved animal who'd found a feast.

Declan was bad for me. I knew it. Knew from the way he held himself in luxury and riches that he was as entitled as the last man I'd been with, and that last man had almost been the death of me.

Still, I couldn't stop. Not even when the thunder cracked right after lightning struck bright and bold over the mansion he called a home.

He ripped his lips from mine only to drag them over my neck, to taste my sensitive skin there, to suck it like he owned it. "No. You don't want to be saved from this. From me. You want it, Everly. All of it."

I shook my head but held him close, ground my hips into his length and moaned loudly when I felt how big he was between my legs.

I wanted his reaction here and couldn't ignore the pull of desire.

My body enjoyed a man taking control, even though I normally avoided it at all costs. "I'm here because I have to be, aren't I? Living with all you people even when I don't want to be."

"Don't want to be?" He lifted one eyebrow, and then his hand was skirting under my dress and into my panties. "Is it the rain making you wet or me?" he murmured against my ear as I breathed in the smell of Declan mixed with rain. Cold, raw, powerful.

Fighting his pull was useless. My body shook with need as though it'd been lost a long time and was finally coming home, back to what it knew, back to what it wanted.

"My late partner's daughter, and she can't even answer... doesn't know which. My wife has no understanding of what really makes her so wet she's dripping down my hand."

His fingers moved against my folds, and my hips responded even though his words were cruel and mean. I didn't care. I knew I would only have him now, this one time, and then I'd find a way to hate him again. "Just shut up and let me feel this," I said practically to myself.

"You want all the control, don't you baby?" he murmured

before he got on his knees, his slacks instantly dampening where his legs touched the ground. He moved my thong to the side and bared me to the cold right before he dragged his tongue over my clit.

My fingers flew through his hair, gripping him immediately, grinding my sex into his mouth. Rushing toward my high was uncontrollable when his tongue flashed across my pussy, knowing exactly how to make me feel good.

But right when I was about to get there, he gripped my wrists and pulled his head away from me even though I tried to pull him back. "Please, don't stop," I whimpered.

"Say your husband's name when you ask for it then, huh?" He slid a finger inside me as he stood, and I moaned, willing to take what I could get. "Jesus, you taste good when you want something so bad, Drop. You always this sweet when you lose your composure? And that pussy tightening around my fingers like they'll give you life. You want life, Everly? You'd better say my name then."

"Please, Mr. Hardy." I knew it would drive him insane, but he was doing the same to me. I felt how he was holding back, how he stroked my clit, how his thumb brushed over it soft instead of rough, how my hips chased each touch, and he smiled like he had all the control.

Here, he did. Here, I loved seeing how he did too. It was almost like my body sighed, relieved in how he took all the worry away by knowing exactly what we both wanted, by steering the ship when I wasn't sure how to anymore.

"Mr. Hardy?" He chuckled darkly, then slid his finger out of me. "I've been waiting to redden your ass for sneering my name like that all the time."

He flipped me over without permission and bared my ass

to the wind, to the rain, to him. Then he ripped my thong from my body.

"Hey, those are my nice ones!" I tried to act frustrated, moving to lift my stomach from his car, but he shoved me back down.

"I'll buy you the whole lingerie store," he growled. "Just stay where you are. On my car, bent over for me. Like a fucking painting in the rain."

I looked at him over my shoulder but didn't move. We studied each other as he stepped back and unbuttoned his suit jacket, threw it off, and rolled up the cuffs of his white collared shirt. It was instantly soaked by the rain, allowing the outline of his muscles, the hints of black tattoos on his chest and his strong biceps, to show through. I saw the man every woman longed for.

The man who was to be mine for a year.

He undid his trousers, pulled himself from them and stroked up and down, up and down. I whimpered at the sight, him drenched with water droplets teetering on every edge and angle of the strong bone structure of his face.

We came from different worlds. He loved control and domination while I wanted to appease the masses and squeak by unnoticed. He was intense and larger than life, and I was quiet and enjoyed the silence.

Somehow, we were all wrong for each other. Yet, I couldn't stop myself from calling out for him. "Declan."

He came immediately, walked up so close, I felt his hard cock against one cheek. I bent farther into it, and he ran one hand through my slit while his other pushed my dress up from my waist so he could explore my breasts, making my nipples bead up once exposed to the cool metal of the car. "I like my name on your lips, Everly."

I thought he was about to reward me, that I'd get his thick fingers back in my pussy. Instead, his hand left me, and then I felt the slap.

Hard, loud, fast, and the pain as bright as the lightning strike.

I yelped at the feeling against my ass cheek, but the zing of the pain instantly made my pussy pulse and drip with pleasure. "Jesus, Declan."

"When you say my name and want it, you beg with *please*, Everly. Say what you want nicely this time."

My body shook. Not from the cold, but from the need to have him. To have this man at the center of my body, in me so deep I could feel all of him at once along with the emotions I hadn't experienced in so long. He'd awakened my pleasure, my adrenaline, my desire again.

"Please, Declan. Please fuck me."

"Drop wants it now. Even willing to beg for it. You on birth control?" He rubbed the ass cheek he'd spanked, kneading it slow and letting the water falling down on us cool it. His fingers continually grazed close to my puckered hole, turning me on in a way I'd never expected.

I nodded fast, "Yes, I haven't..." I didn't want to tell him I hadn't slept with anyone for a long time. "I'm good. Please, please, please fuck me."

CHAPTER 11: DECLAN

"That." I moved so my length was against her pussy as I grazed both hands over her hips to align us. "That, exactly, is what I want to hear every time you want this dick, Drop. The way you actually want what I give. Eligible bachelor who gets you in a way no other man can now. You married me. You wanted this, didn't you?"

Fuck.

Fuck, I couldn't stop.

I'd known the second I saw her I wanted her, but this was raw, feral, fucking unhinged desire that I hadn't tapped into in, quite frankly, maybe ever.

The tip of my dick practically wept to thrust into her, but I gripped it and lowered it to rub my pre-cum on her clit. I needed her to orgasm, needed her to let go and find whatever she needed to hit her high before I buried myself in her. I knew I wouldn't last long after that.

She gasped when she felt it, the cool metal that pierced my tip rubbing over her. She even tried to turn, like she hadn't experienced something like it before.

I hoped she hadn't. The thought of her with anyone made me fucking crazy.

I gripped her hair hard, wanting all of her now, wanting to prove that I would be the one to leave a mark—even if she'd barely given me the time of day over the past few weeks. I kept her lying against my car as I ground out, "The only thing you move right now is your ass so that you can feel my cock on your pussy, baby. I get to see you come against my car, ass up just for me."

She did as she was told, even if we were both going to regret it later. I knew we would. We were stepping over a line we shouldn't. A fucking marriage neither of us wanted was going to get messy fast if we did this. Yet, I rubbed my piercing over her and let her ride my cock fast, even made her work for it by inching away just to see her hips chase it while I murmured filth to her, lost in a desire I couldn't control.

"Such a pretty fuck you are. My *wife*, trying so hard to ride my cock."

"Don't call me that," I heard her murmuring as I put pressure on her clit. "Oh, God."

"Not God," I chuckled. "Your husband. The one you married today. Seems even if you don't like him calling you his wife, you like his cock right between your legs, huh?"

"Just be quiet so I can get there," she muttered, but her ass moved faster against my cock, and I slid it back and forth, up and down her slit, wanting her to get that orgasm without me entering her just yet.

"As long as you say my name when you come instead of that little boyfriend of yours, Everly." The memory of her wearing his jersey as she rode my hand in the SUV was burned into my memory for eternity, there for my jealousy to latch on to at any time. "Say it loud so we all know your husband is giving you everything you want. Going to another man for it won't get you off like I do."

It was just the rain for a moment. Falling around us. Drop after drop. Muting out the world like my raindrop did for me. Then I felt her muscles tighten under me, saw how her blue eyes closed and her neck arched as she screamed out my name, slamming her hand down on the hood as she came for me.

"That's it, pretty girl." I kneaded her ass, stroking my cock against her wet pussy. So wet it had drenched my cock, mixing with the rain. I was so ready for her I could have slid right in, but I needed to praise her. Needed her to know. "So fucking beautiful when you let go and let me give you what you really want." I rubbed a finger over her slit. "You feel how wet you are?" She whimpered, like my hand at her most sensitive part still turned her on even when she was spent. I brought my finger to her mouth. "Taste it."

Her eyes shot open as she looked over her shoulder at me and they were sapphire blue, alive and full of questions.

"You don't hesitate when I tell you to do something, Everly. Now, open." It was the difference between us. She hesitated with everything. I didn't. This was how we'd test our dynamic, see if we liked the flavor.

She opened her mouth slowly, and when she wrapped her lips around my fingers, her eyes fluttered closed, and I knew our relationship was going to be fucked.

How would I stop enjoying my wife, enjoying *this*? I wouldn't, and it was about to make this arrangement very messy.

"Look at you sucking your own pussy off my hand," I said and then pulled my fingers back, knowing I couldn't take much more of her swirling tongue. I went back to working her between her legs, watching what brought her close to the edge again. I was taking notes, filing it away for next time.

Because I wanted a next time. I was going to die trying for a next time.

Her small hands pressed against the black hood of my car,

and then they were inching toward her breasts like she wanted all the pleasure she could get.

"Declan, just hurry. I need you now. You want control? Take it and fuck me." She was getting aggravated, almost in heat with need but still assessing, still learning me. I saw her do it all the time when she worked at the gym. She was smart, she picked up on people's tells, and she used them to her advantage.

Her quiet confidence, the way she studied me, it drove me insane. I wanted to fuck her down to my level, get a reaction out of her when she never gave me one. I loved controlling her unraveling. Loved that she was letting me.

It shouldn't have been this way. I shouldn't have been thinking about who she was or what I wanted from her as I fucked her. I should have told myself this was a one-and-done thing.

Yet, I took my time drawing away from her and commanded, "Say please Declan."

She slammed her hand on the hood of the car and yelled it.

Without my name attached. I smiled. I got to punish her for that one.

I thrust in and she arched her ass out to me like I was stretching her, like the way we fit felt so good she wanted more. I delivered the punishment as I brought my hand down hard again on her ass. I wanted to feel her pussy tighten, experience if she got as much pleasure from the action as I did.

When she cried out and moaned "Declan" as her sex gripped me like a vise, I almost came.

"Say my name again."

"Declan, please move. Please, please, please."

"That's it. Nice and loud. Give me every one of those screams and come for me. The world is going to know you're my wife even if you don't want them to." She did as she was told while drops of rain pelted both of us, and I fucked her against that car harder than I had another woman in forever.

I buried my cum in her right as she hit her high. I hit mine simultaneously, practically blacking out even with lightning streaking across the sky. Nothing could be heard but our breathing and the storm for moments after. I held on to her like she had something I wanted, and I wasn't willing to move, didn't want the moment to end, but she shifted under me as she brought her hands to her dress, so I lifted myself from her.

She straightened up and pulled the fabric over her body. "Declan, I—"

Ringing from my pants pocket sounded off, announcing that Anastasia was calling me. Everly's face, vulnerable a second ago, shuttered off all her emotions, the bright blue in her eyes even dimmed.

"Give me a second."

"No need." She held up her hand and shook her wavy wet hair back from her face. "I can wait in the car or if your guesthouse is open...?"

She turned to look toward the small stone home across the driveaway but surrounded by trees and gardenias.

"It's open, but I'm not taking the call." I silenced the phone immediately.

"You should. She probably has parts of the will she'd like to go over with you too." She was already backing away, putting as much distance as she could between us. "Tell Anastasia I said hello, and if you're informing them of the marriage, let me know what I should say also."

"I said I would discuss it with you if I was going to tell anyone about the marriage, Everly."

"Right. Then, all rules still apply, I think."

"What about what happens between the rules, Drop?" I pushed her. We were already muddying the waters, already blurring lines, crossing them in places we shouldn't.

"Rules are black and white."

"Relationships aren't. And rules change. A change saved you from something, didn't it?" I pointed to that necklace. The way she'd whispered her truth to me showed me Everly had secrets that cut deep, that she hid in the dark crevices of her soul, and I wanted to see all of them.

"Changes can save you, but they can also destroy you." Her eyes shimmered like they went somewhere far off before she glanced back at me. "Anyway, this isn't a relationship. It's a professional commitment of sorts." Her hand was already on the guesthouse's doorknob, the one I was sort of pissed I had at the moment. I couldn't corner her and make her talk to me about this more. I simply had to accept that we were still very much two different people.

"Didn't feel very professional two minutes ago." I combed a hand through my hair, trying my best not to get aggravated by her composure. I'd buried my dick inside her not moments ago, and she was fine walking away from me.

No woman did that so easily.

No woman was like Everly, though.

"Let's just keep our distance from now on then."

I stared at her, saw her for the beautiful woman she was. Quiet confidence, composure even when her estranged father threw a curveball. And my partner's daughter. "I'm not sure what Carl wanted to happen between us," I said softly.

"We're giving him as much as we can," she whispered back. "I don't know that I owe him even this."

"He did love you, Everly." I wasn't sure she saw that.

"You can't possibly know that." She wrung her hands in front of her, but I saw how she leaned in, how she wanted to know more.

"He smiled when he talked about you, was proud of how quickly the athletes warmed to you. Albeit he was pissed about Wes, obviously, but he wouldn't have cared about Anastasia and Clara doing that. In his eyes, you were part of his team."

She gave one jerky nod before she murmured, "I know you were very close. I'm truly sorry for your loss. I know I said that at the funeral, but I meant it. Losing someone is difficult." She stopped for a moment. "I lost someone a while back and... I miss her a lot most days. I hope you let yourself sit with that grief and heal it. If you don't, it will eat at your soul."

"I—" Saying anything would probably bring me to damn tears. I cleared my throat. "I'll miss him for a long time."

She chewed her cheek and then stepped forward to wipe some of the rain from my face. Her touch soothed, comforted, and warmed me in a way I wasn't sure anyone else's could.

My phone went off again.

She snapped her hand away and almost jumped back, her blue eyes refocusing on that distance she wanted between us. She cleared her throat. "Feel free to have someone come show me around when they have time. Otherwise, I can explore myself. I'll make sure to stay in the guesthouse and call if I need something."

"*Someone*? I'll show you around right now!" Jesus, did she have to turn that composure on so damn quickly?

"Call Anastasia, please. I think it's best if she discusses things with you. She obviously wants to. And she's friends with Piper, right?"

My jaw worked up and down as I saw her take a step back toward the guesthouse. "So what?"

"You and Piper are close, correct?" She tilted her head. "You told me once she does your PR? It'll be good for you to be on the same page with them. Plus, I would really like to get my bearings, take a shower, all that."

She needed to wash me away. *Fuck.* Fine. "Right. Well, you have the guesthouse to yourself. My assistant will stock your fridge. You can write her a list of what you want. She'll text you soon to get everything coordinated. Movers will be here in the next hour or so with an overnight bag and will be stopping by with your things throughout the next two days. They'll organize them for you."

She wrinkled her nose. "Hmm."

"And I have a personal chef on staff for meals, so have them make what you want—"

"I can organize myself," she said, halting me. "I can also get my own groceries and make my own meals. There's no need for—"

"I know that, Everly," I said, pacing up and down my driveway. The rain had stopped, but my clothes were stuck to all the wrong parts of my body, irritating me further on top of her nonchalance. "It's a convenience to have them do it. Plus, we can catch up over dinner or breakfast, whenever we're both available. The chef can text you when they'll be preparing things over at my place."

"It'll be an inconvenience for me, actually. And I'll enjoy sorting through my own stuff. Just tell them to leave it out front." A small smile played at her lips. "And Declan..."

Her saying my name had me stopping and looking at her. Curly hair weighed down by the rain, free of makeup in a black dress that wasn't supposed to do anything for her, but she didn't need it to. The statement was her. Her blue eyes, the freckles that sprinkled over the bridge of her nose, the slope of her neck.

Raw beauty.

"Thank you for trying to make this comfortable. It won't be, but trying is best. One day down, 364 to go, right?"

"Right," I grumbled. Why did I feel like a child? Like someone was judging my life and I was coming up short?

She left me on my own driveway, staring after her like an idiot.

An idiot who hadn't even offered her a ride to work.

Sure, I'd miss Carl, but I wasn't above damning him to hell for the shit he was pulling from the grave.

CHAPTER 12: EVERLY

The first morning I awoke as a married woman felt about the same as any other day except there was a knock at my door and a woman with thick black-framed glasses and bright-red lips greeted me as I opened it. "I'm Maggie. Ignore me while we move in your items from your apartment. Mr. Milton had the extra key. You don't have a car, do you?"

"No, but I—" Wasn't it five in the morning?

"Good. We don't have to worry about that. Declan said you can use any of his in the garage."

I shook my head and tried to wake up.

"Well, I have a team here to organize. Go about your day as you like. Also, Declan requested lingerie and work attire." She snapped fingers behind her, and I immediately moved aside as people marched in with clothing racks of athleisure and literal panties of all colors dangling from gold hangers.

"I don't need more clothes." I tried to stop her but she walked past me like I was insignificant.

It was too early to argue, and I escaped to my bedroom when my phone rang. I grabbed it like a lifeline but groaned as I answered. "Mom, it's too early, like still-dark-out early," I croaked into the phone.

"You're fine, Evie. You know I'm an early bird. Talk to me a minute and then go back to bed." She knew me well enough to know I would sleep until the last second I could. "Tell me how things are going."

"Everything is fine. I already told you." It had been via text, however, because I'd avoided talking to her directly. Which was normal. My mother had her own life and we didn't need to talk unless big things were happening. I yawned and stretched before getting out of bed. "I'm staying with Declan as we iron out the details of the will."

"Hmm. Are you dating him? What aren't you telling me?" I wanted to say the same to her. She hadn't ever told me my father owned the yoga studio or our home.

"Not dating him." That wasn't a lie. "It's nothing. There's some nuance to the terms, and I want to make sure—"

"Do you think maybe you should come home?" She hesitated over it, like she wasn't sure she should even offer the idea.

Still, I wondered the same. But going back to my hometown wouldn't solve anything, not now.

And I'd left for a good reason.

"I don't know if that's a smart idea."

"I don't either." She sighed. "When he gets out, I'm going to make sure to—"

"Don't go to the courthouse. Don't do anything. Andy has a lot of ties everywhere. The judge already gave him his sentence." I walked through the guesthouse again, opening the linen drapes to see the gardenias outside my window. To avoid the smell, I'd make sure not to open it. "Plus, we can't keep living with the fact that we don't think he got what he deserved. We have to accept it, remember? You told me that."

Still, moving on from a past sometimes wasn't that easy. It infected the present, made you hesitate about your future.

"Yes, you." She grumbled, "I told you that. I'm your mother. I teach you how to do better than me before I rip someone apart for hurting you."

That was the problem with us though. My mom had reacted badly once in the media. She'd stepped over the line when the cameras were on her, lunged at them when they called me a liar. And, according to my lawyer, they'd never forgiven us.

From that point forward, the attorney thought it best to keep her out of the limelight and made sure every time a camera was on me or I was in the public eye, I dressed the part, held my pain and anger, held my fear, held my heart at bay. My composure was the only weapon I had.

I sighed into the phone. "I love you for that, Mom."

"I hate me for it," she grumbled back as if remembering the day, "but we're through some of the hell, right?"

"Right."

"So," she ventured tepidly, fiddling with her braids, the beads clinking over the phone line. "How are you?"

I shrugged, not knowing what to say but also knowing she couldn't see me.

Still, my mother's intuition was always at work. "He was your father, Evie. It's okay to be sad you lost him. It's only been two weeks. The funeral was hard on you."

We'd all sat in the pews and listened to Melinda and her daughters and Declan and his brothers give eulogies.

The family that he loved, that he built, that he'd surrounded himself with had everything all mapped out. I understood it. I'd done the same already for my mother. We knew she would be cremated and given back to the land like she wanted. We'd talked about her belongings, and she'd said she was giving the studio and house to me.

Now, I questioned all that. Yet, I couldn't question her.

Giving her the burden of pointing a finger at her wouldn't help.

"I'll be fine."

"You don't always have to be fine, Evie," she said quietly. Yet, my mother had always been fine. She'd never cried about the divorce or about being a single mom. She got up, ran the yoga studio, and taught me to do the same all on her own.

"It's just hard to digest it all," I said quietly. "He was trying with me, you know? And now..."

"You can miss the idea of him, baby girl. You have to give yourself grace to miss and to hurt, even though you didn't know what the future held. Maybe you miss your hopes. That's real and you shouldn't discount it, okay?"

I took a shaky breath as I peered around the house. "I know you're right. I just don't like change, and I like to be one step ahead."

"Or a million steps ahead." She chuckled. "It's okay to breathe, to feel, to let go a little."

I nodded. "I'm going back to bed, Mom. You're my sunshine."

"My only sunshine," she replied back. It was the song she'd always sung to me on a bad day, the lyrics we still exchanged as I love yous now. I hung up and tried not to cry, curled up in that bed, and tried to ignore people milling around and organizing my life.

Not much later, the movers and assistant were gone, and Declan knocked on the oak front door. I padded over the plush cream carpet to swing it open. "Hi?" I said, wiping the sleep from my eyes, not sure why he was here.

"Were you still sleeping?" He squinted at me as if it was absurd.

I tried to smooth the hoodie I had on as I took in the

formidable man standing before me, looking as bright and awake as the sun. "I'm not a morning person. Your assistant stopped by though."

He nodded. "You get all your belongings?"

I glanced at the lingerie and clothing rack. "I got more than that."

He hummed. "Wear what you want. Return what you don't. I promised a lingerie store."

I chewed my lip and tried not to melt at how casually he offered an explanation. "I really didn't need it—"

"I really wanted to give it though. So, I did," he said without a worry in the world about it. "Anyway, you always wake up this late for work?"

I shrugged and nodded.

He chuckled. "That's shocking actually." The desire to slam the door in his face grew as his eyes twinkled with what looked like amusement and pure energy that I needed to get from a big dose of caffeine. "You're normally ready to go when you get to the gym."

"Sort of shocking you know that considering you never used to say hi to me or notice me the mornings I work."

He leaned against the doorframe. "I've always noticed you, Drop, no matter how damn hard I try not to."

My heart beat fast at his confession. "Well, I normally have a gallon of coffee. So, I'm up by then." I tried to stifle a yawn and motioned toward him at my door. "Was this a wake-up call or do you need something from the guesthouse?"

It was then I took a minute to look him up and down. Declan normally wore gym shorts and a T-shirt—or no shirt at all—when he was working out. Instead, standing on the white doorstep, he was dressed in a navy suit with shiny gold cuff links and a HEAT pin on his lapel. Clean-cut, tailor-made for him. "Are you going to work or someplace else dressed like that?"

He pulled at his collar. "I have meetings most of the day. My brothers are stopping in, and we'll be talking with shareholders, discussing new designs, ironing out what will happen with the gyms, spas, and resorts in the next year or so."

"Oh." It occurred to me that only Declan and his brothers had been invited, that Carl's legacy wasn't being passed down to me at all. "I guess that makes sense."

"You guess?" He lifted a brow.

"It's mostly your company now, right? It might benefit you to take into consideration all the dynamics."

"Do you think we don't do that already?"

"Melinda is managing the spa. She may want—"

"That woman won't be managing anything." He cut me off. "I talked with her and Anastasia last night. They've given me voting rights because they have a spin class."

Jesus, did they not care about anything other than their damn lifestyle within HEAT? "Okay. Well, I know it's an exclusive access for some but the kids that come now love it. It could benefit HEAT to work in more charitable ventures for them and—" I stopped myself. "I'm sure you know this."

He narrowed his eyes. "I'll make note of it."

I figured he'd forget what I said. "Well, is there anything else?"

"We're leaving in thirty minutes for work. My driver will be here then."

"I don't need a ride. I like to jog to—"

"It's five miles now, Everly."

"Good. I can walk some of that and—"

"Jog at work on the track. We need to discuss our lives for the next year, and I think you're unaware of the fact that yours will be changing drastically once the news outlets find out you're staying here. You can't go jogging by yourself anymore."

That had the retort dying on my lips fast. "The paparazzi," I whispered, frustrated that he was probably right. "But they don't know yet."

"No. I intend to keep things as quiet as I can for as long as I can."

I nodded and glanced out the window. "Would you like some coffee?"

"No. I have enough energy as it is."

As much as I'd tried to avoid the news about him in the last few months, I saw the headlines. Declan Hardy lived a high-impact, fast life that people admired. He pushed his body to the max in any way he could. He'd go bungee jumping on his day off or one day Juna whispered to me that he and his brother-in-law—who was a questionable businessman but also the head of our nation's cybersecurity—were photographed together pushing electric cars to high speeds. Supposedly his brother-in-law had helped calibrate them.

"In that case, I guess I'll take you up on your offer, and I'll be ready in twenty minutes."

"Are you not going to invite me in?"

"I have to get dressed."

He lifted a brow and laughed before pushing off the doorframe and walking right in. "I've seen you naked, Drop. I'd actually prefer to wait here and catch another glimpse."

"Are you always like this in the morning?"

"Like what?"

"Pushing boundaries."

"Sure. People are vulnerable when they're tired. Might learn something new about my wife." He shrugged and smirked at me, like we were suddenly friends.

"I don't... It's too early for this. Don't call me that."

"What should I call you, then? My late business partner's daughter?"

I glared. "Probably better."

"Probably not, since even knowing that, the first time I saw you, I pictured fucking you on the conference table."

"Oh my God." I rolled my eyes but couldn't stop the blush that spread across my cheeks.

"In my defense, I didn't know you would be working for us or that you were his daughter until you were introduced."

"I don't know whether to be offended or—"

"Or turned on? Go with that." This was bad. Playful Declan in the morning was not something I could contend with without caffeine.

"I think you need to go back to your mansion, Mr. Hardy." I shoved him but hated how my heart fluttered as he caught my wrist instead of backing away and pulled me close.

"My mansion feels empty when I know there's a woman in the guesthouse who tastes as sweet as she smells."

"I think we're going to have trouble with our rules if you don't start following them," I said as he nestled into my neck.

"Right. Not sure flirting and stealing a kiss here and there are a part of the rules. I sat up all night thinking about you over here."

"We said no sex," I pointed out.

"And then we fucked," he shot back. "Plus, this isn't sleeping together. Although, I can change that if you want." He eyed the island counter like he had ideas.

"Okay. You need to leave. Your mind is in outer space with alien life-forms this morning." I turned his shoulder toward the door and pushed his back. He leaned his weight into me, and I chuckled. "Come on. Are you joking me? That's not fair."

"What do you mean? You're the one who practically tackled me the first time we met."

"Tackled? Get real. You fell over like a child who'd gotten a scraped knee when you thought I'd break your precious wrist."

"Ah. My Drop does have some sass under that cool, calm composure."

Who was this man, and what had he done with my brooding boss? "Oh, stop." I took that moment to step away from him fast, and he almost fell over without me trying to shove him out the door.

"Good. Not good enough though." He stumbled to right himself. "I'm learning the way you move."

"Learning? How?"

"I see how you scrap around in the ring every now and then with clients. You use their weight against them most of the time."

Why did the fact that he was watching me every now and then warm me in places it shouldn't?

I shrugged. Then, I turned on my heel and went to get dressed, smirking to myself when I saw Wes's jersey in the overnight bag Declan's assistant had left. I snapped it up.

He wanted to tease me in the morning? I'd do it right back. Playful felt good, felt new, felt like something I could be, if only for just a second with him.

I slipped on the jersey as I peeked around the corner at Declan. "I see the SUV outside. I'll meet you out there."

"Fine." He dragged out the word like he was pouting, and

then I heard the door open. I swiped on a bit of lip gloss and spread some cream in over my waves before throwing a change of clothes into my duffel and bounding out the door and into the Escalade.

Declan was on the phone as the driver pulled out. "Then find another way. I want to see every line of that document."

He turned to me, and I saw how the cheeriness drained from his eyes. The twinkle faded away, and his jaw tensed as he continued to listen to the person on the phone.

"Right. I understand the legalities. I just don't care about them...which means you need to not care about them either. Find me a way."

This was business Declan. I saw the NFL player—the man willing to go to great lengths, seeking the adrenaline rush for his team. Then I saw the ruthless businessman—the one who didn't smile and tell you to get the job done next week. He wanted things done his way. And now.

"See that you do," he murmured before pulling the phone from his cheek.

Yet, the Declan in front of me now... I wasn't sure which it was. The player or the businessman, ruthless and angry, ready to get his way.

"Peter, turn the car around."

"Sir?"

"Peter, don't. We'll be late for work," I said with a surprising amount of authority.

"Ma'am."

I kept my composure as Declan clicked a button, and suddenly a black partition slid up between the front seats and the back. With every centimeter of the driver disappearing from view, my heart rate skyrocketed.

In a way I wanted.

In a way I shouldn't.

"You have another shirt in that duffel bag to wear?"

"Not one I'm willing to put on right now. It's for after my workout."

"Then we're going back to the house for you to change, Everly."

"Mr. Hardy," I drawled his name, "this is merely a shirt. Please don't tell me you're going to lose your temper over it."

He narrowed his eyes. "Are you trying to piss me off?"

I pursed my lips, attempting not to smile. He had to know I was going to wear my HEAT sports bra under this at the fitness center. "Are you truly that easy to rile? I'll wear my sports bra there, Declan."

I broke eye contact so I wouldn't burst out laughing right in his face.

"Carl would be so disgusted with you right now." He shook his head in disappointment. "Part of that will was to not have you entertaining the idea of Wes when you're married to me—"

"I'm not really married to you." The laughter bubbled out. I couldn't help it. "This is all so ridiculous."

"Fuck me," he groaned. "What's ridiculous is you thinking that a Cobra is going to be okay with you staying at my place every night."

"Your guesthouse."

"You think he's going to enjoy knowing I fucked you into oblivion on the hood of my car?"

I couldn't stop the flush from overtaking my body. "We aren't telling people any of that. When the time comes, I'll be honest with him and let him know it's a marriage of convenience with stipulations for the benefit of HEAT's corporation. We were doing what my father wanted. No more, no less."

"Isn't it 'more' since I know how your pussy tastes, Everly?"

"Declan, that was— It won't happen again."

"We got a whole year of you and me crossing paths, and you think it won't?"

"Why would it? We had our fun." I straightened in my seat and tried not to even look at him now. If I did, he'd know I was thinking about how he felt inside me, how I couldn't stop imagining it. "And now we have a commitment to fulfill. Let's do it efficiently without changing things or throwing in surprises."

"That's the thing babe, I don't mind a change or a surprise."

"I do. Plus, I know I'm personally no good at relationships."

"And why is that?" He lifted a brow.

Sharing my past with him would mean trusting him to not look at me like most people in my town did. I didn't trust anyone with that yet. "Past is in the past."

I said it and tried so hard to believe it.

I saw how he sighed, how he nodded and tensed his jaw. Good. He needed to put his barrier back up too. "Fine, other than our tax status, our lives stay the same. Nothing else has changed. Easy."

Famous last words.

CHAPTER 13: DECLAN

We managed to stay off everyone's radar the first month and a half, aside from the whispers.

Everly was quiet, insanely organized, and a creature of habit. I'd seen it time and time again since she'd started working at the gym.

She threw her coffee in the same trash as she walked in, wore her watch on the same wrist, even had designated colors for most every day of the week. Red on Mondays, white on Tuesdays, and on Wednesdays, she wore royal blue, my favorite because the color set off her eyes. I was happy to see some of the athleisure I'd sent over made it into her rotation too, although I wasn't sure about the lingerie.

Yet, my dumb ass was still thinking of trying to find out.

Every day she let me drive her to the gym, unless I wasn't going into work or was heading out of town. She'd then let Peter take her in. And she never wanted breakfast at my place, even though I'd invited her. So we'd idle outside her place until she was ready.

Every day, we were cordial. Friendly.

Our tax status was the only thing between us for a whole damn month. Until, on a royal-blue Wednesday, she burst into my office while I was on a call, wringing her hands as she realized what she'd done. I lifted a brow and told the person on the line to wait. "There a problem out there, Drop?"

"You installed pop tabs for the kids to collect. You gave

them something to work toward." She whispered out, "You're on a call. Sorry to burst in—"

"Reschedule my meeting," I ordered into the phone, holding her shimmering gaze as I clicked it off.

"No, it's fine. I—" She twisted the necklaces on her collarbone, worried now that I was giving her all my attention.

"Everly," I tapped my desk and then smirked up at her. "You know in a marriage, the spouse comes first. Technically, my wife comes first. You have something you need to discuss, I'll push a meeting."

"Declan," she whisper-yelled my name, then glanced quickly behind her before closing the door. "That's not a funny joke. Don't talk like that at work or publicly anywhere."

"I wasn't joking. You are my wife." She was also the person I wanted to talk to in that moment more than anyone else. I was going to give her my attention whether she wanted it or not.

She sighed and shook those waves back and forth before she continued, "The kids are so freaking excited. And having the signs that allow for the clients to donate too is really going to be so much help."

I'd taken her advice and discussed charities with my brothers. We looked up a couple of the schools Everly was working with for yoga courses and found some of them didn't have avid gym curriculum or the finances to bring in more teachers and aid. So, we were funding it and helping the kids in the community.

It wasn't something to thank me for. "We needed to be doing more. I wasn't aware that Carl hadn't restructured some of our finances to allow for this."

She combed a hand through her massive waves of caramel and brunette before she grabbed at her wrist and huffed when she realized she didn't have a rubber band to tie it up. It was the one thing she seemed to forget half the time. "Don't downplay it. They... You made their day. And mine." She walked around the desk, bent over, and kissed my cheek.

Were we in fucking high school?

I grabbed her neck and pulled her close to take her lips in mine. She smelled like ocean and sweat and sweet coconut. I growled and spread my legs, let my hands drift down her neck, down her arms, down to her waist to grab hold of her ass. Her hands threaded in my hair as she pulled me closer still, like she was starved for me too. But just as I brushed a thumb on her bare thigh, she stepped back fast, gasping for air. "I didn't come by for this." Her sapphire eyes dragged over my body as she licked her lips. "I just needed to say thank you."

"Thank me on my fucking desk, Drop," I growled.

She tsked but I saw the small smile as she turned around and left.

Finding that I wanted to make my fake wife happy was a damn problem. Because the rest of the day, I walked around like a dumbass with a bright smile on my face.

Dom elbowed me during our last meeting and ground out, "Get your mind off whatever the fuck you're thinking about and pay attention. If you want the press focused on our new sponsorship, you better nail this meeting or they'll be focused on some other shit."

His words killed my mood.

The press was always circling, always waiting for their next target, and I didn't want our marriage to be it. Not when things were going just fine.

* * *

The next week, I idled in front of her house, deciding to take the Bugatti because Peter was off.

Right on time, she came out in the white she always wore on Tuesdays.

We were silent on the car ride like we had nothing to say. Or maybe it was we had too much to say, so much that we didn't know where to start.

Small talk was easy though. "What did you have for breakfast?"

She grumbled something over her coffee. The woman hated discussing anything before she'd downed the whole cup.

"What?"

"I don't eat breakfast in the morning." She slouched down in her seat like she wanted me to disappear so she could enjoy the silence.

I turned onto the highway instead of going straight to work.

"What are you doing?" she grumbled.

I didn't answer, just veered off the first exit and pulled up to a small drive-thru coffee stand. "What do you want to eat?"

"Nothing," she pouted. Like I was inconveniencing her.

Great. So I ordered just about everything on the menu.

"Are you that hungry?" she questioned, her brows furrowed. "Don't you eat at home?"

"I do." I nodded and pulled around to collect the food and pay.

"Oh, Mr. Hardy! We thought it was you in the camera." A young guy stared in the window and a few others peeked around him. "No need to pay. I watched the Super Bowl last year. Huge fan. How's your wrist been? Can't believe they didn't fine more of those guys—"

"Great." I wiggled it in front of him. "Good as new."

Someone snapped a photo. "Can I have an autograph?"

I tried to suppress the sigh. I took her pen and signed a book she had on her. Then someone shoved their phone toward me. "Just sign the back please."

I signed five more things before I pointed toward the gym. "Have to get to work."

They all waved goodbye as I pulled away quickly.

"Here." I handed her the bag of food.

"For me?" she whispered, and when I glanced over, there was a frown on her face.

"You work out hard. Enjoy some food before you do."

"Is it like that most places you go?" she asked as she looked in the bag.

"Most places that aren't HEAT owned."

She hummed without giving much away, like she was digesting what I said. "I think today I finally want to know... What happened to your wrist?"

"Happened during the sport you don't watch," I mumbled, not caring to talk about it.

"Want to share?" she pried a bit more as she took a crescent roll out of the bag.

I should have asked her what happened to the past staying in the past. Yet, I didn't want to. I was going to pry one day, step over the boundaries and break the rules where I could with her. I already knew it.

I admitted what I pretty much allowed anyone to admit around me. We didn't talk about my wrist within the HEAT brand. It was something everyone knew I wouldn't dwell on and they shouldn't either. "Got hit wrong in a preseason game."

"By more than one guy?"

I nodded and ground my teeth together without giving further details.

"You should rehab it." She took a bite and moaned. "I could help."

"I'm done playing ball, Everly. And I was able to play the rest of the season once it was healed."

"So, you didn't give it much time to heal then?" she challenged.

"I have ninety percent of function back and don't want surgery."

"I could get you to one hundred percent with stretching," she said with brighter eyes than she'd had a second ago.

"That crescent roll going to your head and giving you energy already?"

"It is pretty good. You want one?" She dug another out of the bag.

"Nope. I had breakfast."

"So what? This whole bag is for me?" She shook it and the brown paper crinkled in her grip. "I can't eat all this."

"You didn't tell me what you wanted. How was I supposed to know? Next time tell me so I won't have to order the whole restaurant."

"That's when you guess and buy one thing."

"Everly, my wife gets what she wants, and if I don't know what that is, I just get everything."

Her sapphire eyes widened at my comment. She wasn't sure how to respond. I saw her cheeks flush and how she wiggled in my leather seat.

Flustering Everly would be something I was going to enjoy doing for the year to come. I already knew it.

"You need to stop with the wife stuff. Even as a joke." She

wrinkled her nose. "Just call me *Evie* like everybody else." She enunciated it like I didn't know already she wanted that.

"I don't call you that," I pointed out and glanced in my rearview mirror to see an SUV following me.

"Everyone does though."

"Well, your husband doesn't," I shot back because I didn't want to be like "everyone" to her. I maneuvered into another lane and they did the same.

Her long lashes fell over her cheeks as she breathed out. "Declan, you're trying to frustrate me. We both know this is going to be difficult as it is. I don't need you throwing around *wife* and *husband* in private." Then she saw me glance behind us. "Is someone following us?"

"Might be a pap or two."

She immediately tensed, her whole body going ramrod straight. "Honestly, I'm not even sure why I'm going to work with you when I can Uber. This isn't good for either of us."

"It is," I countered. "Gives us time to talk."

"Could give the public something to talk about."

I shook my head, not wanting anyone to destroy the small relationship we were building. "People expect this. The magazines are already printing that we've become close. Haven't you read—"

"No." She said it fast, hard, full of determination. Then she glanced at me, her sapphire eyes vulnerable. "I'm not good with the media. I hate it. I told you that. So, if they're going to write about us, I'd rather not know."

"The media is going to write about us at some point, Everly."

"Okay." She obviously didn't want it to be true.

I hated to offer, but I had to. "You can talk with Piper if

you'd like."

"I'd rather not." She picked at the corner of the paper bag.

I took a deep breath, knowing that I needed more time with her, knowing we'd need a reason to be closer. "Look, I'll have you work on my wrist."

"You will?" Her eyes lit up, and she zeroed in on it. "Really?"

I grumbled, "My wrist doesn't need it, but it'll show everyone we've become friends and will lead to less questioning when I drive you home from work. Last appointment of your day, keep free for me."

"Oh." She frowned before taking a large drink of her coffee and then taking a bite of her crescent roll. "Sounds good."

CHAPTER 14: DECLAN

She stretched my wrist every night for a month after when I was in town.

I'd find her near the weights and have her twist it any which way she thought was necessary that day. After a month of her brand of rehab, though, I felt the tension and discomfort changing in my arm, like she had some magical touch.

Or maybe it was her attitude, the way she didn't care about anything outside the stretching. She didn't ask me about football, didn't care to know how the injury actually happened, and I knew she didn't give a shit if I ever stepped foot onto the field again. She was the complete opposite of every therapist and coach I'd had questioning the progress.

And I saw why athletes throughout my gym gravitated toward her. She didn't care about their job nor their status, just about helping them move forward and heal.

I rubbed my wrist thinking about her as I pulled at the collar of the dumb-ass suit I had to wear yet again for another meeting on the top floor.

Dom snickered when he saw me walking in and fell into stride with me. "How's babysitting your wife coming?"

"Fuck off," I grumbled.

My brother sobered for a minute. "Carl did want what was best for all of us in some way or another. Don't think it's *actually* best though."

"I don't know. Carl had a funny way of getting all the way

to the edge of disaster and then turning it into a fucking dream instead."

"What? Like he did with the HEAT empire?" Dom scoffed. "I loved Carl, Declan, but we worked our asses off to bring it back to life when it was near death. That's why Carl had us invest."

"He had great ideas," I shot back.

He nodded and studied me like he was concerned, his dark eyebrows knitting together as we neared the elevators. "You okay? You were closest to him, even if he was an ass half the time."

I nodded once. Mourning someone even when they weren't the best human on the planet was confusing. You mourned them for what they could have been, not what they were. "Gonna miss the old man, but he's still laughing at us from his grave so I get reminders of him that way instead, right?"

"Right." Dom dragged out the word before he inquired, "So, you gonna be Everly's caretaker for the rest of her life?"

The fucker loved to poke and prod. "You want to take her in?" I turned my gaze on him. "You, Dimitri, and Dex got off easy."

"Did we? What the fuck you two doing over there anyway? You're acting like her stay is a damn diary entry. Just be honest that marriage isn't even fucking that bad."

My jaw worked as we got to the elevators, and I pressed the button. "Everly and I have to work through some stuff. Probate's going to last all fucking year at this rate anyway."

"The lawyers need to speed it along. I can't continue working on the damn resort on the Pacific Coast until they do." He grumbled a couple swears under his breath as the elevator doors closed with us in it. "Carl's will is bullshit on my end.

There's no way to include that damn bakery in it, by the way."

"Clara's?" I couldn't stop from laughing. Dominic had shared that Carl was giving him control of the renovations and design of the Pacific Coast Resort he'd been working on so long as Clara's bakery would be included.

"Fuck you," he spit and shoved my shoulder.

I shoved his back. "Come on, the chocolates are very good." It was my turn to give him hell now.

"Who the fuck cares? She's got blown glass of every damn color in the world through that whole damn shop, Declan. We have a sleek, world-renowned resort being built, and the design doesn't allow for whimsical shit."

We made our way off the elevator and into the conference room to sit down for our first call. We had meeting after meeting scheduled today regarding the shares of the company.

"We're all dealing with our own hell," I said as I looked out the glass window of the office. It overlooked the free weight area, and I saw her down there, explaining some stretching technique to Noah.

She bent over, and I found myself glaring as I readjusted myself in my slacks before a ring sounded from the phone. I slammed the answer button harder than I should have and let the lawyers start.

Hour one. Noah stretched his legs and supposed sore ankle with her. That shit was barely a sprain last year.

Hour two. Wes took her to the shake cafe. I contemplated how I could get him back on the field so I could tackle his bitch ass.

Hour three. I'd had enough.

"I've got to head to another meeting," I said, cutting my lawyer off.

"Meeting or woman?" Dom lifted a brow as he chuckled on his way down the hall with me.

"Fuck off. She's down there with a bunch of boys who can't keep their dicks to themselves."

"You sure she wants them to?"

"Carl would have wanted us to keep them in check." I threw out the best reasoning I had.

"Is that right?" He pushed the elevator down button and waited for my answer.

"We've got a lot of nuances in this will that we have to work on together, Dom."

"I'm sure you do. Work on those instead of the ones between her legs, huh?"

"Watch yourself, brother," I warned.

He took in my stance for a second before he backed down and sighed. "She's got some demons, Declan. I don't know what they are, but I see it when I talk to her and when she lets me spar with her every now and then."

"What the fuck are you doing sparring with her?"

He chuckled. "What? Am I not allowed to?"

"Go over to your hotel, asshole," I grumbled as he walked away.

Instead of pacing over to the woman who was driving me insane, I checked the front desk, made another phone call, and tried to curb the fiery jealousy that had built in me. Of course, my phone pinged instead.

Dom: Declan's about to start the downfall of the Hardy Empire, just making you all aware.

Izzy: What's going on now? I'm the

pregnant sister. Keep me out of it.

Dex: You're like one day pregnant. Be quiet.

Me: Dom's starting shit for no reason.

Izzy tried to call me immediately. I ignored it. My siblings, all five of them, wanted me to rage. I already knew it.

Lilah: Just leave him alone, you guys. He's still trying to get accustomed to a boring, regular old life of a retired athlete.

Lilah: That was mean. Sorry, Declan. You're doing great. Ignore us.

Izzy: Suck up.

Lilah: I have to suck up now. You went and got knocked up with twins immediately after your hubs proposed. You're the favorite who can now get away with anything even if you eloped without inviting all of us.

Izzy: Oh stop. I'll have another wedding but we couldn't help ourselves. Vegas just has that get-married vibe. I'm inviting you to the

> hospital when I have to push these
> babies out.

> Izzy: ...What if they're just like me
> and Cade?

Fuck. My baby sister was the one person in the world I'd talk to at the moment, and only because I knew her mind was spinning. So I called her back right away.

"You're calling me back? What for?"

"Those babies are going to be hell, but Cade's the devil, so he'll keep them in line," I reassured her.

"Oh. Big brother's worried about me. Got it." She sighed and then chuckled. "I'm fine. Cade says be nice to me though."

"Tell him to fuck off."

"He wants to know how the will is treating you and if you need any help yet?"

The man had a way of navigating the world and knowing shit he shouldn't, so I was a bit concerned he knew what was in it because he'd hacked everything he shouldn't.

"Tell him to stay out of my business. He knows better."

"Of course he does," she singsonged.

"You feeling okay?"

"Yes, no morning sickness yet. I'm sure it will come with twins." She chuckled. "I can't believe that I get two. And isn't it crazy they can get all this genetic information from a blood sample now? Like, they tested them both and they're looking healthy already."

"That's all we want," I reassured her. "You healthy and the babies. Remind Cade to take care of you."

"You got it, Dec. And when you figure out that will and the

woman in it, make sure you don't give her too much of a hard time. She seems nice. Plus, since you're married, you have to treat her like Dad does Mom."

I winced. So, she found out. "Izzy..." My tone held warning.

"What? I'm not going to tell Mom and Dad. Or Lilah. But obviously our brothers know, and they weren't going to last long keeping it a secret from me. Plus, I just hacked the court system to see. Anyway, remember what I said. She's your wife now. Treat her like it."

Then she hung up.

Fuck.

Of course they knew. My family spread news like a virus, and I couldn't even worry about it because my wife laughed across the gym at something her fuckboy boyfriend said.

She was meticulously laying out weights to use while everyone else stood around and stared at her ass.

She hummed around with light yoga leggings and a sports bra that showed off her tan skin and curves in a way I didn't want them to. I contemplated if Wes's jersey would have been better draped over her rather than everyone's eyes on that ass. The ass I knew I could redden in seconds if she'd let me.

Four sets of everything. She was thorough when she lifted, rehabbed, even when she stretched during a cool down.

No bigger than a damn fairy, yet she still got it done. Tonight, she managed to deadlift more than most of the women in the facility. Rotating between legs, arms, back, chest, and abs, she pushed her body to the limit. I knew after the bench press, she'd go to trap pulls and that she never asked for anyone to spot her.

Yet, never once was she without a spotter.

Po or Noah or fucking Wes were always there, swarming

like ants around sweet sugar.

Quite frankly, they weren't the only ones.

Men and women loved her. I even saw Clara walking over. She must have closed the bakery for the day and wanted to catch up with Everly. Clara was sweet that way when Anastasia wasn't around.

Or maybe she was addicted to Everly like the rest of us, because Everly had that quiet magnetism that pulled people to her like moths to a flame. And she was always helping everyone. Juna barely covered the front desk when Everly was in because Everly would go up and watch for her every time she had a minute so Juna could read the latest gossip on her phone.

"Two more reps and you're at twenty," Po said from above her as she pushed the barbell up a bit shakier than the last.

If I were a better man, I would have been working out myself, not watching them.

Instead, I watched the woman I was technically married to get a spot from a guy I respected but didn't give a shit about.

"Po! You think you can just take care of my girl because I'm not around?" Wes yelled across the gym while he finished a pull-up, a smile across his face as he claimed something that was actually mine.

My wife.

Even if no one knew it.

"Everly." My voice cut through the weights clanking, the music, and the TVs going in my gym. Women and men looked over. Wes's gaze locked on mine before he reached Everly's side.

One last push with Po standing over her, and she finished the set, pulled herself up from the bar, and smiled brilliantly at all of us. "I did it!"

I glanced back at the bar and then her, sitting there

vibrating with energy from completing a set.

"It's more than I've lifted ever." She clapped her hands together and bounced on the bench with more enthusiasm than I usually witnessed from her.

Po patted her head and then shook it a bit, messing her curls up. "You're killing it, Evie."

"It might be because I have a great spotter."

"He's no better than me," Wes grumbled.

"Wes," Clara chastised like she was a mother hen trying to keep all us idiots in line. She probably was the better one of our group, but that wasn't saying much. "Great job, Evie."

"Glad we could celebrate a rep together, everyone." My voice held menace. "Now, Everly, can we get rehab started before we leave for the night?"

Clara narrowed her eyes at me. "How's having Everly in the guesthouse?"

"Great." I punctuated the word fast, probably too fast because I didn't want to give anyone an opportunity.

"You're staying at Dec's?" Po asked, scratching his head as if something didn't add up. "I saw a news article on that shit but didn't believe it."

"She's staying there." Clara patted down her violet dress and offered, "But you can always stay with us back at our guesthouse if you want, you know, Evie? You're always welcome."

Everly's blue eyes bounced between all of us. I could see her mind whirring so fast, I was surprised smoke wasn't coming out of her ears. She hated not having every scenario mapped out in her head.

"She's fine at my guesthouse. It has more than enough room while we get everything ironed out through probate."

"Damn." Po murmured, "Carl must have left a hell of a

will, huh?"

Evie's gaze flew to mine. Was she nervous I'd confirm or deny? I'd given her my word.

Wes agreed. "I'm having a hard time knowing Evie's anywhere but at my place at night."

This was supposed to be my sanctuary, my gym, the place I felt most at ease. Yet, Wes's words caused my stomach to coil with jealousy, green and twisted.

Everly tsked. "Wes, most nights you're busy anyway."

So, she'd been trying to go over there?

Fuck.

"Everly, if we're stretching my wrist, we're doing it now."

She cleared her throat. "I have one more set."

Clara must have felt the tension because she said, "Come to my bakery tomorrow, Evie. Let's catch up. I'll make biscuits."

Everly nodded and waved as Clara walked away. Then, she totally disregarded my request to start rehab and moved to the pull-up bar as Wes walked up behind her.

"I'll help you with it after rehab, Everly."

She turned to stare at me and tilted her head. I held her gaze, her blue eyes warring with mine. She wanted me to back off, and my ass wasn't going to today. I'd been pushed too far watching her for hours.

Po meandered over and tried to interject. "Let's get this one last set done. Evie's been trying to do ten pull-ups now for a couple weeks. I think you got it in you this time, kid."

"Po," I murmured soft, but it seemed the whole gym heard. "Go home."

Cracking his knuckles, he maybe considered the fight, but after a second, he backed off and nudged Noah. "Evie, holler if you need us."

Wes took another step toward her though. "My girl wants a spot, I'm going to spot, Declan."

"Your girl, huh?"

"Declan," Everly stepped between us. "Remember what we talked about?"

I didn't look down at her. I held her asshole of a boyfriend's gaze until he remembered where he was. So he understood this empire was mine. "Wes, I got your girl for the next hour. She's rehabbing my wrist."

He glanced down at it and smiled like he remembered exactly what had happened. "Benson got you good that day."

"That he did." I shrugged, trying to curtail my rage. "And still, somehow, that season I went home with another ring, huh?"

"Fuck you, Declan," he growled before he walked off.

"Seriously?" Everly crossed her arms over the tits I needed to not be looking at anyway. Then she whisper-yelled, "What is it with you two?"

"You need to break things off with him," I snapped without even an explanation.

"Wes and I aren't even exclusive. There's nothing to break up." She threw out her hands. "Honestly, I'm not getting into this with you because we've set these boundaries already."

"Have we?" It'd been two months since I'd fucked her on the hood of my car, since I knew on paper she was my wife, and since I discovered my dick fit perfectly in her sweet pussy. I couldn't see past the muddied waters to whatever boundary she spoke of.

We were climbing toward something, like walking up steps on one side of a cliff where I'd bungee jump off of. I was anticipating the fall, seeking the adrenaline rush that was

Everly Belafonte.

She had to feel it too.

She stalked over to the elastic bands and pointed to my wrist. "This is all we're discussing tonight."

I narrowed my eyes, but I'd already pulled up the gym's schedule and pushed closing time up an hour. I heard murmurs and groans as I updated it.

"Damn, Dec. Total closedown?" a man threw out.

I shrugged, and Everly immediately twisted her arm to look at her own HEAT watch. "Why are you closing? We still have your stretching and the night crew."

"I'd like the gym to myself for an hour," I told her without giving any indication as to why. Everyone knew I never closed down early.

But I was ready to fuck with all our boundaries now.

The staff around us worked quickly as closing time hit. "Should we go?" she asked softly as she put pressure on my wrist and had me bend it upward toward my body as I pulled the elastic that was restrained by my foot.

"No." I was sweating bullets by the time we were done. "Everyone else is leaving. We're staying."

CHAPTER 15: EVERLY

When Declan had barreled out from that elevator, he'd radiated an energy that was electric, visceral, and almost tangible.

I'd felt his gaze lick up and down my body, and I couldn't help my reaction, not even with Wes standing near. No man affected me like Declan did now. All of this going back-and-forth with him, taking care of his wrist, feeling his skin against mine—even if it was platonic—and then seeing how he took care of me so casually...

He got me breakfast, coffee, a ride to work. He even set up a freaking charity for the kids I taught.

Without hesitation. Without considering the consequences. He just did what he wanted for me, not realizing he was being better than anyone I'd ever been with. And I couldn't escape the thought of it either. Even when my mom called, she'd try to read me the news.

"You were in the paper today, Everly. Declan got you breakfast? I thought you were just staying in his guesthouse."

"I am."

I heard the smile on her lips. "If he is making you happy, I really want to—"

I cut her off, not wanting to get her hopes up. "We're just friends, okay? Nothing more."

"Have you told him about Andy?" she'd asked and I'd wanted to scream that I hadn't, that I wasn't going to.

"Gotta go, Mom. You are my sunshine."

She sighed. "My only sunshine," she murmured right as I hung up.

But the question lingered. My ex in my mind lingered. When Declan made the extra effort, I remembered how Andy hadn't, how he'd always reminded me of his status in the community, how I was lucky to have him.

And Declan was so much bigger than Andy would ever be. Yet, he worked for everything he'd gotten, he didn't quit because he'd already made it, and he didn't shove his reputation in my face.

Even now, he didn't try to skirt around the work. I made sure we covered every base—because above all else, I needed to get his wrist back to one hundred percent to show him I was capable and because he deserved it with how hard he worked—I saw the athlete in him. I admired how he pushed through pain, and I knew it was infuriating and painful to work a small muscle around all the bigger and better ones. Yet, he didn't quit. He just worked it harder, like he wanted to prove no part of him was breakable.

"Last rep, give it your all," I encouraged quietly. The TVs and music and most of the lights were off now that Declan had shut everything down. I planned to get an Uber considering it seemed he wanted to work out on his own after this. He'd never shut the gym down this way, but I realized he'd been working upstairs on meetings with lawyers and shareholders all day. He probably needed to clear his head.

"Done," I announced but didn't let go of his wrist as I massaged it, making sure we broke up the scar tissue right after the workout and allowed for correct healing this time. "I'll get myself an Uber right away. I can wait to shower so you can have some time to yourself." I needed to get away from him too, try to shake off the desire building in me for him even after I'd told him time and time again we couldn't indulge in it.

"You're staying," he said matter-of-factly. "Don't you have pull-ups to do? Ten?"

"I can do those tomorrow." Why had my heart started beating so fast as he held my gaze?

"You'll do them now." He grabbed my hips and turned me toward the bar. Before I could stop, he nudged me forward and walked behind me until I was directly under the metal.

"Declan, I—"

He didn't wait to lift me. His strong fingers held me up like I was a feather, and I immediately grabbed the bar I normally had to use a step to reach. I stared in front of me at the mirror, looking at his reflection behind me. His eyes were on my body, on my form, on how I hung there for him to see.

"Ten, Everly. Give it your all." He repeated my words back to me and then smiled as he said, "Commit."

That smile... It was menacing, daring, and filled with heat that slithered through my body, even in that dead hang position. This was a closed chain exercise that I'd been trying to master for so long. With the hand or foot being fixed in these types of exercises, the muscular growth impact was much more. It's how we pushed our body further, how we made strides for growth.

I tensed every muscle to raise my chin to the metal. Slowly. Efficiently.

"One," he counted. Or taunted. I wasn't sure which. Every time I hit another, he said it without praise, without encouragement.

I pushed harder.

"Eight, Everly."

My body weight was getting the best of me as my arms

shook halfway through this one.

He stepped close and murmured in my ear, "Can you commit, Drop?"

I glared at him as his sea-green eyes narrowed before he raised one arm up and suddenly, I felt the inside of his fist wrap around the bar against the outside of mine.

Then his chest was against my back, his other palm gripping the bar next to mine as he hopped up, caging me in.

Our bodies pressed against each other's as he crisscrossed his calves under my shins and lifted.

My body weight was gone.

The shake in my muscle gone.

The strain of hitting number nine in my reps gone.

"Nine, Drop," he whispered against my neck, and my whole body shook for another reason.

I watched as he pulled me up and then lowered me down again. "Ten."

I bit my lip as his tongue dragged across my neck, and then his teeth latched on to to my ear, and I gasped at the same time I felt his cock hardening against my ass.

"Should we keep going?" he questioned. "Or did we commit well enough for you?"

Commitment.

That stupid word. The way we flirted with disaster and how I knew my heart couldn't handle it had me dropping off the bar fast. He dropped with me, like his body knew mine already, like they worked in sync together even if our minds didn't.

"There's no commitment in cheating the system," I murmured to him, breathless. "I don't even need a spot for pull-ups. You shouldn't have helped."

"Haven't you been cheating your whole workout?" He

lifted a brow at me in the mirror, my back still against his chest. When he pulled me closer and wrapped his arm around me, my hands immediately went to his forearm to hold on as he said into my neck, "Men everywhere spotting you at every turn."

"They're being nice, Declan."

"They can't take their eyes off you." His hand curled around my waist and slipped lower and lower as he shook his head. "I know I can't. I've fucked you and called you my wife."

His skin against my skin, the way he murmured the words, how his voice vibrated down into my bones had me dizzy. I wasn't in control.

"I'm not... I'm not wife material, Declan. I wasn't kidding when I told Wes I can't be exclusive, that I can't even imagine being in a relationship." How could I tell him Andy had broken me?

"We're already married." He said it decisively, like there was no room for argument, like I shouldn't be even questioning it. Then, he walked us both backward until he reached the lat pull-down machine. Each side had a bar that was just within my reach, and he wasted no time grabbing the band we'd been using for his rehab to wrap my wrists tight before threading the elastic right next to the bracelets I had on like an Eagle Scout demonstrating how to tie knots. Before I even realized that he'd restrained me, my hands were above my head, attached to the bar, and every time I pulled, the weight from the machine restrained me.

Declan smiled at his handiwork. "What can you pull, babe?"

"Seriously?"

"Fine." He shrugged and pulled the peg out, only to shove it into the three-hundred-pound weight.

Shit. The adrenaline running through my veins should have been an indicator to stop, but with him, my body didn't want to.

"Safe word, Drop?" he asked before he took, asked before he pushed the boundary.

It was the reason I didn't even hesitate, that I knew I could trust him more than I had others before. "Gardenia."

"Why?"

"I hate the smell of them."

He halted his motion for a second. "They're all around the guesthouse."

I shrugged. "I know. I understand the appeal. They used to be a favorite." I didn't elaborate. The smell of them haunted my soul. They were what Andy had gotten for me once.

"Okay," Declan murmured and dragged a finger across my jaw, soft, soothing, and as light as a single drop of rain on my skin. "Trust me?"

It was just two words, but my whole heart wanted to desperately, and as the air left my lungs, I gave in to whatever this was between us for the moment. I nodded once, and he moved like he always did, without hesitation and without restraint.

He stepped back, the green in his eyes more vivid, full of life, hunger, and control. He knew he had the power now, every part of me hanging there at his will. He walked around me once. "I shouldn't want to punish you for the attention they all give you, Drop. But I really do."

I shivered at his confession. "Do it," I whispered out.

"She commands me like she has a say. Don't you know you're at my mercy, Drop? And I have one goal here tonight."

"What?" I couldn't stop myself from asking. I tried my best

to keep my eyes on him as he circled me again, his stride long, his muscles moving fluidly as he tilted his head to crack his neck as if readying himself for whatever he was about to do.

"Next time you step inside my gym, you're going to remember most everything in it belongs to me..." He stood behind me so we looked at each other in the reflection of the mirror again. "Including you."

"You know I don't really belong to you," I said, even though the idea of it made me clench my thighs.

He grabbed my chin so I wouldn't move my head, so I'd only stare at the both of us, take in how he hovered around me, how I looked so tiny with him standing with his chest to my back. He rubbed himself back and forth so I could feel him. "Look at yourself while you feel me against you."

His hard length against my back wasn't something I could ignore. I knew his cock was throbbing for me, knew right now, right here that he wanted me, that I'd made this man almost crazy with desire. Being at his mercy had my body basically begging for him to get closer. My pussy wanted him in me. I tried to push back against him, but he leaned away.

"Stop teasing me, Declan." I yanked at the restraints on my wrists.

He chuckled. "You're not getting out of anything I tie you up in, Drop. You're mine tonight." He rubbed back and forth over my stomach before dipping his hand low over my yoga pants to rub my clit through the fabric. He worked me up so much that I started to see my arousal coming into view, felt the dampness collecting between my legs. "See how you get wet for me."

I whimpered as his other hand went to the zipper on the front of my sports bra. "Yes." Before he even undid it, my nipples tightened in anticipation.

"So impatient, Drop. Where's that composure I always see from you, huh?"

I bit my lip as my hips moved against his hand, and when he slowly unzipped my bra for my breasts to spill out, I knew I wouldn't last as his hand gripped them.

My whole body careened over the edge, spiraling down into my first orgasm as I screamed his name, all my self-control completely lost. I was losing everything when it came to him. Losing my mind, for sure.

And then his praise came next.

That's when I knew I was about to lose my heart to him too.

CHAPTER 16: DECLAN

I couldn't stop praising her, couldn't get a grip on myself tumbling off the cliff into wanting her for myself. Her body flushed against mine, her pussy wept for me, and the whimpers spilled from her lips like I was torturing her with pleasure.

When she screamed my name, I almost lost it.

"Good girl... Good fucking girl. So good. See how you ride out that orgasm like you can't live without it," I breathed out, lips against her ear, and she bit her lip. I rubbed a hand over her breast, across her pebbled nipple, to watch how her skin quivered. "Look in that mirror. My wife looks beautiful after I play with her pussy, doesn't she?"

I didn't give her time to answer. I turned her around toward me, the bar above her twisting with her wrists restrained to it. I gripped the fabric over her ass with each of my hands and yanked her against me.

"Careful, Declan," she panted. "These are my only expensive ones."

Didn't she realize I was past being careful? That we'd stepped into dangerous territory a long time ago. I gripped them tighter as I descended on her mouth, devoured those lips, took what I'd wanted since the moment I'd seen her that morning. She met my tongue with as much vigor as I gave.

My hands let go to dive into the fabric and grab her ass, but as I did, I realized the one thing most men must have that day—there was nothing underneath her pants. "Fuck," I groaned.

"Are you trying to drive me insane, Drop? How are you not wearing anything under this to work?"

"Declan, panty lines with yoga pants are—"

I was done. Done with her in these pants, with thinking about Wes's eyes on her—any guy's eyes—when she bent over. I gripped the fabric this time and shredded it at the seam.

She gasped out my name.

I wouldn't apologize other than to kneel down and pull them off her as I dragged my nose across her pussy. "You smell like you wanted your yoga pants off anyway. Or maybe it's because that fabric was paper thin."

"They're supposed to be that way to contour to my body and be breathable, Declan. You ruined them!"

"Good. Don't wear anything like it again."

She narrowed her eyes. "Are you going to try to pick my clothes out for me?"

I caught the hitch in her voice as she asked it. Everly enjoyed someone else thinking for her even if she wouldn't admit it.

"If I need to, I will. Monday's red, right? This is a partnership, after all. I can't have you distracting me all day."

"Not happening," she breathed out, then whimpered as I rubbed my hand into her slit.

"Do you make the rules here?" She knew better. I'd smacked her ass for that very reason last time. "Or is it that you want me to punish you tonight too, Drop?"

As I slid one finger into her, I felt how she clenched around me at my words, and I took the opportunity of her gasping at the feeling to slap her ass before gripping her to pull her close enough to my mouth that I could suck on that sensitive clit of hers.

Her hands yanked at the restraints immediately, and she

screamed my name again. I pulled one of her thighs up around me and added one more finger for her to ride. I took a moment to pull back and take her in as I told her, "I'm about to have my tongue in your pussy, Drop. I want your legs around me, riding my face, understand?"

"Untie me. I want to touch you, Declan. Please."

"Love when you beg, baby." I worked her pussy faster and brushed my thumb over her clit. "It won't get you what you want, but I still have to tell you."

She practically started to cry. "Please, please, please."

"Remember the last time I ate that pussy, Everly?"

She bit her lip and nodded vigorously. "On the hood of your car? I do, and I love running my hands through your hair, Declan."

I hummed. "You like to *rush* me, Drop. You don't need control now though. I know how to eat your pussy without your assistance and guidance. I set the pace, and you take it like the good girl you are, right?"

Everly wanted to be ten steps ahead since she was meticulous and a creature of habit, but she wasn't going to be that here. She was going to give up control, feel the spontaneity of the moment, and trust me to give her the best fuck of her life.

"Please, just hurry," she begged.

"We're going to go nice and slow." One lick of my tongue had her shivering as her legs wrapped around me tight. Her hanging there, tits out and ass available to grab as I devoured her sex in my gym: it was a new type of sanctuary. I'd found a new religion, a new mantra.

Everly Belafonte, my raindrop, restrained in gym equipment. I'd kneel and praise her any way I knew how.

I lapped at her core leisurely, trying to memorize every

hitch in her breath, every purr from her mouth, and every time her legs tightened like I'd done something just right. I kneaded her ass and grazed the hole at her backside. "I think I'm going to want to own and control every part of you, babe."

"Not possible," she whispered out, but Everly and I were finding a way to work together. It made me believe we probably got along better than either of us originally thought.

I knew my tongue liked the taste of her pussy, that my eyes couldn't look away from her, and my damn ears liked the sound of her whimpering as she rode my face. As I sucked on her clit, I knew she was close, so close. I registered the weights holding her immobile clatter as she yanked at her restraints.

"Be good, Everly. Come for me loud now. I want to hear the echoes of you through my gym tomorrow."

The coiling of a woman's body, the way their muscles writhed to seek every second of their orgasm, was always ravishing. Yet, Everly was the beauty of a gathering storm over the ocean, so quiet and composed until the lightning struck and you saw the clouds and the rain and the waves of emotion creating brilliance. Seeing what I caused in her, the lightning over what I thought was a calm sea, it made me feel godlike.

As she curled over my head, I stood to loosen the restraints, keeping her legs still around my neck, holding my woman against me as I untied the elastic.

My woman. Just mine.

Her hands immediately went to my hair, her stomach against my face, her body clutching mine like she trusted me to take care of her during her aftershocks.

My hands roved over her back before I laid her down on the bench press and dragged my hands up her arms so I could pull away and look at her there. "I don't think I'll ever look at my gym the same."

"Of course you will. This is your gym. I'm sure you've done all this before." One side of her mouth lifted like she didn't mind if I'd been with other women here.

"You worked in a gym most of your life, Everly. You telling me you've fucked around in one too?" I stood over her and undid my trousers, knowing I couldn't wait much longer for her when she was spread across the bench like this, her wavy hair falling from each side, her tits perky and on display as my gaze dragged over them. I saw how her breath hitched, like she was as sensitive to my eyes on her as she was to my touch.

"No. *I* wouldn't," she pointed out, sitting up on the bench and crossing her arms. "*You* would though."

"We're so different, huh?" I cocked one brow at her, wondering what she really thought.

"Of course. You're driven—you got into the NFL. And to actually play for a team going to the Super Bowl... That's like a one-in-a-million shot, right?"

I shrugged, my hand sliding into my briefs to pull my cock out as I answered, "So?"

"So, I'm a grad school dropout. And I'm sure you've noticed I'm always at the guesthouse—"

"Your house," I corrected, pumping once and her eyes skirted over my body. I saw how color flushed her cheeks, how her breathing increased, and she licked those lips.

"Yes, okay. Well, I'm home every night. I work. I keep to myself. I don't like change or losing control."

"You love losing it with me. I'll teach you how much you can love letting go with me, baby." I walked up to her, grabbed her wrist, and murmured, "Do as I say, and take my cock, Drop."

Her fingers instantly wrapped around it, her thumb

brushing over my piercing. She leaned forward a little and, with her lips so close to the metal, I felt how her breath cooled it. "Did it hurt to get that?"

"In comparison to the amount of pleasure it's about to bring? No."

She smiled. "So you're cocky with your cock then?"

Hearing filth in her mouth made me want to fill it. "Drop, you know better than to question the man who controls you. Now, open your mouth."

She visibly gulped. "I can't take all of you."

I threaded my hands through her hair until I got a good hold. Then I squeezed the curls in my fist, gripping her hard enough that I was able to yank her forward, putting her lips on the tip of me, and then I ground out, "I decide now what you can and can't take. Open, Everly."

Her hips rocked forward on the bench as she did as she was told. Submitting was her kink and telling her what to do was mine. Everly thought she liked control and hated change, but I was about to turn that upside down.

I moved my cock in and out of her mouth, her saliva coating me just enough that I could slide to the back of her throat. She purred like she loved it, her hands on my ass pulling me forward.

She was too eager, too hurried, and maybe she was right, I was too big for her just yet. When she gagged, tears formed over the midnight blue of her eyes, but my dick loved seeing her there, and I couldn't stop it from hardening further, thickening in anticipation of fucking her.

I pulled her hair and stepped back, stopping her from rolling her tongue over me again.

"Turn around and get on your knees," I commanded.

"But I want to finish you—"

"Everly, for the love of God, get on your knees and bend over the bench."

"You may not look at the gym the same, but I know I'll never look at this bench the same again," she said with a smirk.

Her words, although playful, stirred something in me. I'd seen men all over her today, how they flirted with her, how they spotted her, how they wanted her. "I'm going to fuck you here while you stare at all these weights, baby. I'm going to help spot you through a workout of our own so you know how it feels to have me spot you instead of another man."

"What?" she murmured as she did what I said. I knelt down behind her and pressed her down so her stomach was on the leather of the bench, her ass out for me to adore.

"You want other men here with you throughout the day, helping you lift while I sit up in the damn office having to watch? Every time you bend over, they're picturing fucking you. You lay on this bench, they want to lay on top of you. Downward dog and they're imagining grabbing your hips."

"Declan, it's my job," she whimpered as I stroked her pussy again, losing myself in the jealousy of the day.

I smacked her ass once. "And my job is to remind you that I own this gym, that I see everything in it, and that I know when men are eyeing up my wife."

"It's supposed to be fine if they eye me up. This is a marriage of convenience—"

Another smack. "It's not convenient to watch men stare at your ass when all I want to do is redden it, Drop. It's not convenient to picture fucking you on the bench press all day either. Yet, here we are." I pushed her chest farther onto the bench then grabbed her hair to pull her close as I leaned in. "Is this convenient for you?" I wanted her composure gone again, her reasoning out the window.

"We'll get through it," she murmured, and her logic drove me insane.

I growled as I flipped her around so her back lay on the bench. Then I yanked her hips close so her pussy was right on my dick, dripping on me. I rubbed my thumb over her clit, and she shook her head. "I can't again, Declan."

Didn't she realize I was learning her limits here? That I was going to be the one to make the rules, tell her what boundaries she could cross and what ones she couldn't. She was going to learn to let go of that control from now on. I was taking over. "I know your safe word, and you haven't used it. That means I tell you the line, baby. You'll take another orgasm. And you'll enjoy it."

I slid two fingers inside her, and she arched as she screamed and clawed at my wrist. That's what I wanted. Her not knowing whether she was fighting for it or against it at this point.

"Say my name when you come, Everly."

She did. She cried it over and over.

I only gave her a second before I filled her in one fast thrust. I needed her pussy to consume me then, to fit tightly over me with those soft walls and squeeze me like she didn't want to let me go.

I needed her to want me just as much as I wanted her.

I hadn't wanted anything so bad in a long damn time. It made her dangerous and a challenge, but that made her mine all the same. I'd never backed away from that.

Even if I wasn't sure how to keep her yet.

Two months were already gone from us committing.

I realized I wasn't counting down until the end anymore.

CHAPTER 17: EVERLY

The spasms from my orgasm would last well into tomorrow, I thought. There was no way I'd be able to forget this feeling or shake it from my bones.

Declan had infused me with the drug that was him, and I was addicted. When he scooped me up from the bench press and carried me to the locker room, I clung to him harder than I should have because I didn't want to let him go.

"I'm going to clean you up, Drop," he said gently, the hands that had smacked my ass so soft now, like I was a treasure, like we hadn't just had rough sex all over his gym.

"I can clean up on my own, Declan."

He hummed and smiled, nestling his head into my neck as he carried me like a baby to rinse off. The locker room reminded me of a scene from a Greek cathedral with white pillars holding up the tall ceilings, gold faucets at the sink, rustic wood beams, folded plush towels and robes around every corner, and ombre mosaic tiling down the walls of the private shower stalls. A large jacuzzi with dim lighting sat in an intimate nook.

Declan hesitated near it and then grumbled as he walked on, "If I take you in there, I think you'll have trouble walking tomorrow."

I dragged a finger across the collar of his shirt. "I might enjoy being sore."

"Don't tempt me, Drop."

I sighed. "I know. I shouldn't even tempt myself." Because

our boundaries had now all been scribbled out, jumbled around, and rearranged.

He set me on a seat in the shower and undressed, taking his time as I stared at him.

Declan's body had no flaws. His forearms were thick, his biceps round and large, and his abs defined in a way that was near impossible. "What are your tattoos for?"

He came close, so I didn't catch what all of them were. "They're all for my family. Five siblings, one niece, Mom and Dad. About to add two more with my sister's twins."

His hands roved over me as I stared up at him. "Pretty big family."

He nodded. "Full house most of the time when I go home."

"Do you go home a lot?"

He grabbed some soap from the dispenser and pulled me to stand next to him so he could rub it on my back, taking extra care when he got to my ass. "I should go home more. We're all close, though. I try to make it home for holidays."

I gasped when his hand grazed over my pussy. "I can wash myself, Declan."

He didn't stop soaping me up though. He was meticulous and thorough with his hands and fingers as he made sure to rub every single part of my body clean, even kneeling in front of me to rub my feet and calves. "I'm taking care of you now, Everly. It's what I'm going to do when we're together, always."

"I don't need a keeper." My hands fell to his shoulders as his slid up my thigh.

"I know that." His mouth was so close to my clit again, I could practically feel it on me. I stared in his eyes as that hand went farther and farther until he pressed two fingers in me again. My hands immediately flew to his shoulders. "You don't need it, but you like having a keeper. It makes your pussy weep for me, baby."

"Declan, I'm exhausted."

"Give me one more, baby." He wrapped my thigh around his shoulder. "Just one more. I love hearing you panting in the locker room."

I knew this was going to end in disaster. I'd given my body and sexuality to Andy before, let him control me, and he'd made a fool of me, ruined me, driven me out of my own town. "Make it worth it, Declan. Because this has to be the last time."

He chuckled into my pussy and shook his head. "This is just the beginning of us, Ms. Belafonte. I've got you for ten more months."

I dug my nails in as his tongue circled my clit before thrusting into my folds. I rode his face as the shower water cascaded down on both of us.

After I screamed his name for what felt like the millionth time, he let me crumble into him so he could finish washing me up.

"You did so good tonight, babe," he murmured. "So fucking good. You know that, right?"

I took his praise like a fiend who'd never heard nice things before. I didn't get appreciation from my ex, hadn't ever received accolades from my father, and being an only child meant compliments hadn't come often.

Declan spent obsessive amounts of time drying me off before rubbing lotion he'd retrieved from his locker on me, making sure to knead my cheeks with care. I murmured I had extra clothing in my locker.

He shook his head. "You're wearing this."

He shoved a big shirt over my head and worked it over

my body. When I looked down, I scoffed and glared up at him, noticing he wore a smug smile.

"My jersey is best."

"I'm not so sure," I threw back. "I've yet to see either of you play."

"Right. You don't watch football," he grumbled like I was insane.

* * *

The ride home was quiet until my phone buzzed with a text.

I stared at it for probably too long.

> **Tonya: His hearing is coming up.
> Should we go?**

It'd been over a year, almost two if I was counting. But I hated doing that, hated thinking about the night I'd lost who I was, the day Tonya had lost her best friend, the day I'd pretty much died and become someone else.

I didn't want to dwell. So I'd left. She'd stayed.

Tonya was the best friend of a girl who was dead to me. I was someone new. I'd left that life behind, hoping the media and the pain and the hurt wouldn't follow me.

"Everly?" Declan murmured.

I jumped, and his hand went to my arm to steady me.

"Sorry," I murmured and turned my phone off.

"Who was texting you?"

I tried to brush it off. "No one."

He grumbled, "You're a terrible liar."

"It's nothing important to my life now."

And as I watched him comb his hand through his dark hair, I had to believe that. I had a new life here, a stepping stone that could lead me to a life that was better than before. And doing what Declan and I were doing wasn't helping. Not when he was as famous as he was. Not when I wanted my past to stay in the past.

Entertaining our desire could only lead to the path of destruction. The media would dissect our relationship. They'd hold it under a magnifying glass if we were an actual item. It's why we needed to stick to the original plan. Make this marriage a clean one of convenience. Instead, we'd gone between our commitments, outside of them, way overshot them.

And even still, my heart wanted more of it. I wanted him commanding me around. I wanted the change in my life more than I'd wanted anything in a long time. But to want was to hope and to hope was to fear, and I'd seen how hope could be ripped away.

I'd lost the hope of forging a meaningful relationship with my father.

Lost the hope of a future I'd thought would last with my ex.

I'd lost hope in who I was and what I'd become too.

When Declan stopped the car in front of the guesthouse, I knew this had to be the end.

"I've already figured out plans for tomorrow. I'm going to Clara's bakery first thing, and it'll be nice to walk, so don't worry about me."

He studied me, his vivid eyes narrowing. "You always do what you plan, don't you?"

"It relieves anxiety for me." I shrugged.

"You can't plan everything." His voice came out low.

Declan shifted and changed plans when he wanted, indulged in all he desired, and lived a life I couldn't.

"Yes, I'm aware." I needed to plan much better than I had in the past. I shifted in my seat. "But I'm going to try."

We let the silence bounce between us, louder than words in the night. "We're going to be more than a friendly commitment, Everly. You can't avoid that now. This relationship is changing."

I gripped my duffel bag at his words. "What happens when we don't want a relationship anymore, then? Or even better, what happens when everyone finds out?"

"They haven't yet, have they? Let's keep taking it one day at a time."

"I like to plan ten steps ahead," I admitted.

"You can't live everything all planned out, thinking through every scenario. You'll miss half the moments that are made through spontaneous adventure. You're so buttoned-up with plans, I'm fucking itching to unbutton you half the time."

Was I really that obvious? "You don't know if I'm like that or not—"

"Coffee twenty minutes before you leave for the day, you're always on time, no breakfast, color-coordinated weekdays—red, white, blue, green, black. Blue's the best on you, and you should wear it more than one damn day a week. And your lights are normally out by ten. That schedule says a lot about you."

Even if it was boring, my schedule kept me calm, ready for all the outcomes and prepared to take what life threw at me. "Right. Well, sorry. I don't bring many surprises."

He chuckled darkly. "You're full of surprises, Everly. Especially with how you can bend over a—"

"Declan!" I cut him off. "Don't you dare. Oh my God."

He narrowed his eyes. "Come with me tomorrow."

"I don't think it's a good idea. We need to stop—"

"I have an appointment," he murmured, and then he nodded. "You're coming."

"I work, Declan."

"Don't worry about working tomorrow. You'll still be paid, and I'll switch the schedule around."

Just like that. He would cover my wages and take care of my schedule. He maneuvered lives that fast. As I stared up at his big house, I shook my head. "No. Hanging out and fucking in a gym is not— We can't have a marriage with benefits when it's supposed to be one of convenience, Declan."

"Why the hell not?"

He followed my gaze, but his car didn't creep up toward his home. He was parked in front of my place maybe because I never asked to go to his and always turned him down when he invited me.

Or maybe it was because we'd fucked, not made love. Maybe this was still our boundary even if we didn't say it. It had to be, right? I couldn't live in his world, not with my past, and he couldn't be a part of mine. I belonged here, and he had to belong up there.

Sure, he could ask me to change, to belong, to be beside him, but I didn't like change, didn't trust it anymore.

"Good night, Declan." I pulled at my car door handle and hopped out before he could stop me.

As I hurried away though, I heard his window roll down and he called out, "Everly?"

I turned to glance back at him in his stupidly expensive car, and he smirked and nodded toward me. "My name on your back looks best."

With that, he disappeared up the long driveway without so

much as a "good night."

I sat in silence later, tying together another bracelet while my thoughts raced.

My phone beeped with a text from Wes, but I couldn't bring myself to respond back to him. Not when I was trying my best to instead push away the thoughts of my freaking husband's hands on me, trying to forget how he made me feel, trying to tell myself I could never truly be with a man like him. I was from a small town where my ex had made it too hard for me to even stay because of the stories that had been spread about me.

How would I make it here, tied to any of these larger-than-life athletes? The stories would be bigger, the spread wider, and the heartbreak even more destructive.

CHAPTER 18: EVERLY

The next morning, just as the sun broke over the horizon, there was a knock at my door.

I grumbled as I got out of bed, and right then, my phone rang too. I snatched it and speared the green button. "Mom, it's too early."

"I know." She chuckled and then I heard her deep sigh. "Tonya came by yesterday, though, and I figured you should know. She looked lost."

I closed my eyes briefly, willing away the thought, as I trudged to the door. "I can try to call her, but she probably won't answer."

"I know that too." She tsked. "You're best friends. Andy shouldn't have been able to take that from you. It's not fair."

But life wasn't fair. Andy could and had taken everything from me. He'd taken my trust in men, he'd taken my heart, he'd taken my soul, he'd taken my security. And he'd destroyed it all.

With the spread of a single story.

He argued I'd done the same to him.

And the town believed him, a golden boy they knew over a homeschooled girl they didn't. Maybe I'd never stood a chance against the media then, but I'd tried.

The story I told of abuse and assault at his frat party was swept under the rug. Not even the women he'd hurt before me would testify against him. Instead, his family painted a different picture.

Stories spread, friendships broke, the home I loved crumbled, and my life changed forever.

I ran my hand over the necklace I used to share with Tonya, although I knew she never wore hers anymore. "Someone's at my door. I'll call you later."

"You are my sunshine, Evie," she murmured.

"My only sunshine, Mom," I said and hung up just as I swung open the door for Declan.

"You don't look ready." His smile was as bright as the sun and as annoying as an alarm clock at dawn.

"I told you I wasn't going anywhere with you today. I have to go to Clara's and then to work."

"All that has been cancelled."

"I planned to do—"

"Plans change." He shrugged and stepped past me into the house. I noticed he was holding coffee, and it was the only reason I allowed him to continue as he handed it to me on his way in.

He didn't wait for an invitation into my living space. He walked past the living room and kitchen and went right into my bedroom.

"What are you doing?" I stuttered as I hurried after him, setting my coffee on the counter.

He pulled open a dresser drawer where I'd color coordinated all my clothing for the week and pulled out a blue sweater that I wouldn't have ever worn that day. Blue was for Wednesdays.

"You'll wear this," he murmured and pulled out jeans and even freaking lingerie.

"I'm not wearing any of that." I huffed and grabbed the sweater to shove it back into my dresser.

He grabbed my wrist and pulled me close. "Do you really want to argue, Drop? Just about clothing? You like all your clothes, right?"

"Of course I like my clothes." I shook my wrist in his hand, but he didn't let it go.

"Then it isn't a big deal to wear what I like to see you in when I'm going with you somewhere today."

"I don't know where we're going, so I don't especially think—"

"I'm taking care of it," he said, cutting me off. "Put this on, or do you want me to dress you?"

My eyes widened. I couldn't stop myself from reacting when he was being a demanding asshole. "You don't always get what you want, Declan. I told you I wasn't going with you—"

"Right." He sighed, like this conversation irritated him. Then he grabbed my sleep shirt and yanked it over my head. "Dressing you like a child isn't exactly what I had in mind for the morning, but I don't mind getting you naked."

"Are you out of your mind?" I wiggled around, but Declan was a great body handler, although he shoved my sweater on without a bra at all and I wasn't really putting up much of a fight. "You know what? Fine. I'll put it on."

I wiggled the last part of my arms into the material. "Give me a minute, then."

One side of his mouth kicked up, showing one of his dimples. "Finish getting dressed, babe. I'm staying."

"What? You don't think I will?" I narrowed my eyes into slits and poked his big dumb shoulder. He was wearing a white V-neck that hugged his pecs, aviators hanging on the collar. His shirt tapered down to black shorts, and he had on slip-on moccasins.

Business Declan was hot, but Casual Declan was divine.

"I think you might take your precious time. Maybe formulate a whole schedule in your head or map out every scenario this day could turn into." He cracked his knuckles. "I'm too impatient for that. Plus, you need to live without thinking too much about it for a day."

As I stared at him, I wondered if he knew how much I wanted to, if he knew that my mind was swimming with every idea already regarding my mother's phone call. I wondered if he could make me forget it too, if him making the decisions today would allow me a moment where I didn't need to worry, where I felt safe.

My hands crept up over my thighs to my panties, and I hooked my thumbs in slowly.

Declan didn't turn around. Instead, he sat on the soft comforter of my bed and leaned back to watch.

"Not going to turn around?"

"Why would I? People pay millions to have masterpieces in their homes, to stare at them displayed for their eyes only. You naked in front of me is a masterpiece, and I don't intend to ever miss an opportunity to stare, babe."

I let the panties fall and the lace fabric caused goose bumps to pebble over my legs. My body reacted to him so quickly I knew I was already wet. He'd gotten ahold of something I wanted no man to have.

My lust for him.

My desire.

And my trust in him grew. Exponentially. Dangerously.

Declan waited for me, coaxing and persuading in measures. He demanded, but he also offered praise, a safe word, and a way out if I wanted it.

He handed me pants and panties he'd picked out, and I slid them on slowly in front of him.

No words were exchanged. We didn't need them. His gaze on me, watching and lingering where he wanted, was enough.

By the time I was dressed, I wanted to get undressed again.

"Ready?" He clapped his hands together like we were simply going to go about our day.

I wanted to scream, and we hadn't even done anything yet.

"Where are we going?" I turned to my mirror and fluffed my curls.

He walked around my room, taking in everything. "A little place about twenty minutes away." He stopped and grabbed several hair bands that I had in a small jar on my dresser, putting them on his wrist one by one.

I swiped on some mascara and was applying lip gloss but stopped and pointed the applicator toward his wrist. "What are you doing?"

"You always forget these things." He shrugged like it was nothing, but my heart pounded harder and harder against my chest for him.

"I can wear them, Declan."

"You could, but I'm going to instead." Then he pointed at my makeup. "You don't need any of that. Your face is fine."

"My face is fine?" I chuckled and turned to swipe another coat of gloss on.

"You're beautiful." He suddenly was right behind me, his stare taking me in as he leaned close and nestled into my hair near my neck. "Makeup won't change that your eyes rival the color of the sea, Drop. Or that your lips were made to be kissed by mine."

Why did my thighs instantly tremble at his words? I

gulped and said, "Fine. I guess this is all you're getting today since you're rushing me."

He slid his arm around me without hesitation and pushed my curls out of the way so he could lick right below my ear. "This gloss and the way you look...like you just rolled out of bed... It makes me think of having you in it."

"I—"

His mouth moved like lightning, like he wasn't thinking about the consequences, and his length hardened against my belly where I could be reminded of how deliciously big he was. There was no denying him that kiss, even if we shouldn't have indulged. His hands went to my ass as he picked me up, and I wrapped my legs around him as he turned and set me on the vanity. I clawed at his back, pulled him closer with my legs, and met his tongue swipe for swipe.

"Fuck," he murmured as he pulled back for a second. "Forget the plan for the morning. Let's stay here."

I finally willed myself to push him back. "I'm not skipping work and changing my plans only for you to cancel whatever you insisted I attend with you and stay in bed." I hopped off the vanity. "Let's go."

He grumbled the whole way, rearranging his pants and making sure I knew it. I smirked as I grabbed my coffee off the counter and made my way out to his Bugatti instead of an SUV with Peter. "Driving today?"

"I like to drive when I can." He shrugged. "It's too early for the paps to be out. Might as well enjoy a fun ride."

I nodded and took a deep breath. This was Declan. Snap decisions, going with his gut. I wanted to consider every scenario first. If the paps did happen upon us, what would we do?

"Everly"—he tapped my temple as we both stood in front of his car, me not making a move to walk toward it—"stop thinking."

"It's hard for me to do that. My mind is trained to be in overdrive."

"Care to tell me why that is?" he asked as we stood on his massive driveway.

What could I say? I glanced at him and took in his strong jaw, the way he didn't pry since he knew it was important now that he didn't, the way he handled me with care when it was necessary and roughness when I wanted it.

"I should tell you." I breathed, and my hands fisted. "I will tell you. You'll need to know if the paparazzi start digging into my past—"

His brow furrowed suddenly, and then he cut me off. "Tell me when you're ready. I'm not going to have the media push us to share our lives prematurely. I've had to do that one too many times. Until then, I want you to stay here." He pointed to the ground. "In the present, with me. I'm taking care of you today."

"What do you mean?" I whispered.

He stepped close, and his hand went to my throat, where he rubbed his thumb up and down, up and down. "Just let me take care of you today. Let me handle the anxiety, Drop. Let me praise or punish you for listening or not today, huh?" My throat moved under his grip. "I think maybe someone broke your trust. I'm earning it back now, though. I get my chance. So, today, I'm taking control, and you're not going to think about it at all. You're going to listen. Got it?"

Ten more months with him. Ten. We would have to work together, be seen together, endure a lot together. I had to trust him.

This was for the best.

"Right." I nodded. "I can do that."

His jaw worked. "We'll see."

Yet, even as he opened the door for me, I couldn't help but ask, "Will you at least give me a hint of where we're going?"

He smiled as he pushed the button between the visors of the car to open the gate, one hand on my hip so he could lean in. He took his time, rubbing a circle on the bare skin through the hole of my jeans. "Sure, I'll give you a hint, babe."

Then he slammed the door in my face and rounded the hood of the car, dragging a finger across it. One side of his mouth lifted up at me devilishly. I hated that I blushed, and when he got in and pushed the start button, he murmured, "Being shy looks good on you, Everly."

Before I could answer, he shifted into gear and peeled out of the drive. I gripped the dashboard and yelped as he sped past the gate before taking his foot off the accelerator a second later. "There's your hint."

I narrowed my eyes but didn't get a chance to respond because Clara was texting me.

> Clara: I'm only going because you are ... And because Declan asked for me to go because of you. Also, Declan said I shouldn't mention it to Anastasia, that there wouldn't be room.

"You invited Clara?" I asked, staring at my phone.

He nodded, pulling his aviators on.

"Why?"

"Why not?" He shrugged. "You were going to go to her bakery. This seemed like the better option."

"Better than both of us going to work?" I scoffed. "Plus, what's she going to say about us showing up together?"

"That I was trying to do something nice for Carl's estranged daughter? You've been on edge since he passed and felt isolated."

"Is that what you told her?" I picked at a fingernail, not sure whether to be offended or relieved. "I mean, it's good that you did. We can't be telling people anything else, but other than me staying in your guesthouse, I'm not sure it's a good idea to tell them we talk at all."

He shrugged and pinned me with those green eyes. "Is it that much of a stretch, Drop? I drive you to work every day. They know we talk." We didn't actually even talk that much in the car. "She doesn't know I fucked you, but I'm happy to tell her that, too, if you'd like."

"No," I snapped. "Of course not."

He hummed and then made another turn, his grip on the wheel seeming to tighten.

I texted Clara back.

> **Me: Where are we even going? Declan won't tell me.**

> **Clara: He said you'll see when you get there. I'm happy we're doing this.**

"So, you can instruct her not to tell me—make a plan involving me—but you want me to let go and go with the flow?" I blew out a raspberry.

He chuckled and made two more turns.

Clara: It'll be nice to do something that Carl would have wanted us to do together.

Yet, I shook my head vigorously when I saw the track.

"I'm not racing or getting in a race car, Declan," I immediately spit out. "You barely can go the speed limit and—"

"Drop..." He said the nickname, and his hand went to my thigh to squeeze and stop me from rambling all the reasons this was a bad idea. "I'm taking care of you now. I told you not to worry."

I breathed out as we pulled up to the entrance. There were only about five other cars there, and I recognized Clara's immediately—bright red against all the other black ones lined up next to it. She jumped out of the car with a cherry-red smile that matched the red roses all over her jumpsuit.

She waved enthusiastically as I hurried to open my door before Declan could. He glared at me and murmured, "One."

Not sure what he meant, I brushed it off and turned to Clara. "Are you doing this?"

She giggled excitedly. "My dad was so excited about Declan testing the cars. Isn't your sister and her husband coming, Dec?"

He nodded. "They're here already."

Clara jumped with excitement. "I'm literally in love with Cade Armanelli. I mean, no disrespect to your sister but—"

"Wait." I stopped Clara. "You know Cade Armanelli?" It came out a sort of whisper as my heart started to race and my palms sweat. The Armanellis were infamous, badass businessmen who the law could never touch. They were like the godfathers of our century.

"You know who he is but didn't know me?" Declan looked disgusted. "You told me you didn't watch TV."

"I don't, but I have a phone and read the news. The Armanellis somehow evaded and then holstered the law as a tool. They're infamous globally, and Cade is—" I stopped myself.

"Hot?" Clara squealed. "And a freaking genius. Oh my God. Please smack me if I act like this in front of them."

"I'll probably act that way too. We're meeting him? He's like... N-No one ever meets him," I stuttered as we walked toward the entrance. "You're related?"

"He calibrated the car we're testing, and he married my sister," Declan grumbled like he hated the idea of it. "Anyway, I need to make sure it can hit two hundred quick for a brand sponsorship next week."

Clara was practically skipping at this point, and I really couldn't blame her. But she almost tripped and stopped dead in her tracks when she saw another black car pull up. This one was just as expensive as the Bugatti, and the man who got out was just as good-looking as Declan.

Dom's sunglasses hid his expression as he strode over. "You brought the women? For what?" He glared at both of us as Clara's eyes widened.

"Oh, I don't know. Maybe for a bit of fun," she sneered and fluttered her fingers in front of her to emphasize it like Dom needed a demonstration on what fun might look like.

Declan chewed his cheek like he wanted to laugh in Dom's face. "Yeah, Dom. Maybe for some fun."

With that, he hooked his arm in mine, and we walked in. I heard Clara tell Dom to go to hell but didn't look back to see why they were so frustrated with one another. Obviously they knew each other from a time before I was around.

Instead, I focused on the track where everything seemed brighter, faster, and more intense. I saw a white car zooming around that looked a lot like a new sort of electric vehicle. I took in the smell of rubber and dirt and glanced at Declan. "You do this a lot?"

"Enough, Drop." He nodded, his eyes sparkling as he watched the car practically fly by.

Before I could ask another question though, a couple near a sleek-looking car caught my attention. They could have rivaled the sun with their heat, tension, and what felt like hate for one another. They stood there arguing as we approached.

Cade and his wife. She'd been kept out of the news from what I'd seen. Most of the coverage didn't really focus much on them but rather his brother, Sebastian Armanelli.

"Cade, I'm driving as fast as I want around the fucking track as many times as I want or—"

"Or what?" He stepped up to her, dominating her space, his tattoos flashing on his neck like a vicious reminder of who he was.

"Or I'll hold out for this whole damn pregnancy." She saw us as she said it and waved us over.

The woman was bold. I recognized it in the way she held herself, stepping right up to her man like she was sure he couldn't harm her at all.

The love he had in his eyes showed he wouldn't. Yet, he still smiled menacingly at her. "I'd love to see you try and hold out."

"Are you two kidding me right now?" Declan glared at them both before pulling her in for a hug. Izzy had his exact same face shape along with the dark hair. They were siblings for sure. "Quit talking about hooking up with my sister, Cade. Izzy, meet Everly."

She looked me up and down and then pulled me in for a hug as she whispered, "So sorry you had to marry my brother. Hope he isn't an ass the whole time. Cade and I hacked the system to view your father's will. Promise we fucking hate the press so don't worry about that." Then she pulled back with a huge smile on her face.

Brilliant. She didn't look at all apologetic, and she was so straightforward, I couldn't even hate her for it.

This was going to be just great.

"Declan?" I whispered, my eyes widened in panic.

"They're fine, Everly." Declan pulled me close and gave me a squeeze.

"Fine with what?" Dom asked from behind us.

Izzy's eyes bounced from Declan's to Dom's. She wiggled in place like she wanted to unleash a storm.

"Don't start, Izzy," Declan growled and glanced over at Clara.

Izzy immediately picked up on what he was insinuating. Not everyone here knew we were married. "Oh, fuck you, Declan. Dom and I never get to tease you together."

Declan grabbed my hand. "I'm taking Everly on the drive first."

"I want to drive though!" Izzy whined.

"Izzy, you're not getting in the damn car. You're pregnant," Declan snapped at the same time Cade said, "No."

She must not have been too far along because I didn't see a baby bump.

"So what if I'm pregnant?" Declan's sister shrieked. "Dom, tell Declan and Cade they're idiots. This is only the first trimester."

"Izzy," Dom sighed like he was the voice of reason in the family, but his gaze was hard as he reproached her. "None of you should be getting in that car. It's dangerous. And I'm guessing none of you know how to drive stick?"

Clara cleared her throat. "I can."

"Well, then." Cade smiled. "She can drive. As for you, baby doll, you're not driving shit."

"If you don't drive me around this track as fast as possible, I'm not kidding, Cade, I'll be pissed. I already hate being babied this much."

Cade stood staring at his wife like she was the only person in the world, fisting his hand once and then twice before he ground out, "One lap around, woman."

When she jumped up on him, he caught her with one arm, like he anticipated her every move and her legs wrapped around him like a vise.

"Why I subject myself to you two is beyond me," Dom grumbled while Declan rolled his eyes. Obviously neither of them were fully on board with Cade like Clara and I were.

She nudged me, and when I looked at her, she had tears in her eyes. "If a man doesn't love me like that, I don't want him."

I nodded, agreeing with her. "It's really special."

"And rare," Clara added, her red hair blowing in the wind. Her eyes held such a sadness that I found myself leaning in and patting her shoulder.

"But not impossible," I finished. Normally, I avoided hope. Normally, I knew better than to plant that seed. Yet, today, maybe just maybe, Clara and I were on the right path. We may not have been sisters like I'd always wanted, but we could be friends.

We were given directions on how to handle ourselves within the vehicle and then we went to change.

Cade discussed some key mileage markers with Declan and they both worked through what was needed for the launch of this new car brand.

I didn't understand a thing.

Yet, Declan had told me to trust him, and when I sat down in that car and he looked over at me, I saw what must have drawn the whole country to him. Fearlessness. He smiled big and asked, "You ready to ride, Drop?"

My mouth was dry, my hands were shaking, my toes were literally tingling, but I nodded.

"Take care of me, Declan," I said, and he hit the gas.

The car went zero to sixty in one and a half seconds, and I knew Declan was pushing it to its limit. They'd adjusted this car to have smooth tires rather than street tires, giving it better grip to achieve higher speeds as quickly as possible.

I'd tried to listen to more of the science behind it, but it went out the window as my heart threatened to jump into my throat as we climbed to dizzying speeds, speeds that felt impossible, speeds that weren't controllable.

Through our headsets, Declan yelled, "No controlling this, Drop. Just enjoy it."

I gripped my own thighs for dear life as we neared the turn.

Declan winked at me like he was a fucking NASCAR racer, and part of me wondered if he had been one.

He didn't seem at all concerned with our safety, and his confidence had me watching him rather than the road. No wonder he could own the world. He wanted to test every limit, wanted to push so far past comfort zones that he was the only one who had control, and he had the confidence to do it.

I didn't hear what they told him over the speakers or comprehend if we were doing anything correctly at all. I was lost in what Declan was. He'd bottled my worries and anxieties so I could try to enjoy something. He'd brought me along to do this with his family like I mattered too.

And for what?

When we got to the last turn, I smiled as he took it a bit harder, felt my heart lurch but then tumble back into place with a stronger connection to the man who'd gotten it to move in the first place.

When we stepped out of the car, Cade smiled like a villain who'd accomplished mass destruction. "My calibration works perfectly."

"Yours?" Izzy rolled her eyes. "I practically came up with the whole thing."

"You want to tell the news that?" Cade yanked her toward the car.

"No. Absolutely not. I don't want to be in the news at all," she scoffed, and then she smiled at us. "There's bigger news that will be out soon enough anyway."

"What's going on?" Clara narrowed her eyes.

"We've gotta go." Declan threaded his fingers through my hands. "Clara, you can ride with Dom, right?"

"I... Oh. If he wants to be a passenger."

Dom eyed her up and down, and I saw the blush stain her cheeks. "Let's see how good you are at driving, Clara. I have a feeling I won't like it one bit."

She narrowed her eyes.

"Well, since you guys are leaving, it was good to meet you," Izzy yelled as she got into the car. "And Declan, be nice to your *wife*."

My jaw dropped as Cade murmured "That's my girl" right as Declan growled "Oh, fuck me" and Clara barked out "What?"

So much for keeping our marriage a secret.

CHAPTER 19: DECLAN

"You're not telling Mom and Anastasia, Declan?" Clara scolded after she'd opened her mouth one or two times to try to form words. "And what about Piper? I know it's been a couple months, but you two have been an on-and-off thing for years." She glanced at Everly. "No offense."

Everly stood there, back ramrod straight and a mask painted on her face. She almost stared through me as she said, "None taken. I'm seeing other people too. There's Wes and—"

Jesus, I didn't want to hear her even say his name. And now others? No. I cut her off. "We're figuring it out as we go. We haven't told anyone—besides my siblings—yet and don't intend to until it comes out in the press or otherwise becomes necessary."

"Or until our fireball of a sister throws in some dynamite for kicks," Dom grumbled.

"Like I said, we're figuring it out as we go."

Dom paced back and forth and said, "Carl really fucked all of us in the will, didn't he?"

"What's that supposed to mean?" Clara whipped her head toward his pacing.

He stopped and stared at her. "You can't be serious right now... Your bakery in my resort?"

"*Your* resort?" She crossed her arms and stood there in her heels looking about as formidable as Mary Poppins could in her floral suit.

"I'll call you both." I waved Everly into the car. "Until then, keep your mouths shut."

"Declan, it's not a good idea." Clara tried to stop me. "Anastasia is going to find out. She's trying to dig for information as it is, and my mother said she wants to come over tomorrow. You'd better—"

"We're leaving, Clara." I cut her off.

Everly didn't say a thing on the car ride home.

"It's going to be fine," I tried.

She nodded and rolled her lips between her teeth as she looked out the window.

When we reached the gate to my property, I suggested, "Come to my house for dinner."

Her gaze cut to mine, and in it I saw pain. She combed a hand through her hair and tried to grab for the rubber band she didn't have on her wrist. I pulled the elastic from mine and held it out. "Here."

I saw how her brows dipped, how she bit her lip, how she could maybe realize I was going to take care of her, but still she shook her head. "Thank you for this." She held up the band before she tied her waves in.

"I meant what I said when I told you I'm taking care of you."

She sighed. "That's not your job. And thank you for the invite to dinner but I'd rather not."

Part of me wanted to command her to do it, tell her I was the one controlling this situation, but the other part of me knew I couldn't.

She was building up a wall, and I couldn't stop her from doing so. The press was about to try to break us. I knew that better than anyone.

I opened my door but her hand on my arm stopped me.

"I need you to know..." She cleared her throat. "I was in a messy relationship when I moved here. It's not something I like to have define me, but I'm sure the media will find out. So, you should know too."

Thinking of her with any man frustrated me. "If he was taking advantage of you—"

"Some people would say that." She shrugged and closed her eyes briefly, shutting me out from her thoughts. "Most people from my hometown say I'm a liar. So, I'm sorry if that reflects badly on you."

Her words were as soft as raindrops on a window, but they held all the weight of a thunderstorm behind them.

"Is it a story that my PR can help with?" I asked, my body already starting to vibrate with fury at the idea that she'd have to relive whatever hell she went through back home because she was married to me.

My name would be attached to hers when the marriage license came out. My name would put her in the limelight and shine a spotlight on whatever she was trying to keep in the darkness.

She shrugged and opened her door. "Honestly, I'm fine with the press writing whatever they want. I've seen it all, really. I don't want your name dragged down, though. So, I recommend you and Piper do what you have to."

"Me and Piper? Everly, this isn't about me and—"

"Good night, Declan." She cut me off and slammed the car door on the way to the house.

I let my car idle in front of the guesthouse for too long, wondering if I had any right to go in there. Although it was mine and I knew I could go in any time I liked, it felt intrusive.

Her living room light glowed like it did every night, and I sighed and pulled my car into my garage. As I got ready for bed, a smaller light flickered on. It stayed on most of the night.

I worked over numbers, signed deals and contracts, but mostly, I watched those fucking lights that night.

I even went to my pool for a swim in an attempt to clear my head, but instead, my mind wandered to those damn lights.

I called my brothers to discuss more business. Yet, I paced and watched the stupid lights.

* * *

We didn't talk to one another the next morning either, not until the compact tractors with backhoe attachments came through the gates. I watched as they started to dig up the gardenia bushes, one by one, and I smiled when she came out to stare at them, her mouth agape.

She didn't come up to my house though.

She pulled her cell out of her leggings pocket and sent a text instead.

Everly: You're ruining the whole perimeter of your guesthouse.

Me: Ruining? I'm making it better.

Everly: People love gardenias.

Me: Yes, but according to my wife's safe word, she hates them.

Everly: It's going to take forever to get new plants in there, Declan. Those gardenias look like they'd been there for years.

Me: I'm not concerned. Feel free to open your windows tomorrow and smell the fresh air.

I didn't wait to get another text from her. Instead, I went to stand by her side as she looked on and wrapped my arm around her shoulders. We watched in silence. Maybe we knew our time was limited, that the press was about to rip us apart the way I was ripping apart the boundary of our guesthouse, but the moment between us was sacred.

As she watched, one tear drop rolled down her cheek. She patted my chest and then backed away. "I'll appreciate the fresh air, Declan. I've missed it for quite a while."

She walked back into her house and I watched her go, not sure what she meant but sure it had something to do with her past. It took every ounce of restraint not to look her up, not to dig through the internet to find exactly what happened to her back home. But it felt like an invasion of her privacy, an invasion she hadn't done to me. I know she hadn't looked up what happened to my wrist, knew she'd wanted the story straight from my lips.

CHAPTER 20: DECLAN

The rest of the afternoon and into the night, I did the same damn thing I'd done the night before.

I watched her lights.

Tried to work.

And miserably failed.

I even ended up pushing myself harder in the gym than I intended to.

I'd looked forward to getting her in my car the next morning and having a talk with her on our way to work. Yet, when the sun rose, I was ambushed by Anastasia and Melinda at the crack of dawn, both of them doing exactly what Clara said they would.

Digging.

They stopped over with baked goods, like the woman cooked at all. The two of them were vicious in trying to figure out what was going on between Everly and me.

"Declan, you don't have to keep her in the guesthouse. Send her home. Carl wouldn't have cared. He'd done enough for her. Obviously he didn't leave her money for an apartment." She stated it almost as a question, like she wanted to know the stipulations of the will. "I know Carl trusted you and your brothers most. And I know you're always going to take care of us. But," Melinda sighed, "she's not one of us, Declan. She's not even a Milton. We all took his name. She didn't."

Melinda was happy owning most of the spas in the HEAT

empire and having us handle the business. She didn't care to worry about anything other than her social status.

"She's as much Carl's daughter as Anastasia or Clara, Mrs. Milton. I wouldn't turn my back on her even if she—"

The woman laughed and patted her coiffed hair, full of hairspray. "She's not. Carl didn't raise her." Melinda cut me off. "I made sure of it. He didn't go back to see her because his holidays were to be spent with us, and her mother never took one child support payment from him. They had separate lives, and she doesn't understand this one. She's lived in poverty most of her life, probably."

Anastasia put the pie she'd brought over in the fridge and started searching through my cabinets for a glass. "Oh gosh, can you imagine how she must feel here?"

Her mother chuckled. "Like she's won the lottery, I suppose." Then she pointed to Anastasia's glass. "Get me some water, too, would you honey?"

Anastasia flounced back over to the cabinet she'd found my glasses in and grabbed another in that pink floral dress that screamed she was trying too hard. "Declan, would you like one?"

"No." I cleared my throat. "Look, Everly is going to stay here as long as—"

"I wanted to discuss that with you because one or two paps have written about it. It's not big news yet but we need her to go home, Declan. It's not a good look for any of us, honestly. I mean, what if her mother comes to visit?"

So what if she did? Jesus Christ. Dealing with them without Carl as a buffer was much harder than I anticipated.

"Oh, Piper wants us to get together for dinner, by the way." Anastasia didn't care at all about Everly's mom. "She said she'll be needing to come here more often considering the PR shitstorm—"

"Language, Anastasia," Melinda chastised but she was smirking at her daughter. "It is quite a terrible conundrum to have this woman left hanging on us though. I'm wondering if there's a way to get her out of HEAT Health and Fitness without it backfiring on us. It's a member-exclusive club, and she's—"

"She's a great employee, ladies." I tried to quell their bullshit and have them leave without arguing.

"Declan." That quiet voice, so soft and smooth I dreamed about it in my sleep. Yet, my heart fucking froze when I heard it then.

Everly didn't come to my house. She'd never come before. "Everly?"

"Sorry." She cleared her throat and stood tall with her small duffel over her shoulder, her hair framing her face like the masterpiece it was.

I'd outright lost the battle against my attraction to her. I blatantly stared at her lips, her eyes, the damn color of her cheeks as she blushed and tried to catalog all of it at once inside my home for the first time.

"You didn't answer your phone, and your door was open. I'm filling in for Juna early. So, no need for a ride later. I'm going to jog now."

"Wait." I rounded the island counter. "I can drive you—"

"Oh, God. She can jog, Declan. We're visiting. Jesus, Everly. Are you trying to make him feel guilty?" Anastasia accused immediately.

"Of course not." Her eyes narrowed. "He drives me every day, so I didn't want him to wonder where his *employee* was in an hour when he leaves for work."

"Whatever," Anastasia tossed out. "He'd have figured it out. He's not that concerned."

Damn it. I was never a man to yell at a woman, and Anastasia was Carl's daughter, but right then, I considered it and figured, fuck it why not?

But Everly was faster. She was backing out of the room already. "Of course he isn't. I'd never want him to be, either. Just making sure I'm continuing to be that great employee he sees me as." With that, she spun around and jogged off.

I waited until I heard the front door slam before I said what I knew would cause problems.

"You're both aware that Carl had every intention to take care of Everly while he was alive, correct?"

Maybe my voice carried too much frustration, too much anger, too much of the hate I usually held back. I was used to charming the masses, putting on a smile for bullshit pictures, and shaking hands with fucking devils for a living.

It's why I looked for outlets in crazy places. I got my adrenaline rush, exorcized my emotions in the best way I knew how, and then came back to the public eye.

My love had been the game of football. I'd endured Carl's crap to establish a worldwide brand that athletes could feel at home in while also creating an empire for my brothers and myself. Everything else, I didn't give a shit about.

Sometimes I wondered if they forgot where I came from. That I hadn't been born filthy rich, that I still enjoyed the small things.

"Oh, of course we need to take care of her in some way." Melinda flippantly waved her hand but then she nudged her daughter, their eyes darting from me to each other like they weren't sure what had shifted in the room.

It was me.

It was my moral compass, the one I held straight ahead toward money and fame because Carl had been good to me, because I wanted to make him proud, because I felt like mingling with his cruel family was an obligation.

"No. I don't expect you to do that. I'm not even sure you're capable of that, Mrs. Milton," I pointed out. I walked around the island counter and took my time taking their glasses from them and putting them in the sink. It was a blatant end to our visit. "I do expect you to respect the guest I have in my home, though. What's mine is hers. It's her home now for as long as she would like. And if you disrespect her in it again, you won't be asked back here or any place she may frequent—including my fucking gyms, you get me? Now, if you'll excuse me, I've got to chase after her to make sure we didn't offend the hell out of her."

"Declan!" Anastasia squeaked. "Are you serious? Carl would not have wanted this. He always said he dreamed that one of his daughters would actually spend more time with you. He was talking about us, you know?" She smiled, sliding her hand up my arm.

I stepped back. "Anastasia, you're good friends with Piper. She'd never be happy with us spending more time together after—"

"She said you all weren't serious. Right, Mother? You were there!"

Melinda read between the lines. She had pulled her purse on, but her eyes were narrowed, the catlike points of her eye makeup looked more and more predatory. "Yes, Anastasia. I was there. It seems, though, that Declan has other plans. Let's give him his space now. You can talk with him and Piper at dinner when you meet."

I walked right out to my garage as they left, ready to use my car for its main purpose. I sped down my drive and out of the gated community as quickly as I could. It only took me a minute to catch up to her.

Her curly hair threaded through the wind as she jogged, the duffel bag almost as big as her on her back.

I slowed down and pulled toward the curb, hoping no paps were around. She'd been smart enough to wear a baseball cap, but my car wouldn't do me any favors. "Get in, Drop."

She breathed in and out, her running form perfection like rest of her damn body. Why did she look good at everything she did? Even while she ignored me.

"Everly, get in the fucking car."

"I told you I wanted to jog to work, Mr. Hardy."

"Fuck me. Not 'Mr. Hardy' again, woman. I only want you saying that if I'm teaching you a lesson on your knees."

Her gaze whipped to mine as I inched by her in the car. "You think your jokes are funny right now?"

If I told her it wasn't a joke I probably wouldn't win the argument. So I kept it to myself. "Can we start over?"

"Start over with what?"

"The day?" I tried.

"I'd rather not. I don't enjoy mornings."

I sighed and continued to crawl along next to her for two whole minutes. "I'm going to follow you all the way to work at"—I glanced at the speedometer—"eight miles an hour if you don't get in."

"Suit yourself." She shrugged.

"Do you plan on jogging home too?"

"I do." She nodded.

She continued to jog, and I continued to follow, not sure what to say but knowing I had to say something. We weren't really husband and wife, but we'd both committed to one another, and damn if I didn't want to protect her in some type of way from the people who looked down on her now.

"Melinda and Anastasia shouldn't have been over at our house this morning."

"It's your house," she corrected.

"For the next year it's ours. You should be coming and going there as you please. Fuck," I grumbled, getting pissed just thinking about it. "I didn't want you to feel uncomfortable and that's what happened."

"I should have knocked."

"No." She shouldn't make excuses for others by blaming herself. "This isn't your fault."

"Well, if I had knocked and waited—"

I didn't wait for the rest of her reasoning. I sped ahead and whipped my car into park on the side of the road to get out and stand in front of her.

She stopped abruptly, breathing harder than normal, small beads of sweat running down her high cheekbones, glistening in the sunlight while her hair went wild around her in the breezy morning air.

She stared up at me with those sapphire eyes, and in them, I saw pain rather than anger, sadness rather than irritation. My hand instinctively went to her neck, pulling her closer to me. I felt her heat, rubbed my thumb over her jaw, hoped to soothe something in her. "You don't knock to come into your own home, and you don't wait for your husband to finish a conversation with another woman."

"Declan," she breathed out. Looking up at the sky, her eyes

brimmed with unshed tears. "I'm just an employee now. Carl is gone and Melinda and Anastasia find me to be a nuisance, even if, at one point in my life, I wanted to be so much more to them."

"You're *not* just my fucking employee." I wanted to snatch back those words forever. "Look, I'm going to meet with Anastasia and Piper. I'll tell them—"

She chewed her cheek and searched my face, blinking rapidly. Her long lashes caught any of her tears before she stepped back, out of my reach. "You're meeting with Piper?"

I narrowed my eyes at how she straightened, how she pulled at her duffel in front of her, utilizing it for some sort of stability to hold on to. "She's PR for us, and we will need that and a good story when the time comes."

Her head tilted. "Has she always been your PR?"

A sliver of hope ran through my veins that she cared, that she was just a little bit jealous. "Piper has always been around because of Anastasia and Carl. She's Anastasia's best friend. If you want to come to meet with her when we discuss—"

"Absolutely not," she said, cutting me off. "I'm not looking to invade your professional or private life at all."

The fuck? I was looking to invade every part of her and her life. Quite literally.

"Please inform me of what she thinks the spin needs to be. If the story is that I'm to be made the employee who's on her way out soon, fine. I just need a heads-up." She cleared her throat. "Also, I'm hoping to work extra hours to pay you for my half of her PR salary."

"You're not paying me for shit, Everly. And I'm not going to throw you under the damn bus for some bullshit PR story. Are you serious right now?"

"You have status in this community, and I don't want to ruin it. And we should have been this way from the very beginning. I knew this was how it was going to be. I just got lost in..." She waved away our relationship and started to walk around me. "You do what you have to do."

My arm shot out and grabbed her elbow. "What I might have to do is throw you in my car, Drop. You're treating me like I can't be trusted, like we've shared nothing." The thought had me pausing even as my heart picked up speed. It's how I knew I cared for her way more than I should. "You're treating me like I'm nothing to you."

She glared up at me and ripped her arm out of my hold. "We are nothing to each other but a signature, Mr. Hardy. We made a legal commitment, that's it. Let's stick to it and get through this."

"Just a signature?" I'd contained my frustration in worse circumstances, but Everly pressed all the right buttons, and it was the exact wrong time to push me over the edge. "Drop, I can't fucking sleep without thinking about you down in the guesthouse, can't go to work without my eyes drifting to where you're helping a client, and let's be clear, I still taste your pussy when I think about it, still feel your tongue on my cock when I imagine it. You may think you can go backwards and forget my first name, but remember you knew it when you moaned right before I made you come."

Her eyes widened. Then she took a step back, then another, then another toward the gym, away from me, away from the idea of us. "Well, I've forgotten it, Mr. Hardy. I'm an employee, that's all. You said it yourself." With that, she spun and started jogging again.

I should have sped off and left her there with how fucking

enraged I was. Instead, I inched the Bugatti alongside her the rest of the way to work.

She turned to glare over her shoulder once. "You seriously can't still be following me?"

"I might be mad, but I'm not ever going to have my wife jog on her own with the shit you told me the other day about sexual assaults."

"This is a completely safe neighborhood!" she pointed out.

"Even safer given my driving behind you," I deadpanned.

"You're causing a scene." She pointed to the cars behind me.

"Get in then."

Everly was cool, calm, and collected most of the time, but I had to smile when she narrowed her eyes and said, "No."

Cool, calm, collected, and stubborn. She'd made her decision, and she was sticking to it.

And I had my temper and my acting without thinking. So I yanked the wheel, steered the car to the side of the road—again—and got out. "Drop, remember when I told you I make the rules and you listen? That it's better that way?"

She shook her head at me, eyes widening as I came toward her. "Don't you dare, Declan."

She knew I was going to. She wasn't even attempting to outrun me or fight me, either, because she knew my way was better.

I bent and caught her right on the hips where I could raise her up over my shoulder. Hanging on to her legs and walking her back to my car was easy.

She didn't fight.

She just murmured, "This is going to look great in the papers. You carrying your employee to work."

"Maybe I should correct the fucking papers then, Everly, and tell them you're my wife."

CHAPTER 21: EVERLY

He practically threw me into the passenger seat and went the extra mile to buckle me in like I couldn't do it myself.

"I can buckle my own seat belt," I ground out as he did. I hated that I'd been hurt hearing him talk with Melinda and Anastasia, hated that I cared, hated that I hadn't thought over the consequences of running to work right after.

Emotions were to be tamed, controlled, and wrangled into submission.

Be calm. Collected. You can't show anything else.

I knew that. I'd done it back home. I should have been able to do that here. Yet, Declan infected me with a hope of something better, and I'd fallen stupidly for it.

"I'm not sure you can at this point," he growled. "You seem to suddenly want to throw caution to the fucking wind when it comes to safety."

I scoffed at his ridiculous statement, but he didn't give me time to reply as he swung my door closed and got into the driver's side.

We stewed the rest of the way to work as I shuffled around my duffel bag and glanced behind us to make sure no one was taking pictures. "If that really does come out in the magazines—"

"I'm going to dinner with Piper and Anastasia. I'll make sure she knows."

"Right," I seethed, rolling my threaded bracelets around

on my wrist. I couldn't be mad at him for going to dinner with them and yet I wanted to. I wanted to scream at him for it even though it's what he should have been doing. And when Declan pulled into his designated owner's parking spot, separating him and everyone else, it only served to remind me of the vast divide between us—I was an employee, he was the boss.

I got out of the car fast before he could open my door.

"That's two times now you've done that."

"Done what?"

He followed me. "Gotten out of my car without letting me open the door for you."

"I don't need help with a freaking door, Declan. Or anything for that matter." I approached the revolving door and hoped Declan wouldn't attempt to step into the same wedge of glass as me.

He did.

And then he slammed his hand on the glass behind us to stop the rotation. I jumped as I whipped around to see the glare he had directed at me.

"You need help with this door, Everly?" he said, his voice low in warning, like I'd pushed him to the edge of sanity. Me. The woman he'd fucked a few days earlier but then told his friends was just an employee. He held it there, not letting the autorotation continue.

"Are you serious?" I glanced at the front desk where I saw Juna wide-eyeing us.

"Dead fucking serious." His stare held mine, his presence powerful and vibrating with energy.

"What are you even mad about right now that would warrant this public of a reaction?"

"You seem to think I give two shits about the public. The

public cares about me. I don't care about them. If they want to document me having a fit with my wife, they sure as shit can. But what they're not going to do is see you getting away with endangering yourself again. You won't be jogging to work or home from work. If you do, I'm hiring security to tail you."

"You can't think that's—"

"And since you finally decided to step foot in my house, you can join me for dinner every night. Breakfast in the morning too."

"That all?" I said, the anger boiling in me now too. Did he think I would easily bend to his will?

"I will open doors for you, Drop, or I'll keep them closed until you let me."

"Well, that's just immature, Declan." He was being a child and letting his frustration get the best of him. "Is this how you handle your emotions?"

"I can take you to the locker room if you want me to show you how I really handle my emotions when it comes to you."

I pulled at the edge of my sports bra, trying to let the heat of my body escape. "Do you hear yourself?"

"Yes. I'm sick of not being in control. I let your father call a lot of shots in our business, but he's gone. The only thing he gets to control now is our marriage. I let the media push me one way when I wanted to go another. I didn't used to until this empire's responsibility began bearing down on me. I'm about done with letting the press dictate my life."

"We have to maintain public composure and approach this with level heads—"

"You want me to have a level head, Everly, then listen." He didn't wait for me to respond. His eyes were a dark, dark green, like they'd changed with his mood. "The press is about to dig into our relationship hard because we're arguing on the side of a road. So, now might be the time to drop the news."

"Of our marriage?" Why did I sound so scared?

He nodded like we were about to go to war and took a breath. "It's time to take control of it. I'll let Piper know. Tell who you need to."

I didn't want to tell anyone. So, I gulped instead.

He smiled softly. "Now, ask me nicely to open the door for you."

I stomped my foot as I glanced around and realized clients were waiting to get in and out. People's phones filmed him, and I stood there looking like an imbecile. "Please, open the damn door, Declan, so we can get to work," I grumbled and then muttered under my breath as he took his hand off the revolving door, "and next time you manhandle me on the sidewalk, I'm laying you out."

"I hope that's a promise and not an empty threat. I'm happy to be laid out if you're on the ground with me."

"You're totally and completely ridiculous. I say that after assessing all angles and knowing I can't come to any other conclusion because obviously I have to be the logical one here." When I looked at him, he was smiling like he'd won another freaking Super Bowl as he walked behind me. "See you at six for your rehab."

"Looking forward to it, Drop," he said rather loudly as he passed by and nodded to Juna.

"Drop?" she whispered.

"Just a dumb nickname," I said, scanning my watch.

"Are you going to tell me what that was?" She pointed to the doors. "Because I've seen Declan mad on the field and in the tabloids but never here. Here, he's practically the nicest guy!"

"I don't know. He's having a bad day." I shrugged and waved her off. "Go home so you can get your day off."

"I feel like if I go home, I'm going to miss something," she said, her dark eyes the size of saucers staring at me.

"What are you going to miss?" Clara intruded on the conversation, bouncing over with tulips on her dress and an actual flower in her hair. I wondered if she'd plucked it on the way to work or if she went to a boutique to buy it in order to complete her outfit. I wouldn't have put any of it past her.

"Declan yelling at Evie. He nicknamed her Drop and held her hostage in the revolving door to start off the day, so I'm guessing the drama is only going to get more and more intense as the day wears on."

Clara whipped her head over her shoulder as if she was watching out for someone and then whipped back to us. "Weird. Anyway, see you later, Juna." Juna didn't take much offense to Clara dismissing her because she was really in a hurry to get out of the gym. But as soon as Juna was out of earshot, Clara leaned in with a glare. "I'm going insane keeping this secret, Evie. My sister and mom are like hawks when it comes to you two."

"I know it's difficult—"

"And Piper is going to be pissed. She doesn't act like her and Declan are a thing, but if someone's going to replace her, she thinks it's going to be Anastasia on Declan's arm. If it's you..." She practically yanked at her hair. "I'm sorry, but she's going to be furious."

"I'll handle it." I waved a client over and scanned their watch. Then I examined the schedule one last time. "I have one-on-ones after an hour of front-desk duty. I think we just go about our day as if nothing has changed—"

"Were you just jogging down Oceanside Street with

Declan Hardy trailing you?" a young client with blonde hair and excited hazel eyes asked me.

"I'm sorry?"

She pulled up her phone and turned it to me. "Is this you? Are you Everly Belafonte?"

The paparazzi worked fast. So fast, I saw in real time how the views climbed for the video. Someone had filmed us. And with his fame, I knew it was only a matter of time.

That hour standing at the front desk lasted way longer than normal. With me wearing the same outfit as in the video being viewed by everyone, people recognized me over and over.

Once out from behind the desk, I kept my workouts moving. I held two beginner yoga classes and the dozens of men and women were respectful to one another as they helped each other reach perfect poses and hold them. Learning to breathe, control movement, and center yourself had benefits for everyone, especially me that day.

"Great class today," one guy said on his way out as he dropped a few pop tabs into the bin near the door. "I'm happy to hear the charity this year is for the schools throughout Florida."

Glancing at the sign near the pop tabs, I scanned it to see there would be a gala in a few months and sighed, knowing Declan had probably made that happen.

How could I be mad at him when he was like this? Removing gardenias, actually following me to work because he was concerned about my safety, setting up a freaking charity going for the kids in town?

I reminded myself that this was his home, his life, all of his friends who he had to answer to about me being here. After the year was up, I could move. He couldn't really. His fame would follow him everywhere.

I grabbed a towel to brush over my arms just as I saw Wes walking toward my studio. He cracked his knuckles and nodded my way. "How's living with the NFL's golden boy?"

I'd been avoiding his texts and figured sooner or later he'd confront me about it. I leaned against the doorframe. "I'm not living with him. Just in his guesthouse. You know that."

"I know." He pulled at his hair a bit. "Just saw that video of you two."

I glanced at my duffel where I knew my phone was probably receiving texts and calls. "Who knew a video could spread like fire in a dry forest here? Anyway, I'm trying not to let it get to me too much."

"You're something special, Evie. The fact that you're irritated about going viral rather than excited makes you a gem of a woman, seriously." Wes looked more intrigued with me than he ever had before. Like I was an exotic bird to him all of a sudden.

"I don't enjoy attention." I shrugged.

"I love that about you," Wes said, then stepped close. "I miss you."

He couldn't possibly. We'd only been out a handful of times, and since I'd moved into Declan's we'd fizzled. Our interactions were limited to conversations at the gym. He'd extended no invitations and I'd been glad for it.

"Haven't been able to get you to come to my place or even a text back for a while. We haven't done much for almost two months."

"It's been busy and...a lot with Carl passing." I tossed out the excuse easily. The hard part was I hadn't even missed him. He wasn't a bad guy, just not the guy for me. Not even casually. I didn't get butterflies or feel sparks or any sort of emotion toward him at all.

"Can we do dinner tonight?"

"I didn't bring a change of clothes or anything..." Was that enough of a reason?

"We'll go somewhere low-key."

Po's weights clanked behind us and he barreled up right as our watches went off. "Stop hogging Evie, Wes. I've got a one-on-one with her where I need to discuss all the ins and outs of this video."

"Oh God." I pinched the bridge of my nose and Po's broad smile whipped across his face immediately as he pulled me in for a hug.

"Kidding, woman. You know I don't care about that shit." That was probably true. Everyone had an ego here and didn't need to give attention to those who were destined to be a one-minute wonder online.

"We can do a small yoga class if that will help with stretching," I suggested to Po.

He nodded with a smile on his face. "Sure it will help you too. Looks like you need an outlet at this point. Hot yoga?"

"You want to do it or are you doing it for me?" I asked. "I think you could actually use hot yoga to loosen the muscles after playing hockey."

"Whatever helps that fucker's balance." Noah walked up and shoved him, but Po didn't move a muscle.

He lifted a brow. "We should probably let Noah and Wes join considering Noah's dumb ass can't even bend over without falling. Didn't you fall trying to hit the puck last night?"

Although he took it in stride, I saw how Noah's neck tensed, how his stance stiffened up a little. They all cared about their sport and didn't want to lose. "Fuck off. You know it's because I took Johnny's hit."

I waved them on. "Let's go before someone gets their feelings hurt."

"Po knows I've got great balance. Next season, I'm going to kick your ass," Noah pouted and I figured this was the commentary I'd have to listen to through this spring and summer during their offseason.

Wes glanced over at me with a smile and dragged his finger down his cheek. "They're such babies," he whispered to me as we walked to the studio, but Noah overheard him.

"Like a quarterback could take one of us on?"

"I could take either of you." Wes puffed up, but Po and Noah didn't even give him time to defend himself. They cracked up and elbowed one another.

I stood outside the room to swipe my watch, increase the temperature on the thermostat, and log that we were utilizing the studio. I typed in the time and who would be in there with me.

Just as I was finishing it up, Gianni waved at me from the ring in the center of the gym. "You opening a hot yoga class?"

I shrugged. "For those who want a quick workout."

He hopped out of the ring and combed a hand through his dark hair. At six two, he was a tall soccer player, but he moved nimbly from what I'd heard and was good at the game—better than most, actually.

I waved him in right as the locker room door opened and Declan walked out. With the floor-to-ceiling windows overlooking the ocean as his backdrop, he strode down the gym hallway, and I had a hard time looking away. "Hot yoga then, huh?"

"What?"

He tapped his watch. "I'm ready for the workout."

"Declan, this is for—"

"Anyone who wants it, so the schedule says." He breezed past me into the room, and I squeezed my eyes shut.

Great.

It took only ten minutes to warm up the room and stretch. After twenty minutes, everyone was sweating with the poses.

"Gianni, if you came to learn yoga, quit staring at me and get into downward dog." I didn't say blatantly that he was staring at my ass, but he was too obvious not to call out.

"Evie, you know I can't help it," he whined. "Your ass looks like you've been doing yoga your whole life." In his defense, I think he was truly led around in life only by his dick, even if he did have a good heart. The first time I'd met him, he'd hit on me and then completely respected my refusal, explaining we could still be friends. Then, he'd called a girl two minutes later who sounded like she was happy to meet him for a hookup later that same day.

He also was great about immediately yelling at others for doing the same thing. "Wes, you can quit looking at her ass too."

"Fuck you, man. Evie and I have a different sort of relationship."

"And exactly what type of relationship is that, Wes?" Declan hadn't said a word all class though I'd felt his eyes on me. I was aware of the tension in his muscles, and I swear I was attuned to the blood in his veins boiling at this point.

"Aw, man. Can we get past our bullshit? You two are obviously friends, okay? I get it. She's going to be my girl one of these days though." He looked at me with puppy eyes. "Can we go out tonight? It's been too long, babe. And after—"

"After staring at your ass this whole time like a damn creep, he feels deprived," Noah threw out because he loved giving Wes hell.

No one responded to him though because our watches all buzzed at the same time. We didn't brush off the alert because it could be a change in schedule or...big news. Big HEAT news that is. In this particular case, though, it was epic, devastating, catastrophic news.

"HEAT Heiress Everly Belafonte Married to Declan Hardy"

The HEAT PR team released the following statement this afternoon: "Declan Hardy is officially off-limits. He and Everly Belafonte were wed in a small ceremony at an undisclosed location shortly after Carl Milton passed. Sources claim they are committed to their marriage and request privacy as they enjoy their time as newlyweds."

That explains why Everly has been driven to work by Declan and why they've been seen together so often. The biggest question on everyone's minds, though, is how long have they been dating and how did Everly steal him right out from under all of us without anyone being the wiser? Details to come...

My eyes flew to Declan's as each of the men in the room turned his way. Even Wes shrank back with the rest of them. It was as if the alpha dog came to the party and suddenly none of the betas wanted to challenge him.

Declan didn't say anything. I wasn't even sure he'd looked at his watch. Instead, he just crossed his arms and stood there bigger than life, like he ruled the studio, gym, and empire he presided over with utter confidence and power.

"Sorry about commenting on your wife's ass," Gianni grumbled as he literally backed up toward the door. "I respect you and your athleticism. You've done great things for every professional sports league in the country, and I want you to know I didn't mean any disrespect." Then, much like a dog with its tail between its legs, he rushed out.

Po and Noah were next, though they were more protective. I was suddenly their little sister. "You two seriously married?" Po inquired.

"You think we'd lie?" Declan finally responded. "What's it matter to you anyway?"

"I mean, I don't know." Po continued, "Evie's a damn knockout, and she trains us the best. If this was for something in Carl's will... I just don't want her hurt—"

"Everly is more than capable of making her own decisions." Declan cut him off. "Our marriage is our business."

He didn't say more or less. He didn't say he wanted to be married to me, that we were in any sort of relationship, that this wasn't for show.

It shouldn't have hurt. That was the plan. But my heart wasn't listening. *Be calm. Collected. You can't show anything else.*

Declan didn't correct him but motioned toward the door instead. "I have a few things I'd like to discuss with Everly now that the news is out."

Noah and Po immediately walked out of the studio but Wes murmured to me, "I'd like to still see you tonight. Text me, huh?" He didn't wait for an answer and even as Declan opened his mouth, he was already out the door.

"You're not seeing him tonight."

"I *should* see him tonight because he needs some clarification on our relationship."

"Don't we all?" Declan threw up a hand before he started pacing back and forth. "I think it's best for you to come to the meeting tonight with Piper and Anastasia."

"Nope." I halted him right there. "You know that's not in my best interest. I hadn't spoken a word to Anastasia since the funeral until this morning, and Piper is her best friend. I don't belong in this circle—"

"If I do, you do." He strode toward me.

I chuckled and shook my head. "As much as I'd like to make this easier for everyone and agree, Declan, we both know I can't. I might even offend them by showing up."

"I won't have you feeling like you're less—"

"You won't," I clarified, "but they will. And that's fine. I won't encroach on their territory longer than our contractual twelve months anyway, which is why you all should handle it as you see fit."

He opened his mouth to say something more.

"Without me, Declan."

"Without you," he muttered and then he was toe-to-toe with me, looking down at me as I looked up at him. "You realize that for the past couple days, I haven't had a thought without you in it. My mind doesn't work without you in it. My dreams, my nightmares, my subconscious, my conscious... None of them operate lately *without* you."

My throat was closing, tears sprang to my eyes, and my heart felt like it wanted to leap out of my chest into Declan's hands. I'd have to hope he'd hold it carefully, and I hated that I'd started to believe it too.

Yet, I'd be opening myself up to everyone and it wasn't

something I was willing to do.

"Is it bad that every day I'm with you, every part of me is learning that it doesn't want to be without you either?" I took a shaky breath. "It is bad because we'll have to be without one another soon enough, Declan. You know this. And what would you have me do?" I whispered, "Go and frustrate your PR manager so she doesn't want to help us at all?"

A guttural sound came from deep within his throat, and I saw his turmoil as he dragged a hand over his face. "I should just fire her and get somebody new."

"I don't think we have time for that. Plus, you said she's good at her job. She just has to keep the story the same. We're married," I said but air quoted the word married.

He narrowed his eyes. It only took him walking past me to grab a towel and press a button on his watch that dimmed the door's window for me to remember all the things we'd done in the walls of this gym mere nights before. When he turned and grasped the back of my neck to pull me close and drag the towel across my collarbone, I bit my lip to keep from moaning. "Yes, we're married. Completely committed to each other right?"

"Well," I hesitated, feeling the fire in his eyes. "We're committed to a marriage of convenience."

He leaned in close so that I felt the scruff of his five o'clock shadow against my cheek. "We may be committed to a certain timeline with this marriage, but I'm also committed to punching my clients in the face after they stare at you doing yoga in front of them. Should we add that in, Everly?"

No answer was needed from me as his grip tightened and he rubbed more sweat from my chest, then my cleavage. We both knew the answer, and yet my breathing became rapid, and my nipples pebbled as I stood in front of him. Hoping. Wanting.

Aching for him.

A shift in his hold on the back of my neck and his hand was threading through the waves of my hair, urging me to arch into him so he could tilt my face up and descend on my lips. Declan's kiss was possessive, animalistic, and full of control.

He wanted it all now, and I was seeing what made him a world-class athlete and thriving businessman. He dominated and plowed through all my reservations and boundaries. He obliterated my hesitation with the pleasure he delivered with how his hands held my hair tightly, his tongue roved around in my mouth, his lips owned mine.

I folded into him, whimpering and clinging. I took because I knew we wouldn't be able to soon, that this marriage and our secret was about to become a colossal misstep. With that thought, I pushed him away and held my mouth, breathing hard as I closed my eyes, trying my best not to indulge any further. It wasn't realistic, I told myself. "We can't do this. You're having a pissing contest with these men because you slept with me, Declan. And for what? Nothing between us would ever actually work." He glared at me. "Declan, get real. I'm the girl who you thought was a burden without any experience a few months ago. You essentially told my father you didn't want to babysit me and that I was ruining your sanctuary."

"And you were." He nodded, still letting his gaze run up and down my body like he might be picturing me naked.

"Exactly. And my past can ruin your reputation in the press."

"I don't care about the press."

"Well, I do." I tried to keep going. "And we're from different lifestyles. We'd never be compatible."

"You feel pretty compatible when you're screaming my

name."

"You're on another level right now, you know that?" I shook my head at him. "Let's just focus on the original plan. We're together and married if the press asks. For those close to us, we can tell them it's a marriage of convenience."

He stared at me as I paused. I wasn't sure why I did. Maybe I wanted him to demand that this marriage was more than that, that we could be more than that. But he only asked, "Is that what you want?"

I took a deep breath, trying to hold onto my logic rather than following a silly little hope dancing around in my head. "Yes, it's the smart thing to do. You can talk with Anastasia and Piper and see how they want to run with it. I'll let Wes know."

"So, he's that close to you?"

"He deserves an explanation, Declan. I trust he'll be discreet with the information. And as for the public, I don't think they need to know anything else."

He hummed, those eyes searching me for answers he wouldn't find. I was closing the box and locking it before the media came looking for bread crumbs.

I moved toward the door and opened it. "It'll be good for us, Declan. This is the plan."

For another ten seconds, he stood there, a pillar of vibrating emotion, and I wasn't sure what would erupt. "Be home at a reasonable time, Everly, or I'm coming to find you." Then, he walked past me out the door and held up three fingers. "Three times now you've opened the door instead of me."

Why did him counting like that send shivers down my spine?

CHAPTER 22: DECLAN

Dinner with Piper and Anastasia ran later than I wanted it to. I'd even made the effort to go to one of HEAT's low-key restaurants, Vibe, at the hotel across the skywalk from the gym so that they wouldn't want to stay late.

Still, they both ordered drinks and kept talking like I didn't have somewhere to be. As if I didn't need to get home to see if Everly was back from her date with Wes. Instead, I had to pretend I wasn't pining over a girl who wasn't sitting at the table with me.

"So, this marriage is a complete curveball but I'll just run with it." Piper was laser focused on me as she said the words. "It'd be great if we dropped something other than the fact that you're married. I mean, you could do an exclusive interview as a couple or if you want to be honest and discuss Carl's will..."

She wanted all the details. She waited, her eyes trying to cut through to the truth.

"There's nothing to disclose in regard to that. The HEAT empire is secure."

"Has any sort of probate started or—"

"Piper, you're on my PR team." I set down my drink firmly. "You kill stories that don't line up with mine and you put out the ones I want. That's why you're the best, am I right?"

"Declan, it's easier when I know what I'm going up against."

"This time, your job might be a little harder. You'll get it done or I'll find someone else who will."

Anastasia tsked softly but when I swung my glare her way she immediately looked down at her phone. "I'm just so disappointed in Carl."

"Me too," Piper pouted. "I realize we haven't been seeing eye to eye lately, Declan, but Everly over Anastasia? You and Anastasia have been close for years. I'm shocked that he'd have you marry a stranger who doesn't run in our circle whatsoever."

Anastasia nodded her curled hair in complete agreement and it was glaringly apparent to me now how offensive both of them truly were. They didn't see past themselves at all. They were entitled, arrogant, and ignorant.

"Oh my God." Piper's jaw dropped as she looked past me. "She's still going to date Wes?"

Whipping around, I saw her. Lips shining with a bit more gloss than she'd had on at the gym and a bit more flare to her lashes too. Everly waltzed in on Wes's arm looking up at him with a dazzling smile on her face.

Most men probably would have felt jealousy right then, maybe even anger. I felt a damn challenge.

I excused myself immediately and made my way over to them, weaving around the oak chairs and strategically placed foliage. "Everly, Wes. You guys up for a round of drinks?"

My raindrop bit her lip when she heard my voice and her brow furrowed. She adjusted the tennis skirt she must have changed into around before answering. Yep, she knew this wasn't going to go well. "I don't think that's—"

"Oh, Jesus," Wes groaned and rolled his eyes. "I'm never going to get a second alone with her, am I?"

That was the fucking point. "Piper and Anastasia are here. Clara might be stopping by. You know they're going to bother you if you don't sit by us anyway."

Wes sucked on his teeth, flexing his muscles and rearranging the man bun on his head for no damn reason as he weighed his options, not even thinking to ask Everly's opinion. Then, he shrugged. "A few drinks won't hurt. Noah and Po will probably stop by."

"Great." I nodded at him as he breezed by me, beelining over to Anastasia and Piper who were already waving him over. I leaned into whisper to Everly as she walked by, "Guess we'll be spending the evening together after all."

She rolled her eyes like she'd had enough of me. Did she know I was only getting started? I touched the small of her back and saw how goose bumps flew up over her arms. I was thankful for Piper recommending a bigger booth so I could slide in next to Everly and push my thigh up against hers underneath the table. She glanced at me, pursing her lips and shaking her head ever so slightly as if to deter me.

I didn't care, and she was either too stubborn or too intrigued to move away. Instead, when I placed my hand on her leg after ordering everyone a round, she narrowed her eyes at me like she was daring me to continue. I had no problem with that. My thumb circled on her bare skin over and over again. Then, she leaned into Wes to whisper something into his ear before he proceeded to wrap his arm around her shoulders.

"I think I need a shot." Anastasia wrinkled her nose at them.

Me too. I ordered them all shots on top of the round.

Everly chewed her cheek before she picked hers up and clinked it with everyone to down it.

When she shuddered down the gulp, I leaned in. "If you hate it, don't drink it, Drop."

She took a deep breath. "I think we should all have

another," she announced.

There was a challenge in her eye so I dragged my hand higher up her thigh. Her soft lips parted but no other indicator of our interaction was given.

Clara arrived right then, floral pattern all over her dress like she'd burst from a garden, and a smile peeked out when she saw Everly although she tried to hide it from her sister. "So, I saw the news."

"I can't believe it," Anastasia muttered.

Wes sighed as his hand rubbed Everly's shoulder right in front of me, like he had no regard for our marriage, like I wouldn't contemplate breaking his wrist for touching my girl. Then he said, "It's a shame Carl put you both in this predicament. Everly said it won't be for long."

"Did she?" I asked, my eyes on her. So she'd told him the truth on the way over. And yet, why did I still want to pound his face in? I took a deep breath, trying to calm myself and let my hand below ghost over Everly's thigh back and forth. "Well, a year isn't that long to some, is it, Everly?"

Fuck, the fire in her eyes as she whipped them at me was intoxicating.

"A whole year?" Piper and Anastasia said at the same time.

"Well, we're about two and a half months in." I shrugged and squeezed her leg under the table. Surprisingly, she hadn't shoved me away, but her glare could have burned down the whole restaurant.

"Well, at least you can both date other people, right? I mean, do it discreetly, of course," Piper pointed out and glanced at Wes's arm, then turned to Anastasia. "You two still have a chance."

"Anastasia and Declan?" Clara scoffed. "They've never

even been on a date, Piper. Why would you say that after you've been with him?"

"Because Anastasia and Declan *belong* together, Clara. Everyone knows that. I just was a blip on his radar." She smiled at me, and I felt Everly's thigh move under my grip. But she didn't move away. She moved closer, spreading her thighs apart.

When I looked at her in question, I saw that Everly was indulging her jealousy the way I was, that she wasn't backing down even as she smiled, cool, calm, and collected at them. "Well," she said, "Piper does know what the public likes to see, I'm told. You all have a great group here together."

I brushed my thumb across her panties, and she leaned over on the table, placing her chin in the palm of her hand.

"Exactly. It's a tight-knit group too," Piper pointed out, swirling her drink around. "You haven't been around long enough to understand the dynamics."

The dynamics were simple. I'd pick Everly over them again and again.

Wes interjected, "I'm trying to make her understand, guys. She's going to be one of us soon enough because she's my girl. Even if she's gotta do this last crazy thing for Carl's sake. Right, Evie?"

Everly turned to gaze at him, biting her lip while my hand brushed over her soaking panties. When she looked in Wes's eyes, he thought she was looking at him that way, like he caused her to fight for her next breath, like she loved every second of what he was doing.

"You're my girl, right?" he whispered as he leaned down and kissed her temple. "And I got lucky she's not a part of this crew because you're all a damn handful sometimes."

That's when I pushed her panties to the side—to remind

BETWEEN COMMITMENT AND BETRAYAL

her who really got her wet, who took control when she needed. Her eyes widened and she sat up away from Wes, busying her hands with a napkin to tear it to shreds.

Clara agreed with Wes, which irritated Anastasia enough that they all started bickering, which took the attention off Everly for a second. That's all it took for me to slide a finger in, for her to shift enough that I could move my thumb over her clit and rub the bundle of nerves just right, and then her sapphire eyes closed and her hand went under the table to grip my wrist.

I leaned in so she could tilt her head back and act as though she was listening to whatever I had to say. I hope she listened good too. "He's lucky I know how to hand-fuck you under this table so you can remember who you really belong to, or I'd break his arm off from around your shoulder."

Her breathing was too erratic to respond, but I worked her pussy until she got the best orgasm she could and then pulled her panties and skirt back into place before bringing my hand to the table to dip my finger in my whiskey.

She watched as I swirled it round and round, and her cheeks flushed when I sucked the alcohol and her sweet taste from it. "Whiskey's good tonight. Take a sip, Drop."

She didn't even hesitate. I owned my wife's body even if no one thought I did, and I wasn't backing down or away. Nobody saw our exchange as they all argued, not even the man with his arm around her shoulders.

"Why don't Everly and I go get another round?" I announced.

Clara was fast to agree as our only ally, and I stood from the booth, pulling Everly with me.

Anastasia and Piper stood too, but Anastasia was bold enough to lean into my chest. "Declan, let's go dance," she whined.

It only took three shots for her to turn into a clinger, for her to get those doe eyes she thought would work on me. In the past, I used to fold, giving in to whatever she and Piper wanted because it was the path of least resistance, but when I felt Everly's hand sliding from my own, I gripped it tighter.

"I'll meet you out there in a while maybe."

I pulled Everly past them and weaved through the crowd that had formed. The restaurant had already dimmed the lights.

"Declan, you probably should go dance with her."

"I probably shouldn't," I responded back. When we got to the bar, I pulled her up to it and caged her in between my arms. "If I'm dancing with anyone tonight, it's going to be you."

"I don't think so. I'm here with Wes." She lifted her chin and stared straight ahead. "You have an obligation to your peers and the company. Once we're done, it won't be to me. It will be to her, Declan."

"Is that so? And do you have an obligation to him? Is that why you went out with him tonight?" I blurted.

She looked over her shoulder at me. "What sort of obligation would I have with him that you're so worried about, Declan?"

I hummed low. "One where you're in a damn skirt for him, Drop. And wearing lip gloss that I know tastes like strawberries." I stepped closer to her and felt her ass against my cock, my arms brushing against her bare skin. Vibe was filling up quickly, and it allowed for me to get close without anyone questioning it.

"You realize it's a tennis skirt and the only thing I had in my locker, right?"

"What about when I have dinner with you?" I wanted the same treatment, wanted whatever she'd give me at this point. "You going to dress up for me?"

"I'm not sure." She shrugged and turned back to the bar like nothing could faze her. "We haven't had dinner together yet."

"I've invited you to dinner."

"At what you claim is our house? Well, then, it's supposed to be my home too, and I don't really get dressed up to sit at home," she snarked.

The small smile that played on her lips told me she was trying to rile me. And still, I took the bait. "So, you get ready for your boyfriend but not your husband?"

She whipped around and whispered my name fiercely, fire in her eyes, "Declan, don't start with that."

Alcohol. Jealousy. A tiny raindrop that I wanted to control more than life itself. You name it. "You're driving me fucking crazy sitting next to him and whispering in his ear," I admitted.

"That's ridiculous. You were out with Anastasia and Piper who I know you've..."

"Go on. Finish the sentence."

"You've slept with Piper," she pointed out and then fisted her tiny hand like she was mad at herself for having a reaction. "And it doesn't matter. Honestly. Because we are two people living separate lives. And after, you'll probably have to date my stepsister."

"Would that bother you?" I whispered in her ear.

I saw the goose bumps break out over her neckline. "If it did?"

"Then I'd say we need to rethink the commitments we've made regarding this marriage."

She shook her head, worried immediately about changing a course she'd already set in motion. "No. I'm not bothered. I'll get through it."

The bartender walked up and asked for my order, willing to cater to the owner. She wiggled away from me right as my phone rang, and I let her go when I saw the number.

"Mrs. Johnson?" I answered as I watched her weave through a few guys and then catch Noah and Po's attention.

I'd hired someone to dig through the will, to figure out what Mrs. Johnson wasn't telling us and I was guessing that's why she was calling.

"Yes, Declan, sorry to be calling so late, but I wanted to remind you of the stipulation meeting. We've got two weeks until then and I want to make sure you and Everly are getting along." She cleared her throat. "This stipulation won't put too big a wrench in anything but I have heard you've been digging around."

I wouldn't deny it. "I'd like to know what it is sooner rather than later."

"Well, at three months, Ms. Belafonte and you will have to make a decision that will either end your marriage or move it forward. I'd like to think the latter. You two seem so good together."

My blood pressure rose, and I gripped the side of the bar. "Holding a stipulation secret this long with regard to a will can't be—"

"I'll see you soon, Declan. Please be nice to your wife."

I hung up and mashed my teeth together as I called the one person I thought may be able to help.

I pounded his number into my phone as I walked out of the bar. He answered on the second ring. "What do you want, brother-in-law?"

"Do you and Izzy know the three month stipulations of the will?"

"Sure," he said with literally no emotion in his voice.

"What the fuck? Tell me."

"I'd rather not."

"This isn't even legal," I ground out.

"Sure. But when you're willing to make an illegal trust and will legal, it sort of takes illegal actions to make it null and void again. The world's nice and fucked-up that way."

"Fuck you, Cade."

I hung up on him and went back inside to search for Everly. We had two weeks to figure out if we were going to commit to the stipulations and I knew whatever it was, I wasn't losing her just yet. I knew whatever it was, I wanted her to commit with me.

CHAPTER 23: EVERLY

Lust and desire and luxury pulsed through the club. Vibe was decadent with crystals and diamonds threaded through lush amounts of vines and roses, all royal colors woven through the piping up above. With satin lounge chairs lining the corners of the restaurant and the booths made of tufted silks—all royal blue and purples—every customer felt like royalty. Waitresses with flowers in their hair and all-black attire buzzed about making sure top-shelf alcohol was served to all. Food was bought through a swipe of the watch or put on a regular's tab without them having to even offer to pay.

Declan could order shot after shot after shot and never would a bartender ask him for a credit card. To him, it was normal. To me, it was insane, just another indicator of our incompatibility. Yet, when I'd heard Anastasia and Piper holding a magnifying glass to all our differences, I'd wanted nothing more than to prove we had a few things in common.

He knew how to make me feel good, and we both enjoyed that. He may have been my husband in hiding, but the chemistry between us was noticeable. At least to the two of us.

Or so I thought. He'd hung up his phone and hadn't turned to look for where I'd walked off to. Instead, he made his way back to our table, but not before my stepsister grabbed him and pulled him close. She dragged a hand over his jaw and looked up at him lovingly. Piper smiled the whole time, as if encouraging her friend to engage in a relationship with her ex.

She was a better woman than me.

Never would I be supportive of Declan being with a close friend of mine had we actually been together. He stood there, smiling down at her, his body bigger and stronger and harder than most in the crowd. I knew what it felt like up against me, how the hands he now had on her wrists as he pulled them away from his face felt on my skin, how he smelled like sandalwood and rain to me even when it was sunny. I ached for him, even though he wasn't truly mine.

Sighing, I turned to the bar and asked for another drink. "One more shot. Make it stronger than the others you've served tonight, please."

The bartender nodded, completely happy to oblige. Taking a dark bottle of liquor, he murmured, "Rough times when you're getting followed by the owner to work, huh?"

I sighed. "So has everyone seen that video?"

"Pretty much." He lined the rim of the shot with sugar and then followed it up with setting the top of it on fire for just a second before he waved away the flame. "This'll make you feel better. Favorite one of my own. I call it HEAT's Sugar. It's sweet and spicy."

I shrugged. "Bottom's up." It burned while still tasting sweet as it licked down my throat, causing me to shiver enough that he laughed.

"I'm Corbin, by the way. I've seen you working out in the gym a few times. Carl was a good man. Sorry to hear about your loss."

I nodded, letting the liquor and his comment settle in my body before I responded. So many people had been sorry for my loss lately. "I didn't know him that well."

"Sure. You moved here only a few months back, right?"

He leaned over to take another order from a woman next to me. Then, as he grabbed another bottle from under the bar, he smiled softly. "You're just as entitled to being sad as any of them. You probably saw more of him than they did anyway." Corbin chuckled as he looked past me. His words amplified what my heart felt in that moment. And I felt it entirely, wholeheartedly, and it walloped me fiercely.

One glance back into the crowd, at Anastasia still near Declan as he stood by our table now, had emotions bubbling up in me that I really hadn't dealt with in years. People shouldn't cry in public or show that they're falling apart.

Like he could feel my eyes on him, he turned. That deep-green gaze pulled me in like a dark forest wanting to be explored, but his stare was questioning, probing me for more information than I was willing to give. I turned back to the bartender just as I saw Declan take a step toward me.

"You need my watch?" I asked Corbin.

"Your tab's on us when you're here." He grabbed the empty shot off the bar and winked at me before another customer nodded at him.

"It's time for us to go," Declan rumbled behind me.

The heat of him there pulled my body back, but this time I ignored it. "Oh? Is everyone headed out?"

He leaned into the bar. "No. My *wife* and I are headed out. I have something to talk to you about in the car."

"I came with Wes, Declan. You came with women too. We should leave with them."

"Now it's about Wes? Not just discussing what our marriage looks like to him?" He shook his head and rubbed his jaw roughly once. "How did you describe it anyway? You tell him I can hand-fuck you under a table so good that you drip down my fingers even while he sits in the next seat over acting like your boyfriend?"

"Jesus Christ, Declan." Anger and desire warmed my face at the same time.

He breathed in deep, as if trying to quell whatever he was feeling. "Drop, I'm not in the mood. And I know you're not either. Just a second ago, you looked back at me over at that table like you were ready to break down. Like this place is getting to you, and I know it's damn sure getting to me."

"I don't break down, Declan." I peered up at him, suddenly frustrated that I almost had. He didn't know what I'd endured, what I was capable of bearing still, or how I would handle going through it. "I can't break down. Not again. But if we keep doing this, I will. I'll go home with Wes. You can leave."

He hummed. "*We're* leaving, Drop."

Alcohol swirled with my emotions, especially the bold ones, and the combination was dangerous. "I'm going to go dance."

I slid past his body, hard to my soft, massive to my miniscule, dominating to my usual submissive ways. Except we'd clash here tonight because I couldn't stop feeling like their eyes were on him. My stepsister, the one my father prayed I would get along with, literally wanted my husband. Without talking to me, without looking at me, without even acknowledging I was there. I meant nothing to her, and the feeling was about as treacherous as it had been back home when everyone had found out what had happened between my boyfriend and me.

So I'd let the alcohol flow through my veins and drown out the heartache of not just one loss, but that of an entire family. The hope of them accepting me died when his heart stopped beating, and I needed to let go of what wasn't meant to be.

The music beat loud, so I moved my hips to and fro, concentrating on simply feeling the soul of the song for a moment. Declan had turned to watch but didn't follow, his gaze heavy enough on me that he probably knew it's all I felt even as Wes and Noah emerged on the dance floor ready to bust out their own moves in front of me.

Clara laughed when Noah tried to break-dance, and then he grabbed her hand to whip her around the dance floor like they were two salsa dancers. He was tall and an athlete, which most of the time equaled instant rhythm and dance skills. Noah outdid most though. I could tell from the lines he stepped into and how he held Clara that he probably had legitimate training in it.

My mother had always been a dancer, and with me being homeschooled, she'd taught me enough to appear skilled. So when Noah grabbed my hand after spinning Clara out, I did a bit of a curtsy before he pulled me into his arms. A basic two-step turned into a sashay as he got the feel for what I could handle, and then a brilliant white smile, dimples over his cheeks, and a twinkle in his eyes showed me he'd caught on. He pulled me close. "You dance?"

"I used to." I moved my hips with him.

His hand on my lower back kept me steady with him. "Let's show your boyfriend and husband what you're made of then. I'm pretty sure you already own their hearts, but I think Declan's going to bleed out and still crawl to your feet when all is said and done."

"Be serious, Noah," I chuckled, feeling completely comfortable for the first time that night, dancing with a friend who had always treated me exactly as such.

"Oh, I'm serious, Evie. Didn't you ever watch him on the

field when he wanted a damn touchdown?"

I shook my head as he turned me out so I could spin, then pulled me in for a dip.

"He moved viciously on instinct. Most people say he played with heart... I say he wasn't playing at all. He was dominating like a damn animal. When he's pushed and not getting what he wants, you'd better be ready for it. Remember that."

Two more spins and a lift—where we got most of the dance floor cheering for our salsa—later, the song ended, and I smiled at Noah. "And what do they say about you on the sports channels, Noah?"

"That I'm reckless." He shrugged. "I can break a bone in a heartbeat, Evie, and I won't feel bad about it at all."

We were both breathing hard as I pulled him in for a hug before glancing over at our friends. Clara was clapping and Dom had shown up, eyeing me curiously as Wes walked over like a puppy dog, pouting at Noah. "Give my girl back."

Noah winked at me and nodded behind us toward the bar. Toward the formidable man who I knew still sat there, watching. His glare grew heavier and heavier. It was like I could feel it impressing upon me, overtaking my thoughts, clouding them, filling them with dark oil that I wouldn't be able to swim out of.

Still, I didn't look back. I waved to Dom as Noah asked Clara, "Dance with me again, flower girl?"

Clara smirked, but before she could say a thing, Dom interjected. "Clara, shouldn't you be working on the blueprint to show me of your bakery for tomorrow?"

All the light from her smile dimmed as she frowned at him and took Noah's hand. "Blueprint? I have a design. And it's done and completely magical."

He glared at her as she frolicked off with Noah while Wes wrapped his arm around my waist. It wasn't meant to rile anyone, but the posture laid his claim just the same.

Declan's stare pulled my attention, commanding me to glance his way again. A man who owns the world has the ability to shift it with a tiny movement, and Declan owned my world that night. He had me on the edge of a cliff where he knew I was teetering, and when he mouthed Four, I knew exactly what he meant. I hadn't left with him earlier, defying him for a fourth time.

He strode over, his dark jeans and T-shirt doing nothing to dampen how attractive he was with his chiseled chest and arms, veins moving over the muscles like he wouldn't be contained by them.

"Everly, time to go," he ground out.

"Babe, you're coming to my place, right?" Wes spoke against my ear, his arm pulling me closer to him while he kept dancing with me.

Declan didn't give me time to answer. "My *wife* is coming home with me."

The sharp and loud emphasis on my title had Noah freezing mid-dance with Clara as both Anastasia and Piper glanced over from our table where they were enjoying another drink. Everyone froze in shock, even the music seemed to quiet, as the blood rushed through my veins.

Clara was the only one who seemed to know what to do. She wasn't stock-still in her floral dress or her bright-red high heels. She smiled big and patted my shoulder, pulled me from Wes subtly by hooking her arm with mine. "Of course it's time for us all to get home. Evie, it's okay for me to stop over early to look at the mock-ups for my bakery, right? I really need help with those for the new resort going up."

We'd never discussed that before, but reading a room was something I'd been able to do quite well now. "Sure." I turned to Wes. "Will you take me to my place instead? Do you have a driver?" I wouldn't go with anyone who'd had too much to drink.

Even Noah's eyes ping-ponged over to Declan along with Wes's. It's how you knew Declan was the alpha here.

Wes puffed up his chest like he was ready for war, but said, "Of course."

Declan took a formidable step forward, but Dom pivoted in front of him. "Watch yourself in our restaurant, Dec."

Piper appeared out of nowhere and put a hand on Declan's heart. "Stay for another drink, Declan. Anastasia and I will get this round."

I turned on my heel and hoped with everything in me that Wes was following.

I had to leave Declan where he belonged, in a land of fame and fortune without me.

But as I reached the door, I heard him call out, "Everly, that's five."

Those shivers, the ones that only raced through my body for Declan, plagued me again.

CHAPTER 24: DECLAN

"You're losing your fucking head." Dom grabbed my arm and steered me away from Piper and everyone else.

I only looked over my shoulder to catch Everly's ass swaying as she walked out with Wes close behind. I swear she was even walking with more sex appeal tonight because my dick was in full control now.

I ripped my arm out of Dom's. "I'm going home."

"Why? So you can ease your mind when she shows up right away?" he asked. It wasn't to irritate me, either, because his brows were raised, and I could tell he was genuinely concerned.

"That fucker has my girl in his car like he's going to get laid tonight," I snarled as I pulled my phone from my pocket and texted her.

> Me: You better go straight home, Everly.

> Everly: I'm an adult. Don't treat me like a child.

> Me: I'm treating you like my wife. And if your boyfriend puts his hands on you, he better know I'm breaking them.

> Everly: Are you serious? Read that

text back to yourself and let me
know if you want to continue this
conversation.

Me: I'm on my way home and when I
get there, you better be there too.

Everly: I won't.

Me: Then I'm coming to find you, and
that fuckboy is fucked.

"Feel good about yourself right now?" Dom chuckled as I glanced up at him. "Rage texting her will get you nowhere."

"You don't know a damn thing about what gets me somewhere with a woman."

"I know Evie's quiet, but she's smart as fuck. I also know that the news about her history is going to hit soon. Did Piper inform you?"

"Inform me of what?"

"Evie's been in the media before, Declan." He pulled at the back of his neck, massaging it while finishing what he had to say. "I'd recommend you ask her and figure out how you want to handle the news going forward. It's going to be vicious."

The news about the will was enough. "So another shitstorm is headed my way?"

"You're the bachelor of the century, man. It makes sense now why Carl wanted you to marry her. Maybe he knew it would blow up in her face at some point. Just ask her and stop fucking around. This is serious."

I didn't even say goodbye to anyone. Dom's warning sobered me up. The night air was pungent with summer humidity and foreboding of what was to come. I skirted around those who were enjoying being on the beach and got home faster than I was sure Wes could have driven.

I parked in my large garage where five other vehicles sat. All black. All luxury. All of them Everly refused to touch.

Instead, the stubborn woman would rather jog to work when she was mad at me.

And had her damn boyfriend drive her home. As if on cue, I heard the rumble of his car pulling up. At the press of a button, I disabled her ability to open it. Instead, I strode to the side of the gate to unlock the pedestrian door.

"Declan"—her window rolled down—"the gate's not working."

"Oh, it is," I countered before pointing to Wes. "He's just not allowed on the premises."

Fury danced in the blue of her eyes before she responded, "Well, how fucking childish of you."

Her words were potent and visceral, like they'd been let loose from deep in her gut. I leaned against the stone pillar, considering how much she'd had to drink before I responded with, "Say good night, Everly."

Wes may have been trying to convince her he could hold his own, but the man was nothing without a group of men behind him. He was a pussy of a quarterback, used to hiding behind his O-line, and when the opponent's defense got through his linemen, he bitched out half the time. I'd never seen a man throw more interceptions than he had just to get out of being tackled. Even now, he didn't get out of the car to open her door or confront me. He murmured something to her and then kissed her temple.

It was bold enough to boil my blood though, bold enough

to know that after tonight, he'd never have his mouth on her again.

I'd make sure of that.

She slid from his car and made her way past me as Wes's driver turned down my street. Just as she tried to skirt around my body, she stumbled, and I knew the alcohol in her was showing its effects much more than it had thirty minutes ago.

"What did you drink at the bar?"

"None of your business." Her chin was up as she tried to shake my hand from her elbow.

I smiled. "Not happening, Drop. I let go of your arm, I'm throwing you over my shoulder again."

"Go right ahead and try." She turned toward me, squaring up in challenge, and I rolled my eyes as I bent to put my shoulder into her waist. She thought I wouldn't pick her up again, that I'd back down. She was dead wrong.

Yet, as I bent to scoop her up, she swung around my neck, wrapped her thighs around me, and yanked me down to the ground. Our backs hit the grass on the side of my brick driveway with a thud.

"Fuck, Everly."

She flipped over on top of me and then smiled down, victorious, while the dark cloudy sky served as her backdrop. "I told you the next time you manhandled me I'd lay you out. Want to try again?"

Her eyes were narrowed and sparkling, the only things shining as the sky rumbled like it might rain down on us again as she panted on top of me. My cock hardened between her legs as she sat, and when she rolled her hips, I knew the game. She wanted to play, and I couldn't deny her.

I flipped her over this time, and we rolled in the grass.

I took hold of her wrists, but she maneuvered her arm with exactly the right momentum to hit me where she knew my grip was weakest. I grabbed her waist, and she twisted so her legs had me in a choke hold.

Round and round we went, like gladiators. Except I was twice her size, more sober, and my stamina was better than hers, even though she'd probably never admit it.

Her last attempt was futile, but she did get a good head start on getting away. When she leapt up and turned to run toward the guesthouse, I caught her foot, and she was so damn small, it was easy to yank her back. She yelped and fought me the whole way, but I overpowered her swiftly, my adrenaline going now with the need to control her, have her, consume her.

I pinned her again, trapping her wrists in the grass above her head, and she was too tired to fight it. "Use your safe word, Everly. Tap out."

She shook her head slowly. "What if I don't want to?" Her voice was soft as she stared up at me. "I should, but I won't. So, take what you want, Dec. You want your wife out here in the middle of the night? Take me."

I growled, ready to let go and get up, but she whimpered and bit her lip as she pressed her pussy against me. "You're drunk, Everly."

"Yes, and I'm soaking wet for you. I've been imagining your cock fucking me since the moment you got me off with Wes sitting next to me."

Bold. Everly with alcohol was a dangerous combination for me. "Oh, now you like us playing in secret all of a sudden?"

She rolled her hips into me again, and my dick practically throbbed. "My stepsister and her friend want you even while you're doing vile things to me under the table."

I leaned in, one hand still holding her wrists and the other skating down her body. A better man would have stopped, not knowing what stipulations were ahead, but knowing we needed to have our emotions in check. Still, I couldn't.

Would I let her go if whatever was coming our way at that meeting was catastrophic? Or would giving her up destroy me anyway?

The last question twisted in my gut as I stared down at her, those waves of hair sprawled out around her face, framing it in the dimmed light from our home.

Our home.

And she hadn't even slept in my bed with me yet.

"Declan," she whined, her blue eyes had a fire of need in them as she writhed against me. "Please, I need this."

I growled, unbuttoned my pants, and pulled my cock out, not willing to deny her begging. "You get one, Drop. Rub against my cock."

She twisted and rolled against me, locking her legs on my hips, and I pinched her clit while keeping her wrists above her. I wouldn't fuck her tonight, but I couldn't deprive her this fantasy either.

"Maybe I should restrain you more often, have you beg to get fucked."

"Oh..." She wasn't capable of engaging in the conversation anymore. She bucked her hips up and down on me while I tried my best not to take over and take her roughly the way I wanted to. "You feel so good. Please."

I shifted just enough that when I leaned down to suck on her neck and push my hips forward, my cock entered her just right. She gasped as I groaned at how tight she was, her sex gripping me like it missed me.

She didn't hesitate to try to catch her orgasm as her eyes squeezed shut while the rain broke from the clouds to drop on her smooth skin. Her hips moved her up and down on me as she worked herself up and up. I watched the whole time in awe, trying to stay as rigid as possible rather than moving with her. If I did, I'd fuck her all night long in the wet grass outside the house.

Instead, her breathing increased even as she fought to get out of my grip. Her hips bucked faster when I moved one thumb back and forth fast over her clit. "That's it. Keep going, baby."

"Declan," she whined, and I saw her jaw set, felt the anger behind her words as she said, "Are you kidding me? *Fucking move.*"

I chuckled and shook my head as I leaned in to tell her, "No. You want it? Then, shut the fuck up and take my cock like the good girl you are, baby. Take it exactly how you want it."

She let out a frustrated little growl as she tried to free her wrist from my one-handed grasp again and couldn't. I pinched her clit then just as she squeezed her legs tight around me, shoving my cock farther into her. I did it again and again and again to her exact pace of riding me, her movements becoming more and more erratic until she cried out, arching her back and pushing her tits to my chest as I mashed my teeth together, trying to stay in control even while she came against my cock.

I catalogued her every movement and the way her eyes weren't on fire anymore but instead had embers of pleasure and satiation burning there when she opened them. "Damn, you're stunning when your pussy coats my dick with how wet you are, Everly."

"Fuck me right now, Declan. I'm begging you," she pleaded, but her eyes were hooded, her body almost limp.

"You need to sleep off the alcohol, Drop." I didn't wait for her to disagree. I pulled out fast, knowing I couldn't withstand another second in her or I'd fold. Then I kissed her forehead when she protested, sticking her lip out like she was pouting. "I promise I'll fuck you so good tomorrow, you'll beg me to stop if you want."

She didn't answer but I saw the small smirk across her lush lips as I scooped her up to walk her straight into my house.

Only once had she been in here. Only once with Anastasia and Melinda tearing her down. This time would be different. This time, I'd close out the world for a blissful moment before I asked her if she'd be ready to barrel through the rest of this marriage with me, if she could commit even without knowing the stipulation.

I undressed her before I laid her down in my bed, and she didn't help at all, practically already asleep by the time I got myself undressed too. I stripped down too, pulled her close, and willed my cock to try not to fuck her during the night.

CHAPTER 25: EVERLY

I didn't wake with a headache or aches and pains. Instead, I dreamt about his hands on me, the way he talked to me, the way he worked me out in the rain. Then, I woke with his cock between my thighs, hard as a rock, and his arm around me as he snored.

Last night he'd worked my body in a way I'd never let a man, made me beg almost at his complete mercy, and I'd loved every second.

Too much.

My pussy wanted more, wanted him, wanted his cock sheathed in me so I could coat him with my slickness. I was at just the right angle that if I rocked a little and slid my hand between my legs, I'd finish again.

I was so close. So, so, so close.

I rolled my hips and moaned his name, letting my hand glide down my body to between my legs, imagining how he'd made me orgasm the night before.

Suddenly, his hand shot out to grab my wrist. "I thought you weren't a morning person, Everly. But you're grinding against my cock like you are. Stealing an orgasm this early?"

I looked over my shoulder at him and confessed with no embarrassment, "I want you, Declan."

The rumble from deep in his throat rolled through the bedroom, making my pussy clench for him even more.

Then, he thrust his cock right up in me so fast my thoughts

and emotions scrambled everywhere immediately. I gasped, "Oh my G—"

"Your husband, Everly. No one else." He cut me off, wrapping his arm around me and pulling me even closer to his bare muscular chest. With only a bit of sunlight peeking into the room, the birds chirping outside, and his rock-hard body against me, I was lost in our own moment. His hand slid up to my breast where he rolled the nipple between his fingers. "I'm starting to understand why people get married. I should get to go to bed fucking you and wake up with you riding my cock every damn day, Drop."

His words made me dizzy with need and lust. I wanted him that much more as my sex clenched when he thrust his length in me again, hitting every wall of my insides. "I'm so close, Declan," I moaned out his name and he trailed his fingers down to roll them over my clit.

He pinched it hard and then moved it back and forth. My whole body moved with it, his cock impaling me again and I screamed, the pleasure so intense I couldn't keep myself quiet if I tried.

"That's it, pretty girl. My wife doesn't like a damn thing in the morning except her husband's cock. She'll wake up for that," he said against my neck as he let me ride out the aftershocks of my orgasm.

I arched against him, wanting him to feel just as good as me, wanting him to feel the same release I'd just felt. Every time I was with him, I felt more and more bold, like he'd keep me safe even while I put myself at his mercy. Looking over my shoulder, I caught his gaze and blurted out exactly what I was fantasizing about. "Let me take your cock in my mouth."

His pupils dilated, the green becoming more vivid, as his

grip on my hips tightened. His hips bucked so that he buried his length even deeper as he groaned out a fuck. Then, he pulled out of me, shaking his head. "Not today, baby. Today, I'm making you love waking up early in the morning."

With that, he dragged a finger over my slit and I shivered, my body ultra sensitive to his touch at this point. "Declan, I enjoyed waking up already. I want you to enjoy it now too."

"You think I don't enjoy playing with this pussy?" He smirked and then he turned me onto my stomach, lifted my hips and slid a pillow under them. "Hold the headboard baby."

When I glanced at it, I saw the dark sleek posts were solid wood. Then I looked back at him. "Why?"

He positioned himself between my legs. "Baby, you need something to hold onto when you ride my face."

I bit my lip at his words but saw how the tip of his dick now had precum there, how it jumped at his words too like he wanted this as bad as I did. So, I did as I was told.

And right when my hands wrapped around those posts, he yanked my hips back, so my arms were stretched, my back was straight, and my ass and pussy were on display just for him.

"Such a pretty, pretty good girl. Look at that pink pussy, dripping just for me."

I whimpered when his hand slid up the back of my thigh slowly, like he wanted to explore every inch of me before he got to my sex. He massaged my upper thighs and then worked his way up to my ass, squeezing both cheeks and rolling them in his hands. "Declan, please."

"Shhh, baby. Let me take care of you." He said it like he knew what was best for me and I started to wonder if he did as he finally dragged his tongue over my clit and then my cunt, slow and deliberate, just one time before he pulled back and blew on it. It was a sensation I'd never felt before.

I gasped at the cold air hitting my wet sex, my whole body quivering with need.

He hummed. "Yes, look at that. That pussy's dripping for me now, baby."

After that, I heard him growl and suddenly his tongue thrust into my folds, lapping at me ravenously. Holding onto that headboard became necessary as I rolled my hips into his face, my body unhinged with need for another orgasm from him. His hands continued to massage my ass and just when I thought I couldn't take more pleasure, he slid his thumb to my puckered hole and pushed in. I was filled with his tongue in my pussy, his thumb in my ass, and thoughts of him as more than just a contractual husband as I screamed out again, the white-hot pleasure coursing through my veins.

He let me ride out the aftershocks, lapping leisurely at my arousal as he praised me here and there with, "Such a good girl, holding onto that headboard the whole time. I love the way my wife screams my name."

I shouldn't have enjoyed him calling me his wife, but I also shouldn't have had him between my legs. And even still, when he hummed into my pussy and kept licking it like he wanted to work me up again, I shivered in pure animalistic need. Although I was exhausted from hitting my high, I craved his length inside me. "Declan, please. Enough. I just want you now. Please."

I felt his lips smile against my sex as he murmured, "Don't let go of that headboard, baby. I told you I was going to make you beg me to stop."

I started to sit up but he pressed a hand to my lower back, holding me down and then he slid two fingers into me quick, curling them into my g-spot and pumping them up and down fast on it. Every part of me was so sensitive at this point that I cried out immediately and started riding his hand fast, my body chasing its own pleasure now.

"Please, please, please," I said over and over, not sure if I was begging him to continue or to stop and fuck me.

"You begging me to stop already, Everly?" He slowed his pacing like he loved hearing me beg, like he was taunting me to beg him more. "I'm just warming you up, baby, getting you ready for my cock."

He said it as he dragged one hand to my thigh and spread them farther apart as his fingers pumped inside me. I couldn't help bouncing my hips and ass up and down to get my orgasm even as I chanted please the whole time, giving him exactly what he wanted.

He got me to unravel again and it felt like every worry at that point melted away too. I was floating in a cloud of bliss where I couldn't be concerned about how our relationship was becoming messier and messier. Even when I felt him shift behind me and felt the cool metal of his cock piercing at my entrance, I didn't worry one bit that I practically wanted to cry out in ecstasy at feeling my arranged husband's length there. I just moaned, "Declan..."

He chuckled. "Ready to see how deep your pussy can take my cock?"

"Yes." I didn't even hesitate. "Fuck me, Declan. I want it rough," I told him, because I was lost to him at this point, and I wanted every part of him, wanted him to be lost and want me too.

We didn't know what was to come, but I knew I wanted to leave this memory and mark on him now.

"I tell you how rough we're playing, Everly. Not the other

way around," he ground out as he nudged just the tip of his cock into my pussy.

"Do you though? Fuck me rough, Declan. Or can my husband not do that?" It was me using the title now, me taunting him with it.

His hands were already at my hips as he lost it, roaring out as he thrust in me so hard the headboard banged against the wall. He entered me so deep that I saw stars in another galaxy. White blazing stars that exploded in and around me all at the same time as he thrust in over and over again with a bruising grip. We both screamed as we hit our last peak, and then Declan slumped over me, breathing rapidly with his eyes closed.

"Fuck. This bedroom is never going to be the same," he murmured as he rolled to the side of me. "Never, ever going to be the same."

I couldn't help but smile at that. I wanted this memory, would bottle it up for the future.

He pulled me close and kissed my neck before getting up. "What do you want for breakfast?"

His casual question, the way he smiled down at me, shattered the moment, reminding me of the day before and of how none of this actually worked. Knots tightened in my stomach. "We should probably iron out how the public is going to take our news for the next—"

My phone went off on the nightstand, and I saw that Declan had also left a glass of water for me along with my stack of folded clothing.

I mouthed a thank you as I grabbed my cell and stared at the number.

She never called. She didn't want to communicate.

"Hello?" My voice trembled as I answered.

Declan tilted his head in question and mouthed, Who is that?

I waved him off and grabbed the stack of clothing to pull on. Yet, he yanked it out of my hands suddenly as if he had a second thought and walked back to his closet to throw them in there completely buck naked.

"I'm only calling because of the article. It says you're married, Evie," Tonya murmured, her raspy voice accusing over the phone. She had lived down the street from me growing up and had taken probably every yoga class my mom would allow her to, along with learning dance on the side with me after she'd found out I was homeschooled.

She'd been my best friend and my shadow for as long as I could remember until that night.

Now, she only called when big news came to her doorstep about me, figuratively and this time literally.

"It's just a marriage of convenience," I explained as Declan stared at me, leaning against the closet doorframe, every inch of him on display for me to see as he crossed his arms.

"Right. But it has pictures of movers, of him ushering you past paparazzi. Of you both driving to the gym together."

"To be fair, I work at the gym, Tonya. It's just us going to work at the same time."

Declan mouthed her name back to me, and I waved him away. He pursed his lips but seemed to figure out I needed space as he pushed off the doorframe and walked out of the room. "Carl wanted us married but it isn't real."

Even saying those words now felt wrong because I couldn't see what was real or fake anymore between Declan and me.

"But why?" she whispered. It was something no one had really asked me, like they all thought they knew why I was doing it. Declan Hardy was the most eligible bachelor after all. I'd snagged him.

The press yesterday suggested it was for the will, but Declan and Carl's lawyers had done a good enough job hiding the private information. Still, speculation had fallen largely on me wanting shares of the company and Declan holding on to those shares.

"It doesn't matter." My heart hurt telling her that because it did. It mattered that she'd asked. It mattered that she knew in her soul that I wouldn't just sign over my life for one of luxury.

It mattered.

"It won't take them long to figure out about us, Evie. Does everyone know why you're there?"

I sighed and picked at the soft down comforter that practically could swallow me whole with how plush it was. "Carl did. Now, nobody does."

"Evie, I'm sorry about you losing your father." She hesitated over her apology. Once upon a time, she would have been there. She would have held my hand and cried through it with me, felt my pain, shared it, would have tried to take it away. Now, she skirted around it. "I know you tried to escape by leaving here, but—"

"I get it. I can't escape it anywhere I go. I know that. Yet, my father didn't want anyone to know. I think it was his way of giving me a fresh start."

"And now he's gone, leaving stipulations in his will so you don't have a fresh start?" she questioned, prying for the information I promised Declan I wouldn't share.

"It's just a year, Ton."

She sighed. "You shouldn't have done this. You shouldn't even have moved. You did it for me. I know you did."

"That's not true. I—"

"You would have never left your mom's studio, Evie." She cut me off. "You loved teaching there. And you never cared what they said about you. This town has always been a shit show."

I pinched the bridge of my nose and felt the headache coming on now. "It doesn't matter."

"It does!" she screamed into the phone, and then she breathed in deep. "I'm fine. Just stop whatever you're doing and come home. I don't care if I see you here anymore, but you can't just be there, unhappy, because you think the town will forgive me without you here. I'll be okay."

"Will you be though?" I asked because my friend hadn't looked at me for a year. She'd actively avoided me, and then I avoided her when the press went after either of us.

"I'm getting better," she admitted quietly. "It's a lot, but I'm getting better."

"Mom said you stopped by. I called, but you didn't answer."

I heard the sniffle in her voice. "Right." She cleared her throat. These silences. I used to love them between us. The space between always felt so comfortable. Now, though, it was pained, full of guilt, remorse, and distress. "He's going to get out soon. Have you considered calling him?"

"No." I dropped the word with hate, with loathing, with frustration. "I told you I won't."

"You should. You can't let him take that too. If you call him and work everything out, it will be better. What if he's still mad at you when he's released? Andy already took so much from you."

"Like our friendship?"

She waited. More silence. "Yes." She sighed. "If that guy means anything to you, you need to tell him our secret. Because it's not about to be a secret anymore."

She hung up without a goodbye.

And not two minutes later, Declan was standing at his bedroom door, his blue jersey in hand. But it dropped to the floor as he read what was on his phone. My HEAT watch beeped from the nightstand, and I didn't have to glance at it to know what he was reading.

The press had done their job.

The look on his face said it all.

"Is this true?" He held up his phone. My face was all over it.

And the headline read, "Everly Belafonte: One Scam After Another."

CHAPTER 26: EVERLY

"I'm not sure what the article says, Declan." I tried to keep my voice steady and hold back the tremor in it. "So, I can't say. I haven't read it yet."

He stormed across the room as I started to type in the headline, ready to read it myself, but he snatched the phone from my hands.

"No." His voice echoed through the room, so powerful in his anger I knew he felt blindsided and furious. Then, he strode away to put our phones down on a dresser and turned back to me. The fury ricocheted off the walls around us. "You tell me what happened. Who is Andrew Baldeck?"

My ex's name in his mouth sounded wrong, vile. So revolting my stomach churned. "He's a man from my past. We're not talking about—"

"Everly, the rules have changed. The past is now in the fucking present. Let's be honest. It always has been."

"I... I don't know what the newspaper wrote, but I can guess they painted me as a liar, as someone who made up a story because I was a jilted lover."

"Is. It. True?" he asked again, and my heart cracked because I didn't know what he meant.

"Me being a jilted lover?" I looked up at him and felt my throat closing as tears filled my eyes. My emotions were finally bubbling out after I'd held them in for so long. "Or the part where they say my account of being cuffed to a bed by my ex who assaulted my best friend and then me is a lie?"

Declan didn't wince. The fire in his eyes though, it licked through the room at my words. "You know what part I'm asking about. Is. It. True?"

"The sad part is, Declan, I really don't know." I wanted to disappear, wanted to not even ask, but everyone who I'd thought would stand by me, who were supposed to be my friends, turned their backs on me. I'd put on a show for so long, I just swallowed down the hurt and the pain again as I gulped and said softly, "The story was twisted so much over the last year that I really don't know. I can say, the only part of these stories that are normally true about me are the ones they say are false. I don't know what they wrote today, but it doesn't matter. I got as much justice as the system allowed me to get, and the rest is whatever you want to believe for whatever suits your reputation and narrative now. You're more of a public figure than I am. So, if the news is tainting your name, I can make a statement—"

"Stop." He shook his head, closing his eyes and pinching the bridge of his nose. "Just fucking stop."

He grabbed the phone, taking a deep breath and walked over to me with purpose. Leaning behind me to grab the comforter on either side of me, he folded it around me, wrapped me into a cocoon of sheets and pulled me into his lap, curling around me like he could encase me and protect me with his own body. Then he held the phone in front of me. "You're going to see it, but I only want you looking once. Then, I'm having Piper go after every tabloid she can."

"Declan, we don't have to—"

"I'm taking care of you now, Everly," he said with a controlled tone. "Please just listen."

I took a deep breath and read.

"Everly Belafonte: One Scam After Another"

The mastermind strikes again. Everly Belafonte was a graduate student at Edgewood University more than a year ago when she claimed she was assaulted. According to her statement:

"Andrew Baldeck invited my friend and me to a frat party at Beta Zeta Delta. We had three mixed drinks each before he invited us upstairs. We walked into his bedroom and he locked the door. He was my boyfriend, so I trusted that he wasn't doing anything cruel, but when he opened his nightstand to pull out a gun, he wasn't the man I trusted anymore.

He told us to take off our clothes. I kept telling him to think about what he was doing, but he grabbed handcuffs from the drawer too and directed me to put my wrists next to the bedpost. When I hesitated, he pointed at my friend, who was crying. He then grabbed her by the hair and threw her onto the ground. He assaulted her and threatened to do more to her if I didn't cooperate. I promised I would and begged him to let her go. He unlocked the door and told her to be quiet. I told him I didn't want to do more, yet he assaulted me against the bedpost for what seemed an eternity. I was compliant until he stopped, and then I asked him to uncuff me. I told him I was enjoying it, so he did. I fought him for the gun as soon as I was free and called 911 once it was in my possession."

Belafonte's story is just that: a story, according to sources who have claimed Belafonte's friend, who was later name as Tonya Lakeland, doesn't talk to her anymore and that no one at the frat party would corroborate her story. Andrew Baldeck was a D1 football player, straight-A student, and has no record. He claims she "wanted the fame and was mad I'd kissed her friend once. So she twisted this story. Her friend knows it too. We still talk, actually. We were all just having a good time that night."

Baldeck has a parole hearing set for next month after spending over a year in prison for assault and attempted rape—a crime he claims he didn't commit. Beta Zeta Delta refused to comment. According to sources, no investigation of the fraternity house was done.

When asked about Belafonte now, after being told she has just married NFL star Declan Hardy, he laughed. "Of course. It was probably all a big plan so she could cry to her estranged father and get this laid out for her instead. Seems about right."

Is Everly Belafonte scamming us all?

"They're making you look like a fool," I said, and one tear slipped from my eyes. One tear. That's all it took for a mask to drop and for everyone to see you were leading with your emotions. I swiped it away. "Oh God, I do not want to cry over this now. I'm sorry—"

"Sorry?" he whispered. Then he bellowed, "Sorry? What the hell do you have to be sorry about?"

He literally wouldn't let me go as I wiggled in his lap. Instead, he turned me towards him. "Declan, I need to approach this without succumbing to—"

"They twisted your pain into making it seem like you're

some kind of a damn con artist, Everly. You want to cry over it? You're entitled to that," he ground out. His face turned red, so red I nearly reached up to soothe him before stopping myself by snatching my hand back.

"How do you know what they're saying isn't true?" I whispered.

"Are you fucking with me, Drop?" He took my face in both hands as he stared into my eyes, brushing his thumbs over my eyelashes.

"Honestly, I think there are days where even my best friend isn't sure she can believe me, and she was there. The press does a great job of—"

"Messing up the truth. But you had Carl. Why didn't he...?" Declan narrowed his eyes at me.

"Carl didn't know at first. We'd covered it up well with not releasing my name immediately. It's what my lawyers and I thought was best. But over time, most of the town found out. Andy was expelled from school, listed as a sexual offender, and has served a year in prison. Unfortunately, no other women would come forward. There were more. Past girlfriends, dates. They called, sure, and thanked me for being brave." I shrugged. The justice system was broken. There was no evidence for those women. And the evidence there was at one point had probably been destroyed. They didn't keep rape kits that long back then. It'd taken years to implement procedures that helped survivors like us, and even still, societal norms were stacked against us. "But my evidence wasn't great. He was my boyfriend. I went to his frat house willingly."

"What about your friend?"

"She didn't want to testify either." I sighed. "Tonya gets wrapped up in wanting to be a part of the group. She'd kissed him before, behind my back. It was the perfect twist on the story. I was angry, I made up a story, the end."

"Is it true she still talks to him?" he asked softly as his hand rubbed up and down my arm as if he wanted to soothe me. "Was that her on the phone earlier?"

I winced because having my friend talk to Andy was the hardest part some days. "It's complicated. Andy's charming, and his family has money and a reputation. Most of us didn't."

"But Carl could have gotten you a legal team or—"

"I wanted a father, not a payday, so no," I snapped, still irritated that the article was questioning my integrity. "I never asked for a lawyer nor would I have accepted one. We worked with what we had."

"So, what? They bought everyone off while you just endured their shit?"

"In all fairness, I'd been at a frat party drinking with my boyfriend, a straight-A student with no prior legal trouble. Even with my father's backing, I would have had to fight, and it would have tainted the Milton-Hardy legacy in addition to everything else it destroyed of mine. I was a homeschooled loner people didn't trust. My lawyers recommended that I drop the case or take a settlement. Still, I couldn't. So, now I've been branded a liar and jilted lover in the town I call home."

And I should have rejoiced according to my lawyers. We won. Or so they say. I still had to deal with the trauma of that night.

"Everly... How did I not know this?" He swore, and the pain in his voice brought tears to my eyes.

"Because I didn't want anyone to know! My father agreed." I shook my head and looked away from the pity in his eyes. "Do you know what it's like to have your body taken hostage and controlled by someone you thought would never hurt you? To give that trust and then they proceed to do their worst with it?"

"Everly—"

I didn't want his pity or his consoling words. I just wanted to get it out. "I died that night, okay? You asked me once how I knew about experiencing death... That's how. Who I was, who I wanted to be, she died. He stole that from me. I contemplated murder, Declan. Once I got out of those cuffs, I fought him for that gun, held it to his head, and shook while convincing myself not to pull the trigger for minutes. Whole minutes I considered killing someone when mere minutes before that, I'd hoped I would die myself." I quaked with sobs then, and Declan let me break down. Let me get it out. Let me crumble. "He cried as I held the gun to his head, saying he was sorry, that he was drunk, that he was so wasted he wouldn't remember in the morning. But I was drunk too, Declan, and I remember *every single detail.*"

His gaze was locked on me. "I want his full name and address," he ground out loudly, but the volume of his voice didn't scare me.

"Declan." I shook my head. "This has been over for a while now."

"He did all those things to you. He shouldn't go free. He should be dead."

He searched my eyes for how I felt, but I wouldn't hide it. Most days, I wished I'd pulled the trigger after hearing what he did to the others, after they called and cried to me like it could absolve them of the burden and trauma he left them with.

"Everly, fuck." He paused like he didn't know how to say the next words. "I was rough with you last night. I've been rough with you."

"I wanted that from you." I poked him in the chest. "I get to want what I want, Declan. Why can't I, huh? You read the article. The media got what they wanted. Andy got what he wanted from me too. But do I get what I want ever? To move on?"

He petted my hair, trying to take away my pain, but no one could do that except for me.

I sighed and shifted in his lap to look out the window instead of in the eyes of a man I was falling for when I shouldn't be.

"The media never covers the aftermath of a victim." I pushed the blankets off and went to grab the jersey he'd dropped. He let me go, knowing this was important for me. I put my hands on my hips, jersey hanging down my thighs, and faced him. "I'll be honest. Yes, he took control of my body for a few minutes. That's it. Was it the longest couple of minutes of my life? Probably. Have I struggled with my sex life since? Sure. Will I always? I don't know. Either way, I learned that night that I could fight back. That I wanted to fight. That I wanted to survive."

"It's why you insisted on the self-defense classes," Declan said, like he was putting it all together.

"Sure. Among other things. Andy had hit me before that. Self-defense is a gentle reminder that I shouldn't allow that without fighting back. I did for so long. And I jog to work even though there may be a risk of assault, but I've equipped myself. I wear what I want even if I have to plan ahead to quell my anxiety of doing so. I don't think it's fair that I should live with a burden he created."

"Jesus Christ. I..." He pulled at his hair. "I've manhandled the shit out of you more than once, Everly." Regret he shouldn't feel was something I knew I had to blame on my ex, another wrench thrown in for survivors of abuse that their lovers had to endure too.

"And so...what? I have to take a gentle lover now because I'm some victim when that's not what I want? Not only can I not act out, but I should be careful where I go now, be aware of who I love, stay cautious and have every one of those responsibilities put on me? I have to consider it all every day, and I don't want to. I don't freaking want to." I repeated it pointedly, furiously.

I hated that when I glared at him in front of me, his eyes were glassy too. Declan, the man who acted on every emotion was now holding his back from me too.

I dug my nails into my palms, ready to let him know this last thing and then package this up in a box to bury far, far away as a memory I didn't want. "You know, my lawyers said the best way for a 'mixed woman' to fight the media is to stay calm. That I'd done a good job not hurting him when I had the power to. I was praised for not taking his life and having a level head even though he'd taken everything I was from me." I dragged in a shaky breath. "I've made sure to always have a level head now with cameras on me. You'll be able to count on that for the remainder of this marriage, at least. If I cried back then, it would have made me look crazier. If I screamed or got mad, it would have been over. My mom did. She grabbed a cameraman one time to protect her only daughter. You know what they did? Labeled her as trash."

Just that one day had created so much turmoil for us both. I remember how she'd cried, how her braids slid over her shoulders as she hung her head, and I vowed then to never let the media get to her again.

Calm. Silent. Void of emotion. My demeanor was a weapon

in that courthouse that I used effectively.

"You deserve more justice than what you've been given." I saw how the veins on his neck protruded, how his jaw worked, how his knee jumped in fast fury.

"It doesn't matter. I'm trying to live my life the way I want and feel what I want. I won't live in fear or be ashamed of my desire for another person because of what he did to me."

His jaw worked up and down. Up and down. When someone cares for you, your pain is their pain. He was mulling through what I knew most people in my life had to work through, and it wasn't easy. Tonya couldn't even do it.

"I'm still me, Declan," I whispered, not sure he understood that I wasn't ruined, that I wasn't tainted by all this, that I'd survived in the best way I knew how.

"But, baby, you're so much more. Don't you get it? You're the drive to keep going when someone took everything from you. You're the will to survive when most of us would have given up by now. You're all the raindrops in a tsunami of courage and strength." He got up and came to me, lifted his hand to my cheek, but before I could get comfort from his touch, he fisted it and pulled it away.

There it was. That past catching up with me and molding the people around me again. The past followed me everywhere. It shaped the present and the future. A past I couldn't escape no matter how hard I tried.

CHAPTER 27: DECLAN

She'd survived assault, and no one had delivered justice.

The court system had failed her. Like it had failed so many. Her father had failed her too. It all made sense now. Carl tying me to her, knowing how the media would resurface that information. It was clear he expected me to take care of it.

I took her to the guesthouse that same day and tried my best not to touch her until I got my emotions in check. I wanted to rage—red, violent, catastrophic rage. She didn't need that from me. But I was going to. I didn't give a fuck what she said. She operated logically and without emotion because the world hadn't allowed her to feel her damn heart.

I knew I was the opposite. I acted on my first instinct, and I would here too.

Not for Carl, but for her.

That night, I called company after company to make sure those stories were taken down. And I called Piper to tell her to get to fucking work. "Maybe it's best we let the stories ride out and not try to save her image if she's concerned—"

"You let these stories surface, I fire your whole PR firm, Piper. Get rid of them."

Everly didn't come over to eat, although I'd invited her, but the lights at her place burned bright while I swam lap after lap in the pool outside. Way past ten, her light was still on. I knew because I stayed up until three watching it.

I dozed off but woke up at five to get back to it.

"Declan, it's five thirty in the morning," my sister snipped when she answered.

"I need to talk to Cade."

She muttered out, "Of course you do. Just don't do anything stupid." Izzy, the freaking wild child of the family, was warning me.

"Give the phone to your husband," I said and she knew I meant it because a second later Cade grumbled in the background.

"I want all the information on him and his family," I spit into the phone.

"I don't think me giving you that information is very legal," Cade drawled on the other line.

"I don't give a fuck."

"Oh, so now when you want something done it's fine if it's not legal? What happened to me not being good enough for your sister because of my background?"

"I swear to fucking Christ, Cade. You met her. It's for her."

"I've met a lot of people," he deadpanned. "There're a lot of women in the world—"

"There's only one woman you're going to have to see around the family for the rest of your life attached to me and that's my *wife*," I bellowed, losing my patience. Quite frankly, I think I'd lost my mind. "You want to cross me? It will mean you dealing with me and my sister. Izzy will—"

"The information's in your email, fucker. Stop acting like I wouldn't get it for you. You're part of the family now."

"I'm not a part of your family, Cade—"

"Oh, you are. You'll see."

My brother-in-law hung up the phone on me, and I didn't bother picking apart what he had to say. My focus was on her.

Everly Belafonte. The woman who'd stood up for what was right and been torn apart for it.

My phone beeped as I scrolled the email he'd sent.

> **Izzy:** Declan truly is being the reckless child now. Make sure all you Hardy men are watching him. He even called Cade.

> **Me:** Fuck off, Izzy.

> **Dimitri:** Too early for sibling chat. But I will say, Dec, the press is doing her dirty because she married you. You'd better handle that shit.

> **Dom:** Honestly, I got my own problems, but if Declan can't handle it, I definitely will. Everly's my girl.

> **Me:** She's not your girl. She's my fucking wife. I'm handling it.

I grumbled to myself as I stared at the sunrise outside. I had let all of the day pass without calling or texting her or barging back into her place. Now, it was breakfast time. And the clock ticked.

6 a.m.

7 a.m.

8 a.m.

I still hadn't eaten, but I made scrambled eggs and biscuits and cut up damn strawberries, like I was ready for us to have a gourmet meal.

> **Me: Are you coming to breakfast?**

> **Everly: I don't particularly enjoy breakfast, as you know.**

> **Me: You didn't come to dinner either.**

> **Everly: I wasn't sure you wanted me there after everything we discussed. So, I decided against it.**

> **Me: You decided against what I specifically told you we were doing every day?**

> **Everly: Declan, the media is going to drag your name through the mud because of my past. Let's just get through the rest of this year. Sharing a meal every day isn't necessary. I'm going back to bed.**

I stomped over there, unlocked her door, and went to her bedroom.

"Are you kidding me, Declan?" she groaned when I opened the curtains and ripped the comforter off the bed. I had to smile when I saw she was still in my jersey.

Then I threw her over my shoulder.

"Oh my God. Absolutely not." She pounded my back. "What happened to you feeling bad about manhandling me?"

I'd feel some way about that for the rest of my life, but I

couldn't focus on that now. "I'm still me and you're still you. What kind of man would I be if I let another man dictate the relationship I have with my wife?"

I felt her body shaking and realized she was laughing at me as I made my way out of the guesthouse and up the stone driveway. "You can't let anyone rule your world, can you?"

"Why should I when I built it? Now, you're not following the rules. We had a breakfast and dinner plan for the rest of the marriage, and you went against your commitment."

She huffed and stopped fighting as I stomped back into my place. I set her down at the white granite countertop and placed the food in front of her.

"Did you make this?" She lifted an eyebrow.

"What? Is it not good enough?" I spun around and grabbed bacon out of the fridge. "We should have protein too."

She narrowed her eyes, bluer than the blue of my jersey, and then stood. "I can help."

"Stay on that side of the island or I'll be eating you for breakfast instead."

She sat back down with a huff but a small smile played on her lips.

"Good girl." I winked at her and started cooking.

"Stipulations are a week away, Declan. And the press is—"

"Handled. Let's enjoy breakfast and the day, huh?"

She didn't argue. Maybe we were both tired of the bullshit. Maybe we were escaping into the bubble that was our gated home. It didn't matter because I had her there, weaving calm into the flurry of emotions in my head.

"You actually are a decent cook," she said as she crunched into a piece of crispy bacon I set on her plate. "And you make sure the bacon isn't floppy."

"Are you surprised?" I questioned. "My mom is a good cook. She stayed home because nobody was going to give her a job as an immigrant with an accent where I grew up, so she perfected what she did there."

"I read they both immigrated here. You're a rags-to-riches story," she admitted, and I lifted my brow because Everly never went online. It was one thing I respected about her. "Yes, I finally looked you up."

"And what did you find?"

"You're about as big as your ego, which is massive. You've got the world in a choke hold with everything you do. The HEAT brand does well because of you. I stopped reading when they went into your NFL stats and history."

I rolled my eyes because she never wanted to know a damn thing about the sport. "You going to watch some of the preseason games with me? They're starting up next week."

She chuckled. "Nope." Then she studied me. "You know, it's a bit scary how you can touch something and it's like Oprah endorsing it. Have you thought about that? I guess you look the part and act it though, so it makes sense."

"What's that supposed to mean?"

"You look like the all-American boy, and you probably acted all macho in the NFL. People like that sort of thing." She waved me off like everyone in the world loving me was ridiculous.

"What the fuck?" I ground out, annoyed she wasn't more in awe of me like most of the women before her. And yet, I went to sit down next to her, trying to get as close as possible. "I worked hard to get where I am."

"You also have a pretty face with a lot of muscles, dark hair, light eyes, good bone structure. People trust men like you. The media eats that up."

"So, you're saying I got to where I am based solely on my looks. All the touchdowns, workouts, training, schmoozing, and the amount of asses I had to kiss did nothing for me?" I heard myself getting irritated. "I worked fucking hard to get here."

"No doubt. But even if I had worked that hard, I probably wouldn't be where you are."

"I—" Thinking about it, I snapped my mouth shut. "Fair."

"Did you retire just because of your wrist?" she murmured as I wiggled it a bit before taking another bite of my food.

"Not really." I shook my head. "Maybe more because of the press behind it. And my sister had a kid. My family's always been important to me, and I just..." I shrugged as I stared at her. "Do you want kids?"

"Kids?" Her blue eyes widened before she glanced down at her plate. "Sure. I guess. Probably one day. But, like, a lot. Not just one."

I choked on my food. "Why a lot?"

"You have sisters and brothers! I didn't." She shoved my arm like she didn't want me making fun of her. "Was it a lot growing up with all six of you in one home?"

"Hell yes. Especially when I wanted the bathroom over the twins. My sisters are fucking brats." I chuckled. "No, they really aren't. They all have their demons. You've seen how Dom walks around. His ass is the oldest, and it's like he's got the weight of the world on his shoulders. My mom and dad put pressure on him to make sure we all were okay. Izzy and Lilah are married off to— Well, you know...but they love my sisters, so I can't say much."

"Cade would die for Izzy," she said longingly. "I want a

husband like that with a bunch of babies."

"But you like the quiet."

"I do. But I like noise when it's comforting. It's as good as silence when it's the sound of loved ones buzzing around your home."

I silently vowed to take her to my family's Christmas party. She'd absolutely love that chaotic shit. For the time being though, I announced we'd be watching Home Alone instead.

"Don't you have to work or something? Do some investing or shareholder stuff today?"

"Nope. We're relaxing before they throw some other story at us."

She stared at me. Assessing, maybe questioning, I didn't know. Her eyes pried at my soul though, and when she found whatever she was looking for, her smile was brilliant. "I'm going to go get my string to make you a bracelet while we watch."

She ran out of the house and returned minutes later with a little box. In it were strings of all sorts of colors and little tiny seashells. She plopped down on the floor instead of the couch while I searched for *Home Alone* on a streaming service. "Where'd you get those shells?" I asked her.

"I pick them up sometimes on the beach," she said. Of course she did that, looking at all the small things of beauty none of us saw anymore. It made me want to spend all day and all night with her just so I could soak in how good of a person she was.

So, that's what I decided to do all afternoon and all night. We watched a whole damn marathon of those movies while she showed me how to make bracelets, demonstrating the knots over and over again. She made me an all-black one with one of those shells threaded in and tied it to my wrist with such pride,

I knew I'd probably never take the stupid thing off.

At one point, I touched the necklace around her neck. "Who's that one for?"

"Tonya and I have these. She doesn't wear hers anymore." She glanced away. "The red one on my right wrist is for my mom. The others I sort of make for whatever mood I'm in. Ours now match."

She touched her wrist to mine, two black ones that bound us to whatever we were at this point. Friends in a marriage. Or maybe it was one friend and another friend who wanted something more.

I crawled over to her and took my time kissing her, exploring her mouth in a gentler way than I ever had. The air shifted between us, the silence she loved so much becoming loud with my desire for her, my draw to her, my need for her. She let my hand inch up her delectable tan thighs, pushing the fabric of my jersey up until I saw her wet lace panties underneath, covering her sex. When my phone rang, though, she swatted my hand away and told me to get it. "It's Piper. We need to know what's going on."

I needed to turn off the feature that fucking announced who was calling. I rearranged myself and swiped my cell off the table. When I answered, Piper purred into the phone that she'd taken care of everything. It was good news, she'd done her job, and I was thankful for it. I sat down on the couch and let her rattle off the list of magazines.

"Only one is giving us a hard time." She sighed into the phone.

I glanced at Everly and shook my head at her when she started to get up. I wanted her on that fucking floor and this call was ruining it. "Which publication? Actually, it doesn't matter.

Just pay them."

"It's going to be six figures to get rid of it. It's probably best we discuss it over dinner?" She was trying to get me to come out.

"Dinner?" I questioned back. I wasn't processing what she was saying as Everly stood but at my question, my little raindrop spun around, her caramel brown highlights fanning around with her fast turn. "Tonight?"

"Yes. It will look good the press seeing you out and about, Declan. Should I invite Anastasia too?"

Everly had walked back over to me, a look I couldn't quite decipher in her eyes. She kneeled down in front of me, and all of a sudden, her small hands were on my thighs as she held my gaze. I pulled the phone away and said low in warning, "Everly, what are you doing?"

Doe eyes. She did them right. Full of innocence and longing and naivete when she brushed her hand over my bulge. "Just finishing up what I started with my husband so he can go to dinner."

"Declan, you there?" Piper said as Everly unbuttoned my pants and pulled them down, my jersey shifting mesmerizingly over her chest as she did. Then she wrapped her fingers around my cock, and I had to bite my damn fist to not moan into the phone.

"I don't know if I'll be able to make dinner, Piper," I choked out as she stroked me up and down, up and down with a soft but firm grip. When she lowered her head to drag her tongue over my pierced tip, I felt like I was going to explode before we even got started.

"Oh, why? Anastasia was really looking forward to it."

"I don't know why Anastasia would be looking forward to

it. I didn't say I was going," I ground out through clenched teeth right as Everly wrapped her soft full lips around my cock and hollowed out her cheeks.

"She misses us having you all to ourselves, Declan. I mean, do you have plans with Everly?"

Her tongue swirled around as I tried to listen, as I tried to formulate any sort of thought other than that I wanted to fuck this woman for the rest of eternity. "I do have plans. With my wife. For the foreseeable future. So, don't make another plan for me."

I hung up on her and growled loud as I pulled Everly from my cock and shoved her down onto the ground where I could hover over her. "I should fuck your mouth more often. Seems you like taking me there with someone listening."

"Are you going to dinner?" she asked, a frown on her face.

"Jesus, baby, I'm not going anywhere." I looped a finger into her panties.

"Maybe you should," she murmured. Her voice dipped low though and I knew she didn't mean it. There was no way either of us were going anywhere after I'd felt those soft lips wrapped around my erection.

"Maybe. Or maybe I should give you what you really want." I pulled the lace to the side so I could brush my hand over her. "Spread your legs like a good girl, baby."

My wife, the one who normally would have thought this through, didn't hesitate. Her thighs opened for me to see her pussy glistening.

"Wet as always, Ms. Everly Belafonte. You think if your cunt could choose it would be Mrs. Everly *Hardy* instead? It's ready for me every time." Just saying her name with my last attached to it had my cock hardening.

"I think that would be ridiculous considering our plan."

"What plan exactly?" I whispered in her ear before I slid my finger into her.

She wanted to answer, I saw her open her mouth, but I sucked her bottom lip between mine and worked her clit agonizingly slow, so slow she forgot to say anything but *please*.

Over and over again.

"You want your husband to fuck you?" I asked.

She nodded fast.

I worked her up further. "Say you want your husband's cock, Everly. Only mine."

Her sapphire eyes caught my stare. "Declan..." she whimpered.

"Say what you want."

"Fine. I want my husband's cock. God, please."

I was no better than all the men who saw her and wanted her for themselves. Everyone at my gym—Wes, Gianni, all of them. She was a fucking phenom of a woman that I wanted to consume for the rest of my lifetime.

I drove home into her. At this point, her sex was where my dick belonged. Rolling my hips so the friction would arouse her clit, I asked, "How does it feel to be full of me, Everly?"

She clawed at my back, wanting more, wanting it faster, probably wanting what we had before. "Hurry," she pleaded.

"Raindrop, I'm taking my time. Nice and slow." I pulled my length from her inch by inch, letting us both feel every part of each other and then I pushed back in with agonizing control. "We've got all the time in the world. Nice and slow."

She whimpered.

I repeated it over and over until I took not one but two orgasms from her.

I repeated it as I hit my own high.
I repeated it, knowing it wasn't true.

CHAPTER 28: EVERLY

The whole next week, Declan was careful, gentle, loving.

We went to work like nothing was wrong, like the news of my life hadn't dropped around the nation. The paparazzi were handled. Piper wasn't just good at her job. She was the best.

It should have been perfect.

Yet, it wasn't. Declan tiptoed around me, made me meals, catered to me without commanding me, without feasting on me, without doing what he'd always done.

Every night after dinner, he kissed my forehead as I announced I was going home. Then, he let me walk off. Sometimes, I saw him go back into his house, but a few times that week, he got in his car and drove away.

I'd watched for his headlights every night.

I didn't see them until much later, and my heart crumbled at the thought of him with other women, women who probably didn't come with the baggage I did.

I didn't ask. I didn't have the right to.

Maybe that last weekend had been our goodbye. Maybe that was all it took. I'd been zoned as a victim to him now. I felt caged by it, tortured by his kindness, my desires neglected by his soft touch.

We both were quiet on the way to the will reading. He typed away on his cell as his driver turned into the parking lot. But tension vibrated through us both. We hadn't had each other the way we wanted for weeks, and we'd already blurred the lines of the marriage more than once.

"Declan, I—"

He started too. "Everly, we—"

"You go." I waved a hand at him.

Glancing at my left hand, he grabbed it and held it in front of him. "You don't wear a ring to show we're married," he said more to himself than me.

"I don't think you'd want that when you go out; nor would I."

"Why not?"

"If a woman wants to indulge in a relationship with you—"

"They'd have to take my attention off you first, which is near impossible at this point," he growled then clenched his mouth shut, his jaw moving. Leaning to the side, he grabbed a small velvet box from his pocket, a deep red and with gold etching on it. He didn't take his eyes off me as he opened it. Beautiful large diamonds lined the gold wedding band. "I want you to wear this."

I opened my mouth to object, to respond negatively in some way, to tell him this wasn't right but he slid his hand to my jaw and placed a thumb on my lips to quiet me.

"Let me finish. I know you're not supposed to be my wife, but to the world, you're mine, and a man should think twice before fucking with what's mine for the next nine months."

"And what about you?" I countered.

He smiled and leaned close. "I'd like a ring made of that string like the one on my wrist. Black seems to be our color, right?" He tapped the bracelet I'd already made him. "I can give you ring measurements."

I bit my cheek as I tried not to feel his answer in my heart where it could settle and bloom into something like love.

Instead, I gave him a jerky nod as he slid the ring on.

"The stipulations might be crazy, and I've tried my best this past month to get more information, but Mrs. Johnson had it locked down."

"We can figure it out together." I shrugged but felt the anxiety of the reading building, felt my world starting to shift again, and felt my breath becoming shallow because of it.

When we exited the SUV, he rounded the vehicle, hooked his arm in mine, and grumbled, "You didn't wait for me to open your door."

Combing my hair back from the wind, I sighed. "I didn't think we were still doing that."

He stepped in front of me to open Mrs. Johnson's office door. "We're always doing that, Everly."

The elder woman straightened her knitted blazer as she cleared her throat when we walked in and she wiggled her beaded glasses at us as she told us to take a seat.

The other lawyers, dressed in all black huddled in that same corner as last time. She shuffled around a few papers and then dove right in. She didn't spare me five minutes or even a warning before she dropped the bomb on my life. "If you two wish to proceed in your marriage and thus the conditions of the will, at this juncture, it is required that you produce an heir." She sighed and dropped the air of formality as all the air seemed to be sucked from the room. "It's just one baby, and technically you'll be meeting the requirements of this condition as long as you're trying. Carl did tell me it's for the good of the empire and for your reputation, Everly. This should be easy peasy."

"Easy...peasy?" I wheezed with wide eyes.

"Yes, Carl made this the last condition. The terms require you to go see a doctor, send me your visit information, and updates when you start trying for a child. If you can't conceive after six months, IVF would be the next step for the remaining three months of marriage, and then everything is yours."

"If we don't agree?" Declan ground out and I saw how the blood had drained from his face like he'd seen a ghost, or maybe the ghost of the life we'd been living before this idiotic will.

"If you both don't agree, you may divorce after your sixth month of marriage, but it is expected that you try for a child with Ms. Anastasia Milton if you wish to retain majority shares, Declan. Everly, you have your choice of the Hardy brothers to conceive with if you wish to retain your mother's home and business. It's all here"—she held up the folder—"but quite complicated. Anastasia will only be made aware of this caveat under those specific circumstances and—"

She kept going and going and going like she hadn't just rattled off the fact that my father expected me to be a freaking baby factory *with my choice of Hardy brother.* I white-knuckled the chair, tried to take a breath, and bit my tongue until I tasted blood in order to maintain a poker face of some sort.

I turned to the only person here who would know how I was feeling, who would be on my team, who I trusted now. I fisted my hands and felt the ring he gave me on my finger. Declan was watching my every move, his forest-green eyes studying me. Cautiously. Warily. Almost like he'd agree, like he was willing to sign on the dotted line again without thinking this through.

"Declan," I whispered. "You can't honestly—"

"Oh, Everly. Now, it isn't a big deal." Mrs. Johnson reached across her desk and patted my fist with her perfect manicure. I pulled my hand away and folded them into my lap because if I didn't, I'd claw his and her eyes out for staring at me.

"Everly, we're already sleeping—"

"Just because I fucked you doesn't mean I want to have children with you." The words flew out of me fast and were meant to be vulgar, meant to be vicious and cutting. I wasn't thinking about who was listening or watching or judging me now. I wanted a war if he thought this was something we could just dive right into.

"Well..." Mrs. Johnson's eyes widened as if she'd suddenly realized this was deeper than a transactional deal. "Seems the marriage is very convenient, and we should give you two a moment to discuss."

"Mrs. Johnson, we can commit to visiting the doctor's office and go from there," Declan said, like I wasn't even present. Like he thought I was just fine with going with the flow.

I scoffed. "We won't be going to the doctor's office."

Mrs. Johnson slid papers across the table toward Declan instead of me. "Well, if you do agree, it's all here."

She left us staring at that sheet of paper. I didn't look at him. I couldn't. I got up instead and walked over to the side of Mrs. Johnson's beautiful oak desk and vomited into her gold trash can.

He held my hair back and then used a stupid hair tie that he had on his wrist to wrap it up. The gesture brought tears to my eyes, tears of fury and pain and love and hate. I breathed in and out as I stared at that ring he'd just put on my finger. It shined so bright against the dark oak.

"You put a ring on my finger like it means something more to you than some shares and a reputation, but you're willing to agree to this bullshit before deciding *with* me?"

"That ring does mean more." He said it like he meant it. Yet how could he? "Whether you want this or not, it means the same damn thing. But we should move forward rather than shutting it down before we even discuss."

"Or we discuss and then give them a decision. I'll discuss right now. I don't want to have a baby. So we're getting a divorce immediately." I said the words pointedly. "There's no reason for the marriage."

"You told me you did want children and Carl wanted us married for—"

"Who cares what he wanted!" I threw my hands up and turned to stare at him. "He wasn't thinking right. I'm surprised they even allowed him to put this in a freaking will without questioning his sanity."

"Carl had friends in high places. The judge of this town—"

"I don't care." I cut him off. "*I do not care* how he did this because he was wrong."

His brows lifted, and he crossed his arms in his stupid collared shirt. I hate that he looked as good in that as he did workout clothes, that he still looked delicious when I wanted to be furious with him. "He did it to protect you. I know that now. The one way to beat the press is to give them what they want. A new story."

"I don't need to beat the press, Declan. I need to disappear." My voice shook with emotions I couldn't contain now. "All I wanted was to leave my past in my hometown, and now I'm here facing it again—"

"You would have faced it again and again because your hometown means something to you. You can't outrun it. I see that when you talk about it, Everly. You have to change the narrative, control it, and fight through it." He pinched the bridge of his nose before he said, "Carl knew your image would change with a child."

I winced at his words. What a terrible way to see the world and how sad that I knew he was right. The media would eat up that I was pregnant, that we wanted a beautiful family to carry on the legacy. "Or he wanted his legacy protected."

"Probably a little bit of both." He shook his head, and then he quietly murmured, "It can't be that bad thinking of having kids with me, Everly."

I glared at him, thinking about babies with him, thinking about the life I wanted, thinking about how he could be a part of that. "Happily ever afters aren't made this way." My voice cracked even though I whispered it and I hated that tears came to my eyes.

I slid his ring off and he immediately shook his head at me, his gaze hardening as he commanded, "You keep my ring on your finger, Everly."

"I'm not wearing this ring. And you shouldn't have that bracelet on either." I grabbed for his wrist but he held it out of reach.

"You're not taking my bracelet." He said it like he was truly offended.

I almost screamed but stomped my foot and glared at him instead. Then, I used my teeth to untie my matching bracelet from my wrist, holding his fighting gaze with my own. I held them both up and outstretched my arm for him to take the jewelry. "Take them. I don't want them."

"No. Put them back on." He crossed his arms, his tone authoritative.

I lifted a brow. "Absolutely not. I'm never going to wear anything from a man who makes decisions without me. If you think—"

"I said we'd go to the doctor. That's it," he proclaimed.

"Without my fucking say," I bellowed as I threw the ring and bracelet at him. He didn't flinch as he caught them both somehow.

"Jesus Christ, Everly. I didn't think it was a big deal to just go to the—"

"I don't care! It's a baby, Declan! A freaking *baby*. For the legacy of a man I barely even could call my father."

"Drop, he thought what he was doing was right. You wanted kids—"

"Not like this." I stumbled back away from him, using the desk to hold me upright at his words. "Not because my father says so. Not because some fucking will says so. You would do it just for that?"

"No." He shook his head, then growled up at the ceiling. "Yes. I don't fucking know. With you? Yeah, I'd have a fucking kid with you. I don't need to plan it like you, Drop, or think about all the different outcomes. In my life, if it feels right, I move forward. I push the obstacles out of the way, and I get what I want. You've always felt right, babe—"

"But a baby? Like this? Does this *feel* right?" I slammed my hand on the desk and shut my eyes, trying to block out how his words felt in my heart, cracking away at my walls and making me imagine something that couldn't possibly be right. "Because this feels like we're forced, like we don't even have a real relationship and now we're rushing to bring another human into it...for what? A studio and some shares? I won't. I'll find another way."

"This isn't just about a studio anymore. And there isn't another way." He groaned. "I met with the lawyers all last week at night, okay? I made the damn calls. I've had them working on a way of getting out of whatever stipulation I thought would be coming. They told me whatever it was, it would be upheld in court because the fucking judge knew Carl."

"So that's where you were going every night?"

"Yes..." He said it cautiously.

"Why didn't you tell me?" I narrowed my eyes at him.

"You didn't need something else on your plate—"

"Don't ever treat me like I can't handle something, Declan. I've handled shit my whole fucking life." I stepped up to him and poked his chest. "Don't think that because I let you take care of me a time or two, you know how to handle burden better than I do, that I haven't held bone-crushing burden on my shoulders too."

His jaw worked up and down, up and down, but his gaze held remorse even as he ground out, "I'm always going to take care of you, Everly. I won't apologize for trying to—"

"You're not acting like this is even a friendly partnership between us." I pointed to that bracelet on his wrist. "I gave you that because we were starting to operate as a team. We'd committed to that by signing the marriage contract, I thought. Teams share what they're doing for one another, and then they work together. That's a commitment, that's a team, that's a *marriage*. I'm your *equal*, not a damsel in distress and—"

"No. You're not my equal, Everly!" He cut me off, his hand slicing through the air. "Don't you see that? You're so far above me, I'm scared to even touch you right now. You endured a shit ton of pain but still made it out without a single thing to mar your soul. But I know the media, I know how they twisted the story of my wrist, how they said I'd never play again. That shit ate at me for months, how it happened, how everyone lied. And it's fucking nothing compared to what you went through. Carl knew our marriage would bring them back out, and he's put us here for me to fucking change the narrative. So you have to let me try."

I shook my head at him. He rammed straight through everything, wanted to bulldoze into getting his way, and he truly believed he would get it. He did most of the time.

But how could we be sure enough to do it again? And did it matter? Because at the end of the day, I had to want this. We had to *want* a baby.

My heart thumped while my blood rushed around, and my thoughts scrambled everywhere. "I don't know what to do. I don't even know how this is possible." My life was slipping through my fingertips like sand, and I couldn't catch a single part of it.

"Because your father made it that way."

"Do you really want a child right now? Does this sound like a good way to have one?" I searched his eyes and then took in the way he shifted on his feet and then met my gaze with determination.

"We'd make a beautiful baby, Everly." He pulled at a strand of my hair, and I felt it all the way down to my toes. My body still wanted him, still yearned for him, even if my mind told me not to. "We could still have so much good, even if we gave into a fucked-up way of getting there."

"What's the good? A kid born to parents who did this for a studio and an empire?"

He narrowed his eyes at me, like he wanted to say more, like he wanted there to be more. "Go to the doctor with me, and let's just see." He said it with conviction, with confidence, and with authority as he wrapped his arm around my waist and pulled me close.

My body immediately sought to fold into him but I took a

step back. How could I not? Would we be good parents? Could I even get pregnant? What if I had a genetic problem or... Oh shit. And then I blurted out, "I don't even have insurance."

"You what?" His hand in my hair froze, and his brow furrowed. "What do you mean? Full-time employees are always offered insurance."

"I didn't want the extra cost when I got my own apartment. Plus, I'd already gotten preferential treatment and you were so mad I was coming to work at all when I didn't have the credentials. Taking insurance felt—"

A sound from deep in his throat came out before he said, "It'll be taken care of."

"I don't want—"

"You don't want anything, Everly. You don't want my car in the garage or my ride to work or extra clothes or any of it." He spun away from me to pace up and down the office. "You'd rather earn every fucking thing in the world, but the world doesn't work that way. It's unfair and murky and there aren't exact measurements that tip the scales towards right and wrong, okay?" He turned me so he could hold my face in his hands, and I knew he wasn't only talking about the insurance now. "We've just got to give it a shot."

"But what if—"

"Don't think. Let's just do, baby. Do you want your mother's yoga studio and do you want kids one day?"

"Of course. But I can't—"

"Then, we're going to the doctor and deciding the rest later."

I stared at the papers and then fisted my hand before grumbling out, "One doctor's appointment." Then, I brushed past him to leave the office.

He followed me and said, "Put your ring back on, huh?"

"Not happening. You need to earn that ring being on my finger."

CHAPTER 29: DECLAN

I think she punished me with silence. I swear it was the most effective weapon known to man too. That and the fact that she wouldn't wear the ring or the bracelet drove me to near madness.

She didn't come to dinner or breakfast. That ship had sailed for us too. She instead would open her own door to go to work every morning, then slam it extremely hard. I still counted silently every time she did for a fucking punishment later.

Worst of all, she ignored me. Flat out didn't even wish me good morning or say goodbye.

I'd made a decision for us both one freaking time, and the woman was going to go millions of times without talking to me for a whole week. I told her when the doctor's appointment was and practically prayed to all that was holy that she would be ready when I drove up to the guesthouse in one of my less-used electric vehicles to pick her up. I didn't want anyone following us to this appointment.

Thankfully, she appeared right on time and we drove in silence, walked to the office in silence and then we sat in the doctor's office.

In silence.

At least the waiting room had no one else in it and the nurses were cordial. They'd rearranged the schedule for us both and it was confidential enough that they'd made it a private visit.

The doctor asked for my autograph before he handed

Everly two forms to fill in. I took the insurance one with a grunt and scribbled information on there harder than necessary. I was frustrated with the fact that she hadn't had insurance and that I hadn't thought to put her on mine the day we were married.

I hadn't thought about a lot, but I damn sure was now.

I didn't know her middle name was Rose.

I didn't know her social security number.

I still had to write her maiden name instead of mine. "Didn't take my name, and I don't know half the shit about my wife on this form."

"It's for the best," she finally said but only to reassure me of something I didn't want.

"Why is it for the best?" The more I thought about it, the more it wasn't if she was going to be the mother of my child. I needed to know everything about her now. Didn't she understand that?

I wanted a damn kid. With her. Sooner rather than later. It might have been an irrational decision, and I may have made up my mind quickly, but Everly would have to come around to the idea. She had to see that this would be okay, that it could be more than okay.

It was the logical thing to do. Sure it was about the empire and the studio, but more than that, I'd make sure the press painted her in the way she should have been seen from the very beginning. And as I stared at her and pictured her pregnant, rubbing her belly with a small smile on her face as she felt a kick from our baby, I knew it'd be easy to do.

The world would fall in love with her.

I wanted to experience everything with my wife of convenience. Babies, weddings, happily ever afters. The inconvenient part of it was, I wasn't sure she wanted the same.

They called her back and told me I could finish filling out forms before I met them in suite 10. Once I got there, Everly was in a robe, and I sat down to listen to the doctor talk over the birth control she was on. He seemed concerned.

"Wait, what?" I asked. "So you're telling me there are all those side effects? Breast cancer?"

"Well, there are of course others. Everly, you put here you have migraines?"

"I've had some in the past, sure."

"So, if you're considering children, you can come off this birth control. Keep in mind, your period will be irregular for a few months. If you aren't planning on considering children yet"—he glanced at his computer screen—"I'd still recommend a different birth control. With this one, you have an increased risk of blood clots."

What in the actual fuck?

The doctor smiled softly. "And with your migraines, well, they may get worse with this bi—"

"Take out her birth control." I cut the doctor off with my demand.

"I'm sorry?" the doctor said just as Everly blurted out, "Excuse me, what?"

"I said. Take. It. Out. We're not risking her health. And I want a baby with her anyway."

"Declan!" She grabbed my arm and wide-eyed me. "Are you joking right now?"

"You heard what that birth control is doing to you. I want it out. Now."

The doctor cleared his throat, probably not sure how to continue. "Mr. Hardy, it would be Ms. Belafonte's decision."

"Ms. Belafonte." I muttered her last name in disgust, mad

that she didn't have mine instead. "She has decided she wants it out."

The doctor chuckled nervously. "Mr. Hardy, if Ms. Belafonte wants to take out her birth control, she can do that herself. The ring is self-inserted, so..." The doctor swiveled in his chair, glancing between both of us before standing. "If you are looking to have genetic testing to rule out any gene mutations or screen for any unknown conditions, I can draw blood from you both today."

I lifted an eyebrow at her but waited this time, knowing she had to decide to keep the ball rolling or not.

She rolled up her sleeve, albeit quietly so as not to cause a scene, but I saw the fire burning in her blue eyes.

Blood was taken, and the doctor explained we could leave when we were ready before rushing out as fast as his medical clogs could carry him. We were close behind because it seemed Everly didn't want a scene in the doctor's office.

Instead, we sat quietly in the car as I drove us home. And the longer the silence lasted in the car, the angrier I got. She was taking a medication that was detrimental to her health... for what. When we got home, I didn't stop at the guesthouse. I drove straight past it.

"Declan, drop me off—"

"You're coming into our home, where you should be sleeping anyway, and you're taking that birth control out."

"Am I?" She shook her head. "Funny because I'm pretty sure I told you just a week ago to stop making decisions without me. Now, here we are, you trying to make another one, but guess what? This one, I make all on my own." Her cool, calm, collected tone was not going to fly at this point.

"Did you not hear the risks, Everly? You're taking that out

or I'm going to fucking take it out for you." I glared at her.

"Do you hear yourself? You sound so ridiculous." She chuckled, actually chuckled at me. "I've been on it for years."

"All the more reason to take it out now," I bellowed, concerned that cancer could now have a head start in her body, that blood clots may be forming, that she'd get another damn migraine.

"You realize if I do that, we could end up with a baby, Declan," she said and her eyes shook with such a blue vivid fear that I noticed something right then.

"What are you so scared of?"

"Scared of?" She jerked her gaze away from me and shook her head. "Nothing."

I cranked my door open and slammed it shut to go around to her side. I yanked hers open and scooped her up.

She stuttered out, "Declan, I can walk—"

"I know that," I told her as I opened my front door and passed the kitchen, taking her straight into my bedroom where I set her down on the bed in front of me. Then, I kneeled down and grabbed her thighs. "You're not agreeing to a damn thing now except taking this out. I need this out of you. He said someone with migraines is more susceptible—"

"I don't think the side effects were as well known when I first started taking it. I—"

"We can get you another birth control, Drop. If that's what you really want."

She bit her lip and I did everything I could to make her see this wasn't a medication for her. Massaging her hips, I nestled into her neck, "You're taking it out, Everly. I need you to or I won't think about a damn other thing."

"You're that concerned?"

"About you? Always," I said, holding those sapphire blues hostage.

"Okay. But only because I said," she murmured so soft I barely heard it as she tilted her head to the side.

"You sure? Can I?" I said even though I was damn sure.

When she nodded, my hand was already unbuttoning her pants and pulling them down along with her panties. I nudged her back onto the bed so I could pull them over her feet and then I was grabbing her ass to set her on the edge of the plush comforter. She whimpered when my thumb brushed over her clit, and I groaned when my middle finger slid into her wet sex. "Fuck me. I missed you, missed my pussy."

She wiggled closer to me, biting her lip like she wanted to admit the same.

"I'll never get used to how wet you are for me every time, baby."

"Declan, please," she begged, her long nails digging into my shoulders as I started working her. I knew the ring was deep, so I took my time swirling my fingers against her walls on my way up to it. Her breathing became rapid, and her tits swelled right in front of my face as I watched the blush rise over her cheeks. Her hands started to roam everywhere as her thighs shook with anticipation for a release.

"I think I need to see you in my bed much more, Drop. Much, much more."

She whimpered but didn't confirm or deny that she wanted that too.

When I finally was deep enough and felt the ring, I murmured, "This should have never been in my pussy in the first place." I pulled it out, and she gasped at either the feeling of someone else handling her birth control or at my words. "My cock is the only thing that ever belongs in my wife. Say you understand."

She murmured yes over and over as I set the ring aside to throw away later, because I was about to take what I wanted immediately. I licked the arousal from her sex. I drank my favorite drink until she gushed on my mouth, screaming my name in her first orgasm of the day.

I didn't let up. I wanted to reward her for listening, make her understand that this bed was where she belonged, that I'd always take care of her here.

I sucked her clit as she rolled beneath me. "Declan, please fuck me. Please. I can't take anymore."

"I know that's a lie, Everly. You can do whatever you set your mind to. Now, give your husband another one."

CHAPTER 30: EVERLY

He didn't actually make love to me that night. He just did everything to me but that. Then he reported our doctor's visit to Mrs. Johnson, and we went to work like nothing had happened. For weeks, our routine became the same.

No sex. No ravaging. Nothing.

He'd drive me to work, act like a charming gentleman who opened the door for me, then disappear to train a new athlete or go into meetings. The stretching of his wrist was nearly done, but I still met him every night to do our routine. He didn't bother with much small talk. Instead, he'd take work calls through an earbud or let silence fill the room.

"Mrs. Johnson now knows you're off birth control," he'd say in passing. And when I'd try to reply, he'd cut me off. "We can discuss later."

"Mrs. Johnson knows you didn't pick up birth control," he reported a different day. "We have another few months to discuss next steps."

That was it. Efficient. Precise. And committed to the will.

Piper handled the paparazzi because she seemed to know how to twist them into exactly what she wanted them to say. Nothing about my past was brought up. It was disappearing just like Carl had planned.

The only problem was Anastasia had her own ideas about where the story should go. She wrote social media posts about how Declan was doing it all for the family, for the HEAT empire, and even maybe for *her*. Magazines ate it up and became obsessed with what could have been for her and Declan. It had me starting to think that Piper might be helping her, that they hadn't kept their word on being discreet about what Declan and I were really doing.

He seemed to know that too, because he handed me a magazine one day in the car and pointed to it. "We need to be seen together more because the media is focusing on something we don't want them to."

I cleared my throat and tried to start the discussion we should have been having the day of the reading with Mrs. Johnson. "Declan, maybe we should talk about—"

"We can discuss that later. Give yourself time." That was it. He refused to open it up for discussion because he dialed a number on his phone and immediately jumped out of the car once we were parked at work. Of course, that didn't stop him from coming around to open my door for me even while on the phone.

All day, I worked out and considered my options, but nothing stuck, nothing made sense, nothing felt right.

I snuck away from the gym to grab a snack at Clara's after Juna grilled me again about my situation. Clara was humming in the back of her bakery with a delicious scent of cinnamon and chocolate wafting out. She wore an apron with hydrangeas of all different colors flowing over it. The color completely clashed with some of the blown glass she had on the counter of the bakery. And the tables. And the walls.

Yet, Clara's charm was that she could smile and everything worked well together around her immediately somehow. "Evie! Did you come for lunch?"

"Just stopping in. I'd love a snack if you have time to whip up a sandwich."

She nodded and pushed her wavy red hair from her face, smudging some flour on her cheek in the process. Clara in the kitchen was something very different than Clara with her sister. "You got it. Turkey with bacon, lettuce, and mayo work?"

"You know it." I pulled a barstool over to the counter where she had a gold espresso machine and smoothie mixer. Behind it, she housed a few essentials for drinks and had a window into the kitchen.

She rushed around, peeking over her shoulder to ask, "How's the gym?"

"Great. Just got done with a yoga class." I frowned at a magazine near her tablet that had her sister on the cover. The article title screamed at me—"Anastasia Should Have Been His Wife."

"Ignore the magazine!" She clattered around and buzzed up to the front to snatch it from my view and throw it in the trash. "It's nonsense."

"It really isn't." I sighed, although I'd already silenced the alerts that had been chiming on my watch with news. "The world knows it. And so do I."

"The world doesn't know anything, and they definitely don't know you." She stuck her finger out at me.

"And yet we let them define us every day," I muttered.

"You ever look up Declan's Super Bowl story? The last one?" Clara asked as she let the bacon sizzle. "He never let the media define him."

"No. He told me some, and I figured I'd let him define himself for me when he was ready."

"Yes, you would do that." Clara chuckled and came around the counter to pull her phone from her apron. "Just watch."

"Okay." I gave in, wanting to bond with Clara and wanting to find out anything about Declan at this point.

The newscaster was going over the game highlights and announced that Declan had done what no other man could by carrying that ball in for a touchdown *after* breaking his wrist earlier that season. They'd given him one shot to prove he still could handle the ball, and even with the press betting against him, he went in and proved everyone wrong.

Then the newscaster went on to condemn Wes as a clip of him played. "The quarterback of the Cobras instructed his linemen to crush Hardy's hand in the first game of the season, putting Hardy at a huge disadvantage for the year." A clip of Wes yelling "Crush his hand" to his linemen was replayed.

I clicked the phone off as my jaw and heart dropped. Shock and anger flew through me fast. He might not have done it himself, but Wes had encouraged the fight on the field, encouraged his team to mess with another athlete's body. "Was this his last season?"

She nodded as she grabbed the bacon for my sandwich and then brought it out on a bright-pink plate. "Yes, well, the season before that now. He rehabbed and came back to run a record number of touchdowns in a single Super Bowl to clinch the team's victory. And he did that all when everyone said he couldn't."

He'd told me we could get to a place where the fucked-up wasn't bad anymore, that we could make good from it. He honestly believed it. "I don't think he will let anyone define what he can and can't do."

"No, he won't, and you shouldn't either." She tilted her head and wrinkled her nose. "I wish you both would have been given a shot at a relationship outside of the marriage. You would have worked beautifully, I think."

I took a big bite of the sandwich so as not to respond, but I shook my head. We'd never have worked. He'd disliked me and my lack of credentials on sight.

"I saw the way he looked at you before our father passed." She did that now, called him *our* dad instead of hers, and I appreciated how it warmed my soul to be bound to her even in that way. "He liked you."

"I really don't think so," I mumbled as I kept eating.

"Who liked Evie?" Dom waltzed in and glanced at his HEAT watch before coming over for a hug.

"Clara's imagining things." I waved her statement off and hugged him back.

Dom shrugged and grumbled, "That sounds about right."

"Can't blame a girl for being optimistic." She didn't say it with kindness. It held an edge, and I wasn't sure what for.

Dom didn't let me dig in any further as he asked, "You got a ton of work later today or you able to spar a few rounds?"

Taking one last bite, I jumped at the chance, pulling at one of my arms to stretch it right away. Something in me was brewing after watching Declan, and I needed a place to work it out. Dom had gotten into the ring with me before, and we'd both learned how to navigate our weaknesses and strengths. I enjoyed that about him...and that he seemed to be a watered-down version of his brother.

"I can now." I nodded at Dom and then turned to Clara. "Make sure this comes off my HEAT tab. It was delicious."

"It will absolutely not come off your card because this is me trying to get you to visit your stepsister. I realize maybe a lot of people let you down in the past, but I'd like to not be one of them." She picked at a napkin on the counter, and I blushed with her words. "This bakery is safe from the media and from judgment. I hope you'll come here more often."

Clara was trying, so why couldn't I make the same effort? I was allowing the past to control my future, allowing my anxiety of past relationships to taint my new ones.

I focused on dusting off my yoga pants so I didn't end up a blubbering mess in front of both of them. "I'm definitely going to try, Clara."

She rounded the counter and bombarded me with a hug. "Oh, and are you going to HEAT's charity gala? Declan has to go. Be prepared—it's a few weeks away."

There was probably a reason he hadn't asked me. "That's not really my thing."

"It'll be fun." She shrugged and then kissed my cheek. "And don't let my sister's ridiculous magazine articles get to you. We are the only ones who can define ourselves. This life. Not the one on social media, not the one in the press, and not the one in magazines. Remember that."

Her words echoed around in my head as Dom and I made our way into the ring. And when I saw Declan walk off the elevator with Anastasia right next to him, Clara's words clattered around and then flew out my mind altogether.

The media's words. The magazine's words. Even the fact that the will had been made in the first place to keep me safe from the press were each another needle to my heart. I'd gotten through a media slaughter once before on my own. I'd left town and started anew just so I didn't push the pain onto my best friend anymore.

I could define this too, get out of this too. Me. I slammed Dom to the mat, and he wheezed before I jumped up and stalked toward Declan and Anastasia. I didn't let her continue her conversation as she laughed and started to say something more to him, but his gaze had drifted to me storming up. "Wes intentionally had your wrist broken."

"Um, yeah." Anastasia popped a hip and frowned at me. "Everyone knows that. Wes is a weasel but since Declan forgave him, we know not to talk about it." She wrinkled her nose like I'd broken an imaginary HEAT law.

"You didn't tell me that." I held Declan's gaze. "You didn't tell me you were the bigger person with him and still won the Super Bowl against his team that year."

"It's irrelevant what he did. We won," he said, popping the button on one of the cuffs of his shirt and rolling it up slowly. He was doing what I used to do when eyes were on me. He was acting like none of it mattered, like the process behind all of it—how he'd trained, how he'd navigated to that win—wasn't a big deal. "It may have been a fucked-up situation, but we can still make it a good one."

"The fact that it happened still matters, Declan!" I threw up my hands. "What he did, that shouldn't be ignored."

"I know that, Drop. I fucking know." His jaw worked up and down, up and down as he slowly rolled his cuffs before he murmured, "We don't ignore it, Everly. We conquer it, knowing we're stronger than it. If you can survive the past, you can damn sure barrel through any obstacle in the present and create a peaceful place to thrive in the future."

I chewed at my cheek, knowing what he was saying. Knowing that he somehow wanted me to be strong enough to do the same, but I wasn't sure I could. "Some things can't be muscled through, Declan." I meant it for myself, for my past bleeding into my present, for a child being pushed on us without love. For everything.

Didn't he see we were broken and ruined before we even began? Could I really believe we'd get through that? That he'd even want to get through it?

Noah was on the bench press and piped up like he'd been listening the whole time. "Yeah, so anyway, about the gala, you going with your husband, Evie?"

Dom had walked over and draped an arm around me as he stared down his little brother. "Pretty sure my brother will be taking Evie. Right, Declan?"

Anastasia leaned in to whisper between Dom, Declan and me. "Declan and I were just talking about that, and I told him it would actually be best if we went together again. Piper and I discussed it. You know the press actually wants to see it and with this only being a marriage of convenience, maybe it's best we start to show some sort of separation..."

She drifted off with her statement. My heart raced and my body shook with a jealousy I knew I should control. I bit my tongue before I murmured out, "Yes, it probably is for the best."

Anastasia sighed into Declan, her small frame dwarfed next to him as she hooked her arm in his while he stared at me. "You really think it's best?"

I nodded.

"We'll see about that." Dom hooked his arm in mine suddenly, and Declan's gaze flicked to our connection with a flash of warning. "If Declan's not taking you, you're coming with me. My family is going to want to meet you."

"Your family?"

"Yes." Dom turned to Declan. "Mom's still furious she wasn't a witness to your marriage vows, by the way. She said stop ignoring her calls. She's not coming to the gala, but she expects you to bring Evie home in the next month. But Lilah, her crazy-ass husband, their kid, and Izzy and Cade will be here. Lilah said she'd get a handle on the situation for Mom."

"What the fuck?" Declan's hand shot into his pocket to grab his phone as Dom started laughing. "Not happening, Dom. We're on a damn group text. Why the fuck hasn't anyone said anything?"

"Right, but it's been quiet for a reason." He paused to see if Declan would catch on then rubbed his five-o'clock shadow. "We've all been texting on the other group chat about you. I think Dimitri named it, *Declan Didn't Invite Us to the Wedding* or something like that."

"Jesus fucking Christ. Are you all twelve?" He glared at him and then me. "We'll talk later." Then he stormed off like he was going to conquer the world and his family all at the same time.

"Well, that's awkward." Anastasia flicked a nail, not making eye contact with me but instead talking only to Dom. "You know if I ever marry him, I'll definitely invite all of you."

Dom must have felt my whole body stiffen because he patted my arm. But I was off kilter, not minding how I acted and feeling like anything I said to her was self-defense as she passive aggressively threw punches my way.

Facing an attacker head-on was what I was taught. I didn't really have anything to lose at this point anyway. "Oh, Anastasia, I don't think that'll ever happen."

"Why not?"

"Because I'm married to him, and I'd object a hell of a lot to another woman marrying my husband." I felt those words in my bones. They rattled in me like I owned Declan now as much as he owned me. I wanted that, and I wasn't sure what it meant, but I knew I had to figure it out.

A baby needed to be created in love but the questions began with what he'd said to me. Could we fight through the past? Could we make good from bad? Could we conquer how this was starting and where I'd started from to create a happily ever after?

CHAPTER 31: EVERLY

"I'm sorry. So, you think I'm going with you to the gala?" I asked again over the phone a few weeks later.

"A dress will be delivered in fifteen minutes," Declan said in a clipped tone over the phone.

"I don't need a dress." I'd gotten one for attending the gala with Dom. "Dom and I color coordinated a deep blue. Clara brought one to work for me the other day."

"He's trying to fuck with me, and the fact that you even agreed to this is complete bullshit, Everly. We're supposed to be doing this together."

"Doing what?" I pulled at the string of a friendship bracelet. I was on my bed making a black one again. Like the one I'd thrown at Declan and said I wouldn't wear again. I'd made dozens of them. I'd string them together and then throw them in the garbage.

"Being a team through this marriage."

"How are we a team when every time I try to talk to you about the will, you say we'll discuss it later?" I pointed out.

"Fine. You want to talk about it," he growled, like he'd had enough of being cordial and friendly. "I'm coming over then."

"Well, not right now!" I jumped off my bed and paced out into the kitchen to glance over at his house. "I have to get ready for my date with Dom."

"Are you fucking kidding? It's not a date. And you're going with me, Everly," he ground out. "Lilah is on her way, and now

Izzy is too...with Cade. They're making it a family event, which means we're going as a couple. Izzy told Lilah all about you, Drop. I can't show up with someone else."

"They'll still be happy to see you, whether you have me or another woman on your arm," I responded. "We shouldn't lead your family to believe that this is more than a marriage of convenience anyway when we haven't discussed—"

"Yeah, well, you know I don't think it's fucking convenient. Not when I have to stare at you on another man's arm."

His jealousy knew no bounds. "Well, I'll agree it isn't very convenient now that Carl's put a pregnancy clause on our shoulders." How ironic that I would not want the one thing I really longed for because it was being pushed on me. When my snippy remark was met with silence, I glanced at my phone. "Declan, are you there?"

"Would children with me be so terrible?" He suddenly sounded tortured, like he'd been mulling it over in his head for days and days like me. Gone was the clipped tone, gone was the thought of him giving me updates on what he reported to Mrs. Johnson. Instead, I heard his pain, heard that he might want this more than he let on. "Because I've seen you with the kids at the gym, Drop. I see how you love them. I know you'd make a phenomenal mother. And I'd try to be a damn good dad."

I shut my eyes and tried not to picture how he'd taken care of those kids when he'd come to their classes. He was patient and kind and freaking giving. He'd sign autographs and stay extra to listen to each of them tell their stories. They all loved him most. "I know you'll be a good dad, Declan, and you know I want tons of babies. But I want them born in love. And I know I shouldn't want to plan all that but—"

"I don't want your decision now. I just want you to keep

considering it," he said, delaying what I pretty much knew was the inevitable at this point anyway. "We're going to the gala tonight together. So get ready."

"I agreed to go with Dom. You agreed to go with Anastasia." It pained me to mention her, but it was for the best.

I glanced at the blue evening dress draped over the end of my bed in my room. Clara had said I could borrow it a few days earlier when she'd brought it to work. She'd said it was the same color as my eyes.

"Like Anastasia said the day you gingerly agreed to have your husband go with another woman, I took her last year." I knew it and still the admission felt like a spear through my heart. It shouldn't have mattered, but my feelings were too complicated and tangled to unravel now. "It wouldn't look good if I did again. Not with the shit that she and Piper are doing in the papers. You're going with me tonight, Everly. I'm done with the media. And Dom can take Anastasia. She'll understand—"

I think he was forgetting that Anastasia was best friends with Piper, that they knew exactly how it would affect me if Anastasia went with him. It's probably why she asked him specifically. "Piper wants you to be seen with *her friend*. She's protecting your public image. I'd rather you protect your public image, too, Declan. And your family's. I won't be in the public eye once we're—"

He stopped me abruptly by swearing, "You're going with me."

Then he hung up and not two minutes later, he was barging through the guesthouse door. I sighed, leaned against the counter, and crossed my arms over my chest at his barbaric display of trying to get his way. "Feel good about how you just hung up the phone?"

"Are you trying to piss me off?" he said, eyes flashing angrily as he stomped over to me. He was already in a suit, all black and beautifully tailored to his body. The lines of his shoulders far outshone what other men could do with their suit. He caged me into the counter, his chest right up against mine, not handling me gently now at all. "How did I know you were going to fight me tooth and nail about this?"

"Because you know it's not logical for me to go with you especially if we don't plan on being married much—"

"And yet, here I am, waiting for you to get dressed because we haven't made that decision yet, have we?" He glared at me.

I chewed my cheek as he brushed a hand over my jaw, as I breathed his scent, as my heart yearned for him.

"Fuck me, Drop," he murmured close to my ear, and my eyes fluttered closed as I felt his length against me. "I'll dress you myself if you don't start. You're going with me. You might be fine with her on my arm, but I'm not fine with you on any man's arm but mine. Not even my brother's."

"I already told Anastasia and Dom—"

It was a weak excuse at this point. "I'll take care of it."

I bit my lip and nodded as his lips dropped to my neck. I was giving into the night, giving in to him for now because I didn't know if we had much time left after.

"Goddamn, I miss touching you." He said it low, and I felt it down in my heart. We were both holding out with the big decision looming over our heads, but our souls still wanted to be together more than anything else. His hands were everywhere, sliding over my waist, my chest, my arms, and then down to my hands where he groaned as his thumb grazed over my ring finger.

He stepped back for a minute to pull my wedding band

from his pocket and before I could protest, his lips were on mine kissing me, devouring me, owning me. He slid the ring back onto my finger and said against my cheek near my ear, "You're mine tonight, Everly."

My gaze drifted to his finger, and my eyes widened at the string there. "Where did you get that?"

"I made the bracelet you threw at me into my ring." He shrugged.

I bit my lip as tears sprung to my eyes. Right then, there was a knock at the door.

"Fuck," he groaned out and rubbed his hard cock back and forth on my stomach. "Should I eat your pussy on this counter and make them wait?"

"Who is it?" I whimpered out because now I was too turned-on to think of anything else.

A growl came from deep in his chest before he pushed away from me and pulled at his hair. "That's probably one of my sisters trying to bother you before I get to them. I knew I should have never given them the access code for my gate."

He started toward the door, and I blurted out, "Wait. Do they know about the pregnancy clause?"

"No. That's our business." He thought about it for a second, and then a frown formed on his face. "Fuck, unless Izzy told them."

I sighed. "They're family. They should probably know anyway."

"Not if my wife and I want to keep our business private."

I chewed on my cheek and tried not to swoon over that because he deserved to have them in his corner. "You should be honest with them. They're your siblings."

He narrowed his eyes. "My sisters will practically beg you

to have a child with me."

I couldn't help the small smile. "I'm good at defense." I shrugged. "Don't worry about me."

"I always worry about you, Drop," he murmured and then told me, "So, you're going to this charity gala with me, Everly."

It wasn't a question, but I still nodded, and his shoulders visibly relaxed as he turned to open the door.

Izzy in red and another woman in a black evening gown plowed through. Izzy held her visibly larger stomach as a tiny little human that looked a lot like who I assumed was Lilah barreled in. She had curly hair and wide eyes that matched the man walking in behind Lilah. Behind him was Cade, his head bent to his phone.

"Evie, meet Lilah, my sister," Izzy announced as she walked over to wrap me in her arms. "I've turned into a hugger since pregnancy. Plus, we're technically sisters. Lilah, why aren't you hugging us?"

I laughed awkwardly as Lilah rolled her eyes and came in for a weird three-way hug. Lilah's child toddled over and hugged my leg too, like she needed to be a part of it. "Hug!"

I smiled down at her. "Nice to meet you, Lilah. What's your daughter's name?"

"Oh, Carolina." Lilah chuckled. "She's fourteen months and thinks everyone loves to be climbed."

"Carolina, nice to meet you." I squatted down to pick her up as she tried to crawl up my leg. "I'm Evie."

"Ee-be!" She pronounced my name as best she could before grabbing my face and kissing my cheek fiercely. Then she pouted, saying, "Down."

I chuckled and set her back on the ground. Immediately, the child headed straight for the table where there was a vase, and Lilah gave her husband a look. The man didn't even bat an eye or look perturbed at all. He smiled down at his daughter with a look of the utmost love as he maneuvered the vase up onto the island countertop. "Not today, minion. Not today."

"She's very cute," I said to Lilah just as Dom walked in, also dressed in a suit, and Declan walked over to give him a hug and murmur something in his ear.

Dom glanced over at me with a smile. "You ditching me, Evie?"

Izzy heard the exchange and pointed at her two brothers. Then she turned and winked at me, "If you have a choice, which I know you *really do*, go with Dom."

"Izzy," Cade chastised, "you weren't supposed to bring up the will."

"You showed me. So, I'm bringing it up." She shrugged as Declan swore.

"What is going on?" Lilah asked like she wanted everyone to calm down.

My eyes got wider and wider. I wanted Declan to tell his family, but not while I was present.

Izzy's filter was truly gone, though. Her etiquette had flown out the window. She plopped down on the couch and waved over her niece as she announced, "Evie needs to get pregnant to save HEAT shares—any Hardy brother will do. Oh fuck! Declan needs a baby too. So if Evie won't have him, he needs Anastasia. So, I change my mind. I hate Anastasia." She glanced at me. "No offense to you. Now, to her, I mean that totally disrespectfully—"

"Izzy!" Lilah was waving her off. "Please stop."

"What?" Izzy continued. "She's a fucking piranha for an Instagram photo. She tried to take one with Cade one time. I will cut a bitch."

"Babe, I didn't take the photo with her," Cade tried to console.

"You thought about it." She narrowed her eyes at him.

"Only to piss you off." He shrugged and went back to his phone as he sat down next to her and rubbed her thigh.

She shoved his hand off, but he just chuckled and put it around her shoulders where she left it while their niece climbed between them. Cade immediately tucked the little girl into his arm and started playing some baby songs on his phone.

"Anyway, Declan, you want kids, right?"

"Fuck, Izzy." Declan shook his head at her. As I glanced around the room, I saw their looks ping-pong to one another. "You tell everyone about the will?"

"Yep." She popped the *p* and smiled wide. "Except Mom and Dad because they will freak."

Declan walked up to me and threaded his fingers through my hand to pull me into the kitchen with him. "You're really a tornado of a person while pregnant, Izzy."

"There're twins in here, okay?" She pointed and then glanced at me. "It runs in our genes, since you're contemplating conceiving with one of my brothers. Not that it'll affect you, but if you have a daughter, Dec or whoever could pass on that trait to her, and just know, it's double the hormones or something. I'm completely a different human at this point."

"Jesus," Lilah muttered before meeting my gaze and mouthing, Sorry. "She's like this all the time. We can't stop her."

They all laughed except Declan, but even he had a small smirk as he murmured in my ear, "It's going to be okay." Then, he went to fill up a glass of water for Izzy as Lilah walked up and hooked her arm in mine. "Evie and I are going to get ready. She needs time to get dressed."

"Don't scare my date away, Lilah," Declan commanded. "Izzy is already doing a great job of that. And, Drop, this is the big family part I was telling you about."

Lilah yanked me through my bedroom door and slammed it shut before sighing against it. She spun in her sleek black dress and pinned me with a penetrating gaze. "We're a lot for one person."

"That's fine." I shrugged and turned toward my dress still on my bed. "I always wanted a big family."

"Well"—she walked over and dragged a hand over the midnight-blue silk of the dress—"guess you have one for the time being."

I didn't know if I should take that as a slight or a compliment. Did she believe I'd scammed my way into their family? Did she believe everything that was written? "I know you all may be dealing with the backlash of the media from my marriage to your brother, but I hope he's told you that you can handle it however you need to. I don't want to be a burden in—"

"Family's always a burden." She chuckled and then shook her head like I misunderstood. "In the best way. You know that, right? Like, you can't get rid of your parents no matter how hard you try some days."

I didn't correct her. She'd probably known Carl in a much different way than I had. Carl had easily gotten rid of me in a way that families probably shouldn't.

"Well, at least that's how it is with my family," she said as if she knew even without me saying. "Izzy will never leave you alone about that will. I promise you. If you let her keep talking, she's going to keep talking." She wrung her hands.

"I don't mind. I want Declan to be honest with you as

much as possible. I understand you're all family."

"*We're* all family," she corrected. "At least, that's what I want. Standing out on an island against the media because Carl and Declan dragged you into this over some shares is ridiculous."

"And my mother's yoga studio. And he may have thought it would protect me somehow or help me clear my name from my..." I drifted off, not wanting to explain.

She sighed. "So, I don't know what you've been through, but I know the media has twisted it. One day, you'll tell me." She held up her hand when I opened my mouth. "Not now. But when you're ready, because I know what it feels like to hold a hell of a secret inside and what a nightmare it is to share it with the world after you've buried it. Take your time, but know we don't believe a thing the media says, and we won't allow them to drag your name—"

"Let them." I cut her off fast, thinking of my mother, and went to grab some hair cream to put in my curls. Standing in front of the mirror, I said, "It's not your job to—"

"It'll always be the job of family." She didn't let me argue about whether we were or weren't. "Now, let's discuss this will. I'm curious, since Izzy's already told me most of it, do you plan to have a baby this year?"

"Can one really plan that sort of thing?" I winced and asked back.

"That was my next question. How does one go about that?" Lilah asked and then picked at a fuzz on the dress. "I used to hide that I had two miscarriages by Dante, my husband, before we got lucky enough to have one."

"I'm so sorry," I murmured as my throat almost closed at the thought. Wanting kids and not being able to have them felt like a cruel sort of torture not befitting a woman, and yet, women had to endure so much.

She waved me off. "That minion out there reminds me of how lucky I am every day. Still, getting pregnant isn't easy for everyone."

I sighed, knowing the risks and knowing that they could happen to anyone. "Six months of trying followed by three months of IVF. As long as we do both of those things, we're fulfilling our end of the requirement."

"Do you want kids?" She was so straightforward that I suddenly felt like I could be straightforward back.

"I want kids, but I want them to have parents who love each other." I grabbed my makeup bag, but she extended her hand.

"May I?" I'd only ever had Tonya and my mother do my makeup. They'd been the only ones who'd ever wanted to. Handing the bag to her felt like I was handing over some trust or handing over a part of the little girl in me that wanted the love of a friend or a sister.

She patted my hand like she understood, and we sat there while she applied the concealer, the blush, the eyeshadow. "You have amazing eyes that he's probably obsessed with."

"Declan isn't obsessed with me."

"Oh, he is." She tsked. "When I saw him following you in his car on that viral video, that's when I knew. He wouldn't have done that with any other woman. You'd broken him. And you only break someone when they're obsessed with you."

"That's mostly just getting on his nerves." I shrugged.

She hummed and tilted her head. "I need a little more of something." Then she grabbed her purse and dug around until she pulled out a red lipstick. "If that's the case, can I ask you...

Do you want to break him?"

Her question hit me like a freight train as she stared at me with hazel eyes that held me captive. Declan had told me that she and Izzy, although twins, were very different. I saw the difference. She was determined in her gaze, driven with her questioning, and intelligent with where she was leading it. Lilah planned like me. So, I told her what I knew. "I honestly don't know."

"Well"—she pulled the lid off the red lipstick and drew it onto my lips—"I think it's best we find out tonight then."

CHAPTER 32: EVERLY

Anastasia didn't take the switch up well. I heard her yelling through the phone when Dom called her while Declan and I walked out. I'd given Dom an out and said Declan and I could handle it, but he smiled at me like he had the world under control. "I'll take her *and* Clara. They'll both be pissed about it."

Anastasia called Declan immediately when we got into the car, and I didn't let him avoid it. I hit answer when her named popped up on his car's touchscreen and waved at him to say hello. He sighed and grabbed the phone from his pocket to take her off the speakerphone before he greeted her.

There wasn't really a point. I still heard her screaming.

Minutes passed as I watched the ocean and then the city lights fly us by. Halfway through, Declan tucked the phone between his shoulder and ear and his hand went to my leg. The dress was long, but there was a slit he found immediately. I gasped at his touch and his eyes caught mine.

"Anastasia, I told you I wanted to bring my wife."

I heard her say I wasn't really his wife.

That had the grip on my thigh tightening. "Anastasia, let me be clear. Until there's a document saying we're divorced, we're fucking married. Make sure you understand that and make sure Piper understands too." He hung up and drove faster than he should have to the event, like he was on a mission to prove something to everyone there.

When we pulled up to the HEAT Oceanside Resort, the

cameras started immediately flashing at our car, and I glanced down, but Declan stared straight at them. He wanted the world to see us, was ready for them. Before he got out, he grumbled, "Don't you dare open your door yourself."

When he got around to my side, I saw Anastasia wasn't the only one pissed I'd arrived with Declan. As my car door opened, Piper stood waiting to see her friend emerge, and her face dropped as Declan leaned in, I thought, to speak to me. Instead, he smiled as he undid my seat belt. "Declan, do not—"

"Indulge me tonight, huh?" His scruff brushed over my cheek as he pressed the button for the belt. "That call didn't give me a moment to say you look stunning. Fucking divine enough to eat, and I'm going to have a hard time letting other men stare at you and those red lips tonight."

My stomach tightened at his words and heat rose to my cheeks as he pulled me out of the car.

The crowd of press went wild, screaming questions as he and two security guards hustled us in. We only stopped one time, and he murmured for me to smile as he pulled me close, wrapping his arm around my waist. I did as I was told because I just wanted out of there. I felt him kiss my forehead and then wave to a few paparazzi as we hurried inside.

Gentle, calm, on point for the cameras.

"One portion down," he reassured me. This was press. This was media. He was fine with it, he maneuvered it, molded it, bent it to his will.

It's how the night went. One public display of us together after the other. All of them somewhat fake, somewhat real. My mind played tricks on me as he pulled me close, brushed his hand on my back to ask if I wanted a flute of champagne. And when they called couples out to dance, he was already leading me there to move slowly against him as he whispered sweet nothings in my ear. He told me I danced well, I was doing so well, I handled that conversation with grace.

Yet, when Piper and Anastasia approached to tell Declan the event looked amazing, I tried to slink away quietly while they barely acknowledged me. I knew I wouldn't handle them with grace much longer. But Declan wove his fingers through my hand and held me there as Anastasia finally turned to me and said, "Nice dress."

I don't think it was an actual compliment. We were past being cordial at this point, but I still responded with the last ounce of kindness I had left. "Thanks, I borrowed it from Clara."

"Borrowed?" Piper questioned with a raised brow and Anastasia snickered.

"Oh, I'm sure Clara was being generous," Anastasia announced, like I was the charity case that night, as she glanced around for her sister. Yet, Clara had lagged behind with Dom after they'd entered the double doors of the large ballroom. Hosting the party within HEAT's Oceanside Resort allowed for them to set up a stage, food, and tables a lot like a wedding reception would be laid out but much more extravagant. Ice sculptures were made into fountains, waitresses dressed in their own evening wear, all black and silver, and large screens showcased what many of the proceeds were used toward and what the charity endeavored to do next.

"Well, I don't know where Clara is, but she's taller than you. So, she probably bought it for you to wear tonight," Anastasia sneered.

"That reminds me." Declan turned to me and wrapped his arm behind my back so he could rub circles on my skin since the dress dipped so low. "Will I have to have more clothes sent to the house for wardrobing, or will you let our driver take you to one of our boutiques? They can get you the future athleisure styles if nothing is appealing right now. Although you still haven't taken my name, they know you're my wife and want your opinion...and they want you wearing the clothes. You know they are just as much your clothes as they are mine for you to pick from now."

Both Piper and Anastasia's mouths dropped open as I narrowed my eyes at him. Declan knew I didn't care about the future clothing. I barely wore the athleisure he gave me now.

"Not even I have access to future product, Declan," Anastasia spit.

"I know that. I run the clothing lines with a team, and it's only something I trust my wife with." He pulled me close for another forehead kiss and then said, "Excuse us."

"You're poking the bear for no reason, Declan," I told him as we walked toward his family.

"No. I'm establishing a fucking boundary. My wife can have anything she wants and no one has a right to, nor will they ever, disrespect her in front of me. If I need to be more blatant, I will next time."

I sighed because I knew he couldn't be talked out of it. When he wanted his way, he got it.

Lilah, with her baby on her hip and Dante standing behind her alongside Izzy and Cade, looked ruthless and wholesome all at the same time. No one would have contemplated bringing a child to an event like this unless they were above it, and Lilah's daughter wiggled out of her mom's arms, literally throwing herself at Declan like she hadn't seen him an hour ago.

She squished his cheeks as he settled her in his arms and

eyed his sisters. "Don't let anyone talk to Everly while I dance with my niece, huh?"

Then he said he'd be right back and spun away from me, that little girl squealing as her uncle danced her around in circles and threw her in the air for everyone to see. I swear my freaking ovaries almost burst while watching him. He smiled bigger than life, handled her with more caution than the precious football I'd seen him carry in the highlights reel, and murmured in her ear secrets that made the toddler laugh with pure, innocent happiness.

And when he brought her back to Lilah, he pulled his sister in for a hug. "Thank you for bringing the joy of life so we can get through this damn event."

She didn't even roll her eyes. The whole family was enamored with that little girl, and I knew Izzy's babies would receive just as much love.

Born in love.

Wrapped in it, secured in it, protected by it. Maybe the problem was my heart was hardened from looking for it everywhere for so long.

"Ee-be!" the little girl screamed and leaned toward me. "Dance too?"

Lilah laughed and let her lean into my arms as I outstretched them and said, "I'd love to dance with you."

I got the little angel for a whole song, and it was perfect because the violins were playing a rendition of a Disney one. She wiggled with excitement in my arms and her green eyes got wide when I started singing the tune.

She squealed "She's a princess!" to her mother as I handed her back, and I noticed Declan's face wasn't smiling anymore.

I'd overstepped; we weren't really family, and maybe I

shouldn't have taken his niece from them and danced like no one was watching.

CHAPTER 33: DECLAN

Everly Belafonte was stunning, beautiful, and completely and utterly beyond my control. I couldn't control the media interacting with her. Couldn't control the people around her. Couldn't even control my niece's affection for her.

The woman couldn't control people's fondness of her either. I swear, if she were capable of such a thing, she'd have faded into the background so as to not be seen by anyone, hence protecting them from what she thought was her own destruction.

And when I saw Wes approach us, I tried my best not to step in his way.

"Can I have one dance?" he asked her without even giving her a hug. "I haven't seen you in weeks, and I know you're avoiding me because you heard about what happened between Dec and me, babe, but it's no big deal."

Everly stood straighter as if suddenly appalled by him. It was a different version than I'd seen of her. Normally she greeted him with a smile. "No. I absolutely won't be dancing with you."

"What?" He almost stumbled back like he couldn't believe she'd say no.

"You broke my *husband's* wrist," she hissed, and Wes's eyes widened while my damn heart swelled. Hearing her use that title in public had me proud as fuck.

That was the thing about Everly. She held on to what I

couldn't. Didn't forget the past even though she acted like she could. Maybe we all did it a little, tried to move on and conquer it when really it festered in us, making us who we would be the next day. Everly had so much past that I saw the pain in her eyes haunting her some days, and I knew she harbored it deep in her soul like she'd never be able to get it out. Here though, for me and my past, she did.

"Evie, that wasn't what it looked like," Wes stuttered before glaring at me, his eyes menacing like I always knew them to be. "You showed her, you asshole?"

"He didn't show me." She shoved her finger into his shoulder to get his attention. "Clara did. And if I had it my way, you wouldn't even be here." She stopped suddenly and looked at me with new hope. "Can't your wife make decisions on who is a part of HEAT?"

I chuckled and pulled her close. "Not today, Drop. Let it go."

She stomped her foot and scoffed as she glared back at Wes. "I'll never entertain anything with you again after seeing the sportsmanship you displayed. You should be ashamed."

"Oh for fuck's sake." Noah and Gianni walked over just as he threw up his hands, both of them in navy suits like they wanted to match or some shit. "You guys believe this girl? She's pissed about a broken wrist."

"Yeah, man, because it's not hockey. It's football," Noah chuckled.

"Fuck off, man. I get better women on weekends, anyway. I'm not interested in holding out for golden pussy," Wes scoffed, and then it was Everly who grabbed my arm as I stepped forward.

"Stop." She caught my gaze, but Wes was already backing

away like he knew he'd gone too far. I'd make sure he knew for certain before the night was over. "He's not worth it."

Noah cracked his knuckles. "She's right. He's not. Plus, he's been drinking. He'll probably apologize tomorrow."

"Tomorrow he won't have access to communicating with us to apologize," I ground out.

Noah shrugged and then turned to Everly, not there to soothe me but instead her. "Dance with me, Evie. You're the only girl here I know without two left feet."

She didn't even turn to me to see if I'd be okay with it. She stepped out onto the dance floor with him immediately, and off they went, clean lines, beautiful form, and pure sensuality. Noah didn't care who I was. He knew he had the most stunning woman in his arms, and he took full advantage dancing with her.

Did she know she had the whole ballroom enraptured? That Noah probably would date her if he could? That any man would have her here if I hadn't put a ring on her finger—and even that wasn't a surefire deterrent.

I wanted to own her, take her from his grip, and announce to everyone that she was mine, that it wasn't just a fake marriage, that she was truly my wife. Yet, seeing her with my niece had caused something small and ugly to form in my gut, and it felt a lot like doubt. Everly only wanted love in her family, and she deserved it. Carl had wronged her, her ex had wronged her, and her stepfamily continued to wrong her still.

When Noah brought her back to me, I gripped her hand tight as we walked over to our table for the auction to start as we ate.

Clara, outfitted in a red as deep as roses, had offered to lead the charge of the auction that night. I got up to thank everyone for being there and handed the mic off to her. Everly commented that I'd done a good job as I sat back down next to her.

"Good enough for us to leave for the night?"

"Not a chance," Izzy and Lilah said, because of course they were eavesdropping on me murmuring to my wife.

We all listened to auction items as our forks and knives clinked away at the steak dinner, and we sipped more champagne.

Clara finally announced, "Okay, the night is almost over, but we have a surprise. It's the most fun part of the night. We've added a bit of a twist. We'll do the spontaneous portion now."

Dom glanced at me with a lift of his eyebrow. "You allowing any auction items now?"

I shrugged and rolled my eyes. "Clara wanted to put a spin on it."

He hummed and folded his arms over his chest as she explained the rules to everyone. As long as the terms were agreeable to those participating in the auction, people could make requests.

Someone yelled out, "I want a date with Noah Romero. If he fights like that on the ice, I want to see how he fights in the bedroom."

Clara smiled big. "I hope there's no fighting in the bedroom." She winked, and Dom grumbled that this was stupid. "Noah, what do you say?"

Noah was always a team player. He chuckled and shrugged, leaving his date in the dust as he sauntered up there like he didn't give a damn. She must have not cared at all either, because she clapped for him as he hopped up on stage and did a little spin and bow.

When he pointed at Everly, I shook my head. The fuck did he think he was doing? My wife wouldn't be bidding on him. I leaned over and muttered, "Don't even think about it."

With a flute of champagne in her hand, she turned those deep blues on me. "Even if I wanted to, I couldn't compete with what he'll go for."

"You think he'll go for that much?" What the hell was so special about him?

"He's literally a walking dream, and he dances like one too." She must have seen my jaw ticking because she tapped her finger to it before she licked those red lips and murmured in my ear, "In all honesty, I'd pay more for you."

A woman yelled out six figures and her head whipped around, her jaw dropping wide open. Everly probably had never seen the lengths people would go to at a charity auction of this sort.

I expected no other surprise auctions to be announced, but Clara cleared her throat. "An anonymous request for the beautiful woman in deep blue who danced clean lines with Noah." She glanced up from the note. "Evie, that must be you. They want a dance down in the garden under the starlight. What do you say?"

She gasped when she heard her name, and her gaze whipped to me.

I glanced around the room for the anonymous bidder, wanting to make sure I took note of who I would have to obliterate later. A private dance with her wasn't on the table. I set my fork down and wiped my mouth before leaning close to her ear and saying, "Did you fucking agree to this?"

She bit that luscious lower lip and shook her waves of curls. "No, but I can't say no."

"You absolutely can and will." My voice was low and held warning.

Yet, my wife studied my face, took a sip of her champagne, and then patted my thigh before she took a deep breath and met Clara's gaze. "One dance in the garden."

Noah chuckled and leaned in to say something to Dom. Izzy and Lilah whooped while both of their husbands snickered. My hearing, vision—everything—was muted to the outside world. I was singularly focused on Everly. Her back straight, with that wide opening where a man's hand would hold her as they danced; her eyes sparkling, alive with defiance that someone gets to see under the moonlight.

She wasn't giving me the privilege of taking care of her much anymore. The change shook my soul. I'd gotten comfortable having her tucked against me, where I could protect her, command her, make sure I was alleviating her worries.

And when I saw her smile wobble just a second as Po yelled out a bid, I knew the ridiculous charade wouldn't last long. I leaned back and watched Po and Noah and a younger man still on the dance floor go back and forth.

When the bids hit six figures, she gasped, her gaze ping-ponging between the men. Even Dom threw in a bid but quit when I glared at him. Didn't she see the effect she had on everyone? Men wanted to be around her, women wanted to be her, and I wanted her all to myself.

It's when a man hesitates, though, that the serious men step up, sure and strong and audacious.

At nearly $500,000, Clara announced, "Going once, going twice—"

"One million." I held up my paddle without so much as a stutter.

"What?" she blurted out and whipped around to shake her head at me. "No, what are you doing?"

"I'll tell you down in the garden when I get my dance," I said matter-of-factly. She didn't seem to understand that I'd have paid fucking eight figures for her at that point. I was beyond controlling anything.

"Well, that's if I don't bid," Wes grumbled as he walked by.

"You bid on my wife again, I'll end not only your membership to HEAT but your career as well, Wes." I said it casually. It wouldn't take much work.

"How's that?"

"You think I don't know your coach, all your teammates, that everyone doesn't enjoy their HEAT membership? That I can't drag your name if I want to with the shit you've pulled in the past?" I stood from my seat, done with games. Done with people not understanding that Everly wasn't simply a transaction to me. I grabbed his paddle and snapped it in half and set it on the table before I held out my hand for my wife to take.

She glanced around with a blush staining her cheeks as Clara nervously chuckled out, "Well, I guess sold to the possessive husband of the night."

People clapped and laughed, but I wasn't worried about their approval. I pulled my wife to the balcony's doors and opened them to feel the night air on our skin. My brother had done a phenomenal job creating the stone balcony that overlooked a garden of beautiful foliage that could rival the Gardens of Versailles.

I didn't stop to enjoy the view. I pulled her down the stone steps and across the lush green grass into the small hedge maze that had been created for guests to enjoy. It would ensure the privacy I needed now. Here was where I needed to make her understand one thing. Here was where I needed Everly to see only me and no one else.

Away from them.

Away from the bullshit.

Away from a life I'd created but didn't enjoy without her anymore.

"Why did you agree to that?" I said once we were deep in the hedges, the stars and the moonlight highlighting her features.

She stood there in that gown that practically glowed the same color as her eyes, the material hugging her curves and then fanning out below where the wind could blow it softly over her thighs, the slit much too high for a man like me, a man so obsessed with her I couldn't see straight anymore.

"It's for charity, Declan. We're giving kids a future in sports and athletics who otherwise wouldn't get one." She folded her arms close to her chest. "You didn't have to be the one to bid on me."

She thought this was about the money. "Oh, I had to bid on you."

"Why?" She shivered as a gust of night wind blew past.

Already, I'd begun to unbutton my suit jacket. "You're my wife. Everyone in that room knows it."

"Right. Well, it'll be amazing for the kids, but it's not like we're going to be married long anyway because—"

"Do you think my bid was for charity, Everly?" I cut her off as I stepped forward, my anger at her words licking through me fast.

She tilted her head in confusion. She didn't get it yet. "Well, all of them are somewhat for charity."

Maybe it should have been. But it wasn't. This wasn't about my ego either. This wasn't about embarrassment. This was about her and me. This was about the raindrop that turned into a catastrophic storm, drowning me in thoughts of her.

I held her gaze hostage as I slid my suit jacket off my shoulders and threw it over one arm, taking my time rolling up my cuffs, one fold at a time. Neither of us said a word. The only sound was the violins from inside as she licked those red lips, watching me.

Then I stepped forward, and she gasped, but the heat rose over her cleavage and her pupils dilated. The woman's body knew how to react to mine even if she couldn't read what I exactly wanted. Her body knew I was coming for her, that I was about to devour and take what I wanted.

I wrapped her in my jacket and pulled her close by the lapels. "Dance with me."

The stars glittered in her eyes as I saw the same turmoil I felt deep in her soul. She had to feel this, the pull between us and the mindfuck we were dealing with. How was I supposed to let her go if she didn't want a child? How was I supposed to be fine having a child with her when I knew she didn't want one with a man she didn't love?

How was I supposed to give her everything when the will stood in the way, tainting it all? I couldn't tell her this was for real, couldn't force her into this when I knew that she deserved better than all of it.

She tried to step away, but I held her there. "Declan, let's go back inside."

"No, Drop. I'm getting my dance with you. Here in this garden. Tonight. With just the moonlight and my touch on your skin." I pulled her through a bit of the maze of the garden so no one could see us and then my hand disappeared under my jacket where it found the small of her back. I felt the goose bumps there as I pressed my palm flat to nudge her forward.

She stumbled into my hold, and I took her other hand. It was small in mine, fitting perfectly where it was supposed to be. She gulped as she felt my length against her, hard and throbbing for her like it had been most of the night.

And then I spun her, wanting this dance with her even if it meant denying my desire to fuck her right then too. I pulled her back, and we fell into step with each other as the violins built to the backdrop of our night.

I should have let her go back up those stairs, I shouldn't have spoiled myself with a dance while the smell of her swirled around me, with her breath on my chest as she folded into me as our souls mingled together and clung to one another.

It may have been wrong, but her with me felt so fucking right. "That bid wasn't about charity. It was about this. About knowing no one belongs here with you but me. I've had you twice outside in the night. I've looked into your eyes and seen a darkness you harbor that only I want to witness and soothe and bring light to. Why do you think I'd ever give another man that privilege?"

"Declan, it was just a dance."

"It's not *just* anything with you. It's everything. It's my wife in another man's arms, it's her skin feeling his touch, it's her conversation and intelligence being shared. What would you have talked about?"

"Probably the kids we were helping," she said softly, trying to soothe me. She even ran her hand along my chest as we swayed in the wind.

"He'd have seen the love in your eyes as you talked about

those children. You'd share your kindness, your passion with him. Not me. And I don't want you to share anything with anyone."

She murmured my name in chastisement, but I didn't let her finish. My name dripping from her lips was enough to push me over the edge. I took them against mine and kissed her like I should have at the beginning of the night when I'd seen the red painted on them as soon as she came out of her room with my sister. She'd stunned me into silence as she smiled at everyone earlier that night, and my brother-in-law beat me to the punch of complimenting her.

Now, my hands roved over her body, trying to memorize every stunning part of her. I threaded my fingers through her hair, then brushed them over her collarbone, over her breasts, over all the curves of her body until I gripped her ass as I walked her backwards so she was up against the garden wall.

Everly may have wanted to go inside, but as my hand found the slit of her dress and slid into her panties, and she gasped. "You know, Everly, even if I wasn't your husband, you're mine, and your pussy has proven that time and time again. How long have you been wet for me? All night?"

She bit her lip and rode my hand, her hips rocking back and forth, her arousal coating my fingers well enough that when I thrust them into her, there was barely resistance. "I wish I could stop you, Declan. I wish I could just say this is ridiculous and be done." She whimpered.

I wished I could do the same. I knew what was for the best, how she looked at my niece with longing, how she smiled at kids, how she shared with me she wanted them. I knew she deserved it all. Yet, I looked at her sapphire-blue eyes in the moonlight and I wanted it with her, couldn't fathom her having it with someone else.

She arched her tits toward me as I curled my fingers into her and then her hands fell to my slacks. "I need you right now. I've needed you all night."

"I should have fucked you on that counter earlier."

She purred out that she agreed, that maybe she would have had more control then.

I shook my head against her neck as I licked it and let her work my cock out of my briefs. "It wouldn't have mattered. There's no control when it comes to having you. Seeing you dancing all night, seeing how you stood up to Wes, seeing how you were an angel to my niece... I need my wife here in this garden tonight, Everly. I need you."

She threw her leg on my hip and guided my cock to her entrance. I moved the tip of it against her folds and then tipped my hips so I could rub her arousal over that clit with my piercing. She moved herself back and forth, trying to ride me into an orgasm.

I breathed against her lips, "I get you screaming my name before you get my whole cock, Drop." And then I worked her pussy faster, rubbing my thumb over her clit, massaging it just how she liked as I slid my fingers in and out, in and out. She moved her hand up and down my dick in the same rhythm before she squeezed and cried out.

I didn't muffle her screams, didn't try to hide what we were doing, although the garden bushes did a good job of that already.

"That's right, baby. Scream my name so loud the whole gala hears you. Don't they know better than to bid on my wife? Tell them now who you belong to."

She whimpered my name over and over as the aftershocks

shivered through her body. Even still, her hand stayed on my cock and then pulled me forward. I grabbed her hair and whispered in her ear, "I think if I could, I'd have you forever, Everly." And then I shoved into her.

Her pussy gripped me tightly and was slick with her orgasm. She took me whole in one rough thrust, gasping as her hands dug into my shoulders.

I wasn't gentle or even focused now. I thrust deep in her over and over, trying to make it clear she was mine, trying to make her understand she belonged to no one else.

Trying. But as I stared into her shining eyes filled with a brewing desire again, I lost myself to her. I realized she didn't belong to me. I belonged to her.

I fucked her hard, wanting to own her but realizing I couldn't.

She held my sanity, my control, my power, my heart in her hands. She owned me.

My body built toward release, every muscle in me tightening to have her all to myself, to keep her close to me forever, and then I pumped into her one last time before hitting my own high and coming as I swore fluently into her neck. "Fuck. Fuck. Fuck."

She did the same, her arms around my neck now, pulling me close as she whimpered over and over, coming on my cock.

"That's it, baby. Get all you need. Ride my cock like the pretty, good girl you are."

She did just that for one, two more thrusts before slumping into me and kissing my neck.

I held her tight, didn't let her slide down my body just yet. I smelled her hair, rubbed her back, stayed connected to her as long as I could.

I didn't want to leave the garden, didn't want to leave this night and go back to reality. Here, we could be under a spell, lost in the magic of one another, not worrying about outside factors.

Yet, she finally sighed and untangled her legs from around my hips. She rearranged her dress as her gaze held mine with a vulnerability I hadn't seen most of the night. "We're going round and round, Declan, and I don't know if it's right to do that without admitting that I keep thinking about the decision we have to make. We're being reckless by taking what we want in a garden and not discussing our future."

I tucked my cock back into my trousers and tried not to feel an immediate sense of concern at her words. "Or we can keep trying to take it day by day."

"Right. But I don't do that." She sighed and tried to smooth the waves of her hair that should have always been given the permission to run wild. "I... I've been thinking about it all night. Your niece, she's so beautiful, Declan."

"And?" I lifted a brow.

She took a breath and whispered, "And what if we had a daughter like her? What if she had your eyes and my hair and wanted to dance with us just like Carolina? But also...what if we didn't? What if we can't make that beautiful soul because we didn't start with what your sister and her husband started with? We need to love." Her voice shook, and I saw how she tried to have the courage to share the feelings she thought I wanted to hear. "And I think I could—"

"I don't love you, Drop." I cut her off fast. I needed to say it out loud anyway. Maybe if I could convince her of it, I'd believe it myself. I didn't want her love this way. I wouldn't have it be like this. Not with the weight of a will bearing down on us.

She needed to love me and I needed to love her without conditions. To do it under a commitment we made to each other for a damn will would be to betray the one thing she deserved to get. She deserved a beautiful life with no stipulations, with only love, with everything she'd ever dreamed of.

"Okay," she breathed out, and her posture deflated, like I'd taken all the wind from her sails and snuffed out the tiny bit of sun she had started to see on a rainy day. I knew it had to be this way though. "But do you think you ever could?" she whispered, and fuck, my heart broke.

Everly didn't push or need to ask for anything from me. She barely let the world in to see her mask slip and witness her real emotions. She was strong, but in that moment, I saw the vulnerable, soft part she hid from the world. And that part would be broken and ruined if I did what I was about to do now.

"I can't." I shook my head, backing away from her. I couldn't subject her to having a baby with me under these conditions. I couldn't steal the one thing she'd planned for all her life by barreling through it in hopes we'd still become the healthy family she dreamed of.

"I'll get your mother's yoga studio, Everly. And I'll make sure the media leaves you alone."

She stumbled back, clutching her heart. "I don't... I...don't want that from you."

"I'll take care of it. Anastasia will agree..."

She'd told me herself the second time we went into Mrs. Johnson's office and she told us Carl was requiring us to have a child—happily ever afters aren't made this way. We couldn't have this inheritance hanging over our head anymore. I had to take care of it for both of us. Then, we'd have a chance at the dream of a family that she deserved.

I hoped one day she would understand that I'd fallen so beyond in love with her that I was willing to do the one thing that would make her hate me.

Betray her.

CHAPTER 34: EVERLY

One night in the garden, lost in the maze of flowers and foliage, under the moonlight, he'd fucked me like he used to.

Rough, in control, on instinct that was too powerful to tiptoe around. But then he'd stared at me with pain in his eyes as waves crashed on the shoreline and the symphony of violins serenaded the night air. It was a devastating soundtrack to play in the background of his words.

"I don't love you, Drop."

Five words. That was all it took for me to really feel heartbreak. Deeper than I'd ever felt it before. And when I asked if he could, he shook his head and told me he couldn't.

How could I continue a night that's supposed to be beautiful after that? How could I go back inside and dance as if my heart wasn't shattered? I whispered that I wanted to go home. And he didn't fight me at all. He had his car pulled around to a back entrance since it was free of media, and I waited in the lobby hoping no one would see me sneaking out.

The car ride was silent. A painful silence that crushed my soul with unanswered questions and what-ifs, how-could-yous, and is-this-its.

The gate creaked open as we approached our fortress, and I stared at his ridiculously big house where I thought I could somehow make it all work.

"I need to know if you're—" I choked back a sob that surprised us both. His head whipped over as my hand went to my mouth, and I tried to hold back my pain. I shook my head jerkily and wished I would just stop there but my heart couldn't let it go. "I need to know if you're going to try to keep your shares."

"Everly..." He said it with so much pain that I knew I couldn't handle the answer. "This is for us. I can't make this something it's not. I care about you too much. I thought I could, but you deserve—"

"Don't," I stopped him, and I knew I wouldn't be able to contain my emotions. This was my breaking point. "I've handled a lot in my life. But I can't handle it if you say it's for me. Don't you dare." This was betrayal. This was heartbreak.

This was our end. And I guess he was letting me have it, because he let the car idle in silence, not giving me a damn word of explanation more.

"If that's the case, Mr. Hardy, I'd like to give my two weeks' notice."

"What?" he barked out, his eyes widening. Then he hit the steering wheel when he realized I wasn't kidding. "No. You can't quit. Where are you going to go? Back to that fucking town that treated you like shit?"

"It doesn't matter. I don't want to stay here," I retorted back at him and then growled when I felt tears running down my face. Why did I have to cry now? "I can't stand it here, and without you? I'd rather take my chances back home."

"You're not leaving," he said like it was final. "What Anastasia and I do...you have to know, Everly, that has nothing to do with me and you."

"It has everything to do with us!" I screamed. "Do you want to watch me have a child with your brother? Should I call Dom?"

"You better fucking not," he said in a low voice.

"Even if I did, he would never." I cut my hand through the air to emphasize my point. "He would never ever do that to you. You're his brother. And that's what you don't get. I'm alone here. I'm alone everywhere except when I'm with my mother. I have no one else, but I thought I had you. I thought this stupid commitment we made was real, that we'd get through it and wouldn't hurt each other. But I was wrong. So devastatingly wrong." I ripped the car door open and rushed into the guesthouse. When he opened his car door, I yelled, "Don't you dare follow me."

For once, he listened. For once, I was in charge. Maybe he gave me that, knowing he was crushing my heart, breaking me before he left me. Or maybe he gave me that because he was letting me go. Either way, I knew I wouldn't fall apart in front of him.

Or any of them.

I wouldn't let them know they broke me more than I'd been broken before. I was as strong as I allowed myself to be. So, I promised myself I'd get it together in a day or two. I promised myself the emotion I was feeling was only because we'd made a commitment to each other to get through this stupid marriage together. I stared down at his ring on my finger and fisted my hand tight. I'd give myself another day of wearing that too before I took it off.

I fell asleep, tears streaming down my cheeks, broken from his commitment. And then from his betrayal.

* * *

The next morning, he texted about breakfast.

Declan: Come eat with me.

Me: No. Please leave me alone.

Declan: I'll bring you coffee.

His car idled in front of the guesthouse, and I wondered if I could tell him I was sick. Instead, I texted him that Clara was coming to get me. She wasn't, but that wasn't the point.

I couldn't be around him. He had to understand that.

Declan: I'll wait until she gets here.

Looking up at the ceiling, I let out the exasperated sigh I had been holding in, tears springing to my eyes again. Couldn't he just stop? Didn't he get my heart was destroyed?

Declan: Would you like coffee before she comes?

No, I didn't want coffee. I'd have to see his ridiculously beautiful face. And the sad thing was I wanted to. I wanted to crumble into him and beat on his chest and tell him he'd hurt me and then wait for him to grovel and make it up to me. Yet my heart was scared he wouldn't, that I'd have to watch my stepsister have the life I dreamed of with him instead.

The babies. The family. The life with the man I loved.

And how was I supposed to leave that man when I still lived next to him, when he was still waiting on me, still driving me to work, still bringing me coffee?

Me: I made some myself.

Declan: Don't lie. Come get it.

Me: Declan, it'll hurt to see you, and I don't think it's a good idea.

Declan: It hurts me too, but I'll be damned if I let that get in the way of having you in my life. We're still friends, Everly. You still have me.

I'd never been his friend. Maybe Declan didn't understand that about me. I'd never had any of them as friends.

Except Clara. So I did the only thing I could do in that moment that would stop all this. I texted her for a ride. And she immediately texted back.

Clara: Oh, I'm happy to hear from you. I was concerned after we didn't see you the rest of the night. I can come now if you'd like. I'm going to the bakery early to get some new recipes going.

Me: Can you bring Anastasia over with you if she's available? I'm convinced both she and Melinda have blocked my number, but Declan would like to talk to her.

Clara: Sure? Why would Anastasia need to come to talk to Declan? Why

doesn't he call her? Tell me what's going on first.

Me: Just bring her.

Then, I took my time picking out yoga pants he hadn't bought me and pulling them on. I pulled my hair back into a tight bun so I didn't have to think about the way his fingers would thread through it. I put on clear lip gloss and ate some breakfast without him.

I stomped outside as Clara pulled up with Anastasia because we were going to end this charade right now. "I'm not driving with you to work."

Declan's green eyes narrowed on me like lasers focusing their power. "What are you doing?"

"Anastasia, Declan and I are divorcing. He'd love for you to drive with him to work so he can discuss further details with you."

"Everly!" he growled as Anastasia squealed and skipped over to his car, but I was already turning around to walk away.

CHAPTER 35: EVERLY

After a whole week of niceties, I was falling into a good enough routine that I only wanted to vomit once or twice a day when I saw them together. No one asked, but everyone caught on. With the news articles featuring photos of Anastasia in his car now and online outlets broadcasting videos of them walking into HEAT Health and Fitness together, it was pretty obvious what had happened. And yet, no article was printed about me ever.

I guess Declan was making sure of that.

I didn't ask him though. I tried to avoid him completely instead. Yet every night that week, he'd still come to me to have his wrist rehabbed.

"Your wrist has nearly one hundred percent mobility back," I murmured that specific night in the private studio we reserved for one-on-ones sometimes.

"I don't think so," he countered and winced when he bent it this time. It was fake. The man could have probably lifted me up with that wrist and felt no pain whatsoever.

"If you want to keep rehabbing it, you can, but I only have another week left working here, Declan." I shrugged and did an arm stretch on the floor to release some of the tension I was starting to feel.

His brow furrowed in question.

"I'm quitting, remember?"

"No." He said it casually as he rewrapped some of the tape across his tendons to help stabilize mobility while he continued weight training on his forearm. "You never turned in a letter of resignation."

I stuttered out, "But I told you. You knew I was quitting. I'm happy to help find a replacement in the next week—"

"You're required to give a month's written notice or you're liable to be sued. It's in the employment contract for everyone here at HEAT Health and Fitness."

"Well, I'm sure you can make an exception—"

"There's no exceptions when it comes to you," he ground out. "HR has already been made aware if anyone lets you out of your contract early, they'll lose their job."

"Why are you doing this?" I stood from where I had been sitting with him and glared at him.

He took a deep breath. I noted he had dark circles under his eyes like I had under mine, and his gaze looked tortured. "I'm supposed to take care of you. I'm your..."

"You're not anything to me anymore," I corrected. "Your rehab with me is hereby over. I won't be doing your sessions anymore." My voice shook as I said it, but I knew I had to stop this. I couldn't be around him, not when my heart felt love even though my mind didn't want to. And I felt it.

I felt it when I looked at the ring I couldn't bring myself to remove. I felt it when Anastasia constantly idled around him. I felt it as I saw him make a conscious effort to avoid where I would be in an attempt to not hurt me more.

He couldn't have me and her. It wasn't possible. I spun on my heel and left him in that studio as I murmured, "I'll find my own ride home tonight. Please don't wait for me." I'd said that very thing each night, and each night he took Anastasia instead. She'd found a way to spend most of her day at the hotel spa and her sister's bakery, waiting for him anyway.

He catered to her now, not me.

Still, neither of us had acknowledged the divorce papers. I'd called Mrs. Johnson at the beginning of the week to file the petition. I knew he'd been served the papers because I'd asked Mrs. Johnson to arrange a "casual" visit to Declan's office with a process server that everyone in the gym would assume was on the legal team. There need not be any drama, but I wanted this to happen as quickly as possible. Still, it had been days and he hadn't delivered a signed copy to my door yet.

Maybe he'd been busy. Maybe he was figuring out the logistics. Maybe he needed to have Anastasia sign on the dotted line before he had me sign on a much different one.

Thankfully, Dom was at the ring when I walked out of the studio, and he smiled soft at me like he knew everything that was going on. "Want to spar, Evie?"

"Like you wouldn't believe." I grabbed equipment to throw on, took a deep breath, and got into the ring with him.

Here I could count on a different type of pain. And I intended to experience it to the fullest extent.

We worked around and around in there for twenty minutes at least. My head wasn't in the game, and I took Dom's slap to my headpiece without even a grunt. I was seeking pain that evening and he knew it.

It was my right as a human to do that. The more I thought about Declan and Anastasia, the more my frustration twisted up further and further. He acted like he was doing me a favor, like breaking my heart was worth this type of pain, and like him being my friend was best too.

"Evie, you're not even trying," Dom bellowed as his muscled arms fell to his sides, beads of sweat rolling over his bronzed skin. A few heads whipped our way in the boxing ring of the gym.

"Don't get all worked up." I shrugged and then cracked my neck and rubbed my jaw. The sting was there, tingling through my face with the reminder that I could feel but also recover from the pain, that it would drive me if I needed it to. "Let's go again."

"Are you kidding? I held back on that one." He shook his head and started ripping off his hand gear. "Your head's not in it. I'm not knocking you out because you want to keep going when you shouldn't. What's gotten into you?"

"One more." I licked my lips and squared up to him. "You woke me up."

He had. I remembered the feeling, the shock of being hit for the first time, how it ricocheted around in my head like a damn ping-pong of a nightmare. Andy had been good at not doing it often. We'd been together two years, and he'd only hit me four times. Yet, each time was like the first time, and that fourth time in that room was the last time I let it happen ever again.

Self-defense taught me I had control, that I could control the pain even if I couldn't control the other person's actions. I could use their actions against them though. And I could control my own reaction.

He growled before he pulled the gear back into place. "This is against my better judgment, Evie. I have a feeling my brother's going to kill me."

This time when he rushed me, I smiled. My body lunged for him instead of backing away. Pain woke me up, made me feel alive, reminded me that I was strong in my emotions, that I was fueled by adrenaline. When he came for my throat, I used his forearm as leverage and, with a quick twist, carried my momentum to jump on his back and put him in a choke hold. He fell back on me, and I wheezed.

Damn, Dom was trying to show me today that my head wasn't in it.

How could it be after seeing him?

Even with the wind knocked out of me, though, I held tight as he lifted his body and dropped it again, letting his weight crush me. My grip slipped just enough that he took it as an opportunity. Within seconds, he was back on top of me, hand on my neck, body between my legs, me struggling like I wanted no girl to ever struggle.

I knew how to get out of this. I knew what to do and how to prove I'd gotten faster and stronger, that I could take care of myself.

I'd done it before.

Yet, I wasn't given the chance.

Suddenly, Dom was ripped off of me, his grip slipping from my neck so fast, I'd probably get rug burn.

"What the fuck are you doing?" The voice was deep with fury and laced with menace. I could place that voice anywhere. My body instantly reacted to it every time I heard it even as I wheezed for oxygen.

I wheezed only because it was a body's initial reaction to gaining oxygen after being choked, not because I couldn't handle it. I was fine.

Just fine.

"We're sparring, Dec." Dom threw his hands, but he was smiling and shaking his head like Declan was insane.

The smile died when Declan charged him and threw him on his back. They must have done this before because Dom put up an extremely good fight. They flipped one another over again and again before Declan pinned him down and had his fist cocked to punch his brother square in the face.

"Declan!" I screamed and grabbed his arm before he could. "Are you crazy? We're in the ring. There's a bunch of people around. It's a standard self-defense practice and—"

"No more!" he bellowed at me, releasing his brother to come to standing. "You're done with the self-defense instruction."

"Declan, I've been—"

"Everyone hear me?" He walked around the ring and eyed every man in the gym. "You touch my wife, you answer to me. And I'll break every bone in your body before I let you leave my gym. Do you understand?"

No one answered directly. I think they were all as shocked as I was. Before I could say anything, he bent under the rope and hopped out of the ring. "Everly *Hardy*, get your ass in my office, now."

Shit.

CHAPTER 36: DECLAN

"Are you out of your fucking mind letting a man touch you that way?" I fumed when I slammed the door to my office upstairs.

"Are you out of your mind calling me a Hardy when I'm not and acting the way you just did over a standard sparring *in the ring?*" she threw back, and her chastising tone could have brought a weaker man to his death. Truly. She wanted me in hell, and I felt like I was. The fact that I had to tell Anastasia to stop following me on the way to grab my brother off my wife was enough in and of itself to piss me right the fuck off.

Anastasia and her mother were pushing me way too far for the damn studio. They knew they were getting something that held a value to me above all else because they knew I loved Everly. Anastasia and Melinda had both sneered at me, asking if I really would do all this for a woman, if she was really worth it. I'd answered yes without hesitation, and Anastasia smiled like she had me by the balls. They agreed to me buying the studio that Everly held dear for an extravagant amount as long as Anastasia was seen a few times with the cameras following us around. She wanted to go to dinner a few times to discuss it. She wanted this, she wanted that.

I wanted to rage, though, seeing Everly's face.

I couldn't tell her what I was doing. She'd fight me on it, say she'd help figure out a way to do it herself. She didn't want anything given to her for free, didn't want anyone to struggle for her. I saw it in how she'd never driven my cars, how she never took money from Carl, how she didn't ever ask me to get that yoga studio for her.

Yet, it's the one thing I would do. I didn't care about the shares of the empire. I'd figure that out later. First, I was appeasing Anastasia so that Everly could have the one thing that had meant something to her from the very beginning. I was getting rid of the inheritance hanging over our head, and then I was going to ask her on a damn date for real. I was going to make sure she knew I loved her for real.

We were going to start completely over.

I hated that I had to make her think I didn't love her, but it was the only way we'd get through it. I couldn't make her have a baby with me now, not when she'd wanted one in a completely different way.

Seeing her think we wouldn't be together, that we wouldn't be trying after this inheritance went through probate, though, was driving me insane, driving me to madness.

Then, I'd actually come to blows with my brother over him wrestling her to the ground like she was a damn rag doll. Hadn't he read the papers? "Men shouldn't be putting their hands on you that way."

"You used to put your hands on me like that all the time, Declan. We sparred in the ring before and, well, we've sparred while we screwed too," she shot back and then proceeded to pace back and forth in front of the window overlooking the oceanside. "Just because we aren't doing that anymore, doesn't mean I can't do it with someone else."

"What the fuck is that supposed to mean?"

She stopped and turned to me, her eyes full of blue fury, her body vibrating with a tension I'd never seen from her. "You think I give a shit about a rough-and-tumble? I enjoy it. I enjoy knowing I can hold my own in the ring, that there are people out there I trust enough to step into it with me. And as for you and me, it means I fucking loved screwing around with you." She closed her eyes like she was in pain before opening them again. "But we won't have that anymore, just like we won't have anything anymore. So I'll have to find it with someone else now."

Didn't she understand we couldn't move on from each other that easily?

I didn't know if she meant to taunt me, to remind me that another man could have her—that another man *would* have her if I didn't figure out the will—but it drove me insane. I was already wound tight enough to snap, but it happened to be her who snipped the small thread holding me together.

"What the hell did you just say?" I growled as I stepped toward her.

She didn't back up. She pointed her finger at me in fury. "You aren't the man I'll do it with anymore, but you can bet your ass that I will do it with someone else once I'm out of here." Then she spun around and went to the computer on my desk. She typed with purpose and then my printer jolted to life. Before my eyes, her letter of resignation appeared. "Here's your written notice. One month."

When I didn't take it right away, she shoved it into my chest and then grabbed my wrist to slam it there too. She was walking out the door before I realized I was losing her. I was losing everything I wanted.

I grabbed her elbow and tapped my watch before swiping it over the FOB area next to the door. With a click of a button, I shut down the room's cameras and locked the door. Then I spun her to face me. "You're not done with me."

"Aren't I?" She lifted a brow.

Everly wanted a fight. I felt it. She'd embraced her anger and was ready to throw it at me like a fucking fireball. "You don't get to be done with me for at least another month." I slammed the contract down on the desk and then shoved her in front of it. "See, you just typed out one month."

"Working for you means nothing."

"It means everything because I can't live without you. I'm so far in love with you that I can't see straight. You know I go to bed touching this?" I held up my hand and pointed to the string on my ring finger. "And I wake up still touching it, like it can bring me closer to you. I've suffered days with seeing the hurt in your eyes and wanting to make it better, with seeing you pulling away and wanting to pull you back. I. Love. You," I ground out.

She stood in front of me, her eyes wide with shock first, but I saw how her whole body clenched up with my last declaration. "You can't fucking say that to me," she whispered, her teeth clenched together like she was trying to hold on to her anger. After another blink, she bellowed, "You don't get to say that to me!"

She flew up to me, holding nothing back and I felt her emotion unleash in the room, like her heart was shattering as she pounded her fists into my chest furiously. I let her, let her get her hate for me out because I wanted to feel her pain too.

I deserved it.

Then, I pulled her close, hungry for the scent of her coconut shampoo and the feel of her body close to me. "I fucking love you, Raindrop. I do."

"Well, you can't. You literally can't after what you've done.

You've left me for someone else." She shook her head back and forth, her chin trembling. "I can't love you now."

"You don't mean that," I shot back. She couldn't get over me that quickly even if she believed that I was catering to Anastasia, that I was trying to do something more with her. Right? My heart lurched at the thought.

I was appeasing Anastasia by being seen with her only to confirm that I would get the yoga studio, only to confirm Anastasia and her mother would let me buy it out. We'd discussed it over dinners, gone round and round about what they wanted. It was a shit show I knew was going to happen.

I knew Everly would believe it too, knew I'd be slicing at her spirit with a blunt knife.

It wasn't at all true. I hadn't even contemplated it. I'd never have a baby with anyone except the woman I loved. Yet, this was the only way to get her mother's studio, to make sure she wouldn't intervene, to make it all right even if it felt wrong for a moment.

I needed her to keep her distance for now but I'd lost control. Lost my sanity in that moment. And even still, the sanity was slipping again as she shrugged like I didn't mean a thing to her.

So I acted out. I stepped forward and yanked her pants straight down her legs to prove a point. She gasped when I ripped her panties from her too.

Then I shoved her toward the desk and she went, bending over it willingly but she threw out words of hate too. "I might want you to fuck me, Declan. I might need some closure, but I'm still not yours, and we're still done."

"No," I announced loudly with conviction. I pointed to the notice she'd given me on the table. "You just typed out I own you for one month until you leave. Reread whatever you wrote, Everly. If you want, I'll have our divorce papers delivered too. Better yet, here's my phone." I threw it on the desk in front of her. "Call the lawyer if you want."

I started to work her pussy, and she whimpered. It was proof I ruled us here, that I wasn't letting her go that easily.

I didn't wait to thrust my cock in this time either. I pulled my gym shorts down and fucked her hard—no restraint, no hesitation. This was me with her the way she wanted it. My grip was bruising, and her nails digging into the wood would leave marks.

I didn't care. I pulled her dark hair every time I thrust in and out, in and out. "This. Pussy. This Heart. They. Are. Mine. No piece of paper is going to change that. Not after a day. Not after a month."

"They're not," she breathed out. She probably thought I wouldn't hear, but I saw red.

My thrusts became erratic as my hands flew over her body, touching her everywhere, like I couldn't get enough of her. I squeezed her tits and smacked her ass. "How many times now haven't you listened?" I asked her.

She cried out that she didn't know. Surely she assumed we'd both lost count.

"Twenty-one," I said. "Twenty-one times you haven't listened, haven't let me open the door for you, haven't let me take care of you."

"You can't be seriou—"

I smacked her ass hard. And then thrust in.

The loud sound accompanied by her moaning echoed around us again, and I pulled my cock out, letting my piercing ghost over her clit. "Remember your safe word, baby?"

She nodded, biting her lip, but I knew she wouldn't use it. She wanted this, needed it as much as I did.

Pain. Pleasure. Pain-pleasure.

Like a yo-yo being played with in the most delicious way, she cried out and then moaned every time I slapped her ass cheek and then gave her my cock, getting higher and higher, closer and closer to an orgasm.

"Please," she murmured, and I laughed but there was no joy in it. It was tortured. I was lost in the hell of wanting to do the right thing and knowing I couldn't. I couldn't stop even if I wanted to.

"Use your safe word," I commanded because fuck, I had to stop myself.

"No," she said loudly, full of defiance, knowing it would push me further over the edge.

"Drop, I'll fuck you so rough you'll have a hard time sitting comfortably tomorrow. That what you want?"

"It's what I'm begging you for," she whispered out. And then she moaned, "Please."

"Jesus, why do you have to be so damn good? Always my good girl begging me when you know I can't resist." I growled and smacked her ass again, her skin turning that pink color I loved just for me. "I can't fucking quit you even when I try. You've broken me like I've broken you. I need you. Need you at breakfast, at dinner, here, everywhere. I can't fucking breathe without you, will never be able to live without you."

Tears streamed down her cheeks as I landed fifteen smacks to her lush ass. I watched how her skin reddened more and more and how my cock glistened more and more with each thrust too. Her arousal dripped down her thighs, her pussy took every bit of my dick like it was made just for me, and her moans became hoarse. On the last smack, I pulled out of her fully just so I could tease her sensitive skin with my fingers. "You're. My. Wife. Everly. Do you understand?"

"I do. I do. I do," she whispered again and again, and I knew she was coming. I felt her pussy throbbing, pulsing, and then clenching as I slid a finger in her and curled it into her G-spot.

"Good girl." I dragged it out, letting her ride my hand through her orgasm before I positioned my cock at her entrance again. "You feel me here, baby?"

"Declan..."

I brushed a thumb over her bundle of nerves and she gasped as I said, "You're quivering for me right now, Drop. This clit needs me to rub it, huh?"

She didn't answer even as I pushed the tip of my cock in her and she tried to rock back to take all of it.

"You don't get my cock until you say it, baby. Tell me you want me to rub that sweet clit. Tell me you want this, that you're still mine."

She shook her head and bit her lip, but her hips rolled against me, her tender skin warm against mine even as she said, "I'm not yours anymore."

Her words made me lose my mind. I wanted to fuck her so hard, she'd remember who she belonged to, who I belonged to too. "You're my wife. I'm your husband. You're mine. I'm yours, Drop. That hasn't changed."

I thrusted into her hard and fast, wanting her to feel our connection, wanting her to love me like I loved her, wanting her to understand my cock was the only one that belonged in her. When her sex tightened around me, she whined, "I hate how much I miss this, hate that you're right when you should be wrong."

"That's right." I reared back and pushed into her again and again ruthlessly, viciously, with no remorse even as I made the desk quake under us. I wanted her to feel how we made love for days. "This pretty pussy belongs to me."

She nodded and whimpered like she couldn't deny it anymore. "I'm yours."

My grip tightened on her and I knew she'd have bruises later, but I was too scared of this being over and scared of losing her again that I couldn't control it. "Good fucking girl. You're mine. You'll *always* be mine."

CHAPTER 37: EVERLY

He was right. He'd always be a part of me. I'd always be his in some way. But...

"But she's going to have your baby, isn't she?"

"Drop"—his voice cracked and my heart felt pain even as my body felt the pleasure. Pain and pleasure, a mixture that warred in my soul. He was betraying me even though he'd committed to me—"it doesn't matter what's happening with her. You understand that, right?"

I didn't answer. He knew good and well it mattered, but I was too far gone, too close to my orgasm to respond. Then he smacked my ass and I cried out, the orgasm barreling fast through me. "You'd better understand. Because until the divorce is final, don't think for a second you can forget. I'll tear apart any man who comes near you. I fucking mean it, Everly. You're. My. Wife."

His statement had me squeezing his cock tight, my body still reacting to him even though it shouldn't have. His thrusts got erratic before he groaned, emptying his seed where he shouldn't have. Yet, I rolled my hips against him, wanting all of it. If this was our last time, I wanted all of him, every part I could take.

It was only a second later that I heard Anastasia's voice down the hallway. His brows came down hard, and his Adam's apple bobbed as I scrambled away from him to pull my pants back up. "Sign the divorce papers, Declan." As I said the words, more tears sprang to my eyes.

"Everly, I'm not going to." He shook his head, his cock glistening with my arousal still. He didn't bother tucking it back in right away, like he had nothing to hide as he grabbed the back of my neck and pulled me to him. He didn't ask permission or hesitate when he took my lips in his. Even as I bit his bottom lip at first to show I was mad, he just groaned, waiting for me to let him in. My weakness was him. My body responded and took one last kiss. He devoured me, lapping at every part of my mouth like he was memorizing every piece of it.

When I shoved him back, I was panting. "You will sign the papers, Declan, because Anastasia is out there. And I'm not waiting for us any longer. This is over. You've got one month."

I stormed past him and scanned my watch to open the doors fast enough that Anastasia flew in past me and started bickering with him.

I didn't say anything to her. I didn't need to. I wanted out of there. I scheduled an Uber and immediately packed my stuff from my locker to go home. I'd lost control by letting that happen, but I knew it couldn't again, especially when my heart broke a little more with Anastasia there to witness my walk of shame.

I ignored the calls from Declan and my mother as I showered that night, but the call I knew I couldn't ignore came from Tonya.

I answered as I towel-dried my curls. "Tonya, what's up?"

"He's out, and he's looking for you." Those seven words. It was all she had to whisper for my blood to freeze, my hand to shake, my heart to beat out of my chest.

"Why?" I whispered.

I heard her take one breath and then another before she

responded. "He stopped by. He's asking about you and Declan. He's jittery about it this time. I..." She hesitated. "I told him to go to hell, Evie, and I've never done that. He looked so furious. But he left, and I heard he's been going around town asking people about you—"

"You need to leave, Tonya. Come here and let the dust settle." I cut her off sternly. Tonya never responded well to me trying to protect her. We'd been through his brutality together. It bonded us for life but also separated us too.

Cruel.

What that man had done to us was the cruelest thing. He'd beaten me down enough mentally that I hadn't questioned his intentions at first, hadn't questioned how he slowly morphed my self-confidence. Now, the pain we felt when we were with each other, reliving every moment, it almost forced us to be strangers. She couldn't look at me without pain, and I couldn't look at her without remorse and guilt. "Being in that town isn't good for your health."

She sighed. "I know that now. God, do I know it now. I should have testified with you, Evie."

I tried to disagree, to see the good in the place I'd left behind. "I don't know if that's true—"

"Stop defending a town that shoved you out, Evie. Stop defending me. I should have been there for you! I didn't even say he assaulted me. How much of a coward am I?"

I shut my eyes, trying my best not to relive it all.

"I practically shoved you out of town, too, okay? I wanted this all to disappear but it's not. And if I leave, he gets his way. Don't you see that?"

I tried to cut her off, but she didn't let me.

"No. You left for me, but otherwise you would have stayed.

I know you would have. You would have stood tall and silent and fucking made him walk past you every single day because you could take all the pain and not dish it back out. You didn't break like me. Every time I saw you, I was too scared—"

"You don't have to explain," I tried to tell her, but I choked over my words. She was saying everything I'd hoped she would, but I couldn't be there to hug her, couldn't tell her it would be okay.

"I know. You'd never make me explain. You'd never make me do anything—which you should have. You should have made me testify against him."

"Tonya," I chastised, "come stay with me for a month or two. We can figure out someplace safe—"

"I can't," she said, harsher than I thought she wanted to. Then she cleared her throat. "I can't do it, Everly. I love you, but I can't see you and that look you always get in your eyes. None of this was your fault, and I'm just... I destroyed you, and I can't take that back, no matter how much I want to. Just be careful." She hung up without another word.

So, I did the only thing I could do. I sent a text.

> **Me: You have something to say, come say it. You know where I work. You've obviously seen the magazines. Stop bothering my friends. If you want to bother someone, come bother me.**

I deleted the thread afterward.

CHAPTER 38: EVERLY

Every morning for a week, he left coffee on my doorstep. He never texted, but there was always a driver outside too. My heart bleeding out happened in snapshots.

A snapshot of him driving her to work.

A snapshot of him leaving work to walk to dinner with her at the hotel.

Snapshot after snapshot.

He didn't try to talk to me anymore though, and I didn't try to talk with him. But neither of us brought signed divorce papers to the other's doorstep. We couldn't pull the trigger.

My mind was tangled up in other things, especially the moment I got the phone call from an unknown number as I got home from work.

"Everly, so glad I caught you. I don't know how this slipped through the cracks, but I'm checking your medical charts, and I know you said you were on birth control at your first visit, but when we did that bloodwork, everything looked great except that—well, you don't have to try for a baby. You're already pregnant."

"I'm sorry?" I gripped my counter. "*What*?"

"I know. I was surprised as well. Rings are quite effective as birth control, but there's still about nine in a hundred women who get pregnant. Have you gotten your period?"

"No." I knew it'd been probably three months without it. I just hadn't worried. "But the doctor said I would be irregular once coming off birth control and—"

"Well, that about confirms it." The woman sounded excited even as I felt like I was about to faint, about to have my life completely changed. "We'll have you come in for a test to see how far along you are. We're so sorry we missed that with all the genetic testing we were doing. Our new staff must have overlooked putting that in your MyChart. What day works best for you and Mr. Hardy?"

"What day works best?" I repeated, in total shock. No day worked best. We weren't having a child. We couldn't be. We'd been protected at that time. There was no way I was having a baby.

Except I was. And Declan had told me he didn't love me. We had divorce papers in our possession. He was driving Anastasia around. For all I knew, he could be sleeping with her by now.

"Would Friday at three p.m. work?"

"I can come Friday," I said in a monotone as my heart galloped away, trying its best to catch up and pump blood through my veins like it felt me slipping. My vision blurred, and I sat down. "I'll be there Friday," I repeated again and hung up.

I sat there for hours. I didn't reach for the phone. Didn't reach for the TV remote. I simply sat with tears streaming down my face as I considered how I could make this work on my own. I vowed never to tell him. I vowed to raise my child in love, and I knew forcing Declan to stay in this marriage wasn't what either of us wanted.

Plus, Andy was coming. I knew he would.

And when your past catches up to you, you don't run. You fight it off and make sure the blowback doesn't injure the ones you love around you. I needed to handle this on my own so my baby and I could have a clean start.

Declan had been right to leave me behind. He'd been born in love, wrapped in it, secured by it. His family was the epitome of love.

I was born into a home where my mother worked diligently to provide for me and teach me that I could only rely on myself in the world. I longed for love and went looking for it, not knowing I was looking in all the wrong places.

I wouldn't do that to my child. So I signed the divorce papers and went to sleep clutching them as I sobbed.

* * *

The next morning, I folded them up, slid my ring off, and opened the front door to go drop off the envelope. Instead, I found coffee on my doorstep, steaming hot like he'd just left it. My phone beeped.

> Declan: Coffee's there for you. Driver should be there soon too. Have a wonderful day at work. Won't be there today.

Perfect, I thought, but then immediately my mind wondered where he would be even as I went to stash the envelop in his mailbox.

Maybe he wouldn't see it for days. Maybe I could plan where I would move to and pack up before we had to talk. Maybe he didn't care to talk at all. Anastasia potentially could have smoothed all the waters.

His driver took me to work where I did yoga with the kids and then followed up with one-on-ones. I meandered over to

Clara's bakery after work to let her know what I could. "I'm leaving in a little less than a month but I'd like us to keep in touch."

"No you're not," she said in disbelief and then yelped in the kitchen. "Shit. Now I burned my hand." She rounded the corner and made her way to my side of the bar so she could sit down next to me. "What's going on?"

"I'm just done here. My time is up. I don't think I ever really belonged here in the first place."

"You're insane. You're the only real thing around here, and we can't lose you. Noah is finally acting like a real human, and Wes finally has his ego in check. Dom almost got punched—which was a long time coming—and Declan..." She stopped and took my hands in hers. "He'll be devastated without you."

"He's with your sister now."

She wrinkled her nose. "Don't remind me. She's acting like they're together, but..." She got up and went to grab two brownies from the glass case next to the register as she narrowed her eyes and shook her head. "Something's not right. Declan barely talks to her, doesn't even look at her. Anastasia won't even talk to me about their relationship and that means there probably is no real relationship to talk about. They're supposed to go to dinner tonight and she thinks—"

"They're going to dinner?"

Clara took a big bite of her brownie and offered me one. I snatched it because no one turned down her brownies, but I also needed an indulgence now more than ever. "It's probably nothing," Clara grumbled, but we both knew that wasn't true. "Oh, Evie, don't let it get to you. I know he loves you. He's just..."

"He doesn't love me." I shook my head and closed my eyes while I took a big bite.

"Should we drink?" she tried.

I sighed. "No. Can we just eat about ten of these and maybe some ice cream?"

She nodded, her face in a permanent frown, but she did what a friend was supposed to in that moment. She went and turned off her Open sign, cranked up the music, and brought out the whole pan of brownies. "If it makes you feel better, I have to work with Dom in the next few months on the Pacific Coast Resort, and I'm pretty sure I can't stand him, but even so, I can't look away either. The Hardy men are enigmas of our species."

I stuffed another brownie in my mouth and let her continue.

We sat there for an hour talking about men, about growing up, about how ridiculous it had been that we weren't ever brought together on the holidays. A silver lining to my whole stay in Florida was that I'd found Clara.

We walked over to Vibe, and I texted Declan's driver that I would be late. We sat and ate and talked more.

By the time I got back, I didn't expect for my own guesthouse light to be on. Yet, when I went to unlock the door, it drifted open, and there was Declan. The soft light of the living room glowed over his features as he sat in a collared shirt, his cuffs folded up, and a tumbler hanging from one hand.

"You're late."

"Late?" I stuttered out. "It's only eleven."

"You normally turn your lights out at ten."

I chuckled and set my duffel bag down in the foyer, pushed off my shoes, and stared at him, not sure what to think of him being there. "You seem to know everything about me, I guess."

He shrugged and swirled the amber liquid in his glass.

"Want to go get your pajamas on?"

I chewed on my cheek without answering.

"I'm guessing you showered at the gym."

I rolled my eyes and stomped to my bedroom to go get a sleep shirt on rather than sitting around in workout gear. It was late, and I did want to be comfortable. When I reappeared, he was still sitting there, a smile that didn't seem kind at all on his face. Then he stood and pulled from his back pocket the very envelope I'd left him that morning. "See. Creature of habit, and that's the exact reason why I wasn't expecting to find this tonight."

The papers smacked down on my coffee table with a *thwack*. I bit my lip as I took in how he wobbled a bit on his feet, how his eyes looked wild, and how he smelled enough like whiskey to know he wasn't completely sober. "It's not something we should talk about after you've been drinking."

He tsked. "When should we talk about it, Everly? Or were you hoping I wouldn't even come here to talk with you? You thought leaving the papers and giving the wedding ring back would do?"

"Declan," I scoffed and tried to slow my heart, tried to tell my body that even though he was here late at night it didn't mean we were getting anything from him other than a fight. I went to get a glass of water and grabbed an apple from the counter bowl where I kept them. I started to cut it and murmured, "I figured we're over. You're with Anastasia now—"

"I'm not with her." The proclamation flew from his mouth fast. "I can't stand her. I can't stand any damn woman because all I can think of is you."

"Declan, you just went to dinner with her," I pointed out. Then I cut another slice.

"Yep." He took a swig of his whiskey and walked over to the counter where I stood so he could slam the glass down on the granite. "And I drank far too much in order to tolerate getting through the night with her. But guess what, Everly? That's over now. I won't be seeing her again."

He was leaning in close to me, his chest on my arm as I glanced to the side to meet his gaze. "What?" I whispered out.

He went behind me and caged me in before he rubbed his length against me, my nightshirt catching on him and riding up a bit. "My cock doesn't like anyone but you. I did all this for you too."

He wasn't making any sense. I frowned at him in question.

"Then I see those fucking divorce papers and you're not here. Were you with someone else?" His voice was full of wrath.

I looked over my shoulder as he asked and saw those green eyes flash with jealousy. "If I was?" I raised my chin.

He chuckled and nodded over and over before his hand dragged up my thigh and shoved my legs apart. "Let's see, huh?" I gasped as his hand went under my night shirt. I wouldn't deny that he'd find me aroused. "Soaking wet as always," he murmured in my ear and then growled as he turned me around. "You going to eat that apple while I eat you?"

My hands flew to his shoulders as he dropped to his knees and pushed my panties to the side so he could taste me. Everything was more sensitive, I'd noticed, and now I knew why. The pregnancy was starting to affect my body, and I felt his touch on my sex like a bolt of lightning in the middle of a dark night. Fast, hot, electric. "Declan, you're drunk—"

"So? I can't indulge my wife's drenched pussy when I am? I just want a taste, Drop." He lapped at my folds, and I shivered at feeling his tongue against me. "You taste better than the alcohol, baby. I'd rather get drunk on you." And then he dove in, angrily, ruthlessly, viciously nipping at my clit and fingerfucking me while lapping at my arousal like he owned all of it.

I clawed at his head and told him to hurry. I rushed him like he'd said in the past, but I didn't care. I wanted him between my legs instead of hers. I wanted him here instead of with her. I wanted him.

When I orgasmed on his mouth, he held me there as I rode out the aftershocks on his tongue, moaning his name, and then he slid up my body as he put my panties back in place. "Yeah, you weren't with anyone else either. That pussy only spasms like that for me."

"Declan—"

"I'm not having a child with her. I wasn't even seeing her. I just had to act like I was. We're not getting a divorce." He walked over to the papers and ripped them up. Not just into two or three pieces. He stood there shredding them as I watched.

"You're crazy." I told him, shaking my head because I was crazy too for even having a sliver of hope that it might be true. My heart, which had been swimming in darkness for the past few days immediately saw a tiny flash of brightness and went wildly toward it. Hope never left even when all felt hopeless. "You're being drunk and irrational, Declan."

"I'm not." He grabbed his phone and shoved it toward me. "Read this."

"I don't want to." I shook my head, knowing it'd be another headline, probably something about him and Anastasia.

"Please," he whispered. "The papers will be printing it everywhere in a week. I was trying to plan it, but I just need you to read it."

I stared at him but knew I couldn't deny him. His eyes

pleaded with me like it was the last thing he'd ever want from me.

* * *

WILL EVERLY BELAFONTE GIVE DECLAN HARDY ANOTHER CHANCE?

A letter addressed to Everly Belafonte from Declan Hardy:

Everly,

I'm not much of a writer. I'm a retired football player who earned America's trust by catching a ball and plowing through opponents. I ran on instinct and trusted my heart most of the time. It got me far.

I plowed through making decisions for our inheritance too. You gave in to marrying me so I could save the shares of the HEAT empire. I saw you do everything in your power to help me and another person save what they hold dear to their hearts.

You never did this for you. Had it just been for you, you would have walked out and not accepted any of it. For that, the HEAT empire should be forever thankful to you.

I'm forever thankful to you.

More than that, though, I'm forever in love with you. I told you that night I wasn't. It was a lie. Yet, I wasn't going to plow through a marriage with the woman I love. I hope you know I want to watch Home Alone with you, stay up late with you, make bracelets with you, and eat breakfast with you for the rest of my life.

I want the ring on my finger to be made of string forever because we love one another, not because an inheritance directive said to put it there.

I want babies with you, as many as you want. Even if it's a crazy amount like you told me before. Not because Carl said so, but because I want to see a little girl just like her momma learning yoga in HEAT Health and Fitness while her mom teaches her. I want that baby to be mine so damn bad, Everly, it hurts.

I want the happily ever after with you, but I want to get there on our terms, no one else's.

Your portion of the inheritance is safe. I made sure of it.

I hope when you read this, you'll tell me my heart is safe too. It belongs to you now.

Will you give me a chance to own yours too?

Declan Hardy has asked that Everly Belafonte not be contacted for a response at this time. We are honoring his wishes until she reads this.

* * *

"Give me a chance to start over with you, Drop. Please?" "Are you saying you secured my mother's yoga studio?" I whispered, staring up at him with my chin trembling.

"I got all of it. I had to do it that way, had to make you think we were over until I had all this worked out because you wouldn't have agreed otherwise."

"You..." I stopped and took a shaky breath. "You're not having a baby with her?"

"No, Everly. Jesus, I never was." He grabbed my hands and squeezed them like he never wanted to let go. "I couldn't tell you though. You would have told me to stop, fought me on it, tried to not have me put myself out there for you. I hated it, but Anastasia wanted to meet over and over about it. All of this was for you though. That's it. I had to get your mom's studio for you above all else."

"What? Why?" I whispered, my heart stuttering as I tried to figure out everything he was saying.

"Carl didn't fight you when you said no thanks to legal help, when you said no to his money, when you said no to any kind of help time and time again. No one fights you, and it shows they aren't willing to. He should have fought to give you everything before, and I'm fighting to give you everything now. I need you to know that's what families do. I'm going to do that every single day. I fought for the yoga studio, and it broke my damn heart to tell you I didn't love you because I love you more than I've ever loved anything. More than the empire, more than the shares. I'm happy to give all that shit up if I get you and your happiness. So, I backed away long enough to do that. I got the yoga studio, and I need you to give me a chance."

"But you—" My mind swirled, a confusing mix of love and hope and overwhelming emotion pulsing through me. He loved me. He wanted my heart. I had his. My heart was being put back together piece by piece.

"I did everything I had to do so that we can start over. No inheritance hanging over our heads. I need another chance, babe. We need another shot because I'm sick of this bullshit. I'm sick of not having my meals with you. I'm sick of not having you. I'm sick of wanting my *wife* and thinking she's just out of reach. You're truly my wife. Not out of convenience, not because of a will. But because I love you. I can't see straight without you."

"We can't just be married, Declan—"

"So, let's start over." He sounded like he'd take anything he could get. "I'll ask you on dates. I'll do whatever you need. I'll court you for fucking years if you want me to. Just say yes."

"We should probably start from the beginning if we're going to try," I said quietly because I wanted to try too. I wanted to go on a date with him, I wanted to learn every single thing about him. I just wanted him.

I wanted to hope.

And hope was scary, but Declan was worth it.

We should always hope when there's a happily ever after to dream for.

He walked up to me and kissed me senseless, then picked me up and carried me to his house.

He fucked me slow in his bed and told me it was where I belonged.

It's all I wanted.

Except we still had a baby.

And I didn't know how to tell him just then that our happily ever after was already in motion.

CHAPTER 39: DECLAN

"Just get them over here as fast as possible," I told my brother early that morning. "I want that place down as fast as possible."

It only took him an hour to get a demolition crew over to the property and another hour of Everly sleeping for her to wake up completely startled by the sound of banging outside. I watched her surprised reaction as she vaulted out of bed.

"Everything okay?" she stuttered and then whipped the covers off when I smiled and nodded as I read some bullshit article in the news about speculations regarding the Hardy empire. "Declan Hardy, what the actual fuck?"

"What?" I glanced up to see her eyes wide as saucers before I grabbed my coffee and took a sip then went back to reading the article.

"They're destroying my house!"

"This is your house," I responded.

"Oh my God. I have stuff in there."

"I had an assistant make sure it was cleared out before the demo started." I pointed toward the front door. "Most everything of value is in suitcases out front."

"Why are you tearing that down?" She looked stricken.

"You said it made sense for you to start there with me. Now it makes sense for you to start here."

"You've completely lost it. I would be fine living over there and trying to make this work." She shook her head at me, but

I saw the small smile she had, like she might have been willing to plan everything out all the time but she loved that I acted without hesitation most of the time.

"I won't. I won't be fine being without you again, not now. Not ever."

I saw how her eyes twinkled, how she wanted this as much as me. "I'm staying in the guest room, and you're going to have to earn anything more, Declan Hardy."

"I'll earn whatever the hell you want me to as long as you're here, as long as we're in this together, as long as you know I love you."

"You can't start saying that all the time now."

"I can and I will. I think I knew the night you danced with my niece. At least a part of me knew." I took the ring I'd been holding in my back pocket since I'd gotten dressed that morning. "You want a different ring?"

"Declan, I'll wear a ring once we discuss the bab—"

My phone rang and an unknown number popped up. When she motioned for me to answer, I picked it up fast to get rid of whoever was on the line. "I'm bus—"

"Hi, Mr. Hardy. Congratulations again on the pregnancy. We're looking forward to seeing you and Everly on Friday at three p.m. We tried to get ahold of Everly about some forms but were unable to reach her. Could you—"

"What did you just congratulate me about?"

"The baby. Oh gosh did she not tell you?"

I hung up the phone and stared at her wringing her hands together like she knew exactly what the call was about. "When were you going to tell me?"

"I wasn't sure." She chewed her cheek, ready to answer every question honestly but without giving me a damn emotion again. It was fine. I had enough emotion here for the both of us.

"How far along are you?" I asked quietly, trying to keep my blood from boiling over into my voice.

"I don't know. We'll figure all that out on Friday."

"Is it even mine?" I shouldn't have asked, and yet she'd hidden it from me like she didn't want me to be a part of it. My blood boiled over at the thought that it might not be.

"I'm sorry... *What?*"

"Is. It. Mine?"

"Are you kidding me?" She gripped the chair she was standing next to, and her face turned a warmer hue, almost like she was heating from within.

"Why would you keep it from me then? Do you think it's Wes's?" I closed my eyes at his name and pinched the bridge of my nose. "We'll get through it either way."

She took one breath. Then two. Then walked up and shoved me hard. "You want a test, Declan? Let's make sure to get that on the docket for Friday too. Paternity test for you, and I'll get an STD test for me."

"What the fuck for?" I ground out.

"Well, we were never exclusive. I don't know what you two have been doing or what you were doing with anyone else."

"Nothing's happened with any other woman since the moment I met you. I fucking love you," I bellowed, and her eyes welled with tears.

"Well, that's just great. I love you too, and I don't want to fight." She said it with pain, and her voice cracked as one tear rolled down her cheek.

I fucking felt that one drop turn my whole life upside down because I watched as my wife's eyes rolled to the back of her head before she crumpled to the floor. I got to her before she hit the ground and yelled her name out of fear.

She was breathing fast and her skin was hot to the touch, but her eyes fluttered open immediately. "I'm tired. I think I might have a fever or something," she murmured.

"Fuck." I lifted her from the ground and set her on the couch, then called a private doctor immediately. She grabbed my hand when I hung up with him and started to dial 911.

"I'm fine, Declan. I didn't pass out, just got really dizzy. I'll be fine. If you call an ambulance, we'll be at the hospital instead of here, and I don't want to be there all night."

God damn it. Her eyes pleading with me had me calling a whole fucking team of private doctors that belonged to HEAT instead as I took her temperature that registered 103.5.

"It came on fast. It's fine." She waved me off, but when I called the doctor back to tell him about her fever, he answered calmly that this happened sometimes with the flu. Because of her pregnancy, however, he recommended a cool bath. Then I told him to hurry the fuck up and get here before hanging up.

I scooped her up, a man on a mission to take care of not just one person in my life I knew I loved, but two.

"Declan, what are you doing? I just need to relax." Her teeth were chattering already, her body trying to work on bringing down the fever.

"You're taking care of a baby now, Drop. It means I have to do what's best for both of you."

I held her while I turned on the bath water. Thankfully, I'd had a large claw-foot bath installed next to the shower, not that she was going to enjoy the luxury of it all when she realized the temperature. She eyed it with trepidation. "I guess I can relax in the bath."

With her shivering already, I knew damn well she wasn't

going to like this. "It's going to be cold."

"Oh, no." She shook her head and started to back out of the bathroom, but I snatched her and pulled her nightshirt over her head. "Baby, I'll go in with you, okay? Just five minutes. We have to get your body temp down. It's not good for you or for our baby."

"Our baby?" She glanced away. "You said you don't believe if it's yours."

"Even if it's not, it's going to be." My hand spread across her belly because I knew I wouldn't let her go even if she was having another man's kid. "I'll raise it as mine."

She stared at me. "You really mean that, don't you?"

"More than I've meant anything else in my life," I told her. Then I slid my wallet from my slacks and toed my shoes off. I picked her up and stepped into the tub, cradling her like a baby as I sat down in the cool water.

"Jesus," she gasped and clung to me. "Did you put it to zero degrees?"

"It's lukewarm," I chuckled but sobered as I realized she really must not be feeling good. "You're burning up, so it feels freezing cold. The doc will be here soon. We'll get you feeling better in no time."

"Declan"—her eyes met mine as she looked up—"you're the only person since Andy I've slept with." She whispered it softly as she laid against my chest and tried to cuddle into my warmth. My whole body was on fire with her confession. Had she felt better, I would have taken her in that tub.

Instead, I stroked the waves of her hair and held her tight, knowing I would never ever let her go.

CHAPTER 40: DECLAN

Izzy: We're having another niece or nephew, guys!

Dimitri: What? Lilah, you knocked up again?

Cade: She's not. My wife has no self-control and is hacking medical records.

Dom: That's illegal, Izzy.

Izzy: My life's illegal at this point. And you're all a part of it. So, get over it.

Lilah: Focus. Who is having a baby?

Izzy: Declan and Evie!

Me: Do you have no self-control, Izzy?

Izzy: Literally none. You'll see how it is once her hormones kick in.

> **Me: She's sick. So leave me the fuck
> alone.**

Dom called. Then Dimitri. Then Izzy, who I picked up to yell at.

"The whole family's calling me. You'd better handle it," I growled.

"I will. I will. Jeez. Can't you be nice? I'm carrying the next gen here," she pouted before changing subjects. "I can't hold Mom and Dad off much longer though. They don't even care I'm having twins. They think you're avoiding them."

"I am." I shrugged as I stared at my sleeping wife.

"What for? They have to meet her sooner or later."

"I needed to know this was real first, Izzy." I sighed and played with the string of black around my ring finger. It was worn down now from how much I rubbed my fingers over it. She'd have to make me a new one sooner or later.

"And is it real?" my sister sneered, like she knew the answer.

"So real that I'm making sure her fucking abusive ex has no leg to stand on when I expose him for all he's done to women over the years."

She cackled and told me I was the best brother for this very reason. "Here, talk to my husband so you can figure that out. I'm going to go read."

Cade rustled onto the phone and said, "I don't want to talk."

"Great. Me neither. I just want to make sure that prick's family's money won't buy him out of any press we release about him in the next few weeks."

"Andy Baldeck's family has no money left. You essentially bankrupted every company they had that you invested in, which was idiotic if you ask me."

"What would you have done?" I rolled my eyes.

"I would have killed him." Cade didn't hesitate.

"Right. Well, I'm not an Armanelli."

"No. You're a Hardy, but I have a feeling you'll be a lot like an Armanelli soon enough." He chuckled. "Anyway, congrats on the kid."

"Am I going to be godfather to the twins?"

"If I'm godfather to yours." Fucker had to always have something in return.

"Fine," I ground out.

"How's that will treating you? Carl finished fucking you over?"

I nodded. Mrs. Johnson had given me the news that very morning that StoneArm wouldn't be getting any shares of the company now that Everly was pregnant. "I guess so. Not that it matters at this point."

"Did it ever matter? You still would have gotten the shares." He was confident in that statement. He definitely knew something I didn't. "I own half of StoneArm. The Stonewoods own the other half. I would have just given them to you had you asked."

"You motherfucker—"

"You're welcome for the baby and wife, dumbass." With that, the connection clicked off in my ear. There was no point in calling him back. I wasn't really mad because I'd gotten her from it.

She rolled over and cracked an eye open. "Who are you talking to?"

"Outrageous family members," I grumbled and pulled her close to me.

She pushed away and got out of bed quickly, running to the bathroom to vomit. I jumped out from under the comforter and stumbled in behind her as fast as I could. "This flu is insane. I'm calling the doctors again," I murmured as I came over to her to pull her hair back and let her heave.

"No. No. It's just morning sickness." She took a shaky breath. "I think."

"I'm calling them."

She sighed and sat down by the toilet while I dialed more numbers and rubbed her back. The doctor returned and took vitals again. She was twelve weeks along and morning sickness had started with a vengeance. Her fever had broken, but it hadn't provided me any reassurance. I wanted her in bed, wrapped in a cloud of blankets, sipping shakes full of nutrients and watching her favorite shows. I made sure that's what happened for the next three days.

On the fourth day, she glared at me. "I'm going to work, Declan, and so are you."

"Not an option. You're sick," I countered.

"We've both been MIA for almost a week."

"Half a week."

"So what? That's still a long time. My body needs to move. I'm not even sick anymore."

"You threw up this morning," I shot back.

"I throw up every day. That's part of being pregnant." She darted past me, and I would give that to her. She definitely was more agile than she'd been a few days ago. "Where's the suitcase of my stuff?"

I'd been laying her clothes out every day and had already put her toothbrush in our bathroom. I pointed her to the closet where I'd organized some of her clothes while she'd been sleeping. "I put them away."

"When?"

"When you were sleeping."

"You're moving me in here when we haven't even discussed if I should be staying here. I should be at the guesthouse or—"

"The guesthouse is gone."

"Because you're foolish."

"Because I can't worry about you down there every fucking day. I take care of what's mine, Everly. You're mine. The baby is mine. And what's mine stays in my bed next to me where I know they're safe."

"That's ridiculous. We haven't even properly dated."

"Fine." I grabbed her hand and stomped into the kitchen. "First date. Breakfast. What would you like me to make you?"

Her face paled. "I'm not very hungry."

I scooped her up and carried her back to bed. "See. You're sick."

"I just need to munch on a few crackers, and then it gets better. And for some reason, all I want is French fries and ice cream. There used to be this little diner in my hometown..."

I smiled at the randomness of that. "Okay. How about this? You sleep. I get you fries and ice cream. We talk about the gym tomorrow."

She narrowed her blue eyes at me like she wasn't sure she should agree. "One more day, Declan."

I was going to make it a day to last. Within minutes, she was back asleep, and I'd found a diner similar to the one I found on the web in her hometown. I had food delivered immediately and smiled as she woke to the smell of French fries around her.

"Declan, you've lost it," she said, but she was smiling and reaching for the damn food. I had to get the mother of my child to eat, and I'd do it any way I could.

I got one more day out of her before she insisted she was ready to go back to work, that the kids missed her and she missed them. I couldn't argue with that.

She flew into work with her damn yoga pants that were too tight and a sports bra like it was any other day. She nodded and hugged Dom when he approached her, probably to say congrats, but other than that, the day was the same.

She didn't want anyone to know. It was early in the pregnancy, and I understood her need to wait. I tried to not hover. I had meetings to attend and phone calls to make anyway.

For three days we went back to work.

For three days, everyone got along like nothing was different.

Until Anastasia came to my office crying and then tried to beeline into Everly's yoga class. My wife walked out before she could get into the room and folded her arms in front of her. "Yes, Anastasia?"

"You stole him from me." She poked Evie in the shoulder.

"I'm sorry?"

"You stole him, and now you're trying to steal everything."

What Anastasia must have hated about Everly was Everly wouldn't give in and get on her level. Everly had dealt with something so much worse, a whole town against her calling her a liar, and hadn't broken. Anastasia wasn't going to break her either.

"I think I recall telling you I'd object if you tried to marry my husband. I wasn't lying. Even so, if we do have a wedding or a renewal of our vows, I'll invite you. I do want both of you as sisters in my life."

"You're not my sister," Anastasia spat. "I'm... You... If Carl were here, he'd—"

"He'd have made sure your membership was revoked for the way you're talking, Anastasia." I walked around the corner from where I'd been listening. "You're talking to an owner of this empire now. Did Carl ever give you or Melinda the right to do that or give you any type of ownership like that?"

"Owner? She's in a marriage of convenience. She won't get shares—"

"I dissolved the prenup this week. Half of everything I own is Everly's."

"You what?" Everly gasped.

Anastasia did the same, but it was full of menace.

"Everly owns just as much as me now. Do you think it's wise to talk to a HEAT owner the way you are?"

She stuttered out her next sentence. "No... I... You can't be serious."

"I am. And sooner or later, Everly Belafonte will be Everly Hardy, if she'll have my last name. And I expect every Hardy to get the same respect I do. Now, I'll leave you with my wife to see if she revokes your membership. At this point, I definitely would."

I knew she wouldn't. Everly's heart was too big, but I still gave her the option.

She bickered with me the whole way home about it that night. But I quieted her by making love to her all night and we went to work again the next day.

Our life was falling into place. My heart had settled into the damn happily ever after I wanted too. I was seeing that this was what Carl always wanted and I had to thank the man for meddling even if he'd put me through hell to do it.

I was smiling to myself about it when Leo rushed in.

"Evie just left work."

"What?" He couldn't be right. "Explain yourself."

"She was down at the front desk with some guy she told she'd give a session to even though he didn't have an appointment. Dude's not from around here, doesn't have a membership or anything. Evie said it was fine. But then he asked to talk to her some place private. She just went. Looked at me and murmured on the way out that I should cover for her for kids' yoga."

Everly would have never missed yoga with the kids. "My wife, my Evie, said that?"

And my blood ran cold because I'd let her ex fall off my radar after I'd ruined his family's company, hadn't been checking up on where he was located because I was enjoying my wife too much. I jolted up from the conference room table and ran out on the meeting I was in.

Something was very wrong.

And I knew exactly what.

CHAPTER 41: EVERLY

Andy didn't look like prison had aged him even a day.

He stormed into HEAT Health and Fitness demanding I see him. It's the feeling of fear that's as strong as the pain and the anger and the bitterness that makes blood run so cold that a person freezes when they should run. Then the fury wars with the fear and fight-or-flight kicks in.

Today, my blood froze and then burned, the rage taking over. He'd actually come all the way from Wisconsin after ruining my life once like he was entitled to ruin it again. HEAT alarms went off, alerting security that there was an intruder, and without an employee watch swipe, guards would have been at the door, but I swiped the panel quickly, silencing the short burst.

Still, as quick as I was, Noah was training with Po and they both noticed at the same time Leo glanced up from his one-on-one. All three men zeroed in on Andy approaching me, and it was like they fell into a prearranged formation.

A wall of men willing to defend me, protect me, and be the friends I'd missed growing up. As fast as my heart was pumping, it still recognized their display of loyalty.

Andy was a charmer and smiled at all of them. To them, he was a stranger; his face hadn't been splashed all over the media coverage. His family had made sure of it. To them, he could have been an old friend for all they knew. Immediately holding his hands up, he said, "I'm here to talk with Evie." He peeked around them. "Evie, you got a second?"

I chewed on my cheek before I nodded. "It's fine," I told them, because suddenly I wanted him all to myself. There was no intimidation here. I'd trained for him, I'd texted him, I'd actually asked him here. I wouldn't make a scene, but I wouldn't back down again either.

He shrugged at them all and chuckled before he walked up to the counter. "Missed you."

As most of them dispersed, I murmured, "So you came?"

"I did." He narrowed his eyes. "Should I ask for a one-on-one?"

"It'll only end with you on your back, so I'd recommend not."

"Feistier than when I last saw you." He smirked. "Let's go somewhere private then and talk. I have a few questions I need answered."

"I can have a driver take me to my house. That's about it." I shrugged. I wasn't stupid enough to leave with him, but I didn't need anyone else involved.

He cracked his knuckles. "Fine."

I turned to Leo and told him to cover my yoga class. It wasn't like me. I knew it and he did too because his brow furrowed. Still, I needed him out of the facility where something would most likely be recorded.

My driver was always idling outside at this point and greeted us both with an eyebrow raised. "Ms. Belafonte...and?"

"Someone you don't need to know," I murmured as I got in the car.

Andy chuckled and slid in with me. Even his body heat near me made me want to gag. "So, you didn't take his last name, huh?"

"Maybe one day," I told him.

All the right turns to the gated community had Andy tsking. "Guess you did well for yourself for a bit while I was away."

"Away? Is that what you call it now?"

"I can't say anything else, Evie," he ground out, the pitch of his voice changing. I knew that voice. I used to fear that voice. But a sense of calm washed over me as the gates opened to my house. Our driver went around a bulldozer in front of the guesthouse and stopped at our front doors. "You put me in such a bad predicament."

The driver cut him off. "Ma'am, I'll stay right outside if you need anything."

"I won't." I got out and told Andy to follow. "You have ten minutes to ask what you need before I tell you to leave or before my husband gets here. I reckon he's on his way."

"Your husband?" he growled as I pushed the door open and let him walk into the foyer. He glanced at the large chandelier and then sneered at the stairway. "Do you think flaunting your new boyfriend in my face is really something I'm going to enjoy while I'm away?"

"You mean my husband?"

He cracked his knuckles again. It was something he used to do when he wanted to hit me, when he was trying not to. "You're irritating me. Don't act like we're not supposed to be together. I'm done with this little fucking game, and you're going to make it up to me that you had me in prison for a little fucking joke."

"A joke? Andy are you delusional? You assaulted me." I tilted my head.

"I gave my girlfriend what she wanted," he shouted. "You dressed like you wanted me to fuck you that night, so I was about to do just that. When I touched your pussy, you liked it."

"Even if I'd worn lingerie to that party, it wouldn't have given you a right. And I told you I wanted to stop. I said no. I begged for you to stop and think. You kept going. So, I endured it until you took the cuffs off." I tried to make him see. "Do you realize how many women you've hurt?"

"You're all a bunch of whores!" He lunged, albeit carelessly considering I'd made sure to stand right in front of the banister where I could sidestep and let him crack his head into it. He yelped and then ran at me. This time I used his momentum to swing him straight into it again. "Fuck! You bitch."

He turned and barreled toward me but our front door swung open and Declan plowed through, fury in his eyes. His body somehow looked more massive, more vicious than it ever had as he tackled my ex to the ground.

Andy tried to scramble and scrap, but Declan was too powerful, too in control, too dominating for Andy to even get a punch in. My husband beat my ex to a pulp, punching him over and over.

I finally grabbed his arm and said softly, "Declan, he's unconscious."

Declan's eyes were wild as he looked back at me. Then he got up and grabbed my elbow to pull me close.

My body was coiled tight to fight now, though, to register every movement as a danger to me. So, my reaction was instant. A remnant of what I'd dealt with in the past and was dealing with. I jolted back.

I saw the moment he noticed, felt his grip loosen, as if he wasn't sure what to do, and then he tightened it. The frown on his face was one of fury. "He's made you scared of me."

"Not you, Declan." I glanced at the man unconscious on

the floor. "It's just my knee-jerk response to any man putting his hands on me right now."

He breathed out like he was trying to dissipate his anger, and then he rubbed his thumb up and down the arm he had a grip on. Slowly, enticingly, and what felt like longingly. "I intend to spend my life making sure you never have to respond that way again, Everly."

Then, he grabbed Andy by his throat and dragged him towards the back of the house.

"Wait. Where are you going with him?"

"To my backyard to fucking kill him," he bellowed, like it should be obvious.

I opened my mouth to tell him to stop or at least try to plan a course of action, but no words came out. Declan stared at me for another second and then said, "Go upstairs, Drop." Then he paused. "Or stay if that's what you want."

He disappeared through the patio doors. A million thoughts ran through my head, but the only one that stuck was with the baby in my belly. I wouldn't have my husband go to jail for a man who didn't deserve another second of our time, wouldn't have him carrying the burden of this on him forever.

I came outside to take in the scene and saw my husband standing over my ex who was moaning now on the grass. No one had access to Declan's backyard except the birds and the sun. We waited while a cardinal flew by and I smiled at seeing one bird I always saw in my hometown rather than the seagulls I always saw at the beach.

How was this scene so serene now? How was I not scared now? How did I know even without planning that this day would work out perfectly? Declan, the man I love, the man who went with his gut, the man I knew I would spend the rest of my life with was rubbing off on me.

"Declan," I sighed. "You can't kill him."

The beautiful man cracked his knuckles as he glared at Andy and grumbled, "Oh, yes I can, Everly."

"He's not worth it." I shook my head. "We're having a baby. We're going to build a life together. We're not starting it this way."

"Why not?" Declan practically whined but I saw how he met my gaze, how he considered my decision here too now. Declan never hesitated.

Except now. With me.

We were a team now.

We were married truly now.

"She can't hurt me, man. Don't you see?" Andy laughed and then groaned into the grass like his ribs might be broken. The man was a pitiful makeup of a human being, but he still acted like he held all the power here outside.

I smiled with him. I grabbed the emotion this time and felt all of it.

I laughed with him. I laughed and laughed until tears streamed down my eyes and continued laughing long after he'd sobered.

"What? Are you fucking psycho too now?" he taunted.

My smile dropped off fast. "Psycho? No. Not at all, Andy. I'm laughing because you think you have control here like you thought you did the night you tied me up and made me watch you assault my best friend."

"Tonya liked it," he ground out, wiping at his lip that was bleeding. "She'd kissed me before."

"I don't really care what you did with anyone years ago, Andy. It doesn't change the fact that neither of us wanted you that night. The power you thought you held as I sat there, scared... With all that power, I was still able to get away." I got up and walked up to him where he squirmed like a fish out of water. "I still had you begging for your life that night."

"Shut up. You couldn't even finish the fucking job. You got that gun off the nightstand and couldn't pull the trigger because you still love me. You know you do. I should have you get on your knees for me now—"

I knew Declan wasn't going to allow his words. The man I loved grabbed him by his neck and choked him as he growled, "Careful. She gets this because she deserves it, but I'll beat you to death. I don't give a fuck."

"Stop," I said quietly, and Declan backed away, giving me the space I wanted with the man I never thought I would want it with again. "You know, I always tell myself I can move on from my past. I even told Declan to leave our past in the past, but I carry it with me. I carry the pain and the regret and the memory of losing my friend because of you with me every day. I carry the past assault with me every fucking second. I worry and stress and try to plan every single instance of my day so that I don't misstep. I do. Not you. I do. The survivor. Not the assaulter."

"You liked it," he tried to counter.

I scoffed at the lies, glancing at Declan who nodded at me to keep going. "I might have been homeschooled and quiet and looking for love because I didn't get it from my father's family, but I wasn't stupid, Andy. You hurt me. You fucking ruined me. And I won't ever be the same." I took a shaky breath and found Declan's gaze. "I won't be the same but I'll be better. I'll carry my past with me and I'll build a better future because of it. Stronger, smarter, and full of love from a man who deserves me."

"Well, I love you. I know you love me too," Andy said, and his words made my stomach roll. He tried to stand but crumbled to the ground again and wheezed. "I think something's wrong with my chest."

Declan laughed. "No one cares what the fuck is wrong with your chest. Apologize to my wife for the hell you put her through now."

Andy must have realized then that his life was on the line. He started crying, whining, pleading, and apologizing to me over and over.

Declan was beyond forgiveness though. He came to stand beside me and leaned close. "Do you want to take his life or can I?"

"We can't kill him, Declan." I took a deep breath. "He's probably going to sue us as it is. We shouldn't get our hands dirty when you're that all-American dream of the nation."

Declan smiled at me. "I like my hands dirty, babe." Then he kissed my cheek and commanded, "Go back inside."

I chuckled at my husband, and then I kissed him hard and fast before saying, "No killing. We just need to get him out of here."

"I'll take care of it," he murmured. "Give me a second alone with him, huh?"

"Promise to not do anything you can't come back from?" I lifted a brow.

"You bet."

I turned to go inside as I listened to my husband telling Andy, "No one will remember you. No one will care from this moment forward. I'm going to make sure of it. Your family's businesses are going under. I'll manage how the media will paint you in the magazines as a rapist and that's it. A woman's worth was always more than yours, and you got away with thinking the opposite for far too long."

I didn't look back. I went to make bracelets and sit in silence in the living room.

A bit later, I heard Declan come inside but he was on the phone and it was on speaker.

"Cade, I need a favor."

"I'd say no, but I saw who entered your gym, so I'm guessing this'll be good."

"You saw him come into my gym and didn't fucking call me?" Declan said furiously.

"I glanced at your location before I bothered with a call and your ass was going a hundred on the highway to your place. Figured you had it under control."

"Whatever. He's here."

"Don't tell me he's dead. I'm too tired to handle it today," Cade said, bored like he didn't give a shit about my life or anyone else's.

"He's unconscious but still breathing in my backyard. There's a lot of blood." I heard a muffled rustling as I walked up to Declan to wrap my arm around his waist and lean into him.

Then I heard Cade mumble to Izzy, "Your brother lost his mind like you did years ago, and now I have to go clean up his damn mess." He didn't say anything else to us. He clicked off the phone.

"Should I be more worried? We've just committed a crime," I said, not feeling much remorse or sickness or anything really.

"I worry about things," the man I loved said, "not you. You worry about our baby in your belly and that's it."

"There's blood in your backyard," I whispered as two of

Declan's brothers stormed through the front doors. My eyes widened at the fact that they could be liable too. "Wait! Don't come in here—"

"They know, Drop." Declan shook his head and smiled softly at me before he glanced at his brothers. "He's outside."

"You okay?" Dom pulled me close for a hug.

"I'm fine. I'm... Well, we're all going to jail for battery," I blurted out.

Dom sighed and pinched the bridge of his nose. "Honestly, with the way my brother acts before he thinks, I normally would say there should be some sort of repercussion, but in this case, I would have done the same. We're definitely not going anywhere for that fucker out back."

"Cade will take care of it." Declan shrugged and pulled me out of Dom's arms. "Want to go get French fries or ice cream?"

"Seriously?" I glanced at all of the Hardy brothers smiling at me and knew I was finally a part of a family, one that would take care of me in a way I'd never been cared for before. Wrapped in love. "Both?"

"I know the perfect place." He ushered me to the downstairs bathroom, where I showered and got ready with him. We didn't talk about the men traipsing in and out of the house as we walked to his car, because when I glanced at him, he said, "My wife doesn't worry about things, Drop. I do."

He didn't drive me to a place in town to eat. Instead, he drove me to a private airstrip with a Global Express standing by. "Where are we going?"

"Somewhere I've been wanting to take you."

I think getting out of town, away from the burden that had been on my shoulders for so long, and maybe the pregnancy caused me to fall right asleep on that plane. I was in and out most of the flight, hearing him making calls and probably working.

When we landed, he scooped me up and placed me in an SUV, where he buckled the seat belt for me, and once we were out on the road, I knew. "Declan, this is my..."

"Yes...it is your hometown," he said quietly, and then he threaded his fingers through my hand. When we pulled up to the diner I'd told him about, he smiled softly. "And here's your diner, baby."

"My diner?"

"HEAT bought it an hour ago. You needed the fries and ice cream."

My heartbeat quickened as my jaw dropped, and I glanced again at the window. Inside, I saw my mother and Tonya smiling with a sign that read *Let's get married again.*

I turned to him with tears in my eyes. "Declan..."

"You wanted ice cream and fries, right?" His brow was furrowed as he squeezed my hand.

"Yes..." I whispered.

"Good. Because my wife gets what my wife wants."

"No, yes to marrying you. Over and over. Forever and ever."

"I didn't ask, Drop, and I'm not going to." He slid another diamond on my finger. It looked like an engagement one that was a bigger rock than I'd ever seen.

"You're mine. I just need the wedding to let the world know it too."

EPILOGUE: EVERLY

"Should I have brought something?" I scanned the room and saw caterers milling in and out as Clara put out more of her chocolates on one of the long tables. She then rearranged a whole charcuterie platter with what looked like literal roses made from salami.

"What for?" She glanced up at me and whipped her red hair over her shoulder. "We've got salty snacks right here. Oh, crap. Can you not eat deli meat right now?" She glanced at my stomach with wide eyes.

"It's fine. I'll eat around it." I shook my head and chuckled. "Honestly, you brought more than enough for us to eat, and the staff made a crap ton more. The kids and parents are going to be so excited."

I glanced out our luxury box's window, overlooking the whole stadium. We'd set up catering tables within all 125 climate-controlled suites for children within the state's most underfunded school districts who'd never had the opportunity to attend a game before. Declan had made it all possible with his first ever HEAT Charity Football Game.

That newscaster had gotten him just a few months ago when she'd interviewed him for the first time about his letter to me. I remember how she'd started the interview asking if he'd really paid a million dollars to have a dance with me. "I'd do about anything for her."

"Right. That brings me to one of the harder questions we

have. Did you aid in getting her attacker behind bars again? Andy—"

"I didn't have to aid in getting Andrew Baldeck anywhere. The man is a rapist who put himself there." Declan made sure to say those words loud and clear for the cameraman to catch that night.

"I know, but several women have come forward in recent months to—"

Declan's tone turned icy. "A survivor should be able to share their story whenever they feel compelled to do so, am I right?"

"Of course." The host didn't push it any further but I knew the truth. The Hardy brothers and the Armanellis had done whatever they needed to do. The world was safe from Andy forever. Cade had even asked if I wanted him taken care of in prison. Declan had voted for me to say yes. I'd actually thought about it, weighed the pros and cons. He would have deserved it.

Instead, I'd given the justice system one more chance. That night, the newscaster changed the subject fast, realizing Declan wasn't going to give her much on the Andy situation. "So, you'll do just about anything for your wife. Does that mean you'll give your fans what they really want? Would you play Wes Bauer in another football game?" She lifted a brow and smirked. "I hear he was sweet on Everly for a while. We'd love to have that rivalry put to bed."

"There's no reason for it." Declan brushed her off at first.

"Doesn't Everly teach self-defense and yoga to underserved kids in your fitness center? It would be a great charity event for them, don't you think?" she teased him but then waved it off. "I'm kidding. I'm just putting you on the spot because I'd love to see you two go to head-to-head one last time."

I saw that look in his eye, the one where he didn't hesitate and knew right then, they had him. "I'll do it for her and the kids. They need to see I've still got it even if Everly's brought me to my knees a time or two in front of them."

"Really? You spar with her?"

"The first time I met her, she probably could have knocked me out. She stole my pride that day." He smirked. "Then she stole my heart a few months later."

I think the woman was half in love with him at that point. And the world was in love with the idea of a charity football game with MVPs, retired or not.

And Wes agreed to be on the opposing team. The way my husband smiled every time that little tidbit was brought up had me a little nervous to see them play.

"I hope everyone loves the food." Clara stared at the table and then picked up a cookie that was shaped like a cartoon character. "I might have overdone it though. I'm stress baking."

"Why?" I waved her over to one of the leather seats because I was more than tired these days.

She plopped down next to me with a sigh. "Do you think a café or restaurant of mine belongs at our Pacific Oceanside Resort? What if I'm ruining it? We've gone through blueprints and now I'm supposed to fly there and oversee the design and—"

"Wait. Ruining?" I almost screeched at my stepsister. We'd grown so close over the past couple months that I was actually surprised she hadn't shared more with me about her anxieties. It was more than I could say for Melinda and Anastasia who we hadn't even invited to the game.

They'd been angry about that, but less stress while I was pregnant was best. I had to protect my mental headspace for my child now, not just myself. Declan was proud of how I made that decision quickly, not really weighing much else. I was too.

As Declan came onto all the screens, I saw he was wearing a signature blue jersey that now had our HEAT emblem on it. It matched the one I wore with Hardy across the back.

Clara pointed to the television, trying to change the subject. "Let's see what they're saying."

I waved her off. I've never enjoyed football and had already seen how decadent my husband looked. If I stared now, I'd probably never look away. In football pads, he was twice his normal size and looked like a damn beast ready to bulldoze just about anyone. It was the only reason I considered watching the sport a bit more. "Who suggested you'd ruin anything you designed, Clara?"

"Dom freaking Hardy." She ground out his name and then shrugged. "You know he hates my ideas for the bakery, which maybe now needs to be a café or a restaurant. I don't know."

"There's no way that man hates your ideas. He'll love whatever you decide to do, and if for some reason he doesn't, just ply him with your food. No one can turn down your sweets, Clara." I grabbed a blue macaroon with a smirk from the small table in front of me and took a bite, moaning loudly. "Just persuade him with these. They're amazing."

She groaned and shook her head. "I don't think he even eats sweets, Evie."

I narrowed my eyes at her, about to protest, but before I could reply, Dom walked in with a smile across his face that mirrored his brother's. "Evie, my little brother thinks he needs you down on the field as a good luck charm."

"What?" I glanced at the screen and saw Declan waving toward our skybox. "No." He knew I didn't want to be out there where the cameras would be taking pictures of us.

"He said if he's doing this for charity, you have to do it too. Marriage shit and all."

"I'm pregnant and can barely move," I whined, but Clara was already up and offering me her hand as she practically danced in place at the idea.

"This is going to be so cute. You two should do a kiss cam thing or"—she flipped her dark-red hair over her shoulder as she squealed—"have him kiss your belly. The fans will go insane. They're so excited for the little Hardy."

I noticed that she didn't even look over at Dom, didn't say hi, and almost acted like he didn't exist.

"I'm not doing that." I wrinkled my nose but rubbed my belly, not able to avoid her infectious joy about the baby. "Our kid is going to be so spoiled."

Dom hovered over the table of food and said, "Damn right. That's next gen right there. Did you eat anything today? Make sure you're not eating any of this deli meat. Why is it even in here? Don't they know—"

"Oh, it's for everyone else," I cut him off, my eyes darting to Clara who wide-eyed me and then spun around to walk over to the window of the skybox like she wanted to disappear. "Have you tried the macaroons? They're amazing."

I saw how Dom's gaze drifted over to Clara as he said softly but firmly, "I don't indulge in desserts when I can have a real meal, Evie."

I saw how Clara whipped her head around to glare at him, how their gazes met, and the tension crackled through the room. It was a tension I'd started to think they needed to work out. "Well, there's tons of great food here. I'll leave you both to it for a few while I go appease my husband."

I didn't wait for either of them to object. I beelined it out of there and made my way down to the field.

Unfortunately, Wes was the one to meet me by the fifty-yard line after security waved me through. "So, Evie, you couldn't wear the jersey I gave you?" He sneered at me because the man was trying to rile Declan. And he knew exactly how to do it. "Where is it?"

"I fucked her out of it the night you gave it to her, and now it's in the trash where it belongs," Declan growled as he walked up and shoved Wes before pulling himself into the stands and then he hauled me in close. "Should I kill him out there today for you?"

"Not for me." I stared up at him, trying my best not to melt into a puddle as the world around us melted away. His hair curled at the tips from sweat; his face was already dirty, like he'd been rolling around in the damn mud down in the field, and still he smelled like the ocean and my man mixed together. "You're about to push each other around for three hours just to stroke your own egos."

"I'm doing this for all the kids!" He tilted his head toward the skyboxes that I knew were filled with them.

"Mmhmm," I hummed.

"Well that and I want my kid to remember that his daddy still can take down anyone who disrespected his mom."

"Wes isn't worth it," I pointed out, glancing behind Declan to see that Wes had walked off but now there were cameras around us everywhere. Security was forming too, making sure no one bothered us.

"He's not, but you are." He rubbed his hand over my belly softly. Slowly. Taking his time like the world could wait for this game to start. "Our baby is."

I was just a few months away from delivering our little boy and Declan seemed to think everything was worth it when it came to him. He got the best crib, the best car seat, the best sneakers. Declan even had a whole team come in to childproof electrical outlets and the fencing around the pool. Then he'd panicked and asked me if I wanted to move because he wasn't sure this was our home and if I wanted to move back to my hometown.

Yet, HEAT Health and Fitness was where I could still spar with anyone who would take on a pregnant woman. Spoiler alert: no one did because Declan literally followed me around everywhere.

I needed a spot, he was there.

I needed to do squats, he was behind me saying in a low voice, "Good girl. Perfect form, baby. One more for me." It was foreplay that led to way too much workplace sex.

I needed a sparring partner, he stood in the ring and laughed his ass off saying, "No way in hell I'm coming at you while you're carrying our child. You can lay me out all you like." And I did.

Declan Hardy wasn't simply going to be the perfect husband for me. He was the perfect family man and was going to be the perfect father.

Even when he was over-the-top.

"You're making a scene, Declan," I whispered to him as he leaned down, his eyes locked on my lips.

"That's the point. The world needs to remember why I'm here in the first place." He turned to the cameras. "Can you believe I'm doing this for my girl? I thought retirement looked good on me, but she'd rather have me on the field making sure I'm showing these kids how to play ball."

The man had every publicist and photographer laughing and screaming at him. They all knew this game was making the kids' schools millions, and it wasn't only about playing football, but they ate it up. Then, they were telling us to kiss and asking if Declan was going to ruin Wes on the field today. "Is that why you're playing defense rather than offense? You only did that in college," one of them shouted.

Declan smiled big enough that his dimples showed before he kissed me senseless and told me to go back up to the skybox, that he'd gotten the good luck kiss he needed.

When I got back to our suite, the game had begun, and I winced at the sound of men flying into each other at catastrophic speeds.

Declan tackled Wes within the first couple of plays.

One tackle. He pointed to me and mouthed, For my love.

Another tackle. He held up his hand and pointed to the black string he still wore on his wrist and mouthed, For my wife.

He did it over and over. For my son. For my family. He even did one for all his fans. For HEAT.

And the world got the point.

Our marriage may have been arranged at first, but he proved to the world down there that day that he'd deliver hell to anyone who disrespected what and who he loved.

He loved the game. He loved his family. He loved his empire. And he loved me.

Probably about as much as I loved him.

~THE FUCKING END~

BONUS SCENE: EVERLY

"I feel like I should be there." Clara sighed into the phone. "Atticus needs me."

"Your nephew is just fine. Plus, you're working on the most beautiful bakery, Clara." Reminding my stepsister of her priorities was necessary because I knew she was trying to find any reason to leave.

"It's not beautiful. He told me it was a mess yesterday, Evie. A literal mess. He went around and pointed to all the things he wanted to change and then looked disgusted that I had tears in my eyes." Her voice was shaky. "I think he wants me to quit."

I made a mental note to tell Declan that Dom was being an ass to Clara and he needed to lay off. "You're absolutely not quitting. Take a breath. Dom's just a perfectionist until things get done. He'll love the finished product. Don't take it personally."

"That's all this bakery is to me! It's my whole heart. How can I not take it personally? And he won't even try my chocolate." She said it like it was his complete downfall.

Which it was. Her chocolates were divine.

I winced. "Well, we know he doesn't love sweets." I tried to placate her, but I knew Dom despised the idea of her bakery in his hotel on the West Coast. That hotel was his vision, and Clara's style clashed with his. "It'll be fine. Just stay out of his way."

"That would be easier if I didn't have to stay at his place," she blurted out.

"Wait, what?" I practically shrieked.

She just groaned and said, "I'll tell you later. Just, please, pray for me." Then she hung up.

I redialed her immediately, but she ignored my call. So I snuck down my hallway—where Declan had specifically told me not to go. Peering around the door, I saw him rocking our baby back and forth, back and forth. The man was twice my size and bulldozed through everything. Loud, dominating, and larger than life. His muscles looked bigger than our newborn's head, and the tattoos snaking around them could be mistaken as menacing. Yet, when he held our son, he had the softest touch.

He glanced up at me, and one side of his mouth lifted. "Remind me to redden your ass later for not listening to me when I say to go relax. I got him, Drop."

"I know," I whispered. I wiggled the baby gate he'd just installed, and he chuckled before walking over.

"I'm using it to keep you out rather than him in," he said as he turned our baby toward me so I could rub his little head before I got up on my tiptoes to kiss my husband.

"He's my sunshine." I loved being able to say that to my own kid now, the way my mother had always said to me.

"You both make me happy when skies are gray. Now, leave us alone," he growled, and I smiled as I left the room and waited for Noah to come over.

I'd invited him to hang out an hour ago. Finally, there was a soft knock on the door, but I found myself again struggling with another gate. "Declan!" I was fixing to kill this man as I stood there wiggling the dumb thing.

He'd installed approximately fifty of them in the past couple weeks since Atticus was born. For what? I'm not sure. The baby wasn't moving. He cooed at us and breastfed about a million times a day, but he couldn't so much as roll over right now.

"Should I help or something?" Noah frowned at the dumb gate like it was from an alien planet. It might as well have been. I shook it and growled.

"Who needs these things?" I threw up my hands. "Climb over if you want to come in."

Noah chuckled and hopped over it like it was nothing. I

narrowed my eyes at him, knowing he'd just let me struggle for no good reason. I didn't have a second to scold him, though, because Declan rounded the corner into the foyer. "What's wrong, Drop?"

I pointed at the baby gate. "This door has a dead bolt and a screen door with a lock. Is a baby gate really necessary?" I put a hand on my hip.

"Why aren't you relaxing?" He wasn't looking at me now. He was glaring at Noah. "She just had our fucking kid, and you're flouncing over here to hang out? She needs rest."

"Oh, fuck off. She's fine. Look at her. She looks like she never had a soccer ball in her stomach in the first place."

"Excuse me." I stepped between them. "That baby was ten pounds, so you can give me credit where credit is due. It was like a basketball," I said to Noah before I turned to my husband. "And I'm fine. Actually, I'm bored."

"Where're Izzy and Lilah?" Declan scanned the first floor, expecting to see his sisters. They'd come to stay after Atticus was born to help. Declan's mom tried to come, too, but he'd promised her a family vacation over the holidays instead, even when I'd told him it was fine. The look he'd given me was one of fear. He'd said, "You think you like big families, now. Just remember I told you so." He'd never be able to tell me so. I loved having them around.

"They ran to the grocery store." I glanced back at the driveway, thinking. "It's been a while though. I'm sure they'll be back soon. How's Atticus?"

"Of course they did," Declan grumbled. "He's fast asleep, Drop."

I kept staring longingly at the driveway. "If I don't go to the gym or do something, I think I might go stir crazy."

Declan groaned. "How am I supposed to keep you healthy and give you everything you want when those are literally opposite things in your mind, Drop? Your doc said—"

"Oh, look! Izzy and Lilah are coming back." I pointed out at the gate where the car was speeding up way faster than necessary.

It screeched to a stop and Izzy yelled out the window, "Your gate is the worst, Dec!"

We all stared as another car pulled up fast behind them, and my eyes widened when I saw who it was.

Melinda and Anastasia.

They screamed something I couldn't quite make out, and Izzy flicked them off right before they drove through the gates.

"What's going on?" I whispered.

"What's going on is my sisters are on the loose." Then, Declan swore under his breath as he strode outside.

"This is gonna be good." Noah chuckled as he waved me forward. "You go and I'll watch from here to make sure the little guy doesn't cry."

I patted his shoulder. "You're a good surrogate uncle, Noah."

"Surrogate?" He scoffed. "I'm going to teach him how to play hockey, and he's going to say I'm his best uncle before he goes into the NHL instead of the NFL."

I laughed as I breezed past him and stepped outside to where Izzy and Lilah had parked. Melinda and Anastasia scrambled out right after them, no poise in the slightest as their faces scrunched with fury. Anastasia pointed at Izzy first. "You're cleaning up the toilet paper on my lawn!"

My jaw dropped with the accusation.

"Your lawn? Or your mom's? Or we should probably say Carl's," Izzy sneered, and that had me snapping my mouth shut. Had they really done that?

"How dare you?" Anastasia's eyes widened like no one ever talked back to her. "You can't come onto someone's property and vandalize."

Lilah, the Hardy sister that supposedly had always done the right thing, picked at her soft sweater dress. "You should call the cops then. Report that there was a problem. I'm sure you have security cameras. Definitely give them that evidence." She didn't sound at all concerned.

Melinda raised her chin and nodded. "Of course we have cameras. We'll have you two in jail for this by tonight."

"Jail?" I finally stepped forward and Izzy pulled me close with one arm over my shoulder like I always belonged next to her. "What are you talking about? Surely this is a misunderstanding."

"They vandalized, trespassed on private property, assaulted—"

"Assaulted?" Izzy questioned, and then she burst out laughing. "The egg I threw barely even hit Anastasia."

"You threw eggs?" I leaned in and whispered.

"Just a few," Izzy said innocently and shrugged.

"Let's not forget destruction of property. The ketchup on my car is—"

"You can give that an easy car wash," Lilah pointed out. "Do you not know how to wash a car? At least it's not spray paint."

"Yeah, because I've sprayed one or two cars before, and I guarantee you that's harder to get off," Izzy admitted with such a lack of remorse I knew immediately her actions must have been justifiable.

"Declan." Melinda turned to who she thought would be the only logical one. "Your sisters need to apologize. This behavior is unacceptable."

"Apologize for what?" Declan looked baffled, like he hadn't heard any of the conversation.

"They spent hours defacing my front yard and the aesthetic of my house."

"I don't think we have any proof that Izzy and Lilah would do that. They're here visiting Everly and just went to the grocery store, Melinda." Declan crossed his arms and stared at both of them hard as he said, "It must have been someone else."

"We have evidence," Anastasia fumed and pulled out her phone. She scrolled like she was searching for something, and then whispered, "Where is it?"

"Where is what?" Her mother leaned over her.

"The footage is gone." Her eyes snapped up to Izzy's. "You and your boyfriend did this."

"My husband you mean? He married me, honey. And that does mean he'll do anything for me. But erasing some security footage when I can do that myself? Yeah, that's below him. He'd simply tell the police station to not bother him or his wife. I mean, for God's sake, we're Hardys and Armanellis." She hissed the names, said them with such conviction and viciousness that they speared through the air toward the two women who'd always treated me like I was less than they were.

Melinda straightened her knitted pink jacket, a look of fear suddenly in her eyes. "Declan, we should talk. I don't want this to be the relationship we have."

My husband flicked his gaze to me, silently asking me what I wanted. He'd given me the choice of having a relationship with them, but I had stopped pursuing it at all. They hadn't called when I had our child. They hadn't come to the baby shower or small wedding shower Lilah and Izzy had put together for me with Clara.

So I had stopped inviting them, stopped trying. Sometimes the boundaries we set were necessary. Sometimes, those boundaries protected us from the family that never wanted us. Learning to put myself first was easy when my husband put me first too.

"You don't have a relationship with my husband, Melinda and Anastasia." I said it quietly, but Izzy squeezed my shoulder like she knew it took a lot for me to do this.

Boundaries. They were healthy, but they could also be difficult, hard to build, and painful to maintain.

Melinda must have registered how the wind shifted, because she took a deep breath, patted her coifed hair, and looked at me with sadness in her eyes. "I lost my husband, Evie. I don't want to lose you all too."

"Me and Declan? Or just him?" I wrapped my arm around Izzy's back and laid my head on her shoulder. "Because we're all sort of a package deal."

I think her face turned a little green. "Are your sisters going to say sorry for egging our house?"

"Nope," Lilah answered casually but firmly.

"You're all so freaking immature." Anastasia stomped. "I want someone sent to clean up that mess at our house, and I want my HEAT membership back."

Declan walked over to the stone pillar and pressed it so that the gate started to open. "Not happening, Anastasia. You made your bed, now lie in it and leave us the fuck alone."

"I'll have Piper go to every news station—"

His jaw worked as he came to stand behind me, and then he ruffled the heads of his sisters as he said, "Go tell everyone my sisters fucked-up your house. Tell them why too."

"Why would that ever be okay?" Anastasia cocked a hip and glared at him, like she realized he wouldn't take her side. She was ready to fight now, without a mask of kindness.

"It's because you disrespected their sister." He shook his head and pinched the bridge of his nose. "Family, Anastasia. You could have had that with us. With her. Look at Clara and Everly."

Anastasia just scoffed.

"It's fine," I murmured, because it was. "I have my family. And I'm actually sorry you can't be a part of it now, because it's freaking beautiful, Anastasia. And, sure, maybe a little dysfunctional." Izzy laughed. "But it's mine. And it's filled with love not hate."

"I'm not hateful." Anastasia balked like she might consider trying to be a part of it all of a sudden. I considered how she felt, how her actions were probably driven a lot by status, by trying to fit in, by so many things. Yet, it wasn't an excuse.

"Then go home. Forget about me. If you continue to forget, you'll continue to get the inheritance that we control. Do you understand?"

"Declan wouldn't allow—"

"Everly is the one who's been nice enough to let you keep it. If Piper wants to have someone write anything at all about us again, she can write that." Then he pulled me out of Izzy's hold and stared down at me, searching my eyes with his green ones. "Write about how she continues to amaze me with giving you grace when all you've given her is a reason to despise you."

"She won't write that because she's furious you fired her," Anastasia grumbled, but I wasn't concerned. Anastasia needed to grow, she needed to change, and she wouldn't do it until she was ready.

"And I'm furious you're still on my property, making my wife uncomfortable when she needs rest. So leave." My husband delivered his message to them loud and clear. They weren't welcome. They never would be.

"Declan!" Melinda cried. "Your sisters literally came over to our house and—"

"Jesus. I can't believe you two won't shut the fuck up. No one cares. You know what?" Izzy stomped back over to her car and pulled out another carton of eggs, which definitely pointed to them not being innocent. "I've been away from my kids for days now, and I'm feeling somewhat emotional. So, get off our fucking property or pay the consequences."

She opened the carton and held it up for Lilah to take an egg. I really didn't think she would. Yet, she smiled big and grabbed one. "We'll give you to the count of three."

I couldn't stop the tears from springing to my eyes. My family stood by each other, were vicious and ruthless for one another, and were all I had ever wanted.

"Are you going to cry, Drop?" Declan whispered as I heard Melinda and Anastasia getting into their car.

"I might."

He groaned and then scooped me up to carry me like a baby into the house as he yelled over his shoulder. "Don't bother us for another hour, Izzy and Lilah."

"Where are we supposed to go?" Izzy whined but Lilah was laughing.

"Go vandalize someone else's property." He strode up the stairs and then commanded Noah, "Get out of my house. My wife needs rest."

"She invited me over for company," Noah shot back.

Declan stared down at me. "You want his company or your husband's?"

I sighed because he knew as well as I did that I wasn't passing on an opportunity to be with him. "Sorry, Noah."

"Man, fuck you lovebirds." Noah chuckled on his way over the baby gate, then slammed the door shut behind him.

"Guess he knows what I'm about to do," Declan said on his way to our bedroom.

"The doctor says we can't for another couple weeks, Mr. Hardy." I winked at him.

He didn't even struggle with the baby gate into our bedroom as he said, "Right. But I looked it up. I can eat my wife's pussy all I want until then."

... And he did.

ALSO BY SHAIN ROSE

Stonewood Billionaire Brothers
INEVITABLE
REVERIE
THRIVE

* * *

New Reign Mafia
Heart of a Monster
Love of a Queen

* * *

Tarnished Empire
Corrupted Chaos
Fractured Freedom
Shattered Vows

ABOUT SHAIN ROSE

Shain Rose writes romance with an edge. Her books are filled with angst, steam, and emotional rollercoasters that lead to happily ever afters.

She lives where the weather is always changing with a family that she hopes will never change. When she isn't writing, she's reading and loving life.

BETWEEN LOVE AND LOATHING

HE LOATHED HER... UNTIL HE FELL IN
LOVE WITH FAKE DATING HER.

USA TODAY BESTSELLING AUTHOR

SHAIN ROSE

Fake dating my enemy so I can design my dream bakery should be easy ... as long as I don't fall in love with him.

Dominic Hardy might be an award-winning architectural engineer with fancy degrees and considerable accolades, but he doesn't know a thing about baking. He probably doesn't even like sugar.

So when my late stepfather's will states that Dominic Hardy is set to inherit the Pacific Coast Resort he'd painstakingly designed, as long as my bakery can be plopped in the middle of it, it's no surprise he balks.

Yet, my jaw drops when the will further requires us to mutually approve plans for my bakery's design.

His stuffy taste will never mix with my whimsical vibe.

But then Dominic comes to me with a proposal I can't refuse. He'll give me everything I want in my bakery as long as I agree to one thing.

Fake date him for five months.

Keep his ex away by pretending we're in love.

Smile and stare into his piercing green eyes at a gala or two.

Maybe share a kiss.

Nothing extreme.

Five months of acting in love when I really loathe him and his filthy mouth.

Even when he's using it on me.

This should be a cakewalk.

Except there's a fine line between love and loathing, and I think I've made the colossal mistake of blurring it.

Available Now